W9-APD-938

SLEEPING WITH SCHUBERT

A NOVEL

Sleeping *with* Schubert

Bonnie Marson

RANDOM HOUSE NEW YORK

SOUTHERN LEHIGH PUBLIC LIBRARY

NO LONGER THE PROPERTY OF
SOUTHERN LEHIGH PUBLIC LIBRARY

Copyright © 2004 by Bonnie Marson

All rights reserved under International and Pan-American Copyright Conventions. Published in the United States by Random House, Inc., New York, and simultaneously in Canada by Random House of Canada Limited, Toronto.

LIBRARY OF CONGRESS CATALOGING-IN-PUBLICATION DATA
Marson, Bonnie.
  Sleeping with Schubert: a novel / Bonnie Marson.
    p. cm.
  ISBN 1-4000-6041-9
    1. Women lawyers—Fiction.   2. Brooklyn (New York, N.Y.)—Fiction.   3. Schubert, Franz, 1797–1828—Fiction.   4. Spirit possession—Fiction.   5. Composers—Fiction. I. Title.
  PS3613.A7775S57 2004
  813'.54—dc21   2003046605

Printed in the United States of America on acid-free paper

987654321

FIRST EDITION

Book design by Casey Hampton

For my brother Chuck, who left the party early.
Come visit my dreams.

CONTENTS

first movement

Spirited Duet

The day I became a genius I locked the keys in the car with the motor running. This minor delay served its cosmic purpose, I suppose, delivering me right on time for my transformation at the spiritual launch site—women's shoes at Nordstrom.

Christmas in southern California satisfies about as well as chocolate mousse with Cool Whip. Holiday flourishes covered every Nordstrom surface that day, but the sun shone warmly, Santa's suit had sweat stains, and the perfect snow never melted.

Dad and I had a tradition of shopping for Mom together. Knowing her so well, we felt we could combine our instincts to pick a gift she might not loathe. Fat chance.

I found a rose-colored satin luxury that anyone would love. Dad looked at it skeptically, scratching his bushy gray hair.

"How much?"

"Hundred and eighty." I said it casually, like I always spend that much on bathrobes.

"*Dollars?* A hundred and eighty *dollars?* I could buy a house for that!" His face twisted with horror, which our poor saleslady took seriously. She flustered at us apologetically.

"Really, miss, it looks fine to me," he said. "Wrap it, please. Hanukkah paper, if you have it."

The saleslady stared blankly back at him.

Ever since moving from New York to San Diego, my father's jokes zoomed over the heads of store clerks, waiters, and ticket takers. He ached for the verbal volleyball you could pick up on any street corner in the Bronx. I had moved away only as far as Brooklyn, and worked as a lawyer in Manhattan. In spare moments, I fantasized about more creative pursuits and a possible move to palm-tree country. But if ever I were tempted to live in California, that saleslady's blank stare would be a strong deterrent.

We headed toward the dresses, looking for I don't know what. Something for my sister, something for Aunt Frieda. One by one, commission-driven "sales associates" assaulted us with helpfulness. After a dozen *May I help you*s, I grabbed the first dress in reach and asked a saleslady for a dressing room. This made me safe. Nordstrom associates are connected by hidden antennae and territorial threats that keep the shopper safe from other sales associates once an alliance is made. My boyfriend should be so monogamous.

Piano music had been drifting around in my head since we arrived. The volume rose and fell as we wandered around the store. When we drew close to the source, the melodies hardened and cracked like dried clay.

A highly polished baby grand sat on the highly polished marble floor and was played by a highly polished pianist. His honey-colored hair was swept away from his scarily perfect face. Turquoise-blue contacts looked down a surgically carved nose toward a beauty-queen smile with teeth as white as white.

He played the Christmas standards with showy finesse, dramatizing Rudolph and trivializing the Wise Men. His head swayed gracefully with the music, mimicking sincerity. Occasionally, he'd look up to bless us with a smirk and an eyebrow shrug, assuring us he was too good for this banal *dreck* the store made him play. If only he could show us his real stuff.

Normally, I'd accept it all as store atmosphere, but his music was getting on my nerves. Every time I got near him, my head throbbed and sweat slid down my neck. His know-it-all look enraged me and I fought not to scream when he Muzaked *Ave Maria*.

I tried to walk away but his playing attracted me like a spectator to an Amtrak wreck. Occasional missed notes hit my body like flying glass. I outplayed him in my head, summoning the music's original beauty. When he left for his break, I calmly took his place on the piano bench and began to play.

Through all my grade-school piano lessons I'd only gotten good enough to recognize the skill in others. Suddenly I became an *other*.

I was not like a lifeless puppet, nor a remote-control robot. All the movement came from inside. Muscles flexed, fingers moved, and my mind was filled with a comprehension I had no right to possess. I vibrated like a tuning fork as the music flowed outward. Visions slid in and out of focus. My brain engaged in a psychic tug-of-war with an unseen opponent.

It was a lovely piece I played, one I'm sure I never heard before but which felt like an old friend. The melody started slowly and I marveled at the grace in my hands. My manicured fingertips roamed the keyboard at will, gathering up its secrets and pouring them out in exquisite form. The tempo picked up and my heart raced to meet it. I watched my fingers hurling, twisting, and dancing wildly, amazed they didn't pretzel up on me. Then came a light and lilting part pulling on strands of melody remembered from the beginning. The ending left me tear-drenched.

When I stopped, the world of Nordstrom fell in on me again. The response to my music was, like, *totally* Californian. Most of the shoppers shopped on, unscathed by a miracle.

Only a small crowd took notice. They gathered around with enthusiastic words and even requested autographs. An elegant woman in her forties, patrician to her toes, wept into a linen hanky. A gray-haired couple held tightly to each other and offered comments in a language I didn't recognize.

"Hey, lady, how'd you do that?" I turned to see an adolescent boy in trendy, cool-kid clothes. He stared at me, stunned, as if he'd just discovered fire.

"I don't know," I answered. Then the world grew dark, the ocean rushed through my ears, and I gratefully passed out.

<center>~~~</center>

Do people normally dream when they faint? It was the first faint of my life, so I'm no expert. But when Dad's voice roused me a minute later, I had already had a life-changing experience.

My body housed two lives. To protect my sanity I denied it many times but, as I look back, it was obvious from the start. Someone else, some person who possessed more passion than I ever felt, had crawled into my soul with me. Like lovers sharing a bed, yanking at the covers, brushing up and pulling away, we were separate but together and utterly unready for each other.

"Liza, honey, are you okay?" My father helped me sit up as Nordstrom elves scurried to find help. The small throng around me asked one another the usual questions.

"I'm fine, Dad. I just want to go home."

My own sense of shock was augmented by strange responses to the ordinary details of the surroundings. Everything smelled wrong and glaring lights made me throw an arm across my eyes. I gasped at the sight of a woman in shorts.

"Someone's gone for a doctor, Liza. Let's just wait a minute." Then Dad's voice changed from concern to astonishment. "Honey, where on earth did you learn to play like that?"

A stylish store official in a dark business dress broke through the crowd with a medic in tow. Despite my protests, the brusque young man looked in my eyes, felt my pulse, and checked for signs of imminent demise. His quick, assured hands felt cool against my clammy skin. Much as he tried, he couldn't find anything horribly wrong and suggested I go home and take it easy for the rest of the day. If only he knew.

The curious bystanders were pretty much losing interest by then, except for an elderly, tweed-covered gent who chased after me and my father as we hurried toward the exit. He could barely catch his breath when he finally spoke: "Excuse me, miss, but that was remarkable. Really remarkable. Wherever have you been keeping yourself? Where may I hear you perform again?"

Perform a-*gayne,* was how he said it. He was American, but with that Continental accent you hear only in old movies.

"I don't perform anywhere." I was more frightened than flattered.

"Then where do you study? Can't I hear you again?" He looked hopeful, and actually removed his fedora as a show of respect.

"I'm sorry, sir, I really have to go." My response deflated him. "I'm glad you liked that number, though."

Dad held onto my elbow as we turned to go.

"That *number*?" The stranger was following us out the door. I wanted to disappear, but my Number One Fan would not be left behind. "Miss, don't you know what you've achieved? At least take my card and promise you'll call."

"I can't promise that"—I looked at the card—"Dr. Sturtz. I'm not from here, anyway. But I'll keep your card."

He seemed bereft, not ready to give up.

"Where do you live, my dear?"

"Brooklyn."

"May I at least know your name?"

"Liza. Liza Durbin."

Dad was kind while we drove home, allowing me to sit beside him without a word. He didn't ask his many questions, but I was asking myself the same ones anyway, plus some extras. Like why the sight of the parking lot startled me or how come I felt carsick for the first time since childhood. Just the feel of the synthetic seat covers made me squirm.

As we turned into the driveway of my parents' perfectly average suburban home, I realized how un-average I felt. (*Hey, lady, how'd you do that? Sorry, kid, you must mean someone else. You must.*) Only the familiarity of my parents' home kept me semi-sane and earthbound. I sank into an easy chair that was soft and overstuffed, like all their furniture. I scanned the family photos, the smiling faces on every wall and table. I recognized all of them. Would they still know me?

My mother greeted us in a black leotard and knee-length tights. She'd obviously just taught her yoga class. I marveled at her taut, sixty-year-old body as if I hadn't seen it countless times before.

"What are you staring at?" she asked me.

"Nothing, Mom. You look good, that's all."

She eyed me suspiciously. "Twenty years of yoga will do that for you," she said. "I keep telling you that."

In response to my stubborn silence, Mom once again provided details on the many benefits of yoga and how I could easily take classes in Brooklyn. But I was preoccupied, and her conversational train must have taken a turn that I didn't notice. Suddenly she was asking me a question that started with "When?"

"Soon, Mom." It seemed like a good guess. "I'll start again soon."

Mom sized me up through slitted eyes. Uh-oh.

"All right." It was the I'm-your-*mother*, there's-no-escape voice. "What's going on? You look awful and you haven't said a word."

Just what kind of spectacle was Mom capable of making out of my amazing feat? When I was small, she'd call the neighbors any time I blew a saliva bubble or counted to one.

"Liza had a little fainting spell in Nordstrom's, Louise," Dad volunteered.

"A *little* fainting spell? What's little about fainting?" My mother sprang into panic mode, instinctively hitting on food. "Did you eat, darling? Maybe you were hypoglycemic."

"I'm not hungry, Mom."

"Did you go to urgent care? Have you seen a doctor?"

"There was a doctor in the store, Louise. Everything's fine. She just needs to rest."

"I want to hear everything," she said. "I'll make you some chamomile tea, and we'll have something to eat."

No point in arguing. Once my mother has opened the fridge, no mouth goes unfilled. We sat down for a three-course snack. I sensed a spice was missing from Mom's chicken salad, but couldn't say what it was. The fruit salad, though, tasted like ambrosia. As my mother served scoops of cookie-dough ice cream, my father took a deep breath and said, "Louise, something else happened in the store today."

I listened without comment to Dad's tale about the wackoid woman in Nordstrom who commandeered the piano and played like a genius. How could this story be about me?

"It was the damnedest thing, Louise. She played so beautifully, like a Rubinstein or a Perlman." Dear Dad's knowledge of classical music didn't extend beyond "Streets of Laredo," but his praise was heartfelt. "I tell you, this thing came from nowhere, a total shock."

Mom had listened intently, staring at me, leaning toward me, while Dad talked. When he finished, she was silent only a moment before she turned on my father.

"*Shocked?* Our daughter does something brilliant and you're shocked? What's wrong with you?"

Her attention flashed back to me. Her deep brown eyes doubled in size, and her pumpkin-bright hair bristled.

"You were always the best in your piano recitals, Liza. Isn't that right, Max?" No reply. "Everyone said you were the best, darling, and you were. They weren't just saying that."

I lowered my eyes and watched my ice cream melting, little blobs of cookie dough bobbing in the goo. This seemed fascinating to me, and far safer than the conversation in the room.

"Louise," Dad said, settling a hand on Mom's slim forearm, "I don't think you understand."

"I understand that she's good at many things. Didn't she do great in college, and in law school? And she could always draw, too. Why couldn't she be a pianist if she works at it?"

I saw no hope. She would only understand through demonstration. I eyed the black lacquer upright piano waiting for me in their living room, the one they bought on credit twenty-odd years ago. I had insulted it with "Chopsticks," tortured it with scales, and embarrassed it with the *Young Pianists' Beethoven,* the edited version. This time I thought I might make it proud.

Mom and Dad followed me into the living room and I sat at the creaky piano bench. Suddenly, the keys scared me silly. Can a miracle strike twice? Most of me wanted to run away, but my hands dove for the keyboard. They landed in starting position and immediately took flight. The first notes were familiar, instantly linked with the words my mother used to sing to me: *This IS the sym-pho-NEE, that Schu-bert-wrote-but-ne-ver FIN-nished.*

Brilliantly played, with lofty emotion. How'd I do that?

Filled with belief in the music, I moved on through thrilling passages. Torrents of music were followed by sweet pauses. Delicate notes were embroidered into complex patterns. I could hear other instruments that should have been playing: the strings, horns, percussion. I felt the notes as if I'd played them before. Then it changed. Suddenly I was playing something original. I roamed the keyboard, leaving footprints in fresh snow. Improvising, playing with the possibilities. It ended grandly.

Mom got it.

When I was young, I was terrified of the dark. Gradually, the night ghosts turned into explainable shadows and ignorable sounds. No more fears, until that night. A ferocious child-again dread shocked my adult senses. Wild dreams chased me around the bedroom. Loud music yanked me from my sleep. I tossed violently in my sheets, desperately trying to shake off reality. It was reality, after all, that set this apart from childhood fears.

I searched my mind, my memory, my reason, for one indication that the situation was not real. But I could not undo this day of fingers on ivory, impossible music, and something invading my soul.

Hey, lady, how'd you do that?

Was für ein fantastischer Traum! . . . A fantastic dream! Am I real, or is it? Here is a world of brightness, even where there is no daylight. Noise and life everywhere, yet no smell of earth or horse or tree.

Other things are wrong, too. When I reached for the keyboard—dear Lord!—my hands had sprouted red fingernails. I am mired within this frightened creature. Can she even hear when I scream my name?

If I'm dreaming, let me wake. If awake, I must go back to sleep.

I had no problem catching a flight early Christmas morning. Most people were home with their families, so it was just me and the unlucky flight attendants in a half-full cabin of glum passengers. My old fear of flying made an unexpected return. Breathing became a painful chore and my stomach churned as the engines roared at takeoff. I whimpered as I watched the earth shrink below us, then hid my head in the small white airline pillow. At one point I was surprised to discover a pair of flight attendants hovering over my seat, strapping me in with the cooing assurances you give a hysterical child. I must have done or said something to merit that attention, but damned if I could remember it.

My parents were disappointed by my pre-holiday departure, but I couldn't face a house full of relatives. They protested while I packed, and as we drove to the airport, and when I explained for the dozenth time that I didn't want to be around people, even on this favorite family holiday. (My California relatives had long ago switched to Jewish-lite. They always rescheduled Hanukkah for December 25, when it was easier to get everyone together for gifts, latkes, and a nice ham.) At the airport, I made my parents swear an oath of silence concerning what had happened. So I knew I could rely on my mother for twenty minutes, tops, before she'd blab everything. My parents had made a tape of me playing the night before, and I made Dad promise to hide it from Mom until the company was gone. Without that evidence, at least, her story would be taken with a pound of salt.

The cabbie from Kennedy Airport must have been pleased with the hundred-dollar bill he got when we reached my Brooklyn Heights apartment. Too stressed to deal with details, I walked away without waiting for change. I lugged my heavy bags up the four floors, eager to return to my books, my dishes, my African violets, my world. Opening the door, I wondered if my psychic intruder would dare cross the threshold with me. They say vampires can't enter a home uninvited, so I squeezed my brain to envision a crucifix with DO NOT ENTER written across it. It must not have understood English, though. The pushy spirit stayed adhered to my innards as I dropped my big bag next to the old leather couch and threw my satchel on the rickety kitchen table.

I was on home turf again, thank God. Every inch of my little nest comforted me, except for the vague impression that things looked odd just outside my field of vision. I'd twirl around quickly, trying to catch the peripheral view. I half expected to see the melt and droop of a Salvador Dalí painting. But periphery can only be off-center, so the strangeness persisted like an unreachable itch.

I had no fruitcakes or decorations. The messages on my answering machine and a bunch of Christmas cards from friends and insurance agents were all I had to create atmosphere. I listened to my messages over and over. I liked hearing the good wishes. Don't think for a minute that I really wanted to hear Patrick's voice just one more time.

He sounded friendly and familiar. Somehow I thought he'd have picked up a phony-baloney Italian accent.

"Christmas in Siena is incredible. Everything I could want, except I miss you, of course. *Buon Natale,* sweetheart."

Buon Bullshit, asshole.

Patrick's bon voyage speech had been a treasure. "Real love means letting your partner go—to explore, grow, experience other people." Women, by any chance? "If we're meant to be together—and I know we are—we will be. In just six months, at most. You'll be so busy anyway . . ." Blah, blah, blah.

So we'd been in touch since his summer departure, but I can't say I was happy about it. He sounded pretty happy, though.

Patrick Florio and I had been together for three years when he decided to follow his dream as an architect and go live in Italy. Even though he'd never been there, he felt "in his heart" that's where he belonged. I knew in my heart that I couldn't get an extended leave of absence from my law firm. No matter. At least Patrick had plenty of time to absorb Italian culture, study great art and architecture, and complete his comparative study of American and Italian hooters. Little did he know that my missing him sometimes crossed the line into hating him. We were together but not— a theoretical couple.

With effort, I chased Patrick out of my brain, but he kept sneaking back in. I also wasn't ready to deal with my recent musical adventure or the disoriented feeling that followed me around like a puppy. In fact, some heavily rummed eggnog with a good friend was about all that sounded right to me just then. I picked up the phone and called Fred.

"Yeah, sure, I've got eggnog," Fred told me. That meant he would pick up the fixings on his way over.

Fred Wilner was my oldest, most comfortable friend. We'd known each other since college and even attempted a romance of our own once. It was fun, easy, and completely lust-free. We agreed we could marry, assuming neither of us ever wanted sex again.

He arrived with rum and eggnog and a cable-knit sweater for me, which would have been gorgeous except for the egregious mustard color.

"I thought the color would be great on you," he said.

"Why do you do this, Freddie? We agreed no presents, then you go overboard like this?" I slipped the sweater on, not to hurt his feelings. I looked deathly ill in it.

"Liza, I'll stop buying you presents when you stop giving me Christmas stuff."

I wouldn't stop, though. I get enough presents to embarrass a princess, and Fred gets a Radio Shack gift certificate from his uncle Bernie. I handed him a large wrapped package from Max and Louise.

This was what he was really waiting for. With both of his parents gone, he'd glommed on to mine and they were totally thrilled. Acquiring an adult child—housebroken and appreciative—may be the only sensible way to become parents. So Fred had become my parents' favorite child. Big deal. It's easy to be the favorite if the folks haven't endured adolescence and other indiscretions with you.

His package contained a cashmere sweater in a magical shade of blue. How nice. I was tempted to tell Fred that I was a big musical genius, but I forced myself to heap praise on his new sweater instead.

"So how are they?" The sweater went well with Fred's denim-blue eyes. His dark hair curled just above the collar. "Have fun with the folks? I thought you were coming back tomorrow."

"I wasn't feeling so great, so I passed on the family party."

I was barely holding myself together, but I didn't want to scare Fred away. His presence helped me in ways he'd never know.

"Are you okay?"

"Sure," I said. "Besides, my parents'll still send all the presents from everyone."

Fred looked at me closely. "You know, you do look a little pale." It was the egregious sweater, but I didn't say so. "Why'd you really come home early? Kicked out and disinherited?"

The phone rang just then, buying me time to come up with a better story.

"Hello, *amore*." Patrick's voice was honey itself. "I tried calling you at your parents' house. They said you left early. Everything okay?"

"Sure," I lied, "everything's fine. Just wasn't in the mood for a big family gathering, so I ducked out early. It's the kind of thing, though, where you've gotta pretend you're sick to get out of it, or they'll never forgive you."

"Yeah, I know what you mean. I've done that a few times myself," Patrick commiserated.

Across the room, Fred didn't seem convinced by my latest version of why I'd bugged out early. Long distance, though, Patrick had already

launched into a story about himself and what he had done in a similar situation. I pretended to listen.

"Well, did it fit?" Patrick asked, apparently not for the first time. My
mind had wandered, but I realized he was talking about the outfit he'd
sent me from Italy.

"Oh, it's incredible, I love it!" Actually, I wasn't sure what it was. It had
a vagabond Renaissance look involving velvet, brocades, shawls, fringes,
and possibly pantaloons. Definitely not from Nordstrom.

"Does it look good on you? I thought of you as soon as I saw it. Send
me a picture of you in it, okay?"

"No problem," I promised. "Fred's here, I'll get him to take the picture
tonight."

Silence. Patrick hates Fred. Why do I say things to annoy my beloved,
faraway, deserting, self-centered lover?

I changed the subject and Patrick and I mustered up gooey good-byes.
Then Fred helped me figure out my genuine, weird Italian outfit so we
could take goofy pictures. For a little while, I almost forgot to be petrified.

∿

I awoke the morning after Christmas, praying I would feel normal again,
that I could look back on my unexplainable show of genius as a never-
again anomaly. I could live with the prickle of an unsolved mystery as long
as I knew it was gone for good.

After a mercifully solitary start to my day, the strangeness returned
mid-morning. It disabled me. I stayed in my apartment, too preoccupied
to get dressed. Something was inside me that didn't belong, phasing in and
out unpredictably. I knew when it was alert because everyday sounds
made me jump, and the kitchen appliances and bathroom scale became
stare-worthy. Also, a soundtrack ran through my head with musical passages to glorify the brushing of teeth and the rinsing of silverware.

I had a couple more vacation days before going back to work, which
gave me a chance to consider the evidence in private: My visitor was obsessed with music, possessed an Olympian set of senses, and seemed as
scared as I was. Probably not American, judging by reactions to nearly
everything. Maybe not even of this century. I thought about the great pianists first, but that seemed too limiting. With so many instruments play-

ing in my head at once, this pianist was surely a conductor or composer as
well.

My only clue was the "Unfinished Symphony." Even I, with my basic
level of music appreciation, identified that one easily. The other music I
heard was beautiful, but I couldn't be sure who wrote it. Did I hear bits of
Beethoven? Mozart? The possibilities spun around me, dizzying and in-
distinguishable.

In desperate moments, I tried purposely to will the thing away. I visualized it as a virus, urging my body to fight it off like a common cold. As
a last resort before bedtime, I helped myself to vitamin pills, out-of-date
antibiotics, cold tablets, and other stray goodies in the medicine cabinet.
Their cumulative effect was nothing compared to the strangeness I was already feeling. There was no virus, of course.

I had occasional slivers of hope the next day, when I went for up to two
hours without a symphonic note in my brain. During each quiet interval,
I'd tell myself that the whole episode was coming to an end. After all, if I
could return to normal for two whole hours, why not the rest of my life?
Maybe I would *not* wind up institutionalized by rational people who
didn't understand that something real was happening to me. That *Franz
Schubert* was happening to me.

Deep in the night, his name had come to me in a whisper, distant but
clear. At first, I tried to attribute it to dream haze, to push it back in its
hole. In the light of day, the idea kept springing up and waving its hands
in my face. I tried to reject it, nearly deciding that I was delusional, but
that didn't explain my piano performance. Slowly, the reality had glued itself to me: *Franz Schubert was happening to me.* I didn't know if it was good
or bad, only that it was true.

Of course, the only other being who would believe me was Schubert
himself, and we couldn't communicate with words. I sensed, however, that
his fear and confusion were at least as great as mine. Nothing in my world
was familiar to him, not even the century. He was constantly confronted
with startling technology. To alleviate his panic (which rapidly fed my
own), I introduced him to the technology he'd most appreciate—CDs and
the radio.

He was not used to music flowing from impossible, inanimate sources, and his responses were intense. I tested him on different kinds of music. He reacted with magnetic interest to the classics he knew and to the ones he wanted to know. A moving piece could send us both into rapture, but distortions and mistakes in the music (subtle ones I'd never have noticed) caused acute annoyance.

Contemporary music was a great challenge to him, though I suspect he had some understanding through me, just as I understood some things through him. Rock left him agitated, jazz bewildered him, and an old disco tune made my teeth hurt. He was moved by an early Bessie Smith recording, but he also liked some old junk by Gary Lewis and the Play-boys. Go figure.

There was hardly a need to supply music anyway. In any normal day, we're exposed to heaps of it without even trying. Radios everywhere, pass-ing cars with pounding stereos, TV commercials with singing cats, snippets of pop songs when you're put on phone hold. There's always something to hum along with.

Franz's frequent dormant periods were either sleep or, more likely, a voluntary withdrawal from modern commotion. In addition to music, there are the sounds that most of us are oblivious to. Airplanes, car horns, the whir of the refrigerator, the clicking of computer keys, and the rum-bling of the dishwasher were all harshly penetrating to my more sensitive half. It added up to a din, to be taken in small doses.

At night, though, Franz frolicked without restraint. Our sleep was filled with his marvelous dreams, like nothing I'd known before.

Brain chemistry is supposedly ripe for inspiration during sleep. Artists, upon waking, sometimes envision completed works just waiting to come alive. Franz slept in creative overdrive, conjuring music as a full-body ex-perience. He saw sounds vividly, felt them speeding through his blood-stream, smelled flowers and brimstone, tasted every note.

And through this waterfall of new sensations, I realized how insanity comes to people, perhaps to me. A twist here, an alien perspective there, and one day you're not thinking like the rest of the world. It was like dis-covering a new color. How could I describe this nondimensional phe-nomenon to anyone who happened not to be me?

That's why I guarded this secret as long as I could. Yes, it might be a gift and, yes, some people would dog-paddle across an ocean to trade places with me. But to me it was so big and out of my control that it scared me half to death.

Practically speaking, I didn't know what to do next. I was due back at work. Should I go to the office and try to act normal? Walk into an emergency room and demand a surgical exorcism? Scour the Yellow Pages, as if I might find help there?

With wild optimism, I chose work and normalcy. I thought I could pull myself together with massive self-discipline. I'd carry on each day like someone you'd see on a schlocky talk show who harbored a terrible secret for years until a close friend finally asked, "So how long have you been combing your hair to cover that crowbar sticking out of your head?"

The truth is, I was so dazed by my circumstance that people quickly figured something was wrong, even if my crowbar was invisibly nested inside my head. I became ridiculously klutzy with the addition of a second set of reflexes that were not calibrated to my own. The stimuli that I barely noticed would set off alarms in Franz's system. Suddenly I couldn't step onto an escalator in less than three attempts or cross a street without lurching like Frankenstein's monster at a bonfire. Also, my conversations wandered, I couldn't attend to normal tasks, and I had a tendency to hum *way too loud.* This did not help me at the office.

In the highly competitive law firm where I was a hardworking associate, I made a spectacle of myself just by not being perfect. When I lingered an extra hour over lunch (where the *Brandenburg Concertos* played on the restaurant's sound system) on Tuesday, the client I was consequently standing up was instead shmoozed by a mealy new associate named Myles Broadbent. Naturally, at our staff meeting the next day, Myles pointed out how perfectly happy he was to help out any colleague who needed backup. It didn't help that I'd arrived at work in my bedroom slippers.

I left work early that day.

At home I practiced being invisible. Hey, if I could be invaded by Franz Schubert, anything is possible.

I ignored all letters and e-mails, and returned my parents' frantic phone messages with calls perfectly timed to get their answering machine (Tuesday-night Scrabble, Wednesday-night dinner club). I worried about work, called in sick, fretted over Franz, and had a disgusting craving for schnitzel. His thoughts were colliding with mine, and my attempts at solid thinking crumbled like cake. On Thursday night, my friend Fred lovingly coaxed me out of my retreat.

"What the hell's the matter with you? Have you looked in a mirror lately?" Fred stood at my front door wearing a look of shock, so I made a start toward the bathroom mirror.

"No, wait, Liza." He sounded nervous. "Don't look yet. I don't want you to go from scary to suicidal. Let's talk first."

But the mirror beckoned. Fred followed me into the tiny bathroom. I shrieked at the sight of my reflection. Makeup is a dear friend to me, and I appeared to be completely friendless and overwrought. My expensive work clothes lay like rugs on the floor. They had dark footprints on them like in a murder mystery. I was wearing—what, my wetsuit from dive class? With a nice silk blouse and a decorative sheet tied around my waist. I must have been distracted when I dressed. And, of course, that wasn't the worst of it.

My hair has always been my crowning horror. At that moment I could have scared Medusa. It's a gift from my father. His wild thatch was too much for one head. Clumps of Dad's overgrowth leapt onto my scalp at birth, planting hideous hair seeds, stubborn as Bermuda grass. Every morning I do battle with this mop—fluffing and swearing until it resembles human hair. Sometimes I win, sometimes I lose, but this was no contest. I looked at Fred sheepishly (although I think sheep have better hair).

"You also don't smell that great," he said. "Why don't you start from scratch with a shower, then we'll go out."

I was too appalled with myself to turn down anyone else's free advice.

I emerged from the shower to hear the phone ringing. Fred picked up for me.

"Oh, hi, Louise . . ."

I waved my arms and mimed the obvious to Fred. *("I am not home, I am not home.")*

"Yeah, everything's fine."

("I'm away! You're here to water the African violets. Tell her!!")

"I love the sweater, thanks . . . Sure, a perfect fit. I'm wearing it."

("Liar!")

"Sure, she's right here. Let me get her."

("You can lie about wearing the sweater, but you can't tell her I'm not home??")

I had heard that if you smile while you talk on the phone, your voice sounds naturally cheerier. I must have been smiling like Jack Nicholson in *The Shining* because Fred looked frightened. I grabbed the phone, un-smiled, and tried to sound normal.

"Hi, Mom, what's up?"

"What's up? *Where have you been* is what's up. Your father and I are worried sick about you, the state you left in. Are you all right?"

I told her I was fine and offered hearty reassurances, which she disregarded. She wanted details about the music and the fainting. Fred was casually listening nearby, so I went into my bedroom and closed the door.

"Has it happened again?" Mom demanded.

"Happened again? No." Not a lie, technically.

"I've been thinking about this a lot. Your father and I have a theory, don't laugh." She cleared her throat. "Maybe you could be just a teeny little bit like an *idiot savant?*"

I wasn't laughing, but she did make me smile. I commented on my quick descent from being her genius daughter to being a freakish dolt.

"Liza, you know I didn't mean that." I knew. "And Aunt Frieda agrees that something's going on."

"Aunt Frieda, perfect. The world's leading authority on shopping for shoes agrees with your psychological assessment. Case solved. Let's move on."

Mom reminded me, as always, that Aunt Frieda was a sharp cookie who probably knew more than I thought. I reminded Mom of her promise not to tell anyone.

"Frieda is family, darling. She loved that tape of you playing. Anyway, I had to talk to someone about this. Frieda's family."

I pointed out that she could talk to Dad, who was also family and already knew about me. She squirmed past this logic, aiming again for an update on me.

"Well, I've stayed away from pianos, but he's still here."

"Fred?"

"No, Franz."

"Franz? Who's Franz? What happened to Patrick?"

"Franz Schubert, the composer."

It was the first time I'd said the words out loud. I explained that he seemed to be sharing my body.

"Liza, you know that can't be true. Please, you've got to talk to someone about this. A professional."

I wasn't ready to admit it. Instead, I knocked loudly on my bedroom door.

"Mom, that's Fred knocking. We're going out and we're running late. I'll have to call you back."

I surrendered the hair battle and put on a hat, got dressed, and found Fred still sitting in my living room. He didn't enjoy being pointedly excluded from my conversation with Mom, but he was determined to be nice. In fact, he invited me to a recital that night at the Brooklyn Academy of Music. In retrospect, I should have asked what was on the program.

It was a typical classical crowd at BAM that night. Well-dressed season-ticket holders, professors of this and that, college students, Brooklyn's musically enlightened, Fred, and me. Or *us,* depending on your point of view. Franz steered my eyes and ears to every corner of the room, beguiled by the tiniest details. The red-and-white EXIT signs were particularly alluring.

The pianist that night was the music elite's latest darling, Natalie Frome. She was fairly well known among the masses, too. She'd won the Tchaikovsky competition a few years earlier and Van Cliburn fell all over himself praising her. An okay-looking blonde, she was dead serious and on the dull side until she started playing. Then, I swear, she would glow in the dark.

She started with Mozart. I recognized the piece but I'd never heard it like this before. Franz's spirit took off and flew around the room, taking me along for the ride. We sailed on crescendos, glissandos, and heaven-bound strains of melody. I breathed it in deeply, felt the notes in my bones, feasted on luscious harmonies. I saw new colors.

Sometimes at concerts you see serious piano students in the audience playing along on invisible keyboards, their fingers silently working up a sweat. Apparently I was doing this. Fred grabbed my hands a couple of times and, at one point, he said something apologetic to the gentleman on my left.

Fred hissed in my ear, "Try not to play with your neighbor's lap, okay?"

I'd try. But the truth is I was having the time of my life and not much caring about protocol. The program moved on to Franz Liszt for a Hungarian rhapsody. We loved that, too, but grudgingly. I'm not sure Franz and Franz got along.

Finally, Natalie played Schubert. And it happened again.

⌇⌇

I don't think the man sitting on my left will ever go to a concert again. Fred says he howled as I ran over him to get out of my row and reach the closest aisle. Fred further says that I looked like a zombie from *Night of the Living Dead*, staring straight ahead with hands outstretched as I played my unseen piano. Even worse, he says I removed my hat so I looked like a zombie with horrible hair.

As Fred tells it, he and the security guard reached me in a dead heat, each grabbing a shoulder. My approach toward the stage was enough to rouse the crowd and throw poor Natalie off course. I guess I can see their point.

Fred copped an insanity plea on my behalf and the security guard was happy to see me dragged out the exit by my good old pal. I know all this because my old pal was still in my apartment when I woke up the next morning. I found him in my kitchen, waiting to pounce on me with every weird detail of the night before.

"You don't remember a thing, do you, Liza?" Fred handed me coffee, watching me closely.

"Not true," I answered proudly. "Natalie missed three notes in the Mozart."

Fred was not amused.

"Liza, you've got to tell me what's wrong."

"Nothing." Still trying to sound casual.

"*Nothing* doesn't cut it." Fred had never shouted at me before. "*Nothing* is what you say when your turd boyfriend in Italy calls a day late for your birthday and asks why you're pissed. Wearing a wetsuit at home and going zombie in public is definitely not nothing."

So Fred told me the BAM story, then I told him mine.

I know he didn't believe me at all because he didn't ask me to prove it. I didn't have a piano at home, but we could have found one. He could have asked me to play for him. Instead, Fred gave me the standard advice: "Talk to someone about this, talk to a professional."

Naturally he meant Mikki Kloster. It seems everyone in our circle of friends had seen Mikki at some time or other. I went to her for a while and I have to say she was great to talk to, a good listener, and the only therapist I knew who gave actual handy advice. Then she showed up at some of our birthday parties and at a potluck dinner.

I mentioned to some friends that I thought it was inappropriate for a therapist to socialize with clients. You'd think I'd called their children ugly. *We love Mikki, she's important to us.* All I could think of was the dirt she knew about all of us and our interwoven lives. She could easily connect forbidden dots and snuff out a few relationships. But she never did.

"I still have Mikki's number," I admitted. "I guess I could call."

Fred was relieved by my first show of common sense in days. He praised me like a good doggy, then turned to another favorite subject.

"So what are you doing tonight? You do remember it's New Year's Eve."

I remembered, but my date was off in Siena, guzzling grappa with Italian contessas. I had no plans. Neither did Franz.

"Come out with me and Jana," Fred offered. "We're going down to Chinatown for dinner, maybe go to Ruthie's party in Soho. Nothing too thrilling, but you don't need to sit home alone."

"Oh, but I do," I assured him.

Fred clearly wanted to keep an eye on me, but the thought of Franz at a New Year's party was out of the question. And the mention of an evening with Jana was mind-numbing.

Jana was the latest of Fred's imports. Romanian, I think. It seems all

Fred's girlfriends are troubled geniuses—brain surgeons in the old country, waitresses here—with immigration problems and great legs. Jana was one of his less interesting imports, whose obvious mission was to marry into a green card. I saw her as a transparent opportunist and Fred saw her as the Leg Goddess.

"Really, I think I'll just hang out here. I'll be fine." I sort of believed myself. But I decided to take a few slugs of the cold medicine that always puts me to sleep, just to keep me at home and out of trouble.

I did sleep well. In fact, I never enjoyed it more. I had bright, noisy, kaleidoscopic dreams interrupted only by phone calls from my parents, Fred (twice), and my great wandering love, Patrick. He said happy new year in Italian and I thought *vafanculo* in English.

My mother called again in the morning because I had sounded so strange on the phone. Normally, her worry factor would make me crazy, but since I felt crazy already I had nowhere to go with this. Besides, when you're frightened, you want your mommy.

"Aunt Frieda's been asking about you. She'll probably call you."

"Perfect," I said. "I'm sure she can cure me."

"And your sister will be home from Paris on Wednesday. She's dying to see you. Maybe we'll fly out soon and we can all have a nice visit together."

I hung up on Mom, lunged for my phone book, called Mikki Kloster, and told her answering machine that I needed an emergency therapy session on Monday and every day after that, possibly for eternity.

For so many reasons, it was time for me to talk with someone. The situation was already frightening, and bound to get more complicated with my sister involved. If that weren't enough, part of me was starting to enjoy Franz, which was wonderful and terrifying.

We were gradually getting to know each other. I felt slightly more in charge, at least physically. I picked the music, the books, the food we ate—but when I wanted magic, I knew to make room for Franz. His dreams, his imagination, dazzled me without fail.

I wondered if creative giants live with a more advanced set of senses. Or maybe Franz's current form was part of the equation: Removed from the humdrum of paying bills and sorting laundry, his spirit was free to express its spectacular essence. It's hard to imagine a normal, functioning person going through life at this sensual peak, flowering from moment to moment. I realized I couldn't live that way for long. On the other hand, my normal state of mind started looking bland by comparison, like the desert before the cacti bloom.

~~~

I woke up early, and Monday morning slapped me in the face. Work was out of the question, but as a lawyer at Stricker, Stricker & Feinsod, it's considered weak and inconsiderate to call in sick more than once a decade. Better to call in dead, so your work can be immediately reassigned with no hard feelings.

Back when I was a respectable associate, not quite two weeks earlier, I was already used to getting flack for my one "frivolous" quirk. For five years, I'd been volunteering two hours every Thursday afternoon for the Young Writers Project with sixth-graders in a public school in Brooklyn. I was an English major in college and knew I wouldn't be around much creative writing in my law firm, so I made it a condition of employment when Stricker, Stricker & Feinsod hired me. Solid class ranking from a good law school gave me some leverage, so why not? Actually, my colleagues could think of lots of reasons why I should *not* take two sacred billable hours away from the firm for my selfish pleasure. It caused significant whispering and resentment, but I guarded every minute of that writing program.

The subject had come up again right before I left for San Diego at Christmas. Myles Broadbent, our fervent young associate, needed my help with something. I told him I was in a rush to clear my desk and reach my sixth-grade authors to hear their holiday ghost stories. Myles was annoyed, and pretty damn showy about it. His whining got on my nerves, and I was getting a headache, so I may have been a little blunt. People don't like it when you call them anything like "a pathetic little sycophant." They tell the bosses about it, too.

My boss wasn't my favorite person, either. When I was hired at Stricker, Stricker & Feinsod, it was Ivan Stricker (father of the other Stricker) who chose me as his special assistant. He was already ancient, a few blinks away from retirement. At the very least, he would give me some meaningful work to lighten his load. At best, I'd get great experience and would inherit excellent clients from him. Unfortunately, the old guy never slowed down physically or relinquished any juicy work to me. I was buried for long hours under tedious research and cleanup efforts that kept the decrepit Stricker looking good as the firm's honored figurehead. The partners kept me there with promises, decent money, and two hours a week with my writing students.

So even before my adventure with Franz began, life at Stricker, Stricker & Feinsod was not perfect. I had to appear sympathetic as I asked for a leave of absence. Something horrendous and contagious appealed to me. Tuberculosis came to mind. It would be quaintly fitting to call in sick with the vapors while draped gorgeously over the sofa like Greta Garbo in *Camille*. But I'd get caught in the lie, so I opted for emergency leave for personal reasons. Not romantic, but what could they do, sue me? Well, maybe, but not today.

I met with Ivan Stricker first thing in the morning. His office was a caricature of all things Ivy League, with far too much polished wood. I submitted my leave request vaguely but urgently.

"Liza, you know how fond we are of you here." Stricker rested his hands on the desk and assumed the demeanor of a dignified TV lawyer. "We've noticed your recent, um, difficulties. But are you sure you need a leave of absence? It's a significant step."

"Yes, I'm sure."

"Liza, you understand, we all want what's best for you." For the first time, I noticed that Stricker's voice was absurdly high-pitched for his height and heft. I didn't mean to laugh out loud, but maybe Franz did. "Of course, if you take this firm and your position lightly, I don't suppose we can change your mind."

"Please, don't misunderstand," I said. "If there were any alternative, I'd take it. I need some time off, that's all. I'm hoping just a few weeks."

Stricker took notes, then patronized me, wished me well, and turned me over to the enemy. Myles Broadbent could handle my workload for the time being.

It seems the newest addition to the firm was ready to move up. Myles and I had a long meeting in which I handed over files, gave him my phone list, and kissed my career good-bye.

Then I was off to see Mikki.

~~~

It had been several years since I'd seen Mikki Kloster in her professional domain. It was during the death throes of my marriage to Perfect Handsome Rich Guy. Jeff and I met in law school and got together as a natural matter of course. Study partners, *Law Review,* then one day we were engaged. Jeff was sweet and had a great sense of humor, but not a lot of oomph.

We had a perfectly polite marriage that allowed for Jeff's long hours and frequent road trips. Jeff's best friend was also married to a workaholic whose work took her out of town. One day this best friend called with an extra ticket to a Knicks game. Since his wife and my husband were both out of town, I wound up going with him. That's how Patrick Florio and I first got together. Our friendly relationship grew lusty as our marriages dwindled away. I was sick with love, guilt, and confusion when I went to Mikki for help way back then.

"I'm glad to see you again, Liza." Mikki looked sharp in a steel-gray blazer that matched her salt-and-pepper hair. Her office, done in shades of blue, felt cozy. "You sounded upset on the phone. Do you want to tell me what's happening?"

I remembered why everyone liked her. Mikki had a soft humming voice that felt like a hug. She paid perfect attention and made a person feel fascinating. Maybe this was something she cultivated, but more likely it was a gift.

"Well, Mikki, I'm not sure how to explain this. How much do you remember about me?"

"I remember quite well, Liza. But I'm really interested in what's happening with you now."

"Well, it's important that you know me already," I said. "You know I'm not a crackpot, right?"

Right. But I knew I'd sound like a crackpot in a minute. Mikki and I met when I was anxious and neurotic and cheating on my husband. That's unpleasant, but not crackpot.

"I'm possessed by Franz Schubert," I said.

Mikki twitched but kept her composure, even smiled after a moment. Maybe she thought I was kidding.

"The composer?" she asked.

"Yes, of course."

"Of course." She nodded like a good therapist. "Tell me about this."

I spared her no detail. From my first acquaintance with Schubert in women's shoes at Nordstrom to my incident at BAM to my leave of absence that morning. At least she didn't laugh out loud.

"What do you think is happening here?" she asked.

"How should I know? I was hoping you might have a clue. It's not like this happens to me all the time. Have you seen anyone like me before, Mikki?"

I scanned her face for some sign of recognition, deeply hoping she knew more than I did. She revealed nothing.

"Does Franz Schubert mean anything special to you, Liza? Either the name or the composer?"

This unlocked a memory. My mother used to sing me to sleep with famous melodies. Some were classical themes with words set to them, an old technique for teaching children to recognize great music. My mother had learned them from her mother. She wrapped her lovely, shimmering voice around each song and dangled it like a gift over my sleepy head. When I was very young, barely within memory range, I loved the tune to the "Unfinished Symphony."

"So, he was special to you as a child."

"Indirectly, I suppose. I liked the melody, but I was too young to know about Schubert. And it's not like I grew up obsessed with his music."

Mikki gave me a sharp look, as if obsession was exactly what she'd been thinking.

"Liza, how often do you experience this feeling of Schubert being with you?"

"Often? That's hard to say. He's always there but not always awake."

"How do you know he's there when he's not awake?"

"Because I'm never alone."

She asked how this experience made me feel.

"Like the unluckiest lottery winner in the world," I told her.

Mikki wrapped up the session with a synopsis of what she'd heard and made some surprising observations. She insisted I get a psychiatric evaluation. Her point of view made perfect sense, but all the facts were not in evidence yet. How could she take my word for all this? I said I'd consider the evaluation after our next appointment.

DATE: January 3
CLIENT: Liza Durbin

Client believes she's inhabited by the composer Franz Schubert. Does not hear his voice, but experiences his senses and "can play piano like him." Has had two episodes when "Schubert took over," one fainting spell, and has experienced lost time when "he may have been in charge."

Reports no unusual stress, illness, medications, alcohol or drug use prior to this experience. Speaks coherently and answers questions directly. Does not see the "inhabitant" as malevolent—maybe likes him—but is frightened. Too distracted to work, socialize.

I counseled client four years ago on a relationship crisis. Has since divorced and has continued the relationship started at that time. She was well groomed then. Today—expensive silk suit with University of Pennsylvania T-shirt. Makeup looked like it was applied by a child. Frequently moves fingers as if playing piano. Surprised when I pointed this out.

Recommended immediate psych eval. Client promises to go after our next session.—MK

NEXT APPOINTMENT: Thursday, January 6, 11 a.m.

Das Geheimnis, das Geschäft der Frau . . . The mystery, the business of woman. How often did I steal a glance at a woman's bodice, imagining the wonders beneath her skirts?

I know these mysteries now. They are divine and mundane, like a man's.

CHAPTER FOUR

On Tuesday I started writing music.

You hear about religious freaks who speak in tongues or spontaneously write in ancient runes. I was once as smug about those weirdos as anyone.

It seems that Franz missed having a piano and did the next best thing. We could hear everything as we wrote it. This was our recording studio, a perfect rendering in a single take. It would have been wholly wonderful except for one thing: We were on page eight before I noticed I was writing anything.

The kitchen table was covered with laboriously hand-lined paper, and every pen in the place was either on the table or tossed on the floor as unworthy. I realized how easy it had become for me to lose time—to surrender—when I was alone. The phone, a visit from Fred, any human contact was enough to keep me alert and anchored. But without that outer influence, it was becoming frighteningly pleasant just to blend into Franz.

Mom called often, and her tone became increasingly anxious. When I mentioned my leave of absence from work, she had trouble sounding calm. What plans did I have? What about my career? And her favorite: *What am I doing with my talent?*

Loyal Mom. She knew about my "adjustment problems," but believed I could handle them. She was ready for me to share my newfound brilliance with the world.

"Call a music agent. Join the symphony," she suggested. "There's plenty you can do with a talent like yours."

"First of all, it's not mine, Mom." For the fiftieth time. "I don't know where it came from or how long I'll have it. I can't even go to the office; how can I think about playing in public?"

Ah, but I had been thinking about it. Thinking about it a lot.

Franz wanted to play. To create more orchestral work and hear it performed. To rejoin the music world. He didn't say these things in words, but I knew what he felt.

We communicated through feelings, and things made sense that way. When I tried to think with him in actual *words,* everything got complicated. In any case, I knew for sure that he wanted to make music again. But how could a freak like me go public? Not one of my closest friends or family wholly believed what was happening, so what would strangers make of me? Sure, I could impress the crowd at Carnegie Hall, but it's not like they have an open-mike night there. Just making a start seemed monumental.

Sick of feeling powerless and ignorant, I decided to help myself by learning more about my famous guest. I went online, where I could easily scroll through Franz's life and search for helpful info. He was clearly alarmed to see his likeness on the screen, but I was comforted by the words that gave solidity to his existence, and by the enduring admiration he'd earned.

Born in Vienna (*like my grandfather!*) in 1797, the twelfth of fourteen children and only the fourth to survive past infancy. He died thirty-one years later, probably of venereal disease. A contemporary of Liszt and Mendelssohn—and, get this, buried next to his good friend Beethoven. Antonio Salieri, a lethally jealous composer, according to the movie *Amadeus,* said that Schubert "must be taught by God himself." (I blush at that. Franz takes a bow.)

Schubert showed talent from the start, but his family sent him to school to be a teacher because it was a more reliable profession than musician. Still, he composed hundreds of songs called *lieder* just for fun by the time he was seventeen. *(Prolific—nineteenth-century pop tunes?)* Then he met Franz von Schober, who had plenty of money and urged Schubert to quit work as a teacher and come live with him in comfort. This is the fun part—they had a bunch of friends who got together just to sing *lieder* and make music in gatherings called Schubertiads (Karaoke classicals). One of these was a famous singer named Johann Michael Vogl. Schubert played while Vogl sang (*a great surge of joy as I visualize this—must be a favorite memory for Franz*).

At one point, Schubert became the live-in music tutor for the beautiful daughters of a Hungarian count. I liked this, too: Franz composed a lot of four-handed piano pieces during that time, possibly so he'd have an excuse to share a piano bench and cross arms with his favorite young countlette.

By 1819, Franz was on his first concert tour with his old friend Vogl. They were a hit. Schubert was by then a master of orchestration as well as songwriting. He was highly productive and happy until late 1823, when he started feeling ill. Franz kept writing, but his music had a sadder, more reflective tone.

As for his famous "Unfinished Symphony," his eighth, people still wonder about that. It starts with two movements and that's all. There should be two more. Since he'd written that much by 1822, what became of the rest? Theories: He considered it complete after two movements and stopped writing. Or he finished the work but removed two movements and used them with another symphony. Or the last two movements were lost when he sent the manuscript to his friend Herr Hüttenbrenner for safekeeping. Franz focused on this name on the computer screen, and it felt important.

Schubert died without a wife or known heirs.

Franz Schubert became my full-time occupation. His presence permeated everything, and I got the impression he wasn't leaving soon. Luckily, I had a little money to sustain this unexpected leave of absence from reality.

It was the gift of my grandma Helen. By the end of her long life, she'd accumulated a respectable pot of cash. Mom and Dad were financially blissful since they sold their five sporting-goods stores to a large corporation. My sister had married into barrels of money. I was just the overworked lawyer with no husband to take care of me, so Grandma left it all to me.

"I know you make a living," she said to me at our last Thanksgiving together. "Use your salary to pay your bills and buy necessities, but promise you'll use my money for something that makes you happy."

"Maybe I'll make it my vacation fund," I told her. "I could toast you in Paris and Tahiti."

"Yes, vacations are nice," she said, not quite convincingly. "Maybe you'll want it for something else, too. Something really important to you, something you don't know about yet."

"Surprises can be nice," I said.

So here I was, surprised. This was certainly important and something I hadn't known about before, but I still wouldn't call it nice. The nonstop effort to make sense of things was grueling. Normalcy seemed like a luxury, and I easily lost track of time, decorum, and other minutiae as Franz barreled through the mundane details of living.

I was brooding about this when my apartment buzzer sounded and I opened my door without thinking. It was Fred. He immediately apologized for not calling first.

"No problem, Fred, I just wasn't expecting you," I explained. "I thought you were the pizza guy."

"The pizza guy?"

"Yeah, I ordered from Picurro's on Henry Street."

My fine, strong friend looked about to cry.

"Liza, you're naked."

We were both in tears then. Fred offered to stay over that night and I let him. He went to sleep on the couch, but I may have cried out in the night. Fred was in my bed when I woke up, wrapped around me like a blanket.

He took the day off to babysit me, and I felt gratefully grounded with my old friend beside me. We walked the neighborhood bundled in winter layers, and bought food at my favorite market. I felt almost like the old me, but somehow enhanced.

The phone was ringing when we got back to my place. On such a good day, I thought I could be nice to a long-distance telemarketer. But I have my limits.

"*Bonjour!* We're ba-ack, *ma soeur.*" Cassie sang her words, and threw in French with a stinko accent, to boot.

"Already? How was Paris? Leave any clothes in the stores for the next tourist?"

"Come on, Liza, I'm not that bad. Besides, you're supposed to shop at Christmas."

"Oh, I must've misunderstood. I thought the idea was to shop for *other* people at Christmas. Silly *moi.*"

"Who says I didn't bring something nice for you? Come to the house this Saturday and see."

My sister, the fashionista, can dole out pretty fantastic gifts when she wants. Besides, a trip to her house might be just what I needed.

I said I'd come if I could bring Fred. I heard Cassie's eyes roll. To cheer her up, I said I might bring someone else, too.

"A date?"

"We'll see."

Fred was already laughing when I hung up. A trip to Cassie's could be fun as long as Fred was there to offend her. Fred is the opposite of fashion-forward (even his shoes look wrinkled), and he's not going to marry me. Cassie saw him as an impediment to any chance of me meeting "someone worthwhile," no matter how remote that possibility.

Fred knew Sister Dearest quite well from hearing my completely objective stories about her, and from social gatherings I dragged him to through the years. He always accepted my invitations to her house—out of morbid curiosity, he said—but he had reservations this time.

"She's not exactly good for your mental health."

"Okay, she can be a black hole in the karmic universe," I admitted. "But she's my sister. And this time she has something I want."

Don't think for a minute that my sister Cassie has a whole lot that I

want. However, we've always eyed each other's assets with the deepest interest. She's the tall, svelte redhead that skimpy black dresses were invented for. I'm the dark voluptuous one, the eternal icon of womanly
glory, if history had stopped in 1962.

Cassie is a career princess. She was fussy and demanding from the start,
a noisy annoyance to my young ears. While I demurely marched through
school with high grades, she made a commotion cheerleading and being
gorgeous. Even her hair was good. Especially her hair. Red, wavy stuff that
permanently inspired my mother to dye her own to match.

And Cassie and I were sisters at heart, with strong loyalties and clear
boundaries about certain things. Usually.

In my sophomore year at Cornell, I met Barry Whitman and did a
long, luxurious free fall for him. He had classic good looks, was the witti-
est person I ever knew, and had a great sense of adventure. On weekends
we explored the wilds of upstate New York and got in scarier fixes than I
ever encountered in the New York City subways. No mountain too high,
no cave too dark.

Cassie started at Cornell the next year, and it was the nicest time of our
lives together. With no parents there, we weren't competing for attention
or rewards. I liked showing her around, and she liked hanging with up-
perclassmen. It wasn't long before she acquired Wilson, her own adven-
turing boyfriend. We were part of a crowd that saw leisure time as a swell
opportunity to risk life and limb.

I was scheduled to spend spring semester of my junior year in
Barcelona. Barry didn't want me to go, but I was deep into feeling my independence as a woman and secure in my love. I wrote him nearly every
day and phoned twice a month.

In early March, Barry called me in tears. Really, they never meant it to
happen. Wilson had left Cornell, and there was this ice-camping trip and
Barry and Cassie wound up sharing a tent—for warmth, that's all. But
things had changed, and I was away in Barcelona, and no one wanted to
hurt me but blah, blah, blah. They got married the following year.

My parents bought the newlyweds dishes, towels, a Cuisinart, and a
week in Saint Bart's. Barry's parents gave them a Remington.

Maybe people who have always been rich don't think in practicalities.
Cash is a tacky gift and everyone has housewares already, right? On the

other hand, a zillion-dollar statue of a reared-up horse and rider is always in good taste. As it turned out, Cassie built her world around that Remington.

Barry would not come into family money until after graduate school at Columbia, so they started out in a tiny apartment above a Chinese restaurant on the Lower East Side of Manhattan. Cassie intended to continue school part-time. But she looked at the stately statue in their funky living room and decided it needed a more fitting setting. She got a full-time job working with a publicist in the garment center and made a bit of a name for herself. She was stolen away by Donna Karan, and they moved to digs that were better showplaces for the Remington.

When Barry finished his MBA, he started work at the family bank. After paying his dues for nearly six months, he was promoted from vice president to senior vice president. Family money passed hands. Life got easier. Cassie and Barry moved to Great Neck. She set aside a flowering career to have two perfect children. The family soon wound up in that bastion of old Anglo money, Upper Danville on Long Island. At last her Remington could feel at home among Persian rugs, signed Picasso lithographs, a Fabergé egg, and one Steinway grand piano.

Sie ist stark . . . She is strong, with supple limbs and long, long fingers. Every day she feels robust. She expects it.

In my last years, I was so sick and feeble. What might I have done with a body such as hers for a full, long life? What might I do?

CHAPTER FIVE

DATE: January 6
CLIENT: Liza Durbin

Client appeared agitated. Clothes a little better, last remnants of manicure gone, biting her nails for the first time since grade school. Piano
playing gestures continue. Delusion has escalated—brought "proof"
she's inhabited by composer Schubert, pages of handwritten music.
Claims these are the writings of Schubert.

Client refuses psych consult unless I go with her to sister's house
Saturday.—MK

NEXT APPOINTMENT: Saturday, January 8, leave here at 12:30

Fred is a stellar human being, and not just because he's my only friend in
Brooklyn who actually owns a car. He showed up at noon, checked me for
inappropriate attire, then we picked up Mikki on the Upper West Side. She
was reluctant about this outing until I offered a hefty day fee for her services.

Mikki looked just right for a winter's day in Upper Danville, dressed in a long camel-hair coat with paisley scarf over a black cashmere turtleneck, pinstriped woolen pants, and expensive boots. I looked so-so in old black pants, a burgundy sweater, and my favorite down jacket.

The ride took almost two hours because of traffic. It didn't help that there was no noticeable connection among Fred, Mikki, and me. I muttered about the weather while Fred grunted about traffic while Mikki recounted the details of a book she was reading on famous cannibals. It wasn't until we got off the expressway and reached the world of Upper Danville that we all shared an interest.

As many times as I've been there, it's hard to be blasé about these old estates, most of which can't be seen from the road. High stone walls edge the properties, and tree-lined driveways crawl on for ages before they reach home base. Occasional stables, rolling grounds, and glimpses of WASP grandeur still got my grudging attention and apparently were enough to make Mikki sit up straighter and fix her hair. Even Fred looked around as if hoping to spot something not meant for peasant eyes—like the chauffeur's daughter and the heir apparent canoodling under a tree.

To get to Cassie's, you turn down a storybook lane and drive to the end. Amazingly, her home is not the largest in the neighborhood, having only seven or eight bedrooms, formal dining and living areas, plus assorted rooms, each reserved for some essential such as the billiards table, the model ship collection, and a Navajo loom. The place was designed for glossy magazine layouts, eerily immaculate for a home with two young children. Even with a fire blazing in the hearth, there was no distinctive scent to declare who lived there.

So, not exactly cozy, but we were there with a purpose. I rang the bell.

I had played it out in my head for days. How we'd begin, when to play, and all the possible reactions from Mikki and company. But I was not prepared for what happened.

"SURPRISE!" The sudden explosion of family stopped me short. Cassie, Barry, little Cameron, pouty Brittany, and—beaming with triumph—Mom, Dad, and Aunt Frieda, too.

"Tell the truth, you knew, didn't you?"

"No, Mom. How would I know?"

I looked around for an escape hatch. Nothing. They all knew Fred, but Mikki was an unexpected sight, so a great fuss was in order.

"A *therapist*, really? How interesting. Is that how you know my Liza?" My subtle mother was relieved to have a professional on my case. She'd be pulling Mikki aside for a private talk at the first opportunity.

"*Oh, Li-i-iza-a.*" My singsonging sister thrust a large, Frenchly wrapped package in my hands. "I think you're gonna love this. Open, open, *o-o-open it!*"

It was indeed a stunning thing. An ankle-length chenille sweater coat of navy and fuchsia with traces of gold thread. Sadly, it was a bit tight around the top and it was probably meant for someone taller. Like Cassie, I suspect. Mom must have told Cassie a powerfully pitiful story about me to make her part with this treasure.

So probably everyone in the room knew about my "problem." They were there for a show. Personally, I could have waited awhile, but Franz was about to jump out of my skin.

The imposing black Steinway sat in front of a wall of windows that looked out on a sad-sack winter lawn, desperately in need of snow. A struggling fire burped and hissed in the hearth, and the Remington stood aloof at center stage. Subdued tones prevailed. As I walked to the piano, Brittany said something about it being hers, *ya know,* but she was quickly shushed by everyone over the age of eight.

Sitting down, simply touching the keys, felt like all the joy in the world. The first chord washed over me like heaven, and every nerve in my body lit up as the melody revealed itself. The sound turned into dancing lights, soft caresses, the wild teacup ride at Disneyland. We were on a journey through an exotic landscape. I felt the room around us changing. The fire grew stronger, the colors richer, the people more beautiful. The Remington leaned toward us.

But the most spectacular show was behind closed eyelids where no limits exist. I saw, heard, and felt things we have no words for. When it was over, I looked around at my greatly changed family and friends. They would never see me the same way again.

. . .

I would have played forever, but at some point hunger won out and dinner was served at the long dining-room table. Sitting down with my family, I realized I was exhausted, and my back hurt like hell.

Everyone's eyes were on me. After the lavish praise and gushes of amazement, it was hard for people to find words. Yes, it was great, but it was scary and bizarre, too. Not one person there could accuse me of having been a musical giant, or a musical *anything,* until then. They wanted an explanation. Thank God for five-year-olds.

"You play too loud, Aunt Liza." Cameron held his ears and made a smiley face. "I can play, too, but Britty won't let me."

"Why should I? They got the piano for me, *ya know.*" Brittany was blessed with dominant-princess genes.

Cassie jumped in with her sternest reprimand. "Okay, *mes enfants,* we really want to hear about Aunt Liza. Didn't she play beautifully?"

"Britty thinks she's so great 'cause she takes lessons." Cameron turned his soulful eyes on me. "Aunt Liza, will you teach me to play loud?"

"There's nothing I'd rather do, sweetie." I meant it, too.

"Well maybe we should talk about what you're gonna do next, honey," Dad said. He was there at the start of this, and he had been worrying ever since.

"What do you mean, what does she do?" I wouldn't recognize my mother without an opinion to state. Her red hair burned brighter as her conviction grew. "Liza has a great career ahead of her."

My father was not convinced that I wanted that. Neither was I. A large family discussion was brewing.

"Can I have a lesson now?" Cameron was close to pleading.

"Liza, this is the kind of gift you need to share with the world. Think what could be learned from you." Aunt Frieda intoned the voice of a noble scientist. I pictured my brain floating in a jar and a research team trying to make it hum.

"You know, turning pro is not the worst idea I ever heard," my sister threw in. "God knows where this came from, but it's got to be worth pursuing. Sure beats being one more single lawyer in Brooklyn."

"I can play *Für Elise,*" Brittany announced. "Wanna hear?"

They were all talking on top of one another, elbowing to be heard. Barry had been quieter than usual, though, so he had our attention when he finally broke in.

"There are a lot of people who would take advantage of you, Liza. You don't know this business. I'd be really careful about finding the right agent, the right lawyers."

Poor Barry long ago bequeathed his adventurous spirit to the young and naïve of the world. He clasped his worried hands on the table and kneaded his knuckles nervously.

Then Fred coughed for attention. "It's not just other people's reactions I'm worried about. This situation is very hard on Liza. It's not easy to feel taken over by someone else."

There, he'd said it out loud, so there was no turning back. I delivered the Cliff Notes version of my tale of Schubert and me. Just saying the truth out loud was emotional for me. I got teary about the joyful parts and convulsed with sobs about my deepest fears and dangerous lapses. My outpouring was met with thick, silent concentration, except for the occasional *Oh, God* or *Jeez.* My nearest and dearest were not ready to call me insane, but it was also hard to swallow my story. On the other hand, they believed absolutely that it wasn't me playing the piano.

This painful scene was mercifully ended by the commotion of Brittany's impromptu performance of *Für Elise.* Hideously played, Franz wanted to chop off her hands. I loved her with all my heart for the distraction.

DATE: January 8
CLIENT: Liza Durbin

Wow. She's not delusional but I have no idea <u>what</u> she is.

Went with Liza and friend Fred to the home of sister Cassie, brother-in-law Barry, 8-year-old niece Brittany, 5-year-old nephew Cameron. Surprise family reunion with parents Max and Louise, and Aunt Frieda (all from California). They were sincerely amazed when Liza played piano—she was <u>brilliant.</u> No way she could develop such talent on the side—doesn't even own a piano.

Must read up on multiple personality—she's not one, but same emotional trauma may apply. Maybe consult with expert on multiples? Try hypnosis? Past life regression? Black magic? Not urging her to see a psychiatrist anymore. They'd prescribe antipsychotic drugs—but that's for when you want the "delusion" to go away. Not sure about that now.

Family insisted on Liza staying with them a few more days. Dynamics could be interesting factor—concern, exploitation, smothering, all possibilities. Need to keep her focused on how to manage internal struggle around "inhabitant."

Wow.—MK

NEXT APPOINTMENT: Thursday, January 13 (I hope)

They always mean well. So how could I turn down a few more days at Cassie's when my folks and Aunt Frieda had schlepped all that way just for the pleasure of my company and to gawk at me like I was Bobo the Talking Chimp? Besides, they had the piano, an urge to pamper me, and a fridge full of comfort foods. I live to please them.

Fred was nice enough to drive home alone with Mikki, and Mikki was nice enough to shelve the psych evaluation talk. She was awfully quiet throughout our gathering, though she surely didn't miss a thing. She observes everything so completely you can almost see mental pictures streak across her forehead.

When I walked Fred and Mikki to the car, it was clear I'd gained status in her professional eyes. No longer a client, but a *case*. Mikki realized I wasn't just crazy, and she was working on possible theories. Her experience with multiple personalities would help here, though it's not quite the same thing. Still, she said some of the behavioral manifestations resemble those she'd seen in other "multiples."

The truth is, I hoped Mikki would find I wasn't unique. Uniqueness isn't all it's cracked up to be, especially if you're frightened all the time and you've never heard of someone like you before and you don't know who you'll be in the morning and you can't even take a shower in privacy and you're going so crazy that a few more days with La Fashionelle actually sound grand to you.

"Look, Liza, you're gonna be here a few days, you can't run around in the same clothes all the time. A little shopping'll do you good. Just you, me, and Mom, like the old days, except it's my treat this time."

When she put it that way, especially the treating part, Cassie's plan sounded pretty good. Shopping was a revered custom in our family anyway. The proven remedy for rainy days, compensation for birthday acne, a way to make up after family fights and hissy fits.

We left the guys at home and sailed off in Cassie's Jaguar to raid overpriced boutiques and quaint shoppes. Aunt Frieda—a woman of too much jewelry, too much makeup, too much everything—heard they sell shoes on Long Island, so naturally she came along. Princess Brittany missed out because it was a school day, but Cassie planned to buy piles of loot for her so she wouldn't feel deprived. All in all, we were a formidable expedition.

Cassie frequents the kind of shops I put in the museum category—fun to browse through, but you've got to be kidding. Nobody spends that much on clothes. Nobody. On the other hand, Cassie is a well-known somebody, so she buys with abandon. It helps that every slinky little nothing looks great on her and the salesladies pull customers in off the street just to have Cassie prance around in their ooh-la-la clothes. Her gorgeous red hair adds insult to envy. But don't think I hate her for this. After all, those long lovely legs blob out into size-eleven feet, and you've got to love that. Anyway, it was Aunt Frieda who suggested shoe shopping.

"I absolutely must get navy sling-back patent leathers to match that purse I got at Saks. Where should we go?"

Naturally, shoe stores have always been Cassie's nightmare. She flinched at the suggestion. It makes sense. She had to start mail-ordering shoes from the big-and-bigger catalogs by age twelve. Even ordering custom-made shoes from Italy, she learned, couldn't replace the simple joy of having a salesman make twenty trips to the stockroom just to find your perfect pair. I felt bad for Cassie and suggested she and I leave Mom and

Frieda to the shoes while we continue the clothes hunt. It also gave us a chance to talk.

"How long do you plan to keep this thing a secret?" Cassie asked, as we burrowed through stacks of silk T-shirts. "Because, *entre nous,* I've been thinking of possibilities for you. Barry thinks I'm crazy, of course, but I say you should make the most of this thing while you can."

So nice to have a sensitive sister. Despite my blubbering soul-baring of the day before, she chose to look at the bright side. Like how to cash in on this "thing."

"You already said you don't know how long this will last," she continued, plucking flowered panties from a bin. "I say make a CD today so if it goes away tomorrow, it's not a total loss."

Now this I had to ponder. I was far too fragile to go public, but her point was taken. The music could be lost at any moment, and that would be a shame. I told her I'd think about it, that something private and discreet might do.

"*Private?* Are you *crazy?*" Again, that sensitivity. "What makes this thing so wild is that it's you. *You!* Not some music nerd from Juilliard. Just an ordinary lawyer from Brooklyn."

"Maybe I want to stay ordinary, Cass. The music's amazing, not me. If anyone deserves credit, it's Schubert—and I don't see that happening."

But I didn't have Cassie's vision. She had it all worked out for me. We needed to record my "act" immediately—with witnesses to prove it was just me. If the thing stayed with me, it would be a great beginning. If it left me, we could still market the DVD and CD as curiosities.

"I'm not a freak show," I snarled. "And don't plan my life for me, thank you."

"Hey, this could be great fun for you, too. I was thinking the world could use a hot, sexy pianist." I kind of smiled. "And you could use a new look." Smile gone. "So let's just stop in the French Courter and have a little look around, *oui?*"

Mais non. The French Courter is a tasty boutique offering the elegant version of Frederick's of Hollywood. I laughed out loud.

"Come on, Liza," Cassie wailed. "I'm serious. You could pull it off. You got all the breasts in the family. I mean, sure, you could lose ten pounds, but you have time to work on that."

She was already pulling things from racks and throwing them in a dressing room for me. Like all the men I know, Franz had pushed his internal off-switch about ten minutes into our shopping trip, but some part of him seemed suddenly happy. So I decided to have a little fun, too. What could it hurt to try on a few slip dresses?

Let me count the ways.

Long, lanky types like Cassie look alluring in tiny, low-cut numbers. I look like a slut.

Renoir painted me. Babylonians carved fertility goddesses that bear a strong resemblance to me. But you will never see the likes of me next to wafer-thin supermodels in magazines these days.

"I look stupid," I said.

"No, you don't," Cassie assured me. "You just look fat. Try something else. How about this?"

She held up a short satin royal-blue dress with spaghetti straps.

"I can't wear that. There's no place for a bra."

"Try it without, Liza. The color's great. We can always get you a strapless bra."

This is the kind of thing willowy creatures can say. We who shop in the Womanly Section of Victoria's Secret know different. If you have silicone breasts, no problem. Those babies will stand up and smile with no help at all. Not so with the real thing. Fully unfurled and left to their own devices, my natural beauties could destroy weak men and lay the mighty low. As a lawyer and the proud owner of a brain, I had long since opted for a tailored look that I liked to believe was professional yet chic.

"I'm not wearing this thing, ever," I said, slinking out of the dressing room.

"Wow, you look great in that, totally hot." Words I never wanted to hear from my sister. "Let's take it home, just in case."

"I'd never wear it." Adamant, dismayed by her reaction. "In fact, I hope you'd shoot me dead if you caught me in public like this."

"Shut up, Liza. I hate you. I wish I had half what you have. *Sacré bleu!* Women pay megabucks for breasts like yours. And, believe me, no one expects Franz Schubert to have tits like that."

No argument there. I thought my situation came with enough absurdity of its own, but Cassie saw still greater possibilities. She'd been up most of the night plotting it out.

With her brief but impressive experience as a publicist, Cassie felt compelled to put her skills to work for me. With any luck, she said, I'd soon have a performing career. That's what the new image was all about.

Of course I would be tastefully, yet enticingly, packaged, she promised. Definitely not pop or classical, let's call it nouvelle classique. The right performance venues, guest pianist with great orchestras, prestige talk shows, lectures, benefits, awards, the eventual book or two, and a hidden private life to keep the mystery alive.

So simple. Bobo the Talking Chimp could do it.

I let her prattle on for a while, probably because inane talk goes well with shopping. Then I told her that I'd rip her lips off if she didn't stop talking. We gathered Mom and Aunt Frieda and stopped in a dozen more shops on the way home.

When we got back to the house, there was a great to-do of showing off new shoes, modeling clothes, and giving Brittany her lavish due. I was as relaxed as I'd felt in weeks. My family can be intense, but I'm safe with them. If I'm dressed all wrong they just tell me so, and if they get on my nerves I can shriek at them. Things are okay even when they're not.

So I wasn't afraid of being swallowed whole, at least for the moment. As my anxiety waned, so did Franz's. When I approached the piano, we sat down together, and leaned into the music like wildflowers reaching for the sun.

＝＝＝＝

Sie ist reizend . . . She is lovely, but so thin. I try to tempt her with Wurst and Nudeln, but instead she looks in the long mirror and kneads her thighs like dough, as if she could reshape them. She does not even appreciate her magnificent hair. If she could see the plain and pasty thing I am!

And she is charming. People choose her for her friendly nature and amusing ways. She does not need music to attract friends.

To have such gifts as hers!

The next few days at Cassie's were filled with music, more shopping, and lots of talk around the kitchen table.

There are people who demonstrate deep concern by giving advice. Whether they have any clue about what to do is not the point. They have to feel they're helping. So they give the only thing they have—words.

"Your uncle Seymour had the same thing," my mother announced. I stared back in amazement, as did Cassie, Barry, and Dad. Seymour was my mother's late brother who, I believed, was most famous for marrying Aunt Frieda.

"He joined the Navy after World War Two. Before Korea," Mom said. "A year later, he becomes the Navy table-tennis champion."

"And how is that relevant?" I said.

"What do you mean, how? How does Seymour, who never played table tennis in his life, become a world champion?"

"Navy champion, Louise," Dad inserted. "And I also don't see a connection."

"What's the difference? He suddenly developed a gift."

"Mom, isn't it possible he practiced in the Navy?" I tried to bleed the irony from my voice. "Maybe he played table tennis before, but you didn't know. Besides, it's not exactly the same as being inhabited by a dead composer."

"I see a connection."

Actually, my mother had cultivated her own surprise talents later in life. After years of raising kids and pleasing the customers at Durbin's Sporting Goods, she used early retirement as a time to flourish. She went from yoga dilettante to serious devotee and instructor. And she followed her lifelong flair for sewing and embroidery to create pretty stunning fabric art. Good galleries sold her pieces.

"Mom, you had hidden talents like Uncle Seymour," I said. "You might as well say that's the same thing."

"Don't be ridiculous. It was different with your uncle."

"Sorry to disagree, Louise," my father said, "but I think you're nuts. Seymour was nothing like Liza."

"And the Schubert theory *isn't* nuts?" Mom gave in with a shrug. "Maybe we're all going crazy."

On Wednesday, Aunt Frieda added her thoughts. I was packing to leave when I heard her clanking down the hallway. (Frieda never gained weight, just jewelry.) She walked in the room and closed the door behind her.

"So, how's the family genius doing?" A face like a schnauzer and a voice like a dental drill. "Can you stand one more opinion, Liza?"

She got serious and sat me on the bed beside her. She held my hand for the first time in years, and modulated her normal bullhorn volume.

"You won't laugh if I tell you something?" she said. "I always thought this could happen."

"You always thought people could be inhabited by dead geniuses? You're not talking about Uncle Seymour again, are you?"

"The Ping-Pong nonsense?" she said. "Nah. That's your mother's idea."

I asked Aunt Frieda if she'd actually seen inhabitation before.

"I'm not sure." She licked her lips as she thought it over. "I might have seen something. Anyway it seems familiar to me, and I believe in it."

"What exactly did you see, Aunt Frieda?"

"I don't know, it was such a long time ago. Not exactly the same, I'm sure. Who knows anymore?" She waved a floppy hand in the air, making a bevy of bracelets jangle. "I don't think you're nuts, that's all I'm saying."

She obviously had a story to tell. I pressed her for details, but got nowhere. Hard to imagine the blood oath powerful enough to keep my aunt Frieda from telling a secret.

Frieda and I had shared secrets before. She was my ally as I was growing up. As we sat holding hands in Cassie's guest room, I studied Frieda's face, trying to retrieve the person I knew back then.

She was always an assemblage of bold colors, shiny accessories, and perfume. I used to think of it as pure pizzazz. Did her flamboyance turn crasser with age, or had my perception changed? Frieda made herself an easy target for careless snobbery. Not everyone saw her true-blue heart, but she rescued me from humiliation when no one else even noticed.

The Durbins were a family of nightingales, and we used to spend Sunday nights singing around the piano while Aunt Frieda played from *The Great American Songbook*. I belted tunes from the bottom of my feet, gave them plenty of zing, copied the trill in my mother's voice. By the time I was six or seven, my parents encouraged me to accompany on the kazoo. But singing was my favorite.

Then one day: "Mommy, make her stop, she's singing in my ear!" Depend on a sibling to volunteer criticism. "You stink, Liza."

I remember how the grown-ups paused for one awkward, telling moment before trying to soothe my feelings. Too late. Cassie had spoken the truth. I became the family's designated listener, vowing never to sing in their presence again.

Only Aunt Frieda understood my devastation.

"Liza, honey, people don't like my voice either," she told me later in private. Even her speaking voice sounded off-key. "Let's team up, sing together when no one's around. How would that be?"

That was great.

~~~

I took the train back to Brooklyn over general family protest. Franz hated to leave the Steinway, but it was time to check in on my life.

I purposely had not taken any calls or checked my e-mail, but I couldn't ignore the blinking red light on the answering machine. Myles Broadbent, that ambitious legal pup, left pleading messages concerning details only I could explain to him. *Not as ready as you thought, Grasshopper?* Several friends called more than once wondering if I had fallen off the planet. There was a greeting from Fred, a call from Mikki, and one strange message from Patrick.

"I'm missing you terribly, *deliziosa*. You've sounded distant lately. I'll be back soon. We have a lot to talk about. Call me. *Ciao*."

He did sound lonely and sadder than usual. Probably he'd realized he would not be marrying the contessa of his dreams, so he was ready to return to my warm bed in Brooklyn. As usual, our relationship's path did not present itself clearly in my mind.

We started with infidelity, after all. Not against each other, but against two perfectly fine spouses. If not for Patrick's extra Knicks ticket, we might never have had a single hour alone, not one accidental brushup or whispered comment. But we did go to that Knicks game. Soon Patrick was wild for me and wanted to show it. I loved being with a man who thrived on bold feelings. He enthralled me with superlatives that didn't exist in my husband's sensible vocabulary: I was his heart's echo, the Milky Way in his bed, the answer to his only question. And he cooked for me.

Not the occasional omelet, but meals to make the gods sob. This was food to smear on the lips, swirl with the tongue, dribble down hungry arms. Immeasurable, perishable gifts for us both.

Patrick and I found ourselves united in the righteousness of love and destiny, sorry to cause hurt, but desperate to be inseparable. So we got together, caused hurt, but the inseparable part hadn't come to pass.

The thrill of our secret romance dissipated in the toothpaste and coffee stains of everyday life. I expected that, looked forward to it in the course of a full relationship. Unfortunately, we had not counted on the baggage of our inauspicious start. We each knew that the other was capable of being unfaithful. It was the unspoken criticism that either of us could always lay on the other (or ourselves), an underlying theme of mistrust. On the other hand, it was important that we be happy forever after—else why did we break two perfectly good hearts to get here?

With the ingredients of love, mistrust, guilt, and hope thickly binding us, we still had not gotten married. We weren't even living together. Yet I loved Patrick day to day with more assurance and depth than I'd ever experienced. I believed our commitment was growing, right until the day that Patrick told me about Italy. Then all my uncertainty and regret roared again to the surface. (Look what happened when I left Barry and went to Spain!) Patrick couldn't understand my outrage over his plan. He said he felt secure enough to leave temporarily without hurting us, that it was a sign of our relationship's strength. It's the nature of insecurity that I could not entirely swallow his explanation. But I needed to keep trying.

With Patrick hinting that he'd be home soon, I wasn't sure how I'd react. Still, there was a great white sale going on at Macy's and it wouldn't hurt to buy new sheets, just in case.

The next time I saw Mikki, there was a strange role reversal. I became the expert.

Mikki was full of questions for the only person she believed to be inhabited by a dead genius. She had to learn from me before she could offer useful guidance.

"Our reflexes are still out of sync," I said. "Sometimes the phone'll ring and Franz jumps at the sound, and I wind up dropping a plate."

"So you're physically out of sync, yet you can play intricate piano pieces."

"I'm not much of a factor when we're playing. He's in charge and I don't have any instincts or inclination to override him, except in moments of panic."

"How about on the intellectual level? How do you communicate? Words, thoughts? Do you hear the tone of his voice?"

"No. No words," I said.

"Is it all emotional, then, or do you share specific thoughts and ideas?"

"It's both, but without words. Anyway, his words would be German, wouldn't they? Old Austrian German, I guess. But it doesn't matter, we understand in other ways. How do you explain that?"

The good therapist: "How would *you* explain that?"

I compared it to a dream state, where we rely on images as much as words. That's when we skip the running narrative that our wide-awake selves use to catalog everything we see and do and think. Some people purposely try to lose words during deep meditation, and infants dream before they have words. People say their dogs dream. I wasn't sure if my communication with Franz was a move up or down the evolutionary scale.

"So, communication on a prelingual level," Mikki said with interest. "A neat twist on telepathy. This could be its natural occurrence, maybe the only way it could really exist."

A spooky thought occurred to me. "What about channelers? Those wackos with nine-hundred-year-old spiders speaking through them? You don't think they're for real, too?"

"I never thought so, but we should take a closer look," she said. "There's someone I can call."

"Call a channeler? Are you serious? Because I'm not sure that identifying with that subculture would be the best thing for my mental health," I said. "Unless you think we can hook up with Mozart for the Dueling Pianos Tour."

Mikki missed the therapeutic value of sarcasm. She preferred to hear how I was coping emotionally with our coexistence. I confessed that I was getting used to Franz's presence, which scared me more than anything.

"He's this huge being, a creative genius," I explained. "His mind is fuller than mine, and he works on so many levels at once."

"You're bright and creative. Can you learn to keep up with him?"

If only. Any serious creativity I had was gravely stunted in law school. The decline had started long before that, really. I was an honor student in high school, so I got tracked into math and science. No room for lightweight electives in the schedule. I studied creative writing in college but got practical and wound up in law school. Eventually my arty side was limited to encouraging schoolchildren to write and going to gallery openings with my friends. Not one thing in my makeup or experience prepared me for a life with Franz, who was off the creative charts.

"I'm hearing that you're anxious," Mikki said. "What are you afraid will happen?"

"I'm afraid I'll get swallowed up and disappear."

"Well, I think we've found an area we need to work on right away," Mikki said as she checked her watch. "I want you to think more about coexistence and fear, and we'll get into it next time."

. . .

I didn't really need Mikki's instructions to think about my fear. What I could use was instructions on how *not* to think about it.

Sometimes I'd slip into a comfort level with Franz and suddenly my pronouns would slide from "I" to "we." That's when the world was richest, and being a genius was a joy. But as I grew more comfortable, Franz grew more comfortable—and stronger. I was afraid one day those sliding pronouns would shift back to "I" and it wouldn't refer to me anymore.

Mikki wanted to see me the next day, but I put her off until Monday. My folks were still at Cassie's and I already needed another dose of family to assure my identity. Just a month ago, it would have been unthinkable to spend two weekends in a row with Cassie and crew. But family roots are filled with the kind of power I needed.

DATE: January 13

CLIENT: Liza Durbin

Uncharted territory here. Client is communicating with inhabitant on a prelingual (sublingual? nonverbal?) level. Need to get linguistics texts, maybe consult with someone.

Must help client address emotional struggle with inhabitant. She fears being overcome by a bigger persona. Should establish balance in case this is permanent.

Will find out about channelers—who knows?—MK

NEXT APPOINTMENT: Monday, January 15

Î became Voodoo Woman. I carried a bag of charms, rags, and tokens at all times. Mikki told me to do this.

I saw Mikki right after the weekend at Cassie's. It had been an intense family experience, with countless reminders of who I am and no question about where I came from. My family blessed me with plenty of free advice on how to run my life. There was a consensus for me to move into Cassie's, where there was plenty of room and always somebody around—just in case. This was clearly not Cassie's Plan A, but she nobly admitted its merits. I did not.

Even with all that family around, I was slipping more. Franz and I would play piano for long stints, and I'd be lucky to remember half of it. Playing left me physically and emotionally drained. My body ached, especially my back, arms, and neck. I could barely stand afterward, yet it was hard to tear myself from the piano.

Retelling this in Mikki's office on Monday, I could see her concern. That's when she told me about Sensory Heightening Orientation Options. She had developed it a few years earlier for a client with multiple personalities and had great success with it.

Since memory is often aroused by senses instead of words, the idea of SHOO is to keep plenty of props around to trigger memories in emergencies. If I found myself drowning in Franz, I could whip out a piece of my past and stay afloat on that.

I went out to Long Island yet again the next day, ostensibly to say good-bye before my folks left, but covertly to raid the house for SHOO fodder. I casually asked for favorite photos, borrowed a scarf from my sister, took Cameron's hairbrush, stole my mother's perfume, and helped myself to all kinds of nonsense that only I could love. They'd never miss these things, and I didn't want to alarm anyone. Besides, this was my secret stash, the start of my voodoo arsenal.

SHOO kept me sane, somewhat. My oversized handbag contained my "blasters"—memory sparkers that worked only for me. If I ever got mugged, some guy would be stuck with my Girl Scout wilderness badge, a box of macaroni and cheese, a hanky drenched in Shalimar, a nasty old troll doll, and other embarrassing stuff.

I rented a piano, too. Why shouldn't Franz be happy? When you're sharing a body, it's *got* to be better to have two partially content souls than two that are struggling and strangling each other. So the piano was a terrific surprise.

"What the hell are these people doing here? I didn't order a piano!" Fred had been home, asleep in bed, so I probably should have called first.

"Why are you sleeping so late on a weekday, Fred? It's after eleven." I was frankly annoyed at finding him home.

"Not the point, Liza, definitely not the point," Fred rumbled. "These people are building a piano in my living room. *That's* the point."

I'd let myself into Fred's apartment with my best-friend key and the piano pros moved in the used baby grand in pieces. We'd pushed the sofa and chairs against the wall to make room. They were screwing on the last leg when Fred woke up. It was a Thursday and I thought he'd be at work. On closer scrutiny, he looked awfully pale and his eyes were glassy.

"Are you sick, Fred? I'm really sorry I woke you." Insincere contrition did not move him. "Look, I know it's an imposition, but I didn't have a

choice. No one in Brooklyn delivers pianos to fourth-floor walk-ups anymore. We're just lucky you have a first-floor apartment."

"*We* are? Please explain how this makes *us* lucky."

This had to be Franz's bad influence on me. I'm not above imposing on
a friend, but normally I call first.

"You're right, Freddie. I'm the lucky one. I have a best friend with a
first-floor apartment, and it happens to be you. I saw the piano and was
too excited to wait. Please forgive me."

"You could have asked, or at least called, for Christ's sake."

"Yes, you're absolutely right," I said. "Next time I show up with a
piano, I will definitely call first. We'll only play during the day, when
you're at work, I promise."

I pointed out that the piano did wonders for his apartment, which was
filled with the remnants of college days, a few art posters, and inexpensive
furniture. The piano added panache.

"Maybe it would help if you played at my next party." Fred was teeter-
ing toward surrender. "I could impress women if I had you serenade us on
first dates."

"First dates, new women? What happened to the lovely Jana? De-
ported back to Slovaboobchek?"

"Only if you turned her in." Fred looked grim suddenly, as well as sick.
"We're taking a little hiatus, that's all. We'll see how things go when she
comes back from Maui. She went for a week with this friend of hers, an
immigration lawyer."

"The one you'd like to smash with a sledgehammer and feed to
wolves?"

"Yeah, him."

I commiserated with Fred, suggesting that a break from Jana might be
good. As we talked, the movers finished assembling the molasses-colored
Baldwin. The store's elderly piano tuner was giving it a test run. He played
scales, ran up and down the keyboard, and threw in a shake of ragtime.
Then he got out his tools to make final adjustments. Fred winced with
every note.

"You have the flu, don't you?" I observed brilliantly. "Temperature?
Headache?"

"I feel like my body's been through the clothes dryer. My head's about to explode."

"Poor baby." I pressed a palm gently to his steamy forehead. "I'll play quietly."

~~~

My routine included playing with Schubert at Fred's, getting shrunk by Mikki, fending off family advice, avoiding friends, and jolting myself with voodoo blasters to keep sane. I still wanted to get to the Young Writers Project on Thursday afternoons, but I had already missed two meetings due to overwhelming weirdness. Quite a life.

Fred's neighbors quickly noticed the new commotion in their building. The at-home crowd included one harried mother of baby triplets, a retired history professor, an outgoing widow, and some shadowy types I saw but never met. Their reactions were mixed.

The mom was too terrified by her brood to relax and enjoy anything. She could not hear music, just the racket from downstairs that kept her kids awake at naptime. At least once a day she banged on the woodwork to make her point. I can't blame her. We were one more addition to the noise that already devoured her apartment.

Professor Hoffman wore a faded suit with sneakers every day, and tried to catch me whenever possible for a friendly interrogation. Where do I study, who were my teachers, when do I perform, would I be interested in an older man? I was vague about all but the last. Lucky for Mrs. Pardo, the widow.

Mrs. Pardo was a human Chihuahua, complete with bug eyes and jumpy ways. She dropped by a few times on minor pretenses (could I recommend a good podiatrist?), but she was really aching to know who Fred's new roommate was. Her daughter was about my age, single, and Fred appeared quite taken with her when they met, she told me. I explained that I was not a roommate and wasn't involved with Fred, thanks for dropping by, so long. She wasn't buying it.

Hoffman and Pardo quickly formed an alliance (a spy network?). In my lucid moments, between piano raptures, I saw them through the window. They'd stand outside on the front stoop in the dead of winter. Sometimes other neighbors from the block would join them to listen. On a warmish day I could draw a respectable crowd. But Hoffman and Pardo were usually in their own conversational huddle. They claimed to be great music lovers and to admire me completely. But they were clearly suspicious about the mystery musical wonder in their building.

This sublime daily existence was interrupted unexpectedly and permanently by my whining apartment buzzer one cold February night. A stranger wanted in.

"Who did you say you are?" I yelled into the speaker.

"Pretsky. Greta Pretsky. A friend of the family, so to speak." She had a vague European accent.

"I have lots of family. Who sent you?"

"I'd rather not say." Oh, that's persuasive. "It is very important, Miss Durbin. You'll be glad I came."

I ignored her. She buzzed again.

"I'm sixty-four years old, five feet tall, you have nothing to be afraid of. I teach piano at Juilliard. Please let me come up. I've heard we should meet."

I knew at first sight that Greta Pretsky was a liar.

Five feet tall, my ass. She was an Eastern European pixie who stood about eye-level to my waist. Still, lots of people lie about such particulars—even about their weight at times (though I'd have no firsthand experience there, since I truly believe that socks and a glass of water add an extra eight pounds, minimum). I let her obvious fib pass and ushered her in.

"Who sent you, Miss Pretsky?"

"It's Mrs., may he rest in peace. Doctor, actually. And it's not important who sent me. I've heard you're quite astonishing." My mother, for sure. But how did she know Greta Pretsky the Juilliard professor?

"What's important is that I find out about this 'miracle' for myself, yes?" she said.

Her demeanor struck me as dubiously sweet. Gray hair with a little blue rinse, a plump cozy body, and apple-dumpling cheeks. Her eyes, though, were steel-gray without a trace of blue, and I sensed more of a glint than a sparkle. This was a woman who had spent her life being underestimated.

"What have you heard about me?" I asked. "You might not find my 'miracle' believable."

"I've seen many unexplainable things in my life," she said. "The only thing I'm sure of is this—the more things we believe are possible, the more things become possible. You agree, yes?"

Could it be? A genuine open mind? She didn't seem to be mocking me, nor was she awed. Dr. Pretsky appeared to be fully focused, interested, and ready to hear my story.

She listened to the whole thing with intensity, interrupting only when I left out key connecting thoughts or she had a question. Not a single *Oh, wow*, or *Holy moly* out of her. Finally, she asked me how conversant I was with music. This was not the usual reaction to my tale.

"I don't understand most of what I'm doing. To be honest, hardly anything."

"You must become familiar with the language. Musicians speak another language when they talk theory and technicalities. To share what you know, to make the most of this gift, you must be able to communicate."

"I'm not sure about sharing."

"Nonsense. Of course you will." No room for objection, or even hesitation. "Come to Juilliard, to my studio, tomorrow, early. First thing in the morning. We'll get started, yes?"

I must have looked petrified. Dr. Pretsky tilted her head and smiled, a soft smile that made me smile back.

"Let me see your hands," she said.

She appraised them carefully, front and back.

"Extraordinary," she said, with a whiff of envy.

I saw that her fingers seemed long for her stature, but they were dwarfed by mine.

"I know that this is scary for you, Miss Durbin." She rested a hand on my arm. "But being scared won't make it go away. If you stay scared, you will waste it. Here is my card. Come to my studio at Juilliard tomorrow morning, as early as you can, so we have privacy. The rest of the world will find you soon enough, yes?"

We shook hands at the door. If she hadn't treated me to that sweet smile again I might have ditched her card. But fear was getting me no-where, and I had to trust someone.

I dug an old teddy bear out of my voodoo bag and slept with it all night.

———

Ich lasse mich nicht wegjagen . . . I won't be chased away. Her toys and charms are nothing compared to her own ferocity. I struggle every day to be heard, grateful mostly for her ignorance.

CHAPTER NINE

Why did she believe me?

I woke with the obvious question goose-stepping through my brain. Why on earth did Greta Pretsky believe me? Was Mom so persuasive or was my story too outlandish to be invented? Maybe Mom sent Greta Pretsky the tape we made that first day and was afraid I'd be angry. And how did my mother know Greta, anyway?

Everyone else needed a piano demonstration first, but Dr. Pretsky was ready to believe me. Maybe that's why I chose to believe in her. Also, I knew there was more to her story, and I was dying to hear it.

The clock next to my bed glowed greenly in the dark. Five-fifteen. Too early to take the subway up to Juilliard. I drank hot coffee and stared out the window into the dark. I can look across a small courtyard and right into other apartments from my living room. No lights on yet, no neighbor to send a silent good morning to. So I went to my bedroom, where the one tall window faces Manhattan. Standing on a chair, in full giraffe stretch, I could just get a peek of the skyline, where lights always burn and someone's always awake.

My back and neck ached from days perched at a piano. A little outdoor exercise appealed to me.

I had walked over the Brooklyn Bridge before, but never at dawn. Imagine the sight. New York straight ahead, glowing from within, bulging with dreamery. Soon the giant would wake and the daily chaos would kick in. Already the docks and garbage trucks and food markets must be bustling, but I couldn't see them from the bridge. At first light, it was just me and a few hardy walkers and cyclists on the pedestrian overpass. No traffic, no noise, not a hint of chaos.

I walked through the Lower East Side, up through Soho, and toward Greenwich Village. Franz was up and alert, not missing a sound or smell. I wanted to experience it through his senses. He and I slid into the *we* state—effortlessly and by choice this time. The city became richer, dirtier, brighter, more of everything. We'd stop, head turned up in tourist pose, to stare at glorious buildings I'd never once noticed. Each one had a symphony in it. We sniffed outside a bakery door, caressed the granite of a stoic building, then sat for a while on a hard green bench in Washington Square.

A bearded old man in an oversized coat was setting up his chessboard in the park, eager for the day's first challenger. A black teenager in ski cap and gloves jumped off his bike and approached the man. He took a seat and they started playing without a word. A pretty NYU student in high purple boots walked by with her Irish wolfhound, and the boy was distracted for just that moment. So was the man. Aside from that, nothing existed for them except the game.

We wandered up Broadway, admiring the exotica in store windows. Then suddenly it was nine-thirty, time to pick up the pace. We crossed to Fifth Avenue and charged uptown like an express train, no wasteful stops planned. But I can never pass St. Patrick's Cathedral without a look inside. We walked up one aisle and down the other, nodding at each saint. The vaulted ceiling waved at God, and the daylight through stained-glass windows was transformed into wisps of heaven. An angel sang *Ave Maria* in the voice that Franz wrote it for.

Franz would have stayed at St. Patrick's all day. I had to resort to my voodoo bag just to make him leave.

And suddenly it was eleven, and Juilliard was still a long way off. I grudgingly hailed a cab.

"Juilliard, please, Sixty-sixth and Broadway." Just saying it out loud made my innards crawl.

"You are musician?" Friendly driver, definitely foreign.

"No, not really. I'm going to see someone at Juilliard, though. I'm a little nervous. Very nervous, really. Sort of a musician, I guess."

"Sort of musician? That's funny, ha! I am great musician." He laughed at his own words. He was well over forty and had deep brown skin with patches of charcoal gray. His accent was from a galaxy far, far away, and his voice was thick and spongy.

"I sing now for you."

I braced myself for frog belches. I heard, instead, mahogany and spring-water.

It could only be African. The rhythm was as interesting as the melody, and he added clicks and claps occasionally. I imagined it as a folk song about drought and love. While I found it lovely, Franz was completely enraptured.

For the first time it occurred to me that I hadn't been much of a musical guide to Franz. He'd heard music in a haphazard way since he emerged, mostly stuff I knew and happened to like. But he'd missed almost two centuries of music. Even when he was alive, he couldn't have heard much from the world beyond Europe. I decided to be a better host.

The cab stopped, and it was a struggle to leave our driver in mid-song. I heard myself asking for his name, and did he have any tapes or CDs and could we keep in touch. He was Moreno Abdi from Kenya. He sang ancient songs, plus originals of his own. He happened to have CDs for sale—*sixteen dollars, only for you*—and he gave me a phone number. Moreno seemed genuinely pleased with my enthusiasm. Why not? I was a musician, sort of, and Juilliard-bound.

Cornell has a great campus. Marvelous old buildings woven out of granite and ivy. Stunning grounds, a funky college town, and a knock-your-socks-off gorge. The first time I saw it, I danced around the campus, giddy that they'd actually accepted me.

But the Juilliard campus, *that's* really something else.

It's Lincoln Center for the Performing Arts, to be specific. Which means the Metropolitan Opera, the New York City Ballet, Avery Fisher Hall, and all the rest. The buildings surround a wide plaza with fountains, the classic romantic backdrop seen in Hollywood movies. I'd been there many times—grabbing the cheap seats as a student and, more recently, for extravagant nights out. That's how it should be. An air of intimidating excellence shall prevail, where the shiniest stars present their wares and you feel honored to pay outlandish prices just to be there. And here I was, sneaking in without a ticket.

I found the Juilliard building easily, picked up my visitor's pass, and ran for the elevator. Fourth floor, to the right. I passed a long row of small, windowed rooms. Muffled music of all kinds escaped closed doors and mingled in the hall. I asked a tall kid with a trumpet to point me to Dr. Pretsky. Her studio was an ordinary classroom with a piano, and I nearly knocked her over as I charged in.

She had her purse and a bundle of books under one arm and was buttoning her heavy cardigan, ready to leave. No smile for me today.

"Is *this* what you consider first thing in the morning, Miss Durbin?" My mother's tone of voice exactly, but foreign.

"It's not noon yet, is it?" This was a question, not a wisecrack.

"No, it's not noon, but the morning is gone. I canceled my morning appointments for you and you don't even know what time it is."

"I'm so sorry, really. I got up early and left before dawn, and I don't know what happened, but I'm really, really sorry." She looked disapproving but relieved to see me. "Let me buy you lunch, Dr. Pretsky. At least let me do that. We can talk."

The only ordinary things in the Juilliard cafeteria were the food and the tables. The people resembled exotic birds ready to unleash a song or fly out a window. Between conversations, they vocalized, stretched, rehearsed lines, or scribbled notes. Most intimidating were the dancers, impossibly thin girls with elegant swan postures, laughing with their young princes and chowing down on fries. One swan with long black hair had a ketchup blob on her chin that she wiped away with heartbreaking grace. Her toes pointed outward, even when sitting.

"I've got some books for you here," Dr. Pretsky said. "The basics, yes?

You don't have time to become an expert overnight, but you cannot remain completely ignorant."

"Is that Itzhak Perlman over there?" I said.

"I want to hear you play, of course, but my afternoon is fully booked and I'm going to the theater tonight. Can you come after that? Later is good, not so many people around."

I was awed. "Yes, it *is* Itzhak Perlman! Does he teach here? You know him?"

"What time can you be here?"

Perlman sat with a middle-aged Asian woman dressed in black. He was excited and gesturing, laughing at times. She looked like a thunderstorm.

"Miss Durbin?"

"Eleven. How's eleven? Late enough?"

She nodded, then looked at her watch and left abruptly.

I sat there a long time, feeling like a warthog among butterflies. What made these people different? Did they have gorgeous genetic code to make them more creative and charismatic than other earthlings? I could make music now, but I wasn't born special. I was the lichen on a giant redwood, the last coat of paint on a yacht—serviceable, but useless on my own. I searched their faces for something familiar. Maybe Shakespeare or Maria Callas had nestled into someone's soul and ignited the kind of artistry that gets you into Juilliard. I saw nothing. Franz was looking, too, but at something else.

This world was his. These were the artists he knew, friends from another life. He fell in love a hundred times or more.

I don't know why I felt compelled to "practice" before seeing Dr. Pretsky again. What could I do—improve on Schubert? He could maybe brush up on his scales or memorize something nice? Ridiculous, but that eagerness to please the teacher must be an ancient survival skill. It occurred to me that this feeling might be partly Franz. He was about to play for the teacher, too, and could be adding his anxiety to mine. He'd deny it, but really he hadn't been heard or judged by a discerning ear in a long, long, *really* long time. Can't a genius feel insecure?

In any case, we played passionately for nearly two hours before Fred got home. I was in a nice sweat by then. Playing piano with so much intensity is a physical and emotional workout. My back cried in pain, and my arms were limp.

"You've got a groupie out there," Fred announced, as he walked in and steered me toward the window. It was dark out, so my small crowd of fans had left for the day. He pointed to the one straggler, a tall skinny teenager, shivering at the bottom of the stoop. He was heavily bundled and scarved, but his hands were ungloved so he could work a small tape recorder.

"Could you ask him to leave, please?" I said. "That's just too creepy. Tell him I'm finished and I don't like being taped."

"Great, thanks, sure. If he's a psycho murderer and I come back dead, you can have my Rangers tickets."

"Don't worry, dude. I got your back."

Fred scared the guy off without a fuss. The psycho murderer was highly embarrassed and sent apologies to me. But I took a serious look at Fred's back for a moment.

It wasn't much of a back, to tell the truth. Fred's on the small side of average, an occasional tennis player, always meaning to work out more. He had the soft curly hair and fine features usually seen on Hollywood types. Not effeminate exactly, but not a face to scare psycho murderers with.

I wondered what crazies might be attracted to my new and extremely loud talent. Practicing in his apartment brought Fred into my circle, complete with possible dangers. Any good friend would mention this outright and give him the chance to bow out. But that would leave me alone and even more vulnerable. You see my dilemma.

"How was work?" I asked.

"It sucked, of course. That's all it does, lately, is suck."

Fred was the erstwhile darling of Ads Up, a small but surprisingly hot ad agency in Manhattan. The supercharged creative team drew clients with deep pockets who liked edgy, head-tilting concepts. Fred excelled at head-tilting and was persuasive with the clientele. He won awards. All was happy. Then the owner's son joined the agency and became everyone's new boss.

"I think he's autistic," Fred announced. "The guy's been with us three months and still hasn't learned our names. He stares out the window while you talk to him. And just *try* to use irony in a concept! It's like singing to a computer."

Fred was close to the ranting zone. He needed soothing.

"There's a good production of *Ain't Misbehavin'* I've been wanting to see. It's a weeknight, so maybe we can still get tickets. I could call and see," I offered.

"I'm getting my résumé together, that's all, I've had it. I'll take Jake with me, too, and we'll take some pretty good clients along."

"It got great reviews," I said. "I'll treat."

I called the theater as Fred vented on. I got us the last two seats together, not good ones, but seats. I told Fred we'd have to hurry to make it, and should probably take his car.

"*Ain't Misbehavin'*? Tonight?"

"Sure, it'll be fun. But we have to leave now, Fred."

"Okay, thanks," he said, "that's really sweet of you, Liza. A night out would be good."

On the way out, we bumped into Hoffman and Pardo just coming in together. His shirt had a bright orange smudge that matched her lipstick. She had adoring bug eyes for him and a death-ray stare for me.

"Going out, I see. Well, that's nice, dear." Mrs. Pardo's voice stung like ice. She did not like me stepping out with her daughter's imaginary future husband.

"Just for a little while, yes," I said sweetly.

"Will we see you here tomorrow morning then?"

"Yes, I suppose so," I said. "Maybe in the same clothes, if someone gets lucky." Fred looked more surprised by the notion than Mrs. Pardo.

We practically jogged the few blocks to Fred's Mustang. As we got in, Fred said, "Where to, m'lady?"

"The Vivian Beaumont Theater, Lincoln Center."

Fred drove us into the city in lunatic-cabbie mode. He passed cars any which way, terrified pedestrians, and barely nodded at traffic lights. He was wonderful.

Between harrowing moments, Fred gave me the shocking news that he and Jana were through. She had drifted into the Maui-tanned arms of the nice immigration lawyer. They didn't mean for it to happen but blah, blah, life goes on.

We stowed the car in a lot, ran like crazy, and fell into our seats just as the house lights dimmed. Only then did I remember Franz's strong reaction to our last live music adventure. Fred grew suddenly nervous, too.

Thank God for bad seats.

On the far side in the back row, Franz's gyrations were a spectacle only to the beleaguered few around us. Our unusually polite neighbors waited for intermission before lodging complaints.

Sitting still was hard, though. *Ain't Misbehavin'* is all music—lusty singers belting the hell out of Fats Waller tunes. Swingy, contagious stuff that makes your soul sprout feet and learn to dance. And it all seemed so *loud* to Franz's 1800s, unamplified sensibilities. The stimulation level rocketed. I clutched my voodoo bag to my heart, sucked on a Tootsie Pop, and allowed Fred to throw his right leg across my knees to pin me to my seat, which was somewhat helpful. We still managed a sitting jitterbug through "This Joint Is Jumpin'"—and who could resist rolling the programs into drumsticks and banging them on the seat backs? Toward the end, we wept through "Black 'n Blue."

If you ask me, the whole thing was immense fun, but Fred looked fried when it was over. I didn't even ask about the slightly black eye he'd acquired. He's clumsy sometimes.

When the show let out, I insisted on buying us dinner at a restaurant across the street. It was a little late for Fred on a school night, but he was a good sport. He shushed me as I relived highlights from the show. We had big bowls of pasta and heady red wine, so Fred was more than ready to go when our check arrived.

"Listen, Fred, do you mind if we just stop to see a friend for a few minutes?"

"Now? Liza, it's nearly eleven."

"Don't worry, she's right around here. Over in Lincoln Center, Juilliard actually."

"I'm exhausted, Liza. What's this all about?"

I explained about Greta Pretsky. Fred was annoyed that I hadn't mentioned this late-night appointment before. Maybe I was too nervous earlier to bring it up, or I was afraid he wouldn't drive me into the city just for this. Anyway, I was glad to have my buddy with me even if his nostrils looked permanently flared.

Standing outside the Juilliard building, Dr. Pretsky could have been an elf waiting for a sleigh. She wasn't expecting Fred, and they gave each other the witchy eye. Then she led the way upstairs to the practice rooms. She said that it would attract less attention than using her studio.

There were a few students playing even at this hour. We took the room farthest away from anyone else. The plain, bedroom-size enclosure had a piano, some chairs, and black metal music stands. The dull blue carpeting and matching draperies on the walls provided some soundproofing, Pretsky explained. Then she gave Fred the important job of leaning against the door window to block the view inside.

"If you don't mind, I'd like to tape this," she said.

"No, that's fine. I just don't know how well I'll play. I mean, I hope it's okay because—"

"Just play, Miss Durbin."

We did.

As always I was ravished by the very act of playing with Franz. But there was a difference. For the first time, I felt the rush of risk taking, like running through an unmarked door.

When we finished playing, Dr. Pretsky stared in dismay. I didn't blame her. We'd played the stiffest, awfullest version of "Ain't Misbehavin'" you ever heard. Franz needed to work on his swing.

"That's not what you wanted, is it, Dr. Pretsky?"

She glowered.

"Perhaps an impromptu would be better? The E-flat Major?" she said.

Didn't ring a bell to me.

"Could you hum a few bars?" I said.

She came to the piano and played the opening bars, until Franz practically pushed her aside. Then he fell gratefully into the music.

Picture a swan dive from airplane height, except you have no parachute and you know you *can't* be hurt. You'd yield to ferocious gravity, marvel at the view, flap your wings, and add loop-the-loops as you swooped through virgin air.

I watched the performance from above. Fingers on ivory, blurred with speed. Countless notes, intricately connected, each one distinct. Patterns and rhythms, loud and soft, natural as rain. Franz and I landed together with orgasmic pleasure.

Dr. Pretsky smiled, not sweetly this time but genuinely. Teary eyes, truth to tell.

Fred stood loyally against the window, my barrier against the world. He smiled, too, but with a sleepy yawn. Way past bedtime and making *ready-to-go?* gestures.

I was getting up when Pretsky slid into my place on the bench.

"At last, it's what we thought," she said. Then, without waiting to explain: "Listen."

She played a short segment from the middle of the same piece. Good, but not quite right.

"That is the way most people play this section," she told me. "There are other discrepancies, too."

"I don't think you're completely wrong, Dr. Pretsky. My impression is that Franz just improved it."

Fred found this amusing. "The new and improved Schubert? Makes great ad copy."

Dr. Pretsky withered Fred with a look. "Naturally, we may find mistakes or misinterpretations that have occurred and have been passed along with each printing of the music. I had anticipated that much, but improvements are another story," she said. "I'll want you to review all of Schubert's work in modern print, see where we've gotten away from the original intent. We'll mark improvements separately, yes?"

She wanted to hear more, and Fred wanted badly to leave. I promised him *just one more,* then we'd go. I meant it, too.

~~~

Time flies, right? It was getting light out when we left Greta Pretsky and Juilliard. We retrieved the car, paid the exorbitant parking fee, and headed back to Brooklyn. Fred had given up his guard post at the practice-room window well before dawn and had enjoyed two hours of contorted sleep on the floor. I felt exhilarated, but Fred was disheveled and grouchy.

"Don't grumble at me, Fred, you're the one who got some sleep at least."

"I'm the one who has to be at work in three hours. I feel like I slept in a Dumpster. Could you not be so cheery?"

"Hey, you should have stayed awake, then. Always better to stay awake straight through than just sleep an hour or two. Didn't you know that?"

Grunt.

"Well, you missed some really great music anyway. Think of that."

"I'll buy the CD."

Fred left me at my apartment building, where I collapsed fully clothed in bed. I slept right through my ten o'clock appointment with Mikki. She woke me with a phone call, just to make sure I was all right. I gave her the full update: Dr. Pretsky believed in me, we had a work plan. We're going to meet at Fred's apartment most days to play in privacy. She'll also get me a pass to use the Juilliard library and archives for Franz's research and to educate myself.

We were finally rolling into action and I felt good about it, even if Mikki sounded like she swallowed a dust bunny.

I marveled at how much my sense of "normal" was altered that day. I had just spent the night at Juilliard, playing music via Franz Schubert, and it seemed like the only natural use of those hours. Back in my apartment, I felt either bored or amused by things that usually seemed pressing. Monthly bills, dirty laundry, an empty fridge—the fundamentals had become incidentals. My intellect said I'd get in trouble with this attitude, so I made myself attend to necessities. Still, I felt off course—my internal compass was not pointing north.

I checked my answering machine for two days of messages. Among them was Myles Broadbent in a tizzy. *Erase.* Mom and Dad, concerned. *Sigh, erase.* Patrick with a garbled message, ending with "Love you." *Listen twice, will erase soon.* Sister Cassie threatening to visit. *Oh, God.* I returned her call first.

"This really isn't the best time for a visit, Cassie. My schedule's crazy and—"

"It's no problem, really, *chérie.* I'll be in the city on Friday anyway," she persisted. "We can go shopping, catch up on things. Time to plot your future, *n'est-ce pas?*"

"No, absolutely not. I'm not up for shopping."

"I've got to get Brittany a new dress for the party. Something for me, too, of course. You're still coming, aren't you?"

"What?"

"Brittany's birthday party, a week from Sunday. You promised her!"

"Oh, sure, then I'll be there."

"You might as well come for the whole weekend. Come Friday, in fact." Then she added, "Bring that nice Fred with you."

Bring that nice Fred?

Ich schaue in den Spiegel und sehe sie . . . I look in the mirror and see her. Who am I without my face?

And I have her hands, her body, her staccato stride. In every way, I am improved by her. I should be grateful. How is it possible, then, for me to envy something that I possess?

One of us is a thief.

I spent the afternoon playing piano at Fred's, but left before he came home. He had had quite enough of me the night before at Juilliard.

Alone in my apartment, the silence chewed on my nerve ends. I was cast off from my own life. Fred was the only friend I'd seen in two months, and that wasn't going so well. I couldn't talk to my parents or sister without the F-word coming between us. *How's Franz? Is Franz still with you? What are you and Franz going to do?* I didn't feel like a lawyer anymore and I certainly wasn't a musician. Soon my secret would be out and what could I expect from the world? Adoration, ridicule, and everything in between.

I called Mikki and we talked for an hour.

"My biggest problem is knowing that this could be permanent, that my real life's not coming back," I said. "The people I knew, my friends, they're already replaced by new people. And my new friends are only interested in me because of Franz. *(No offense, Mikki.)* Even if Franz leaves, my legal career is probably irretrievable. And if Franz stays, Mikki, if he stays . . . it's all out of my hands."

"I hear you grieving, Liza," she said. "The life you knew may be gone forever. That's a natural reason to grieve."

"Yes, that's what it feels like."

"Are you still volunteering at the school, the writing program?"

"Franz hates it, I think because he doesn't understand. He's bored. It's hard for me to concentrate with him resisting and making music in my head."

"What will you do about that?"

"It's a team project. The regular teacher takes over when I can't make it," I said. "To be honest, I'm afraid I might act strange, and I don't want to scare the kids. I've gone exactly three times since Franz showed up."

"Stick with it, if you can, Liza. It's a connection to the original you," Mikki said. "How will these fears and reservations of yours affect your other plans? You've made certain commitments."

I told her I was trying to accept my role, but it was hard to be happy about it. She asked if I could see my situation as a gift. But that word didn't fit.

I'd had the most incredible highs of my life playing with Schubert, but it was wrong to think of my circumstance as a gift. This was not like receiving a sweater that I could wear once, then stick in the bottom of a drawer. I didn't get this gift. This gift got me.

"Your life has been drastically altered and you had no choice in it," Mikki said. "Let's set aside the things you can't change. What decisions are still in your hands? What can you enjoy?"

I considered my unexpected and unavoidable career change. It's funny how the little details take over. Suddenly I let myself fantasize about recordings, wardrobe, money, agents, touring. Incredible that this had anything to do with me, but it got me focused on something else anyway. I made a long to-do list that ended with: *Send flowers to Fred.*

~~~

I spent most of Friday with Greta Pretsky at Fred's place, while he was at work. She showed up with books, recording equipment, and a sense of urgency.

She taped everything we played, and replayed parts she wanted to discuss. The ordinary Sony tape recorder hurt my pride. I expected something grander, more suited to Schubert's stature. He, on the other hand, was tickled with the fantastic tool at his disposal. He put a dorky grin on my face and found excuses to work the miracle contraption.

I still couldn't talk with Pretsky on any sophisticated level, and she was frustrated by my slowness in picking up her lingo. She wanted to know if I'd read the books she loaned me. I hadn't gotten to them yet.

"No? You have more important things to do?" she said.

"Well, they may not seem important to you, but I still have my own life to worry about."

"Have you even tried?"

In fact, I had. But Pretsky's "basic texts" were dense and unreadable, like trying to ice skate through mud. Through Franz, I could interpret any musical notes written on the page, but I was a pitiful mouthpiece for him. I told Pretsky I'd try again.

"In the Juilliard library, you'll find everything you need. I expect to see you there this weekend."

Yes, Mom.

I wanted to find out more about this formidable woman, but she brooked little chitchat. Either she found me unworthy of the truth or was addicted to privacy. Despite our close contact, Greta remained vague about how she found me, and showed no personal interest in my life.

"Why are you doing all this this for me, Dr. Pretsky?" I was rubbing my aching shoulder after our long practice. She took over the massage with textbook efficiency.

"I am not doing this for you." She knew just how to work the kink out of my neck. "I do this for Schubert, for the music."

"Yes, of course. What was I thinking?"

Greta ended the massage abruptly. She spoke to me from behind.

"I'm sorry to disappoint you, Miss Durbin. We would not even know each other under any other circumstance, yes? I'm sorry, but it's true."

"But you know about this, don't you? You know about being inhabited."

"It's a great mystery."

Greta walked across the room to put on her coat and gloves. Her mind had moved on to something else already.

"Greta, please, at least tell me this—do you think this will be permanent?"

"No."

"Do you know that for sure?"

"No."

Out the door, end of discussion.

It was nearly five, so I ordered Chinese and had a swell dinner table set for Fred and me by the time he came home. It was meant in the spirit of friendship. Fred was in an ungrateful mood.

"It's Friday night, Liza. You should have asked."

"You have a date?" Other women are so inconvenient. "That's great, Fred. Who is it?"

"It's no big deal, Liza. Just someone I'm meeting for a drink."

Fred . . . *mysterious?* Come to think of it, he had a perfumey smell about him.

"Please, Freddie, not Jana again."

His head retracted like a turtle's.

"Jana who ran off with the immigration attorney? Good job, Fred. She's one in a million."

"I don't need your permission to go out, Liza. Thanks for the dinner, but I have to change now and run."

"We're on for next weekend at Cassie's, though?"

He was noncommittal. Such a busy fellow.

I left Fred's apartment so he could go on his stupid date. There was a small box of Godiva chocolates on the stoop with a piece of paper taped to it with just my name written on it. This was the third gift from someone in my front-stoop fan club. I slid the box in my pocket, drew up my collar, and started for home.

Even in the winter, I like walking through Brooklyn Heights. Recent snow had been pushed aside by city plows, edging the streets with piles of crunchy once-white trim. Sidewalk slush was hardening into icy abstract paintings. The sun, a shapeless glow in a hazy sky, slid gracefully behind the solid brownstones. As it got darker, the windows grew brighter from within. It's the peeking hour. The time when people without blinds put their lives on display for the rest of us.

This was a solid neighborhood of three- and four-story brownstones, tall trees, and pampered backyard gardenettes. Was I the only one with a bizarre secret? The people looked so normal. Comfortable families, working singles, and retired teachers live here. Writers and artists, too, who like the homey feeling and lower rents compared to Manhattan.

At night you can look right into their living rooms and downstairs apartments. Everything about these normal people interested me—what they hung on the walls, where they placed the furniture, whether they overwatered their geraniums.

It's this familiarity that I love. I know the buildings, the fire hydrants, the initials scratched in the corner mailbox. I'd wave to Mrs. Whitaker, joke with the Parker kids, and nod to the regulars at the Montague Street Café. I feigned disinterest when I spotted the likes of Norman Mailer at the bookstore. Hey, he's my neighbor. My neighbors are nice, nonthreatening, normal types.

Unless there was someone else whose soul has been invaded. How would I know?

Maybe my neighbors had other secrets as strange as mine. A tail growing from an armpit, the knack of raising cockroaches from the dead. But dread of discovery keeps secrets safe. Soon I could be the star du jour. Would my fellow freaks envy or pity me? I might become their patron saint, the martyr who went public. I would hang from the scaffold and absorb the collective praise and punishment for our freakish secrets.

But that day was not here yet. I could still revel in anonymity, proudly wear my normal looks and feel safe in the bosom of Brooklyn Heights. A few blocks from home, I stopped in at Klein's Deli. He had his back to me, reaching for a tray of cinnamon buns.

"Smells great, I'll take two."

"Sure thing." This was not Mr. Klein's peculiar sandpaper voice. The guy turned to face me.

"Oh, it's you, Miss Durbin." I looked up at a tall, skinny teen behind the counter.

I'd seen that face before. A stack of small Godiva candy boxes sat near the register. This was the mass murderer who frequented Fred's front stoop. He still came to listen to me, but hadn't brought the tape recorder since the incident with Fred the Fierce.

"Did you leave chocolate candies for me?"

"No," he answered too fast. "Well, yes. I took them from here, but I'll pay for them."

I told him there was no reason to leave me gifts at all.

"Okay. I'm sorry. Did you find the M&M's, too?"

A group of women came into the store together, but I wasn't ready to leave the mass murderer yet. The customers leisurely fussed over chocolate truffles versus raspberry scones. Then a man with a crying child came in. It was ten minutes before I had another chance with the murderer.

"How did you find me, and why are you around so much?"

"Are you kidding?" His eyes widened. "You're awesome. A friend of mine lives in the building next door. I heard you when I was over there, I just keep coming back."

I asked why he wasn't in school in the afternoon.

"I usually come after my last class," he said. "Well, sometimes before, but usually after."

"Don't your parents care that you stand outside the house in the freezing cold until dark?"

"They don't know. Well, the housekeeper, she knows. My mother's away."

"Vacation?"

"Sort of. If you call four months a vacation. They're at my stepfather's house in Aspen."

"Are you a music student?"

"Sort of, I guess. I sing. I have a voice coach. I used to play piano, too. Now I play flute, but I like piano better."

I asked why he switched.

"My mother played flute in high school."

"So?"

"That's what I said. But she said I'd like it and bought me a flute. She says I'm ungrateful 'cause I don't like it as much as piano."

I wondered why he couldn't play both.

"They refused to take the piano when we moved from our old place. Paul—that's my stepfather—he says the piano's too loud, and my mom said it wouldn't fit."

"Well, if you've got a small apartment, I—"

"It's giant, much bigger than the last one. Mom meant it wouldn't fit with the décor."

This kid was equal parts sad and sweet. Not a murderous bone in his body. I liked talking with him, hearing about someone other than me. But Mr. Klein was not so happy about it. He rasped at the kid to get back to work. I just had time to ask his name. Danny Carson.

He came to listen more often after that and assumed crowd-control duties for the front-stoop crowd. *Clear the way for Miss Durbin, please. No recordings, sir.*

DATE: March 2
CLIENT: Liza Durbin

Liza still swinging between grief/fear/depression and excitement about new career. Advised her to stay with one task at a time, day by day—no point in rushing the grief process.

Client spends time studying at Juilliard and playing piano. Has new "friends" to help her—Greta Pretsky pushing her to perform—Danny Carson, teenage groupie—This weekend client is going to her sister's house—will get more free advice there. I'll make an appointment for me and Liza to meet with Zazer.—MK

NEXT APPOINTMENT: Monday, March 7

———

Wir sind unzertrennlich dennoch einsam . . . We are lonely yet inseparable, isolated for such different reasons. I ache for her at times, but my compassion simply makes it worse. I have not done this thing to her, but she fears me, maybe hates me. This circumstance was set upon both of us.

Who is savior, who destroyer?

How embarrassing. It was like going to the library at Cornell, where I first spotted the devastating Barry Whitman, my semi-fiancé until he married my sister. I used to find excuses to go there, sneak up behind Barry in the stacks, offer a candy bar to share. Who could resist? This time around, each trip to Juilliard was a chance to brush up next to Chase Barnes, the gorgeous professor who deigned to notice me.

I'd gone to Juilliard on Saturday, as Mama Pretsky ordered. The Lila Acheson Wallace Library doesn't miss a beat. They claim to have 50,000 musical scores, 20,000 books on art, music, drama, and academics, not to mention more than 15,000 sound recordings. I'd set aside three whole hours in which to lose some ignorance. Probably not enough.

Dr. Pretsky had given me a reading and listening list. I started with a small pile of introductory books, just to get familiar with terms and language. I already knew how to read music (torturously) and understood some Italian musical terms, thanks to Mrs. Wolf, my grade-school piano teacher. *Piano, forte, allegro, andante,* and the rest hadn't changed since

Schubert's day, so we could both read those. If I summoned a visual image to go with a thought, Franz could get that, too. But if I didn't understand the vocabulary or the concept I was reading about, we were both out of luck.

Feast on this sample about "augmented intervals" from the *Oxford Concise Dictionary of Music:* "The German 6th serves as a convenient pivot for modulation, since it may be approached as based on the flattened sub-mediant in one key, and quitted as based on the flattened supertonic in another (or vice versa); also by enharmonic change (see *Interval*), it can be transformed into the chord of the dominant 7th of another key, and . . ."

This probably made sense to almost everyone at Juilliard. Any fresh-man could draw mental images, hear it, make it all perfectly clear to Franz. I was useless.

Deeply frustrated, I grabbed reference librarian Sylvia Waits, explained that I was new there, and asked where I could start. The petite, perky woman was eager to help.

Do you want music history, theory, composition? Sure, all that. *Are you interested in counterpoint, twelve-note atonal?* They're nice. *Western European?* Yes, definitely. *Classic, contemporary, jazz, symphonic?* Something with a little of everything, I think. Anything about Schubert, too. *I see . . .*

Obviously, when I'd told Sylvia Waits I was "new here," she thought I was new to Juilliard, not new to music. Once she realized the extent of my ignorance, she took a more creative approach.

"You might try some children's books," she offered. "Just to get started, you know. *A Child's Classical Handbook,* that kind of thing. Would you like to see some?"

"Sounds about right."

I felt like a kid sneaking a look at *Playboy.* Cradled in the center of a grown-up music text, I thumbed through colorful, illustrated, easy-to-read books. It helped, but I had such a long way to go. The last time I felt like this was in law school. The textbooks and legal documents boggled me at first but I became fluent in that language. Unfortunately, it took three years.

As I scanned the books for useful bits, I was aware of someone looking my way. Staring at me, actually. I caught him at it, on and off, for a while.

Then I stared back. This was no hardship, as this man was absurdly handsome and beaming right at me. I took the short, scary walk to his table.

"Do I know you?" I asked. "Or are you just friendly?"

"I'm friendly."

"Oh," was my brilliant rejoinder.

"And I'd like to know you," he said.

When did honesty come back in style?

"Juilliard's not that big," he said. "I thought I knew the other faculty and most of the students by sight. Which are you?"

"Not exactly either. But definitely more student. Not enrolled, though. It's hard to explain."

"Don't explain, then. I'm Chase Barnes." He extended a beautiful hand for shaking. "I teach musical theory and composition."

He was late thirties, maybe early forties. He had true-blue eyes with a lush trim of dark lashes. The well-drawn jawline met proudly at the cleft in his chin. His blue cotton shirt looked stunning, filled as it was with powerful arms and shoulders. Wavy, honey-frosted hair just tipped his collar, the sideburns were a tad long and sexy. I introduced myself.

"You looked very engrossed in your reading," he said. "But you were playing pretty loud table piano, even for here."

I looked at my busy fingers, deeply into the thumping habit by that time.

"You're a pianist?"

"I'm studying with Greta Pretsky."

"Ah, Greta the Great. Now that I think of it, I've seen you two together. Is she grooming you as her most glorious find yet?"

"She's helping me in lots of ways."

"Yes, you said it's hard to explain. What kind of music do you play?"

"Schubert." Was I supposed to tell him that? "Mostly, that is. You write music?"

"Yes, mostly postmodern," he said. "And also a few things people actually like, with multicultural influences. Today I'm looking at some research on a geometric algorithm for assessing melodic differentiation. Pretty interesting."

His nose and mouth were perfect, too. Did I mention that?

"I'd love to hear you play sometime." I think he said this twice.

"Me? Sure, maybe. We'll see."

Chase Barnes tilted his head at me (enchantingly) and said he had to run. He hoped we'd meet again.

Me, too.

On Sunday, I went to the library for just a little while, but stayed a long time. He never showed.

The next morning I spent a full hour on my hair and makeup. I played at Fred's until almost three, then ran up to Juilliard again. This time I saw Chase in the cafeteria, but he was talking to one of those snotty, gorgeous, skinny dancers with silky hair to the waist. I might have guessed I wouldn't be the first woman to notice Chase Barnes. At least he waved at me.

It started pouring Monday night, and by Tuesday afternoon the city resembled a flushing toilet. Which was lovely, compared to the sight of my rain-zonked hair. Of course, that's when I ran into Chase in the hall outside the library. The skinny dance snot was at his side.

"Liza, I was hoping I'd run into you." He smiled grandly. One hand rested on the toothpick's shapely shoulder. "I want you to meet Katje Merrin."

We swapped formalities.

"Katje's a dancer," Chase explained. "I'm writing a performance piece for her. You must see her dance, she's extraordinary."

I said I'd love to, and he believed it.

"Are you a dancer, too?" Katje said this with a straight face, bless her paper-thin heart.

"No, I play piano."

"Are you faculty?" she asked.

"Let me clarify, Katje," Chase chimed in. "She's the special student of Greta the Great."

Quick, knowing glances passed between them. Katje released an impressed "Wow," said I must be terrific and that she'd like to hear me play. Then she had the good idea that I could play sometime while she danced. Chase followed up with industrial-strength music babble. After a few interminable minutes, Katje had to run to a class.

"Do you have time for coffee, Liza?" Chase asked.

I'd just had two cups.

"Sure, I could use one," I said.

We settled into a corner table. For once I wasn't mesmerized by the crowd there, just the face across the table. Even Franz seemed taken with Chase.

"How do you like working with Greta?"

"She's . . . Greta the Great, right? I mean, it's fine."

He wanted to know who I studied with before. I promised him he wouldn't know her.

"Try me."

"Clara Wolf. A wonderful teacher, the best I ever had."

Chase didn't know her. He folded his arms, appraising me closely. He asked if I was a prodigy.

"Not exactly," I said. "I'm more of a late bloomer."

"Let's sneak off to a practice room. I can't wait another minute."

Greta had told me not to tell anyone about Schubert. She warned me about the fuss that might follow, especially among the Juilliard crowd. So I played for Chase and never mentioned Franz.

His whole beautiful self moved with the music, glowed with joy. He hugged me by way of applause.

"Greta's finally found her star," he said. "She's been looking for you for years."

"Please explain that, Chase."

"Greta was a concert pianist herself. This was decades ago," he began. "She played major concert halls, had a following, the critics loved her. Then she acquired a duet partner. They say he was fantastic. Maybe they were lovers. Anyway, he wasn't her husband. They didn't stay together long. He took off on her suddenly and she gave up performing altogether. She's been teaching since then."

"How good was she?"

"Hard to say how good she could've been. She's so tiny. Her fingers can't reach much more than an octave. But they say she was excellent. Now she's like most teachers, she wants a protégée to carry her flag."

According to Chase, the lofty world of Juilliard has its Byzantine side. Faculty members can be ruthless in their self-promotion and cutthroat in competition. Sometimes that competition has to do with training the prodigies. They spot the promising ones and vie for allegiance. The triumphant professor grooms the student to become a stellar artist who reflects on the mentor.

Greta Pretsky had her share of near-hits. Promising students who wound up as solid but little-known artists. A few flared, then failed. And Natalie Frome.

Natalie was the world's latest piano wonder, the one Fred and I saw at the Brooklyn Academy of Music. She came to Juilliard as a teen marvel and studied with Dr. Pretsky for the first three years. Then the faculty was joined by Lorenz Marsters, the suave pianist who filled concert halls and graced magazine covers. He wasted no time in snatching Natalie away from Greta. Why not steal Natalie? She had good training and astonishing talent. Plus, the fifty-something Marsters had the male itch to exchange his used wife for a younger model, preferably the adoring kind who wore evening clothes well. He had the good taste not to dump his wife immediately and marry his protégée; he waited nearly three months.

Natalie Frome had been Greta Pretsky's mountaintop. She missed the summit by a hormone.

"Let me hear something else," Chase said. "A modern piece."

"I stick pretty much to the classics," I said.

"You need to broaden your repertoire then, don't you think?"

It hit me then. "I know classical music by heart, Schubert mostly, but I believe I can read any music."

"You *believe* you can?" Chase twisted his perfect lips as he considered this. "Where are you in your training, anyway?"

"To be honest," I said, "I didn't play for years. I just started again recently. I've got a lot to brush up on."

"Here's my impression, Liza," Chase said. "You have a stunning gift which, for one reason or another, you ignored all these years. You could perform anywhere, but can't hold up your end of any intelligent conversation about music. Just nod if I'm right . . . Thank you. So exactly what planet are you from, Liza?"

"Brooklyn," I said. "We all play piano like this in Brooklyn."

That night in Brooklyn, while most people slept, a surprise blizzard brought our world to its knees. Thursday was called off due to nature.

Brooklyn Heights wore it beautifully. Picture Alaska with brownstones. I made my way to Fred's place through thigh-high snow. Every mailbox, branch, car, windowsill, and garbage pail looked stunning in white. Icicles hung daringly from nooks and crannies. Snow fell gently, whispering and swirling, a quiet symphony.

Fred greeted me at his door with hot chocolate and a pair of mukluks, preheated next to the radiator. He didn't go to work because of the snow and we both were ready for a stress-free day together.

"*Alien* or *Ghostbusters*?" He waved the cream of his DVD stock at me.

"Let's start with *Alien,* save the heavy stuff for later."

We nestled on Fred's couch, stuck our feet on the coffee table, and watched movies until way after dark. No one went near the piano. Even Franz seemed content in this toasty nest. Maybe he missed his own old friendships and relished the warmth between Fred and me. Everyone felt calm and rosy that day.

When I got home, I had a message to call Greta Pretsky right away.

"We've set a date," she announced.

"You're getting *married*?"

"Oh, please, Liza. A date for your debut, of course."

Yikes.

"It's March thirty-first. That's a Thursday."

"You can't be serious."

"I was lucky to get a date before August," she said. "We only have this one because Evan Wald—you know, the Scottish cellist?—broke his arm and had to cancel."

"But it's so soon." *Yikes.* "Where will it be?"

"Carnegie Hall. I played there. You will like it."

second movement

Appassionato

The roads were plowed and passable by noon Friday, so Fred and I took off for our weekend at Cassie's. Fred started out in a chatty mood, but all I could think about was Carnegie Hall. I rolled the words around in my head, scrambled the letters, imagined them in French. How could Carnegie Hall be happening to me? Fred's eyes ballooned when I finally found the nerve to tell him about it.

He had loads of questions about how they'd promote the concert, when I'd record, who was my agent, and other terrifying details. Cassie had tormented me with the same questions on the phone that morning. As Fred interrogated me, I kept trying to change the subject to him and Jana, but he'd switch it right back to me and Franz. We finally gave up on talk and quietly enjoyed the bumper-to-bumper traffic.

As we left the expressway and approached Upper Danville, winter waxed magical again. The snowy fields beckoned me the way a playground calls to a child. Luckily, I had taken my cross-country skis with me.

"You brought those things with you, Liza?"

We shivered outside my sister's front door as she offered this warm greeting.

"And hello to you, too," I said. "You think we could come in?"

"Sure, but leave the skis outside, please."

"No problem," I said. "I still can't believe you live out here and don't have a pair."

"Right, as if I don't have enough to do already."

Cassie disliked cross-country skiing. She saw it as the wimpy second cousin to downhill skiing, at which she excelled.

I left my skis leaning against the house and we followed Cassie to the kitchen. We were slurping the last of our hot coffee when the kids came charging in with Barry. They looked delicious, bright and shiny with cold-weather cheeks.

"We built a fort, Aunt Liza. Can I show you?"

"Cameron, you just got in," Cassie said. "You can show your fort later."

"I can play 'The Spinning Song' with no mistakes," Brittany said.

"You little genius," I said.

"Can Fred come look at our fort?" Cameron was dying to show it off.

"Hot baths, get going!" Cassie bellowed like a train conductor announcing a station, and the kids ran off to their rooms.

Barry put a jacketed arm around me and said, "It's great out there, Liza. You bring your skis?"

I forgot to mention this part. It's not only that Cassie doesn't cross-country ski. Her husband does, and we like to ski together.

"When does Liza *not* bring her skis?" Cassie answered for me. She sounds so petty at times. "Remember when she brought them on Labor Day?"

"Actually, Barry, I was thinking of going out for a little trek," I said. "Get some exercise after sitting in the car."

Fred reminded me that it wasn't that long of a ride. He didn't relish being left alone with Cassie.

"I'm still dressed for it." Barry said. "Let's go."

My ski overalls felt roomier than usual. This new lifestyle of anxiety and dead-person inhabitation was a good weight-loss plan. Add a little exercise and I could be divine.

We put on our skis and Barry made a lewd comment about how luscious I looked. He sped away before I could react to his wildly out-of-character remark. Odd how everyone who knew about Franz naturally assumed that *I* would be changed. If only they could see their own behavior: Barry flirted with me for the first time in years, my sister couldn't get enough of me, Mikki made me the center of her universe, and my parents thought they were Mary and Joseph.

Barry and I skied most of a mile without seeing another person outdoors. It was almost four, and everyone with good sense had opted for warm kitchens and hot cocoa. They'd left their marks on the day. Sled tracks raced down a hill, crossing and colliding. Two horses rode together, then ran off in different directions. A snowman wore a hat intimating he went to Princeton.

"The Kembels' mare has a new foal," Barry told me. "Wanna have a look? It's not far."

It was a little farther than I expected. By the time we reached the Kembels' place, I couldn't remember being cold. The uphill slope to their stables rewarded me with a nice, sweaty zing.

A black mare stood guard in the corral. The crisp white blaze on her nose suggested rank, like a colonel's eagles. She occasionally nuzzled the springy colt hovering around her legs. An alert border collie watched over them both.

It was the perfect scene to watch in silence. Barry broke the spell with the last words I wanted to hear.

"This isn't how I thought life would be," he said.

"Huh?"

"My life," he said. "I thought it would be different."

(If I just don't answer, maybe he'll stop. Please, Barry, please, don't say another word.)

"I never planned to go straight to grad school and have a family right away."

(Shut up. I mean it.)

"I thought we would travel together the world and have adventures."

(We?)

"Hey, Barry! This is a nice surprise."

We both looked up to locate the owner of a loud, hearty voice. A tall, athletic-looking man, presumably a Kembel, approached us with great strides. He shook Barry's hand and introduced himself to me as Dave Kembel.

"Why don't you two come in and have a glass of something? Sara would be glad to see you and, Barry, there's an investment I want to ask you about."

"Another time, Dave. I just wanted to show Liza the colt. We've got to get back to the house before Cassie calls the cops."

Dave gave Barry an understanding wink.

We turned to leave. Before Barry could say another foolish word about his imperfect life, I challenged him to a race back to the house and sped away. My lungs came close to exploding, but I refused to slow down enough to talk. Barry stayed gallantly in range, wasn't even working hard. I was gasping for air, bent over in pain when we reached the house. He offered a manly hand to help get my skis off, just brushing my left breast in the process. I assumed it was an accident. Franz rolled his eyes and shook my head.

Fitting with the weirdness of the day, we walked in to find Cassie and Fred and the kids wriggling around on the living room floor, a mass of happy squeals. Based on the birthday balloons and other regalia scattered about, I guessed they were taking a break from party preparations. The Beach Boys rocked from the stereo as Fred called out dance moves: "Roll once to the left, twice to the right! Arms in the air and flap, flap, flap!"

∿∿

MISS BRITTANY WHITMAN INVITES YOU TO CELEBRATE
HER 9TH BIRTHDAY WITH HIGH TEA & LOVELY SURPRISES

VELVET & LACE
SATURDAY, MARCH 5, FROM 2 TO 5 P.M.
24 MYLES LANE (MAP ENCLOSED)

In Cassie's circle, a child's every birthday calls for a Sweet Sixteen, bar mitzvah, and Oscar party combined. Cassie told me that one boy had real soldiers leading the charge of the paintball teams. At another party, four white horses pulled a little princess in Cinderella's carriage—the original one, no doubt. And for Brittany Whitman's birthday, she and her ten closest friends were being treated to beauty makeovers and glamour photos.

I had foolishly brought casual clothes for this affair.

"What are you *doing,* Liza?" To hear Cassie's tone, you'd think she caught me eating worms. "It's eleven-thirty and Arla will be here any minute. You're not even dressed."

"As you can see, Cassie, I am dressed. A sweater and jeans are actually considered clothing to most people. And who's Arla?"

"I *told* you this was a beauty party."

"No, you didn't."

"*Sacré bleu.* You never listen to me. Everyone's getting a makeover," she said. "Arla Shay is the hair genius from Shay Salon. She's bringing Gilda to do makeup and we've got Lance Bellows coming, too—the fashion photographer. Everyone gets a glamour photo."

"Little girls *like* that?"

"Are you kidding? It's all they think about. Don't worry, it's the kid's version of everything. Nothing too grown-up. Of course, you and I get the full treatment."

"Oh, goody."

Cassie informed me, however, that I'd need to wear something nice to get the full effect. She seemed oddly pleased when I explained that I hadn't brought anything nice. The perfect solution occurred to her, in fact. That little blue dress we bought at the French Courter, *chérie.*

"I told you I'd never wear that."

"Don't worry, you'll look great. I think you've lost a few pounds. Even Barry noticed."

"Cassie, I'm not wearing a spaghetti-strap slip dress when it's twenty degrees outside. Forget it." I could see from her face that some concession was called for. "I'll check your closet for something else."

La Fashionista got visibly nervous as I rummaged through her clothes. She wanted me in my own blue satin dress, the one she had picked out for me. She did *not* want me stretching out her good stuff.

We finally agreed on a red long-sleeved knit dress. Cassie was disappointed, but at least I picked something she wasn't planning to wear again. Just one problem remained.

"You didn't bring *shoes?*" Cassie is easily shocked.

"Of course I brought shoes. Doc Martens or ski boots, take your pick." I could plummet no lower in my sister's esteem.

Cassie's many shoes were arranged in her closet by color and season. Not being blessed with size-eleven feet, however, they were useless to me. Instead, I turned to Soledad, the family's eager-to-please au pair. She loaned me a pair of black heels with sexy straps, which looked perfect with the dress. Even Cassie approved.

"You don't look horrible," she said. "But it's a quarter to one, and Arla's been waiting forever. They'll have to do rush jobs on us. They've set up shop in my bathroom. You go first."

"They don't need to make me over, Cassie, really. That's for Brittany and her friends. I can help with the party, and you go get gorgeous."

But Cassie was already running downstairs, calling for the caterer, so I located Arla in Cassie's palatial bathroom. Being a top professional, she hid her fear as she approached my hair.

"What great piles of curls you have, love!" Arla sounded hip and British. "Too bad we don't have time for a proper cut. Mind if we trim the bangs?"

I let Arla do as she pleased. She swooshed the hair away from the wrong parts and planted it where it belonged. She wielded clips and brushes with surgical skill and tossed in hair spray and a few muttered curses before she was done. Then Arla handed me off to Gilda the Makeup Goddess, who added the final touches. Not too bad.

The men in the house were awed silly by me when I came downstairs for the party. Fred whistled. Barry froze solid. Cameron said I looked like his favorite lady on the *Schoolhouse Sing-Song Show,* the pretty one, not the one who looked like Grandpa.

Hats off to Cassie, I can't remember a better party. Brittany looked adorable, as did all her friends, none of whom actually wore velvet or lace.

As the guests, who were all Ashleys and Taylors, handed birthday presents to Brittany, she gave them each a gift bag. Inside were beauty products for the under-twelve set. Glittery stuff to paint on faces, scented nail polish, peel-off tattoos, flavored lipsticks, and a necklace for each guest with her name spelled out in beads. The family playroom bubbled with little-girl noises.

"Do me! Do me!" A little blond Ashley said, thrusting a jar of Ghoulie Green nail polish toward me.

So Ashley and I did each other's fingernails, followed by toes. Every female in the room, including Cassie, exchanged acts of vanity with knowing, girlie pleasure. The beauty mavens from Shay Salon worked the crowd. Gilda poofed a spot of pink on each cheek. Arla did one special hair trick for each girl, like a Pebbles ponytail spouting from the top.

Meanwhile, Lance Bellows set up his lights, props, and backdrop in the den. As each guest reached perfection, she posed for the wonderfully pretentious photographer. When the kids were finished, Cassie and I each sat for Lance. I made dramatic faces and showed off my green nails. Cassie stuck out her tongue and went cross-eyed.

Before everyone left, Lance promised to send us each a framed photo within the week. I want Cassie to plan all my parties.

The next morning, there were six inches of fresh snow on the ground, winter's last harrumph. I bundled up and quietly crept downstairs. Leaving through the front door, I heard the first sounds of a household waking up. A morning cough, a flushing toilet. I quickly pulled on my skis and set out, as alone as I could be anymore.

It was still snowing and the world glowed whitely. Franz and I merged with the scene, ignoring peripheral vision to block out skis, boots, mittens, poles.

A few brave birds sang out, either sturdy winter stock or early arrivals who'd been hoping for spring. The long skis slid through the snow in steady cadence. Cold air filled my lungs, then exited in bright, lively puffs. My heart sped up and pounded loudly as we settled into a pace, three heartbeats to each stride.

Snow. Breath. Glide. Ba-bump, ba-bump, ba-bump.

Franz turned everything into music. The grainy sky wept in sad, slow strains. Crisp white meadows sang in high, bright passages. Birds punctuated the melody with haunting cries. We saw the day in full composition, sculpting it into sound. A slow opening, a lively section, slower again, then the grand finale. *Snow. Breath. Glide. Ba-bump, ba-bump, ba-bump.*

That morning Franz Schubert created the *Snow Sonata,* his first original work since 1828.

Der Titel ist "Für Brittany" . . . The title is "For Brittany," a birthday gift.

We left Upper Danville with weird good-byes. Barry took me aside and made weak excuses for any embarrassment he might have caused. He said he'd always found me exciting, even before the Schubert thing, but anyway he and Cassie were just fine, so let's forget what happened, okay? Then he kissed me way too tenderly. Cassie walked us to the car and whispered something to Fred that made him snort-laugh.

Then Cameron rushed up with a handmade gift, a snowball to take back to Brooklyn. Brittany called me her favorite aunt. She was wearing the birthday locket I'd given her, which was the one Aunt Frieda had given me way back when.

Back in Brooklyn Heights, Fred and I ate dinner at Kingfisher. We were getting along better, so I confided about my little crush on Chase Barnes of Juilliard. Fred knew who Chase was.

"How could I forget?" Fred said. "One of the dumbest fights of my life was over that guy."

"Over *Chase*? Chase Barnes, the musician?"

"If you wanna call him that. Jana dragged me to see him one night." Fred shook his head at the memory. "It was some modern neo-crap. I have a pretty high tolerance for that stuff, but his noise drove me nuts."

I had never heard Chase's music. I charged to his defense.

"Well, maybe you just didn't understand it. He's very highly regarded, Fred. He writes serious music."

"Yeah, well this thing had a really stupid name, too. *Four Reasons to Clip Potatoes,* something like that. They had a piano, a hammer, and two dancers onstage," he said. "All I know is that it stank. I wanted to leave at halftime, but Jana insisted on staying. She even went to a lecture by him afterward. I should've known she was insane then."

At least we agreed about Jana. Besides, I could have sweet dreams about Chase Barnes without Fred's permission. I changed the subject and asked about work.

"It's getting worse," Fred said. "The boss is still a jerk. Jerkier than ever, actually. Jake's ready to pack up his pencils and make a break. It used to be fun to work there, but—"

"Can't you quit, Freddie? You've got a great portfolio and your clients love you. Maybe it's time for your own agency."

"I've been thinking about it." Fred looked away, scrutinizing the air. "You need a lot of cash to start a business. *A lot.* Or you need a huge cash-cow client. I can't just quit and see what happens. I need money coming in every week."

"What about a partner?" I asked. "How about Jake?"

"He's more broke than I am." Fred sighed heavily. "Look, let's not talk about this anymore. Too depressing. How about dessert? Share the pro-fiteroles?"

It had been a good, mostly relaxing weekend. I started tensing as I fumbled for my apartment keys. I pictured Carnegie Hall waiting on the other side, dreaded everything that had to happen in the next weeks. I was so preoccupied that I didn't notice the obvious until I dead-bolted the door behind me and turned on the hall light.

Someone had been in my apartment.

As I scanned the rooms, subtle changes nicked my senses. The energy tilted a different way, the walls made room for somebody else.

There were other clues, too. Dirty pots and utensils were soaking in the sink. A *Sports Illustrated* lay open on the coffee table. The heat was up way too high, and a dozen red roses sprung from a coffee can on top of a bookcase.

I opened the bedroom door and discovered a picnic, trimmed with champagne and crystal flutes. It was gorgeously arrayed on bed trays set on my new linens—the ones I'd bought at the Macy's white sale.

"I came back just to have this gnocchi with you," he said, "to see how perfect it could be."

Patrick raised his tall body from the reading chair and extended his long arms to fold me in. He smelled of kitchen spice and pleasure. I scolded him for not calling first, told him that I'd just had dinner. He responded with a low, happy growl.

"Fair warning, scrumptious—it's eat or be eaten."

I had no idea I'd be so happy to see Patrick. Silly, inordinately happy. I'd been a big baby before, moping and complaining while he was gone in Italy. He always said he'd come back, that I was his love, and here he was. Plus, he knew nothing about Franz.

We spent the night romping in bed. Franz—who was comfortable with Fred and laughed at Barry—grew nearly faint in Patrick's presence. He hid like an ostrich, his senses shut down tight. Fine by me, of course (though in my kinkier moments I wondered what Franz's super senses might add to the mix).

Between bouts of pent-up sex, Patrick and I found each other again. Our conversation spread in all directions, like marbles falling from a jar. Italy, architecture, food, music, the law. Life without sex, love without touch. The weather, the Knicks, the state of our lives. How could I have forgotten the ease I felt with Patrick, the reasons we were together?

Patrick Kaplan Florio. His ancestors dipped into a dozen gene pools to assemble him. I retraced the face I'd known and missed. The dark hair and fair skin, the blue eyes and unmissable nose. The Scottish side didn't appear in his name but it, too, showed up on his face.

He had my favorite body type, too. Six-foot-three, broad shoulders, perky butt, and no unsightly hair on his back. He liked me, too.

By Monday at breakfast, he still didn't know about Franz.

Maybe this was part of the thrill of seeing Patrick again. I was still just me. Inhabitation by a dead composer is not the kind of thing you discuss with a boyfriend overseas, so I'd waited. Even with him there, I felt no great rush. I told him about the music, though, that I'd taken a leave of absence from Stricker, Stricker & Feinsod. I said I was practicing seriously and that he'd be surprised by what he heard.

"Honey, that's fantastic. Amazing. I always suspected you had hidden talents." Support with no qualms. *Thank you, thank you.* "I couldn't imagine you spending the rest of your life as a lawyer, but a musician, wow . . . are you really good?"

"Pretty fabulous, actually."

"A musician . . ." Patrick caressed the word. "That's really something."

His enthusiasm made me wonder what I'd looked like before to him. A wild woman sewn into a corporate suit? But, no, "wild" was an exaggeration. Professionally, I'd followed a predictable path from college to law school. Law was not my passion. It was a *why not?* choice at the end of college. I'd never once felt the excitement about law that Patrick showed every day about architecture. We could walk through any neighborhood and he'd spot an unusual façade and, bingo, his day was made. I could read a thousand legal briefs and never smile.

"This is such a surprise, Liza. How come you never told me about your music?"

"It wasn't that important before."

He beamed at me as if I'd said something brilliant.

"You know, I'm still just me, Patrick. I'm not a better person than before. Why do I get the impression you're liking me more now?"

"Don't be silly. It's exciting, that's all."

"You mean more exciting than being a lawyer?"

"Well, yes," he said. "Sorry, but in my opinion, yes. And, hey, you sound excited about it yourself. Do you know you've never told me a thing about your work before? Not a word, except for complaints about the firm or the other lawyers. What does that tell you?"

Volumes, I had to admit.

"Anyway, I can't wait to hear you play. And this is all gonna work out great, honey. Couldn't come at a better time."

"Better time? What do you mean?"

"You're an artist. You're not tied to a desk sixty hours a week."

Patrick had an aversion to staying in one place the rest of his life, doing the same thing. He always said he needed more freedom than that, and he wanted us to explore the world together. I had been charmed by his vision of shared adventures. With Franz on board, though, all scenarios got more complicated.

"Listen, I may go back to Italy," Patrick said.

"You can't be serious."

Patrick had come home bearing gifts. Heavenly chocolates, a small oil painting, a gold pin, truffle oil, and other Italiana. I noticed they were scattered around my apartment, along with all his luggage.

"Patrick, have you even been to your apartment yet?"

"I came straight here," he said. "I didn't want to miss a minute with you."

This made me ask how long he planned to stay.

"Don't worry, sweetheart, I'm not going anywhere yet. But I had to re-sublet my apartment, just in case."

"You gave up your apartment again?" *Stay calm, don't commit a felony.* "Why don't you just tell me what's going on, okay?"

"It's good news, really. I got a job offer in Milan, starting in April. It's a conservation and renovation project in northern Italy. Actually, they'll contract for my services through Gekas and Benedict here, so I'll still be employed with the firm when I come back. Gekas figures he already got good return on my leave of absence, just by me bringing home this contract. They have some things for me to work on here until the contract starts in Italy."

"How long will you be gone?"

"Up to a year, maybe, but I didn't accept it yet. I was waiting to talk to you. I want you to come with me."

Carnegie Hall and Italy, too. Opportunity knocked on every door, and I was too big to hide under the bed.

"That's why the timing is so great. You can be a musician anywhere. In fact, this'll be perfect for you. There's all the music you could want in Europe."

How could I answer? I wasn't ready to tell Patrick all the complications. I needed more time with him and me, Franz-free.

I sat down on his long, sturdy lap and wondered how I got so lucky. "I need time to think about this. It's a big decision."

"I understand, take your time. Just one thing, sweetheart. Mind if I live here for now?"

Patrick's reappearance served as an unexpected reality check. It came two and a half months after Franz's arrival. While my situation was no less strange or disturbing, I realized how far Franz and I had come together. Patrick, who knew me as well as anyone, didn't remark on any obvious strange behaviors. I'm not saying I was in total control, but I was definitely stronger than before. I also believe that Franz had learned how to manage his end better, and to show some respect for my life.

If anything, Patrick seemed delighted with any changes he saw in me. I'd like to think it was all about me, but Franz contributed an irresistible zest to us.

I also saw Patrick differently. He did come back as promised, and wanted me to live with him in Italy. Maybe we wouldn't fail, after all, at the relationship that brought down our two marriages. Maybe I could stop imagining Patrick with beautiful Italian women—that would do us both a world of good.

So I had temporarily passed for normal with Patrick, but this reassuring milestone also added to my burden. How could I add Patrick's needs to my life while dealing with Franz, Carnegie Hall, and an unpredictable future? He'd have to know the truth eventually. But not yet.

When I saw Mikki the next day, she was in a tizzy. She seemed more alarmed about Carnegie Hall than anyone. Would I be able to cope? Was I ready? Will I tell the world about Franz?

I told her about my reunion with Patrick, about how Franz and I seemed to move together better. She was glad to hear about it, but had questions about our future.

"I'm concerned that you haven't fully integrated your relationship with Franz," she said. "You need to be prepared emotionally for whatever happens. I want you to talk with someone who's dealing with a similar situation."

"You've found someone else like me?"

"Not exactly." Mikki took off her tortoiseshell glasses to look deeply in my eyes. "It's something we talked about before."

Oh, no.

"Her name is Patty Flanders, and she's not exactly like you, but she deals emotionally with another being."

Don't say it.

"I know how you feel about channelers." She *said* it. "But Patty Flanders is special. She's lived with this for at least ten years, and she's written several books. I've spoken with her.

"Most important, Liza, she seems to have accepted her situation, turned it into something positive. She maintains good relationships, feels optimistic, has a sense of control and purpose. She's written several books. She feels unity with her—"

"Her *what*?"

"I believe she calls it her entity."

"Lovely. Ya hear that, Franz? You're an 'entity.'"

"I know how it sounds, Liza. But I believe you could benefit from talking to her. She can't prove her entity's existence the way you can, but she believes in it just as strongly. Unfortunately, there are no support groups for people like you. It's worth investigating."

We set up an appointment for Friday. Just what I needed, one more thing to dread.

~~~

For the first time in a while, I looked forward to going home. Patrick would be there. I would walk in and find love sprawled across my living room couch. Schubert would not be discussed.

My wandering boy had picked up vats of new recipes in Italy. The aroma of red sauce welcomed me home. The dinky kitchen table sparkled with the elaborate settings, like a mutt with a diamond collar. A nice cabernet breathed for our pleasure. Patrick made so many things better.

"Dinner's on in twenty minutes, *amore*," he announced. "Drinks to be served shortly. Proper attire is casual nudity."

"And me with nothing to wear."

I took off my shoes and sank happily into the sofa. Then I made a hideous mistake: Phone messages and mail should always come *after* the relaxing, romantic dinner.

I stupidly pressed the "play" button on my answering machine.

"*Bonjour,* Liza, it's time to make *pla*-ans." At the sound of my sister's singing voice, I lunged for the phone to press "stop." Lucky I'm quick. I had to protect Patrick's innocence. When he got busy in the kitchen again, I lowered the volume and continued listening.

"Carnegie Hall, big sister, Carnegie Hall! Call me tonight and we'll make plans to get together. We have a lot of decisions to make. I've got some ideas I'm dying to tell you. Call me. Don't for*ge*-et. Call."

The next message was from my mother. They'd made reservations to fly out for my debut. Everyone's excited. What should the mother of the star wear? I didn't listen to the other messages. Instead, I turned to my mail. A bunch of bills and one large padded envelope.

My name was handwritten on the thick manila packet and there was no return address. Inside was a copy of *Classical Music for Dummies.* No note enclosed.

I thumbed through the book, a cheery history of music with definitions and explanations for people like me. Dummies. Somebody knew exactly what I needed.

"What did Cassie mean?" Patrick joined me on the couch and handed me a glass of wine. "That stuff about making plans. What are you two up to?"

"Oh, just Cassie stuff. Life's one big event after another with her."

"Is that all? She sounded—"

"I'm starved. Is that food ready yet?"

White bean soup, pasta puttanesca, and salad with red onions and mandarin oranges. (Franz's compliments to the chef.) Patrick and I played footsie under the table and forgot about the dessert.

DATE: March 7

CLIENT: Liza Durbin

Everything is changed. Liza is scheduled for Carnegie Hall March 31! Have scheduled Friday meeting for client with Patty Flanders (Zazer). Liza is reluctant, but this is essential.—MK

NEXT APPOINTMENT: Friday, March 11

Wie kam ich in diese Zeit, an diesen Ort? . . . How did I come to this time, this place?

These people live with marvelous invention and comfort. Even the children have staggering knowledge, yet it still takes each person thirty years to gain thirty years of wisdom. Their lives remain messy, naturally.

I could easily have obsessed on my rioting emotions, but there were all the practical details wanting attention. Greta Pretsky was more intense than ever when I saw her at Fred's on Tuesday morning. We had so much to accomplish in the next few weeks.

In addition to artistry, playing piano is physically demanding. Greta treated me like an athlete in training, scrutinizing every aspect of my posture, position, and movement. She said I was in no shape for concert life and insisted I start a daily routine that included push-ups and yoga. If that weren't enough, Franz constantly pulled at my lovely long fingers to stretch them just a bit further. He made mental music all the time. My body and mind were being reshaped from every direction by bossy interlopers.

"We must discuss your concert program," Greta said.

"I don't know where to start. Can you help me?"

"Of course. I brought some suggestions." She gave me a handwritten list to look at.

"They're fine," I said, after a cursory look.

"Don't be sloppy, Liza. Read it carefully."

Many of the pieces were familiar by name or number, but only one made me jump. "Lebensstürme"—for four hands.

"Greta, what's this? This thing for four hands? I'm not *that* good, am I?" She looked almost shy.

"Only if you want," she said.

Greta led me to the piano where we sat side by side on the bench. She had the treble end, I had bass, but we began playing the *Lebensstürme* as one.

The music returned to Franz at once, and Greta was a concert pianist at heart. We swayed, wove, mingled our senses, felt communion as our usual barriers dissolved. We were two spirits spinning one tale.

I was so exhilarated when we finished, I hugged Dr. Pretsky. She was obviously uncomfortable with my show of gratitude, so I gave her what she really wanted.

"I'd be honored to play that with you in concert."

"Thank you."

She allowed herself to relish this decision for a quick moment. Then she was back to business.

"We need to think about practicalities. We'll place an ad in the *Times* and send news releases about your debut, but we'll say you're unavailable for interviews, yes? You're not ready for reporters yet, so I will answer their questions."

"Of course."

"The publicists for Carnegie Hall and Juilliard will help us, too. We'll send personal invitations; I have an impressive mailing list. You'll draw a respectable crowd because it's me, and it's Carnegie Hall. I can get the respected critics to review you. What about your friends and contacts?"

I offered to supply the names of everyone I'd ever known. More important, I told her that Cassie was on the job.

"My sister has hideously rich and important friends," I said. "She's sending personal invitations with little notes, like 'Wait till you hear my big sister play!'—things like that. She also bought a big block of tickets to give as gifts. Oh, and she's trying to get a friend of theirs, John Doyle, to come. I guess he's a somebody."

"John *D.* Doyle?" I'd never seen Greta so impressed. "From Sony Classical?"

"Cassie says we should send him a tape, too. She thinks she can get him to listen."

Greta nodded, almost happily.

"Good, that's good," she said, still nodding. "Now, we have many other things to do, yes."

Her face tightened as she ran through an overwhelming to-do list. Her severity jarred me and made Franz grouchy. I tried to relax her, start an actual conversation.

"Tell me about the 'Unfinished Symphony,' " I said. "Do you think the rest of it exists somewhere?"

It seemed as though she'd been waiting for the question. She recapped what I had read once before, the old tale about the missing movements being left at a friend's house.

"Huttenberger, something like that?" I said.

"The Hüttenbrenners. They were brothers, one was Schubert's lawyer." Greta tilted her head as she scrutinized my face. "Have you had thoughts about this, Liza, or dreams? What do you know?"

I had to admit that I had no thoughts about Hüttenbrenner at all, though the symphonic theme frequently came to me. Greta asked me more questions until she was convinced that I had nothing worthwhile to say. Then she left suddenly, as if she just remembered the stew boiling over on her stove. I was glad to see her go.

Franz and I played for a while longer, riding the music for pleasure. I tried to remember proper posture, position, and movement, but I was lax without Greta's incessant reminders. It was fun to play without her, but my body paid for it afterward. Another reminder of how much I needed her.

I finally took a break to stretch my crabby muscles. Through the window, I saw Danny Carson, my teen fan, on the front stoop. It was a sunny afternoon, but brisk for standing outside. I asked him in for hot cocoa. He asked why I always played Schubert.

"I like Schubert. What, you don't like Schubert?"

"Yeah, I guess. But there are, like, thousands of other composers. Why just Schubert?"

"We all have our favorites." Danny had a point, though. "Who do you like?"

"I used to like to play Chopin," he said. "I gotta get in the zone to play Chopin. It's tough."

I'd been fooled by his lost-puppy pose. Chopin's not for puppies. I wanted to know what else he played.

"I was just starting to play jazz. Doesn't matter anymore. I still sing, and I listen to all kinds of stuff."

He called off some favorites. Coltrane, Miles Davis, Cyrus Chestnut, Sarah Vaughan, Mingus, Marcus Roberts, Joni Mitchell.

"Not just jazz, either. I have all kinds of CDs. Classical, rap, reggae, Celtic, klezmer, you name it. Wanna borrow some?"

"Thanks, sure," I said. "Why don't you surprise me with something?"

He did. Danny walked over to the piano, closed his eyes, and started playing "Clair de Lune." Not perfect, I realized, but wonderful. Franz had never heard it, having died long before Debussy was born. The music grabbed him by the guts.

What is it about the arrangement of notes, a choice of tempo, the skip from one key to another? It's only sound. You can analyze it scientifically, put it in writing. Yet one tune makes you dance, another breaks your heart.

The day Schubert heard Debussy, we moved to a higher level of rapport. He wanted to hear more, needed to know what else he'd been missing. I wanted that, too. Danny would be our partner in this.

"Your folks are jerks," I said.

"No kidding," Danny said.

"You can play my piano anytime. Well, almost. I'm getting ready for Carnegie Hall—"

"*I knew it!*"

"But I still have to take breaks. You can play then."

"Awesome. Thanks."

I asked him to bring me a CD next time. Something that I'd never heard.

I looked forward to spending the night at home with Patrick. He'd gone to Westport to visit his mother for the day. When I got home, he called to say that he'd be staying a couple of nights. His mother wanted some time with him because he'd been gone so long. They had family business and other catching up to do. Also, she could keep him away from me a little longer.

Patrick's mom, the former Rose Kaplan, was born on the Lower East Side of Manhattan and converted to blueblood when she got married and moved to Westport, Connecticut. After Patrick's father died, Rose froze in the posture of family matriarch and moral leader. She did not condone premarital fun, and barely tolerated the postmarital kind.

Rose Kaplan Florio and I would never have been best buds anyway, but she had strong feelings about me as the married woman who carried on with her married son. She also happened to adore the daughter-in-law who got betrayed. I had hoped Mrs. Florio would get used to me, but our relationship barely survived a certain incident at a family gathering. She was talking with her sister when I walked in and overheard her referring to me as "Patrick's Brooklyn tart." I believe she overheard me saying "Self-righteous bitch" to her face.

She may have been part of the reason (not a good one, I admit) I was determined to make things work with Patrick. She may also have been a warning sign to me. I tried not to consider her at all.

The bed seemed too big and full of echoes without Patrick in it that night. But I slipped into sleep with the great Franz Schubert, who treated me to dreams of dancing with Debussy.

Patrick should not have left me again so soon, even for a few days. I missed him, of course, but I was also used to my independence. It was nice when he called me first thing in the morning to say delicious, intimate things that set me humming. I tried to remember his sweet words when I ran into Chase Barnes in the Juilliard cafeteria the next day.

"Did you get my present?" he asked.

"Present?"

Chase Barnes sat down at my table. It's not like I minded seeing him, but don't think I'd gone all the way to Juilliard hoping I'd bump into him. After all, I was loyal to Patrick again.

"You must have gotten it by now," he insisted. "Please don't be offended. I got the impression you could use a book like that."

A musical dummy. He definitely had my number.

"You're obviously gifted, and that's what counts, right? I actually consulted a little on that book. I got your address from the phone book and I just thought I'd send it over. Hope you don't mind." He seemed sweetly concerned about offending me.

"Actually, I like it. Thanks."

Actually, you saved my life. Thanks.

He had a cup of coffee and a large pastry that he tore in half to share with me. His smile was so winning, his hair so tousled, I would have eaten half a sneaker just to share it with him.

"So, Liza, anything new to report?"

"Well, the usual this and that," I said. "Playing, reading, studying."

Also, my boyfriend's back from Italy, so, dear Chase, our simmering flirtation will never explode into a frenzied passion the likes of which our galaxy has never seen. So you may as well stop flirting.

"That's it?" he asked. "No other news?"

Did he know about Patrick?

"Most people would mention a Carnegie Hall debut." He leaned close, whispered congratulations in my ear, then kissed me on the cheek.

"Oh, sorry, yes, I was going to tell you. How did you hear about it?"

"Heard it through the vine. Greta the Great's putting everything she's got in your basket." He took my hands in his. "Let me know if I can help. I've been through this. It's scary getting out there, but it's worth it."

"I'll remember that during my heart attack."

"Don't be silly, you'll do great." He squeezed my hands warmly, then took his back. "By the way, what are you playing?"

"Schubert."

"That's it?"

"Schubert, yes, that's it." Franz was picking up some of my thoughts here and snapped to attention. "Is there something wrong with that?"

"No, lots of musicians specialize," he said. "You might show your range, though, by throwing in something else."

We were quickly reaching my discomfort zone.

"Possibly something contemporary—"

"Good afternoon, Dr. Barnes. Hello, Miss Durbin." Greta Pretsky appeared at our table. I hadn't heard or seen the elf-woman approach. She grabbed a chair and dragged it to our table.

"Many things to discuss, yes?" she said, interlacing her fingers and planting her hands center stage.

That was enough to send Chase off to an urgent meeting. Greta and I sat in clumsy silence until our coffee was gone.

⌇

Patrick came back from Connecticut in good spirits. His mother had left for two weeks in Palm Springs and she lent him her Cadillac in her absence. Aside from the parking hassles and constant fear of robbery or dents, this presented some nice possibilities.

"Let's get away for the weekend, Liza, wha'd'you say?" Patrick had brought home a book about romantic country inns on the Eastern seaboard. "Weather's getting better, maybe we could do some hiking."

"I don't know, I have a lot to do these days, Patrick."

"Just a long weekend, sweetie." He hugged me from behind and curled over to nuzzle his cheek against my neck. "It's not like you're working. Surely you can spare a few days for us."

Tempting, but.

"It's mud season, Patrick. Why don't we go next month, when things are dried out and a little warmer?"

"We can go south," he said. "Virginia or Maryland. Take a look, I bet there's something you like." He handed me the lushly photographed travel book.

I thumbed through the pages with distant interest. I could think of only one really good use for the borrowed car. Might as well ask.

It took less than two hours of persuasion and empty promises to make Patrick agree halfheartedly that it would be okay for me to borrow his mother's car. He conceded that he would not be happy coming along on the kind of girls-only day Mikki and I were planning. He agreed to put off the long-weekend idea until April.

The Cadillac was not my first choice, anyway. I had asked Fred about his car, but he had plans of his own for Friday. In any case, Fred was not so happy with me again. He said I neglected him as a friend whenever Patrick—or any other man I liked—was available. Sad but somewhat true. As soon as someone adds another day to my week, I plan to change all that.

I reached Mikki's Upper West Side apartment in the state of terror that is normal for me when forced to drive in Manhattan. She was waiting outside in a brown leather coat, dark pants, and a jaunty felt beret on her salt-and-pepper head.

Mikki climbed into the passenger seat and quickly settled into the Cadillac's lap of luxury. She stroked the leather with overt affection and told me to drive toward New Jersey.

"*New Jersey?* What kind of channeler lives in New Jersey?" I asked. "Is she channeling Jimmy Hoffa?"

"Of course not, that would be silly," she said. "We're going to Clupperville. It's in the country, sort of. I have the directions. I hear it's pretty."

Once you get past the infamous oil refineries of northern Jersey, the state gradually looks and smells much better. The directions guided us through the ultra-quaint town of Clupperville and down a country road. We turned in at the roadside mailbox marked "Flanders," where a severe-looking thirtyish woman stood browsing through the mail. I stopped the car and gave a friendly greeting.

"You're Franz Schubert?"

I gave Mikki a *thanks-a-lot, bigmouth* look.

"I'm Liza Durbin, and this is Mikki Kloster."

We climbed out of the car under the woman's squint-eyed examination. She shoved a pile of mail in an armpit and offered a painfully firm handshake. She had an enormous nose with complicated nostrils. Her prematurely gray hair drooped down her back, a sure sign of New Age convictions. We walked together up the front porch and into the house.

It's hard to say what was wrong with the house. The corners didn't seem exactly square, and the floor and ceiling may have sloped just a tad. The furniture looked like it was dropped in place by a tornado, with a sofa facing a wall, a lone table with no chairs, and large pillows strewn randomly. The effect was disorienting, but that wasn't the worst of it.

"What's that smell?" I asked.

I immediately realized that this question was an extremely rude way to begin an acquaintance. Mikki discreetly covered her nose, but her eyes were watering.

"What smell?" Our hostess sniffed.

I caught myself before laughing. Considering the size of her nose and the vileness of the stench, she could hardly fail to notice it.

"I'll tell Patty you're here."

"I'm sorry," I said. "I assumed you were Patty Flanders."

She gave me a pitying look. I thanked the gods that she was not Patty Flanders. On her way out, she plunked down a questionnaire on the one table and handed me a pen. Aside from the usual name, address, and everything else about me, I was expected to state why I was there and what I hoped for.

Franz Schubert is living in my body. My therapist made me come here. What else could I say?

The real Patty Flanders came in a few minutes later. She seemed like the normal one in this household. Classically pretty, mid-fifties, with short, strawberry-blond hair, wearing a flowing silk ensemble. Very Junior League, but Democrat.

"I'm so glad you could come. You've already met my dear friend Aries, I see." Patty's low, resonant voice warmed me inside. Franz felt a definite tickle. "Have you completed my questionnaire?"

"Yes, but I don't think my HMO covers channeling."

Aries disapproved of my crack. Patty chuckled as she took the questionnaire from my hand. She nodded several times as she read it.

"If you could just sign at the bottom," she said. "It's a standard release."

"You mean, so you're not responsible if I get eaten by a twelve-foot troll?"

"Don't worry, dear." She took the signed form and winked at me. "I haven't lost a patient yet. I've asked Aries to bring tea for us. She's baked something special."

Aries emerged through the beaded curtain carrying a tray of herbal tea and health-food muffins made of twigs and pebbles. I had no appetite, anyway. I had spotted the source of the pervasive smell—little mounds on the floor suggesting untrained pups on the premises.

"I can see you're uncomfortable, Liza," Patty said. "I understand how enormous your new gift must seem to you. It was hard for me at first, too, my dear, but you'll be grateful for it one day."

"Let's get started," Aries said tartly.

The meditation room was in the back of the house. It had big windows covered by batik fabric, burning candles, a multitude of crystals, and, yes, the obligatory incense (which at least made it smell better than the living room). There were several chairs around an oak table, a Persian carpet, and strains of Enya calling to the spirits. The scene would have been too predictable except for the posters and photos everywhere celebrating one subject—dachshunds.

Miniature dachshunds, to be exact, posing in show stance. Miniature dachshunds playing fetch. Miniature dachshund puppies as big as my thumb and half as cute.

"Everyone comfortable?" Patty looked to us for consent. "Then I shall summon Zazer."

"NO!" It was more a blurt than a yell and it came from Mikki. "Just to clarify, the reason we're here is to allow you and Liza to share your feelings and experiences."

Patty turned her full and obviously wise attention on me. She asked to hear about my gift.

"As you know, it's Schubert. Franz Schubert," I said. "He's come to live in my body."

"You are channeled by genius. You must have a wonderful old soul to be so blessed."

"Well, I don't know about channeling."

"Your cynicism is a sign of a closed and simple mind," Aries barged in. "You cannot possibly comprehend in whose presence you sit. If Patty is benevolent enough to speak to you through Zazer, you should feel honored to listen."

"Aries, dear, please remember that Liza is new and tender," Patty said. "Give her time."

Patty then explained that she spoke best through her entity. She preferred to call on Zazer to share his wisdom.

"Couldn't we first talk about everyday sort of things?" I said. "Like about living with another being inside you. How do you deal with that?"

"I thank Zazer every day for his presence, but it's a lonely path, my dear. My husband didn't understand, neither did my children. Even old friends could not accept this change in me."

"So can I ask how you acquired Zazer in the first place?"

"The usual way."

With that, Patty's eyes rolled up behind her lids. She slumped in her chair, hummed through her nose, and swayed slowly.

"Channeling usually starts with a trance," Mikki whispered to me.

Of course. The usual way.

Suddenly Zazer was among us, barking in the hideous yip-yip of tiny dogs. It was purely undignified behavior for Patty but apparently normal for Zazer. Mikki and I were speechless, and Franz was hissing in my ear. Aries took over.

"Zazer, we are honored to be in your presence," she said.

"Blessings, my children. I greet you on behalf of my race and ancestors from Caninus IV in the Gamma Quadrant. We bring you the light, the love, the answers you seek."

Patty had picked up a strange accent, part Hindu and part Yiddish.

"Throughout history you have searched the stars for our existence. You do scour your planet for proof, while all the time we are here. Your companions, your highest gods, we live in your homes and sleep at your feet. Yet your human prejudice does prevent you from seeing us."

Patty drew up her legs to squat on the chair, then planted her hands between her feet. Aries patted her back with large worker's hands. She had a Zazer tattoo on her wrist.

"You do not acknowledge our superiority, yet do you embrace us, care for us, shower love and affection upon us." She scratched vigorously behind her right ear. "Would that you treated one another so well. Would that you recognized the gods among you and followed in our path."

She let loose a pitiful wail, which sounded more like a tea kettle than the howl of a worthy hound. My heart went out to the dignified Patty of just a few minutes ago. At least my entity could do something presentable.

"For two thousand years have I set my example of love, loyalty, and trust. My first companion, my false disciple, embraced the message but did steal it for a jealous god."

"There are *more* gods?" I wanted the whole bizarre spiel by then.

"Long did I dwell in Nazareth with Him, lived the mystery of the lost years at His side. The horrors of adolescence did I endure with Him, yet did I loyally guide Him to manhood."

"Oh, for Christ's sake," I said.

That drew more wails from Zazer. Aries rebuked us with a look.

"Scoff not!" Patty yipped. "He stole our Word. My race is not a vain one, yet do we demand what is ours. The message is *ours*. Your reverence is our due!"

At this point, I squeezed Mikki's hand as we both struggled not to laugh. Zazer growled.

"Though you do mock us, still do we love you. Witness as we share our blessings."

Aries opened the back door on cue. We heard the patter of little paws. Soon we were swarmed by miniature dachshunds jumping on our calves and licking our ankles. They looked like Tootsie Rolls with legs.

Then I spotted Zazer on all fours. There was no more resemblance to Patty Flanders, and Zazer looked awfully ready to sniff my crotch.

"*That's it!*" I shot up and jumped away from the table. "Time to go. You ready, Mikki?"

We yelled our good-byes as we ran to the car with a squad of little gods nipping at our heels. We should have watched our feet as we ran through the living room. As we drove off, Mikki said, "What's that smell?"

———

Was ist das für ein Geruch? . . . What's that smell?

Spring was flirting with New York on Saturday. Patrick and I declared it a holiday. We strolled around Soho, had dinner in Chinatown, and frolicked in bed late into the night. I felt almost normal again. Better than normal, actually, because of Patrick. Even Franz enjoyed him. I briefly allowed myself to be happy, hopeful, and deeply in denial. It ended the next morning when I woke to find Patrick standing over my bed waving the *New York Times* arts section in my face.

"When were you planning to tell me about *this*?" he asked.

"What?"

"Carnegie Hall, Liza, that's *what*."

"Right, Carnegie Hall, I was going to—"

"But you didn't, Liza, did you? What, did it slip your mind?"

"It just happened. I was going to tell you. Of course I was going to tell you."

Patrick looked everywhere but at me. He couldn't seem to locate his own feelings about this.

"What else don't I know, Liza?"

I couldn't answer.

"I'm going out for a while."

He threw on a jacket and left. The ceiling caved in, spikes sprung from the walls, my illusion of safety flew away like ashes.

Patrick had been my only close relationship not overtly tainted by Franz. Soon he'd know about that, too, one way or another. Even Patrick could not be expected to accept my invisible twin in our bed, at the break-fast table, behind my eyes, living in my head. Without Patrick, I might slip into the permanent *we*—Franz the genius and Liza the lost. I was halfway to a good wallow when the phone rang.

"Liza, you've been holding out on us." The voice was familiar. "A little secret you couldn't share with us at the firm?"

Ivan Stricker, of my erstwhile law firm. "Hi, Ivan. Nice of you to call. I guess you saw the ad."

"Me and the rest of New York. Feinsod called me right away. This is big news. We're all very proud of you, Liza."

His reaction surprised me. I was pretty sure they'd forgotten my name.

"We'll all be there, of course. We'll buy a block of seats and invite clients, they love this kind of stuff." He was talking as much to himself as to me. "Can't hurt the image of a firm to have a concert pianist on board. Practically a partner, at that."

Practically a partner? Call-waiting beeped before I could pursue that.

"Knock 'em dead, kid—you're gonna be a star!" Fred gave it a hokey Hollywood delivery.

It didn't end there. People called all morning. Friends I hadn't seen in ages, my fifth-grade science teacher, a college roommate, two old boy-friends, and a man I'd once changed my phone number to escape. They all expressed honest amazement. Many showed a sincere interest in free tick-ets. Only my sister found fault.

"You see why you need me?" Cassie said.

"I'll always need you, Cass. You're my own darling sister."

"Okay, smart-ass, tell me exactly what this ad does for you. For your *image,* Liza."

"From the phone calls I've had this morning, people think I'm pretty cool."

"Those are your friends, Liza, people who know you. They just can't believe it. But how does this ad pull in the public, make a total stranger want to see *you*?"

I admitted I hadn't studied the ad yet.

"Sure, if someone happens to know this Greta Pretsky—whose name happens to be in there *three times*—that might help. But we want people to come see you, Liza, *you*, not some—"

Call-waiting again—Aunt Frieda. As she exclaimed over me, I thought I should probably take a close look at the ad myself. That's when Patrick came back. I hung up and gave him all my attention.

He stated the obvious, that he had brought home hot bagels and a bouquet of spring flowers. The flowers were for him, but I could have a bagel.

I apologized deeply to Patrick. The morning had clarified the extent of my thoughtlessness. I showered him with my regrets, and tossed in a bit of pathos borrowed from Franz.

"I don't want you to torture yourself over this," he said. "I just want to know what it means. Where the hell am I in your life?"

"You're right in the center, sweetheart, right where you belong." The phone rang then, as if on cue, which gave me the opportunity to dramatically ignore it.

Patrick put his hand on mine. "Okay, let's start over. Tell me about this."

He slid *The New York Times* across the table to me. I looked at the ad for the first time.

PRETSKY PRODUCTIONS PRESENTS

AN EVENING WITH SCHUBERT

THE DEBUT PERFORMANCE OF AN EXTRAORDINARY PIANIST

LIZA DURBIN

CARNEGIE HALL

MARCH 31, 8 P.M.

RARE GUEST PERFORMANCE BY GRETA PRETSKY

"Liza Durbin is my highest achievement as a teacher."—Greta Pretsky

"Holy shit, Cassie was right," I said. "Greta's name is in here three times."

"Who is this Greta Pretsky?"

"She's my teacher, sort of," I said, "but not in the traditional sense."

"What is she, then?"

"I'm not sure. I have to think about that."

The next day at Fred's apartment, I mentioned the ad to Greta and told her about the many calls I got. I was steering toward a discussion of the ad's content, but she insisted that we stick to practicing. Franz and Greta soon had their first artistic disagreement.

Greta was in the habit of scrutinizing everything we played, in case Franz Schubert needed her help. We were playing with gusto when she said, "You can't play it like that. You've made changes. People will think you are making mistakes, or you are not serious."

"I don't control how Franz plays, and they're not mistakes. He feels pleased, believe me."

"It may be better than the original, yes. This does not matter. People will not appreciate your changes. If you make these changes at your debut, they will be most critical. You must build your reputation first, make sure people understand."

Easier said than done.

Franz sailed through music on sheer enthusiasm while Greta demanded rational restraint. How could I alert my nonverbal entity to the tortuous relationships between artistic freedom and professional critics, marketing plans, the audience, recording contracts, and music snobs everywhere? Should I even try to limit him?

I had an appointment later with Mikki and decided to ask her advice. At the very least, she would have some ideas for communicating with Franz about it. I promised Greta that we would figure something out.

Greta broached another topic: "Have you thought about your encore?"

"Encore?"

"It is not written on the program, your choice entirely," she said. "I have some thoughts."

She handed over her list of thoughts. A reasonable list, to be sure. I hate to be a skeptic, but she may have had a special interest in one selection for four hands.

She said the *Grande Sonata,* a lovely piece for four hands, would be nice, that's all. She stood before me, looking tiny and vulnerable and uncharacteristically coy. Of course, she had worked endless hours with me and put her own reputation and money on the line, and it would be a knockout of a finale anyway, so why not consider it, yes? But, really, she said, I should not feel any pressure at all, no way. The one four-handed piece we agreed on for the middle of the concert was plenty for her, more than enough, really.

Mom herself could not have set me up better.

∿

The forces were gathering around my Carnegie Hall debut. Rose Kaplan Florio of Westport, Connecticut, was corralling her suburban cohorts to attend a gala evening starring her son Patrick's brilliant pianist girlfriend. No longer the Brooklyn Tart, I'd become a celestial catch.

Ivan called from Stricker, Stricker & Feinsod to say the firm bought 150 seats for esteemed clients and colleagues. Don't let them down, please.

Danny Carson told his friends at school about me, so my front-stoop groupies grew in number and plunged in age. Danny tended the crowd like a herding dog. *Make a path, please, let Miss Durbin through. No, she doesn't give autographs.* Sometimes, after Greta left, I'd invite Danny in to play piano. His friends hooted wildly. They swore they'd be at my concert, cheering from the cheap seats.

When the weather was warm enough, I'd open the window while I played, luring still more admirers. Dr. Hoffman occasionally treated the crowd to free lectures on classical music. Mrs. Pardo would gaze adoringly at him while the others ran for their lives.

One morning my sister came to town and took me to Emporio Armani on Madison Avenue, where she bought me a pretty spectacular dress. The sleek new me looked damn good in the long-sleeved, black velvet, V-neck, V-back number. Not overly sexy but definitely tasty.

And my parents called that same night to say they were flying in a week before the concert. They would have the time of their lives bragging about

me to old friends and cherished enemies in the Bronx. Mom and Dad reserved a room at Castellano's Fine Italian Restaurant for a private party
after the concert. It was for invited guests only, plus anyone else in the
world who cared to express boundless adoration of me and to fawn over
the family responsible for my success.

DATE: March 14
CLIENT: Liza Durbin

Carnegie Hall just over two weeks away—everyone wants a piece of
Liza. She's forgotten the Zazer incident for the moment, asked me to
help with a conflict today between Franz and Greta. Creative visualization comes to mind—picture what she wants. Or maybe she needs to
learn more direct communication with Franz. Learn German??—MK

NEXT APPOINTMENT: Wednesday, March 16

========

Sie ist sehr ängstlich . . . She is so anxious. They all are. Something important
is coming. Why do they doubt me?

CHAPTER SIX

Mikki gave me odd advice.

I told her that Franz wanted to improve his work, let his music evolve, but that Greta wanted him to play exactly what was on the page. I needed a way to communicate with Franz about this. Mikki's advice was to sniff a vial of ammonia whenever Franz strayed from the course. This would be unpleasant for both of us, but it would probably keep him in line.

Mikki's been so right about everything else (well, except for Patty the Doggy-Style Channeler) that I almost tried this. I decided against it because I didn't want to be at war with my inner pal. Also, I wasn't sure who was right. Greta made a good point about building credibility, but didn't Franz have a right to alter his own work? This couldn't be easy for him, either. If my independence was compromised by him, his was barely existent. Despite Mikki's advice, my loyalties were with Franz. I chose negotiation instead of battle.

From the beginning, Franz and I had a relationship based on alien frames of reference, with almost no vocabulary to rescue us. But we were learning about each other and moving more in rhythm. I knew him to be highly visual and I used that as our common ground.

I envisioned scenarios, flung silent movies in the air—doing things his way, then Greta's way. Seeing how Franz could regain his voice, write new *lieder,* compose symphonies, rejoin the realm of great music. I know this approach worked because something amazing happened.

Franz talked back.

He barged into my visual fantasy with one of his own. It was a vivid image, a picture of us playing, I could hear the music. We tinkered with the scene—bargained, bantered, and composed a new vision. We took our bows, saw our path. Not a word passed between us.

We reached a compromise that nobody knew about but us.

∿

In those hectic days, Patrick was my at-home stress-reduction wizard. He came to hear me practice at Fred's occasionally and was suitably blown away. Mostly, though, we went our separate ways during the day. I rehearsed full-time, and he busily worked at Gekas & Benedict. When we got home at night, we lounged and chatted and ate well. Patrick showed interest in every detail of my day, wanted to know what my experience felt like. I listened back as he groaned about the tedium of returning to workplace politics after his blissful months in Italy.

Every night before bed, he rubbed my back with rose oil. Patrick, my love, my warm harbor. Except for one thing.

"Honey, have you thought about Milan?"

"Patrick, I haven't had much time to think about it." We were eating spinach ravioli in truffle sauce. I put down my silverware and pushed away my plate. "I mean, really, you can't expect me to add that to my things to worry about. I'm sorry."

"You're right, I'm sorry I even brought it up." He shifted his long legs around in the chair. "I wouldn't bring it up, except they called today from Milan. They want a schedule. If I don't go, Gekas and Benedict want to send Cohen, but I don't think the client will go for that."

"I know you want an answer. I'm sorry."

More shifting and fidgeting.

"It's just I have to start making plans. The Italians made a big deal of asking me to work on this. This is a real plum for an American. But I don't want to do it without you. Unless that's what you want me to do."

"Patrick, I know this is a big break for you. Let's talk about this after Carnegie Hall, all right?"

Patrick looked ready to say something. The Italians had wanted him to start in April. They still didn't know Patrick was waiting for me. Patrick still didn't know about Schubert. We couldn't keep staggering down this path for long. Too many people knew about Franz. A friend or relative would eventually mention Franz in front of Patrick and then, *oops!*

Each morning I vowed to tell Patrick everything, and by evening I fell languidly into our surreal domestic play. Patrick never guessed at the strangeness of my inner life. He simply saw me as Liza, blessed and late-blooming. I loved pretending he was right.

"Milan could work out, Patrick." I didn't know if I was lying. "We'll know more in a few weeks. I promise I'll make a decision soon."

I meant it, too. But several nights later Patrick brought the subject up again. He was nervous about blowing his big opportunity and wanted to know if I'd had any new thoughts on the subject.

"No," I said firmly. "I told you I needed time and I do."

"I'm sorry," he said. "I promised not to pressure you, but I have to ask. Sorry."

Then he sat there looking contrite and sweetly patient. Oh, so very patient. So very fucking patient with me. That was my breaking point.

"Right, you're sorry," I said, "but that doesn't stop you from nagging me, does it?"

"Liza, I'm trying to be—"

"What, *patient* with me? Are you trying to be patient with me, Patrick? 'Cause I don't really feel I need your patience, thank you."

"Dammit, Liza, I have a life, too, and—"

"Sure, you've got a life, and didn't you take your life and drag it off to Italy for six months without me? Where was I in your life *then?*"

"Liza, where is this coming from? You know why I went, you know I want us to be—"

"Look, just don't be handing me your goddamn patient looks, okay? I'm dealing with a lot of stuff, you can't even imagine. Just be *patient* with me, can you do that, all right?"

I stumped him with that.

"I guess so, sure. Patient?" Patrick annoyed me with his conciliation. "Honey, let's just calm down a little. Let's have dinner, okay?"

"Fine," I said, "but I think I'll go have mine at Picurro's."

I'm proud to note that I was deeply ashamed of my behavior later that night. I came back bearing apologies and cheesecake. Patrick missed the cheesecake because he was in bed when I got home, but I whispered my *so sorrys* in his ear as I crawled in beside him later. He took up most of the bed with his extra-long body, and I didn't even complain when he pulled the covers off me.

After that, I balanced my irrational reaction to Milan by becoming hypercritical in other crucial areas. *Patrick, the salt shaker goes on the* right *side of the pepper. Patrick, the* pink *sponge is for the sink, the yellow's for the counter. Patrick, why are you acting so perfect?*

Don't think for a minute I would subconsciously sabotage a good thing because of insecurities and an irrational fear of failing. Though it's possible my conflicted feelings about Patrick, Franz, and Milan left me unusually susceptible to the charms of Chase Barnes.

Because of everything else I had to do, I wasn't going to Juilliard every day. So I was unintentionally playing hard to get with Chase. Apparently, absence makes me irresistible.

"Where have you been, Miss Rising Star?" Chase was smiling gorgeously at me. "We're honored to have you in our midst again. May I join you?"

"Please do." I removed my books from the table in the Juilliard cafeteria, making room for Chase and his coffee. He was eager to hear every detail of my preparations.

I told him about all the to-do my imminent performance was causing. Tickets, clothes, promotion, programs, fans, family, festivities. As I recited it out loud, I hated how little it all had to do with music. A person could gag on that much tinsel.

"I guess this sounds trivial to you," I said.

"No. It all comes with the package," Chase said. "Are you ready to play?"

"Yes, absolutely. And my sister sent a tape to John Doyle—"

"John *D*. Doyle?"

"Yep. Sony Classical. He liked the tape, and I think he's coming to the concert."

Chase gave a respectful whistle. He said everyone either knew John D. or wanted to. It took Chase years of serious work and reputation-building before he got to record for Sony Classical. He'd made six recordings and John D. still barely acknowledged him.

"I don't think John D. really gets my music," Chase explained. "He doesn't like it or hasn't really listened to it. Maybe you can put in a good word for me with him."

"If you need my good word, you're in bad shape, buster."

He smiled and drew closer to me.

"Are you still playing all Schubert?" he asked.

It hadn't occurred to me to play anything else, and I told him so. Chase shook his head at my simplicity. He took a sheath of music from his leather satchel and waved it at me.

"I dare you to play this," he said. "I've titled it *Pantheon,* and it's ravishing. Would you play it for me, please?"

This time Chase took me to his classroom studio. I sat at the piano and he set the music in front of me, then walked across the room. He could see my face but not my hands.

Of course, Franz could read music, but we hadn't strayed much from the Schubert repertoire before. Franz jumped at the challenge.

Beautiful? No. Ravishing? Maybe. Mostly it was exhilarating.

Years ago, I'd gone white-water rafting in Colorado. That's what came to mind as we played. The music followed a wild course, carved through stony walls, bathed in icy waters. It had a natural flow that sounded like improvisation but had an elegant, inevitable structure.

"I knew it," Chase said. "I knew you could play it."

If only he knew. Playing was no trick at all. Franz read music the way I read comic books. The notes on the page made perfect sense, we followed them magnetically around the keyboard. Understanding the music was harder.

"What do you think, Liza? Ready to enter our musical century?"

"I'm not sure, Chase. I don't even know if I like it."

Franz had heard plenty of contemporary music by then. He once made a clumsy attempt to copy Fats Waller by ear. This was his first serious effort to explore something so vastly alien. Concepts of melody, rhythm, form, harmony, and beauty were prismatically split and rearranged. Franz's openness staggered me as he reimagined the passages, unwove the work, and searched for its core.

It makes sense that Franz's gift would endure within any time frame. If Einstein came back after a century and a half, wouldn't he still be a genius?

"It's fascinating, complex music," I heard myself saying.

"You were meant to play it, Liza," he said. "Why not play it at Carnegie Hall?"

"You can't be serious."

"You can do anything, Liza. You're the rising star." His enthusiasm put me on edge. "It would make a breathtaking encore, really show off your range. You'd make your mark with it."

I must have looked frightened, because he switched his voice to a coo.

"Don't worry. I know you're Greta's star. You want to please her," he said. "I understand if you can't play it."

He waited for me to answer, which I didn't. He stroked my cheek softly.

"I was drawn to you from the first, Liza," he said. "Not just for your looks, for something I saw inside you."

"What did you see, Chase? Please tell me."

See Franz. Please say that you see Franz.

"You're different, Liza, that's all I can say. I'm sure we're supposed to do something together. I've known that from the start. *Pantheon* is my gift to you, play it or not."

Then he kissed me.

Ich erinnere mich gut daran . . . I remember this well, when my own feelings were hidden from me behind warring thoughts and imagined peril.

I can feel clearly what's in her heart. I want to help her. But even if I could, she would only add my thoughts to her ball of confusion. She's no more ready to see than I was.

I remember too well.

CHAPTER SEVEN

THE BROOKLYN BUZZ
Thursday, March 17

Hitting the Heights with Norma Stein

Would I let you miss the best music in Brooklyn Heights on St. Patrick's Day? Here's a clue: It's not in a pub.

You've simply got to stop by and hear mysterious super-pianist Liza Durbin, who opens the windows daily at an apartment on Spice Street near Montague. She gives free concerts for those of us in the know. I spent an hour there yesterday and, trust me, this gal's the real McCoy.

Liza's loyal listeners pack the sidewalk by 9 A.M. I was there when the dark, elusive siren arrived. Her sea of fans parted to let her through. Our secretive genius doesn't talk much, but her followers have their own theories about where she's been keeping herself.

"She debuts in Carnegie Hall on March 31," said Dr. Leonard Hoffman, a retired history professor, "but she's probably thirty-five and no one's ever heard of her as a musician. I can't find a single mention on the Internet, nothing in newspaper archives. How can that be?"

How, indeed, dear readers?

"She lets a foreign woman into the apartment most days, supposedly her teacher," Hoffman confided in me. "But there could be another connection. Theoretically, that is."

Such as, Dr. Hoffman?

"Some of the former Eastern Bloc countries trained their musicians from childhood the way they trained their athletes. At one time a classical musician who could pass as American would have been invaluable to the Communists. They could train someone for decades to become the perfect musician and spy. Such things may still happen in other countries where we have enemies. I'm not saying this is what happened, of course."

A Spy Grows in Brooklyn? Too good to be true.

Another neighbor, who asked to be unidentified, added to the mystery.

"She only plays Schubert," the agitated woman told me, "and *he* was from East Germany."

Now, I never personally heard that Franz Schubert was a Communist, and I doubt that Liza Durbin is one, either. (*Are* there still Communists?) In fact, I print this conjecture purely for fun, folks. As you know, I'm paid to blab, and I deliver.

The only thing I'm sure of is that Liza Durbin plays piano to knock your socks off, and you can hear her for free and you should. And Liza, babe, if you're reading this—give me a call and let's talk. My quest for the truth never ends.

(P.S. Tell your lawyers I'm kidding about the spy thing.)

～～

"Thirty-*five*? They said I'm thirty-five?" Patrick had just shown me our local entertainment news rag, ruining my breakfast. "I knew Hoffman hated me—"

"Not to mention he practically called you a spy, dear."

"And that imbecile Pardo. *East Germany?* Could she be more moronic?"

"Honey, this is not *The New York Times*," he said. "They print anything in these stupid columns. That's what Norma Stein exists for. She

writes silly stuff to entertain Brooklyn and apologizes before you can sue
her."

"You think I should sue?"

"Sure, sue for millions."

Patrick was not properly outraged.

"Face it, Liza, Norma Stein's been around forever, and don't ask me
why, but people love her. The column's too ludicrous to respond to. Just
count it as free publicity."

He was right. I gave in, but not happily.

"They called me thirty-*five*."

When I got to Fred's apartment later that morning, Danny and his
friends had cut school to mill around the front stoop with cheery homemade signs lampooning Hoffman and Pardo and making death threats
against Norma Stein. That made me feel better.

It was the reporters and photographers who made me nervous.

Somebody obviously reads *The Brooklyn Buzz*. There was even a local
TV crew there, no doubt looking for a wacky story to wrap up the evening
claptrap with. Greta had gotten there before me and was handling them
with her usual warmth.

"Miss Durbin cannot be interviewed at this time," she announced.
"However, I will be available to talk with you at two o'clock. Thank you,
good-bye."

"Thanks a lot, lady," said one bored reporter, "but who the hell are
you?"

"I am Dr. Greta Pretsky, young man," she announced proudly. "Do
your homework."

Someone noticed me, and the crowd promptly turned its communal
back on Greta the Great. Half a dozen aggressive mouths spewed questions at me at once. A serious-looking woman took photographs and a
video camera was aimed up my left nostril.

*No, I'm not a spy. Do I look like a spy? Yes, I know this woman, she's my
teacher. No, I can't stop for questions, but you can talk with Dr. Pretsky later.
Yes, I am a member of the New York Bar. It doesn't make me a bad person.
Well, gotta go, guys. Big gig coming up, Carnegie Hall, y'know, ha, ha. Thanks
for coming.*

I sounded like an idiot, flustered and flippant. Cassie had been wanting to rehearse me for the media; Greta had told me not to speak to them at all. I hate when everyone is right but me.

Safely inside Fred's apartment, Greta showed rare concern for me.

"You are okay, yes?" she said. "We sent news releases, but they were supposed to contact only me or Mrs. Mishkin at Carnegie Hall. I don't know how they found us here. You are okay?"

"I guess you don't read the *Buzz*."

A copy of *The Brooklyn Buzz* sat on Fred's breakfast counter. Fred had left it there for my benefit, along with a congratulatory note written in secret-spy code (LIZA, HOLD THIS UP TO A MIRROR!!). I directed Greta to Norma Stein's column and waited for a storm.

I don't believe I'd ever heard Greta Pretsky laugh. She was out of practice and it came in wheezes.

"A *spy*?" she said. "They think you are a spy!"

"Funny, huh?"

"Funny? They think this is a story. Imagine if they knew the truth, yes? That would be a real story."

She reacted like an old pro who knew about celebrity and publicity and foolishness. She also wondered who called Norma Stein in the first place. I named my suspects. Minutes later we were banging on Hoffman's door. He answered with Pardo (the floozy, snug in his bathrobe) at his side.

"I am Dr. Greta Pretsky," she said, planting her tiny frame like a forty-foot oak in the doorway.

"Of course," said Hoffman. "May I introduce—"

"No need, I know who you are," Greta answered. "You think I don't see you every day, I don't know you are obsessed with Miss Durbin?"

I would have sworn that Greta never gave them a thought. Hoffman and Pardo denied being obsessed.

"I am a professor at Juilliard at Lincoln Center. Believe me when I say we have impressive legal resources at our disposal. If you interfere again with my pupil or continue to spread your insane theories, you will find out for yourself about my impressive legal resources."

"But we didn't do—"

"Good day," said Greta the Greatest. We marched away in superiority as the shocked pair wasted their breath on outraged denials.

My Upper Danville sister does not see *The Brooklyn Buzz,* but she does own a half dozen televisions. Cassie spotted us on the local news and wasted no time calling me.

"It's a good thing you lost that weight. At least you didn't look too fat."

"Hello to you, too, Cassie."

"From now on, your hair and makeup have to look good, always. *Always,* understand?"

"Right, I'll apply for a head transplant immediately," I said. "No thoughts on the spy theory?"

"Well, it's a start." She sounded strictly serious. "It's not the image we want, but people are talking anyway. You'll have to do interviews someday. When do you want to rehearse with me?"

"When it snows in the Sahara. I'll check the weather and call you back."

"Funny, Liza. Too bad you didn't sound so witty on the news."

Point taken. We made a date to meet in the city. Have some lunch, review the plans, train me to answer simple questions without humiliating myself and millennia of Durbin ancestors.

The last thing Patrick and I did that night was think up good spy names for me. First thing the next morning, the phone startled me out of a bizarre dream and the real strangeness began again.

"Liza, I'm glad I caught you."

"What, caught me before I woke up? It's six-fifteen, Fred, of course you caught me."

"Sorry, there's a bit of a commotion over here. Your fans are out front," he said. "Thousands of them."

"Thousands?" I sat up in bed.

"All right, hundreds, I don't know." He sounded a bit snippy, frankly. "I do know the police consider it too many people to be blocking a public street. They don't want any free concert today. I thought you should know before you head over here."

The police knew about me?

"You're a star, babe. You were all over the news last night, so they're all over my doorstep this morning."

Patrick rolled over and asked who was on the phone. I told him I was a big star.

"So you'll skip the practice today, right?" Fred said. "Hey, I know you're busy, but Ruthie and Peter and Dan want to take you out for drinks this week. Celebration before the big show. How's Wednesday? Six-thirty at Nonie's Grill."

I hadn't seen my friends since Franz descended on me. I nearly cried. "Wednesday's perfect."

"By the way, you really pissed off my neighbors," Fred said. "What'd you say to them?"

"Greta talked to them, not me. Mrs. Pardo wants you to marry her daughter, though," I explained. "Just marry her and we'll be okay. So, am I in the papers today?"

"Her daughter? Listen, Liza, we haven't had time alone together. I left you messages a couple of times this week, but—"

"Sorry, things have been crazy lately."

"Can we get together later this afternoon?"

"Sure, no problem, Freddie. I'll call you."

I brought a stack of newspapers to my appointment that day with Mikki. There were mentions of me all over the place. Except *The New York Times,* of course, which wasted its space on wars and politics and such. But I was a natural for the tabloids.

I got down on the floor, spread the papers around, and cut out articles as Mikki psychobabbled at me. She didn't appreciate my divided attention, but, after all, I had solved my latest problem on my own.

"Franz liked my solution better than yours, that's all," I said. Mikki looked mildly distressed but said she was happy to hear it.

"I just hope your 'secret agreement' with him holds," she said. "This is a critical time in your career and, most important, your relationship with Franz."

"You know what's scary, Mikki?" I stopped cutting newspapers for the moment. "There are pictures in these papers that weren't taken yesterday.

Someone shot these days ago and gave the pictures to the papers. Look at this one. I wasn't wearing that yesterday. It's an ugly picture, too."

"Liza, what you did with Franz—envisioning different scenarios— I was going to suggest that approach to you as a backup, you know." Mikki was insensitive to my concern about the ugly photograph. "It's called creative visualization. I'm sure I've mentioned it to you before."

"Someone's been taking pictures of me when I don't know it, Mikki."

She was still taking indirect credit for solving the artistic differences between Franz and Greta as I stuffed the news clippings in my bag and left for home.

The frightening facts: Someone was taking pictures of me when I didn't know it. An ad ran in *The New York Times* before I saw it. My sister made all kinds of plans for me. Greta pressured me to do an encore with her, Chase also wanted the encore, and there was a dead composer who went to the bathroom with me. How could I pretend to retain a shred of self-determination? The best I could do was go home, hide under the blankets, and call it a day.

I cried into my pillow for hours that night. A major meltdown, long in the making, tore through my body. Patrick held me, rocked me, then finally left me to my terror.

I wondered where my behavior fell on the continuum of human insecurities. Not many people are tested this way. There's no way to know whose character might be strong enough to stand against a full-spirit invasion by Franz Schubert.

Growing up, my parents praised me for all things possible. At home I believed I was the prettiest, smartest, most talented child in the world. But I went to school and met the world. The adjectives applied, perhaps, but not the superlatives. When my mother called me her "A-plus Girl" and my teacher saw me as more of a B plus, a certain discord set in. When a cute boy told me I looked like a baboon, I started building my doubt pile. I finally built a nice house out of that pile. I was always smart and pretty enough to do well, but the margin of error—the question of superlatives—dug a ditch around me.

Franz made me a superlative. No one could doubt it, not even me. And what did that leave of the original me? Every day of our lives we attract success, failure, titles, identity. One day I took a test, the next day I was Liza the Honor Student. I missed a catch in softball once; I became Liza the Girl Who Can't Catch. I took a test a few years later and became Liza the Promising Lawyer. It all sticks like lint to the bare soul that attracted it. Bits may fade or get covered with new bits, but they don't just blow away. They're not supposed to. We all walk around with the lint that explains us.

I was glad I'd become a genius rather than a bag lady, but I had a life of my own once, with friends and work and few aspirations. All by myself, I'd made something that was not bad at all. It was snatched from me and replaced with something infinitely better, which I had no choice but to hate.

On the continuum of identity crises, I was falling off the planet.

CHAPTER EIGHT

I didn't get out of bed until Sunday. Patrick lured me out with choco-late.

I shuffled to the kitchen in a disgusting state of bed rot. My beloved was bent over the stove, removing a batch of brownies from the oven. The apartment smelled like paradise.

"Have a good sulk?" he asked.

"Yeah, pretty good. I think I'm done for the moment. Nice to have a man around who bakes antidepressants from scratch."

He had a glob of chocolate on one cheek. I had to lick it off because he didn't save me any batter to sample. Patrick came close enough to hug me, then scrunched his nose and retreated.

"Shower first, brownies after," he said. "I'll help with the shower."

An hour later, sated with love and chocolate, I heard my answering machine click on. No phone, just the click, then no message. Patrick ex-plained that he turned off all the ringers and put the voices on mute some-time during my wallow of the previous day.

"Lots of calls?" I half-wanted to know.

"Only everyone you ever met. Plus a bunch of reporters you don't want to know," he said. "By the way, were you supposed to call Fred back yesterday?"

Oh, damn.

"I'm thinking you should get an unlisted number, honey, being a big star and all." Was Patrick starting to enjoy all this? "So, how about coffee and the paper?"

An imposing stack of Sunday newspaper sat on the hall table. I wasn't expecting anything silly about me in America's snootiest paper, but you never know.

I made a point of going through *The New York Times* in order, not rushing to the Arts & Leisure section. Patrick got there first and grabbed my attention with a wide-eyed expression not seen since Buster Keaton in the silent movies. Full arm extended, he pointed at the shocking sight.

There I was, pictured in an eight-inch ad that was absolutely not created with the approval or knowledge of Dr. Greta Pretsky. Her name appeared just once and my sexy self filled the rest.

PLAYING WITH PASSION

LIZA DURBIN DOES FRANZ SCHUBERT

8 P.M. THURSDAY, MARCH 31

CARNEGIE HALL

NOUVELLE CLASSIQUE FOR MUSIC LOVERS

A GRETA PRETSKY PRODUCTION

You should have seen me. My hair and makeup had looked that good exactly once in my life—when I was beautifully lit and captured on film by Lance Bellows, photographer to the stars and to Miss Brittany Whitman's birthday gaggle. I remembered the shot, but there was something different about it.

In this version, I was lying across the lid of a grand piano, face toward the camera, head resting lightly in one hand, body sensually arranged like lush, fertile hills. I didn't remember that pose. Also, I was wearing the blue satin slut dress my sister bought me, the one I swore I'd never wear in public, let alone for photographs. And, incidentally, it clearly was not my body. I'd recognize those size-eleven clodhoppers anywhere.

"What have you done, you fucking maniac?"

"You saw the ad?" Cassie sounded excited on the phone, almost giddy.

"You attached my head to your body? Your slinky, stupid body with the big fat feet?"

"No need to be nasty, Liza." The catch in her throat was for my benefit. "Anyway, we stuck my body on *your* head, not the other way around. I'm perfectly aware that you're the celebrity around here, if that's what you're worried about."

"Sure, Cassie, that's all I'm worried about," I said. "Not another care in the world but that."

A defunct composer took up residence in my brain, and my sister was still crazier than me.

"I just wanted a little dignity, Cassie. Is that too much to ask? For that matter, is it too much to ask you to ask me first before doing something like this?"

Cassie calmly explained that she couldn't ask me first because I would have said no. She was very clear that "dignified" was not the look we were going for.

"We're *not*? Strange, *we* didn't know. I think I owe more to Schubert. A dignified image, at least, so we're taken seriously. So people will actually listen."

Cassie noted that barely six hundred people in all of Manhattan had bought tickets after seeing Greta's dignified ad the week before. Nobody knew me—why should they be interested unless we gave them a little tease? This was the best way to be sure Schubert was heard.

"But this ad, Cassie, it's tacky. I look like a stripper." Okay, I actually looked great. "And 'nouvelle classique'? I'm puking. Who's gonna take that seriously?"

"Fred said the same thing, but I—"

"Fred?" There must be a million Freds in the galaxy. "You mean *my* Fred?"

"*Oo-ops,* my mistake," Cassie said. "He was going to talk to you yesterday. Didn't you two talk?"

I grabbed my jacket and headed toward Fred's.

I could see the crowd outside his apartment from a block away. They swarmed the sidewalk and flowed into the street. The regulars were there and plenty of strangers, too. Obviously they were drawn by the recent publicity and by that Frederick's of Classical ad in the *Times.* Disappearing seemed the best idea.

I called Fred from my cell phone. His answering machine fielded my sarcastic message. He was wisely screening his calls or had already escaped his apartment. Either way, who could blame him? In the beginning, Fred probably found Franz's appearance exciting, amusing, maybe even scary in the fun way. Unfortunately, he'd been dragged into the downside more than once. But nothing excused colluding with my psycho sister behind my back.

When I got home, Patrick asked about Fred the Traitor. He tried not to look smug about his pseudo-rival's fall from grace. In fact, Patrick was in an awfully good mood. He suggested we forget the bimbo ad, the reporters, Fred, and the rest. Nothing could please me more.

We took the subway to Central Park, rented rollerblades, and wobbled happily around the reservoir. Later we feasted in Little Italy. We held hands everywhere and made out on street corners. Patrick actually got me to laugh about my sexpot ad and I deeply appreciated its effect on him. He thought I was hotter than hot. Maybe all of Manhattan did. Maybe my sister would lend me her body for the concert so as not to disappoint the horny section at Carnegie Hall.

Patrick and I were still cuddly and warm as we let ourselves into the apartment that night. Fred had left several messages, anxious to talk with me, of course. I didn't call back because we were having too much fun. Better to wait until morning to fully enjoy Fred's apologies and wretched regrets.

~~~

Fred stopped by my apartment the next morning, not as apologetic as you might think.

"The hell with you, Liza," he said.

Patrick had left us alone in the apartment to work things out.

"For the tenth time, I'm sorry it happened this way." He sounded more cranky than sorry. "I tried to see you, I left you messages, but you're too goddamn busy to return a simple phone call these days."

"Tell me this, Fred. Why my sister? Why *Cassie?*"

"Well, you know I quit my job at—"

"You quit your job!"

"Yes, Liza. I told you I did. I told you more than a week ago. You just don't listen anymore. Jake and I left Ads Up and went out on our own. We found the cash-cow client we were looking for, so we could leave. She's more like a silent partner actually."

With extreme reluctance, my brain pried apart forbidden neurons and let the truth enter.

"*Silent* partner? In your dreams, Freddie. My sister, your cash cow, couldn't be silent if she were dead."

"Don't talk about her like that," he said. "Cassie's not that bad."

Here's what I learned: Cassie contacted Fred to find the right photographer for Brittany's birthday bash. Being an advertising pro, Fred would certainly know the right person to call and, oh, by the way, wouldn't it be lovely if she and Fred got together, maybe help old helpless Liza make something out of her situation instead of wasting it like an uncashed check? He needed some persuasion, probably a nanosecond of it, but finally they made a secrecy ("let's be sensitive about this") pact, and Fred gave her Lance Bellows's number.

Fred and Cassie (*not* Jana) had been having hush-hush meetings. They'd grown closer and he appreciated her more. They had meaningful talks and envisioned how we could all meet our lofty goals together. She wanted to revive her career as a publicist, he wanted to branch out and needed a rich client. I would certainly want whatever they brewed up for me.

I was furious with Cassie, but I knew I'd get over it. She would continue to be my sister, just as she did after she stole and married my boyfriend in college. I was destined to love her with sibling tenacity. It was tougher with Fred because I had chosen to love him.

Friends can have any combination of traits, appealing and appalling, as long as they feel connected. I had been happy with Fred as my closest friend, even though he liked action movies and had owed me two hundred dollars since college. But betrayal has no place in friendship. I told Fred how angry I was. He swore he'd make it up to me, even came close to crying. I knew I'd forgive him, but I needed time to get there. I'd have to get over the fact that Fred had changed while I wasn't looking. I had to get over the fact that I'd been too busy to notice.

I don't believe Greta Pretsky saw any possible way she might get over my new classical vixen image. Since our affiliation had become well known, it was okay for Greta and me to discuss the matter in public at Juilliard. Apparently it was okay for her to have a big old tantrum in the hallway there, too. She raged and turned colors and threatened to cancel the concert. I tried to calm her down, but everything I said lit her up again.

"You think this might be *good*?" She made my suggestion sound silly by repeating it. "Good that you look like a sex queen instead of a serious musician?"

To tell the truth, I was getting to like it a little. You wouldn't believe the phone calls and attention I got, and Patrick found me more irresistible than ever. Even Franz responded to the picture, but I didn't like to dwell on that.

"Why not keep an open mind about things?" I said. "At least people are buying tickets."

"You've humiliated me and shamed Schubert. That's what's on my mind, Miss Durbin."

"I understand. It was a shock when I saw it, too. I never would've allowed it, but it's already done, so let's make the best of it."

"I hope your sister has no other surprises planned, yes?"

Not wanting to think about that, I distracted Greta with questions of a musical nature. We went to her studio to review a few things. She took the opportunity to gently bug me about playing the four-handed *Grande Sonata* with her for the encore, especially since I'd let her down and all. I was feeling guilty anyway. Greta didn't deserve to be embarrassed by me. She also was not open to apologies or mushy shows of gratitude. I wasn't sure I could ever please her, which was purely frustrating. By the time I left her studio, I was ready for a snack in the cafeteria. I absolutely was not hoping to run into anyone special.

I was so busy being in love with Patrick again that I hadn't thought about Chase Barnes in days. Well, almost.

"There she is—dangerous spy, goddess of the keyboard, Schubert's own siren," he said. "I'm guessing that Greta wasn't happy with the new ad."

"You've got keen intuition."

"That, plus a dozen people heard her ranting at you in the hallway."

"Did you think the ad was awful?"

"Not my call," he said. "It's an attention-grabber, I'll say that. Hell of a picture, too."

I attempted a demure look. Chase smirked at my effort.

"I have a copy of my music for you," he said. "You know, *Pantheon*. Thought I'd better give it to you, just in case."

I said I couldn't promise anything. He gave it to me anyway.

"I know you're still considering it as your encore, Liza, and I appreciate that." Such a pleasant voice. Nice jawline, too. I bet he didn't have a snooty, holier-than-everyone mother in Connecticut, either.

"Whatever you do is fine with me. It's just an option for you. So, do you feel like playing?"

I felt like playing the-shepherd-and-the-milkmaid with him, but that's not what he meant. We went to his classroom studio. I knew Franz needed to play Chase's piece again. There were things in it that he wanted to hear again, passages he was ready to absorb. It was nearly overwhelming.

I finished playing and Chase was at my side again, congratulating me in my favorite way. Everyone has more confidence on a second kiss, and ours was glorious. But I love Patrick.

I told him I had to leave immediately. My parents and Aunt Frieda had flown in that afternoon and we were meeting everyone for dinner downtown.

We met at Chops, a numbingly hip and popular Asian bistro, famous for overpriced cuisine styled to resemble Vietnamese gardens. The maître d' led me through the crowded bar to the multilevel dining room. Ceiling fans shaped like palm fronds stirred the air and intimidating art graced the walls.

My parents yodeled their greetings. Cassie and Barry threw hellos from their end of the table, and Fred waved a spring roll at me. Brittany and Cameron demanded bear hugs. I took the empty seat between my mother and Patrick.

Patrick?

Of course Patrick was there. I told him to be there, but not until seven. I'd clearly told him seven because the rest of us were getting there at six-thirty. That would allow plenty of time for me to warn everyone not to mention Franz. (The kids might slip, anyway, but who would believe them?) So Patrick was a surprise.

"Wow, you're early," I said. "Never saw you anywhere so early, sweetie."

"That's funny," Patrick said. "I was the last to show up until you. It's twenty after seven. Where were you?"

Twenty after seven? Impossible. Yikes. Impossible. *Shit.*

"Sorry. Has my family been entertaining you?"

"Oh, you know, just catching up on things."

Patrick hadn't seen my parents since he left for Italy or, as my mother liked to put it, dumped me "like yesterday's trash." She was not excited to hear about his return and exceedingly not excited to learn he was staying with me. After three years, she still could not believe I gave up an actual husband for nothing more than a boyfriend, and a wandering one at that. Ditto for Dad.

I squeezed Patrick's knee in sympathy.

"You didn't mention to your parents that I was offered a job in Milan, did you?" Patrick's voice was quiet but strained. "Or that I asked you to come with me?"

"I was waiting for the right time."

"Don't bother," he said. "They asked me what's new and I said I was waiting on your decision about Milan. Imagine their surprise."

Yes, imagine.

Brittany announced to all that she could play "The Spinning Song" without mistakes.

"Maybe you can teach it to me," I said.

Conversation around the table moved in great waves after that and did not happen to land on Milan again. It floated through soccer meets, Carnegie Hall, ticket sales, Mom's last gallery show, in-flight movies, and touched down once in the Bronx.

"I have a surprise," my father announced. "We're going to the store tomorrow, all of us." He could only mean the original Durbin's Sporting Goods in the Bronx.

"Who's all of us, Max?" My mother hates surprises. "Our girls are busy. Maybe they don't want to go to the Bronx."

"Louise, honey, it's all arranged," he said. "Cassie knew."

"I don't know, Mom," I said. "It could be fun. I haven't been to the home store since you guys sold everything. Doesn't Cousin Alfie still run the place? Maybe he'll give us free stuff."

"Never mind the free stuff," Dad answered. "Just let 'em buy tickets to your concert, him and the rest of those bums."

Those bums were Dad's friends and neighbors until five years ago, when they sold their stores to a corporation that wisely kept the original name, the look, and as many staff members as possible. Before the sale, my father had presided over the original Durbin's Sporting Goods six days a week for more than thirty years.

Dad's brief career as a Yankee shortstop was barely noted in the record books, but unforgettable to him and to us. He prolonged his celebrity and sports love by opening a small shop on 161st Street. The store sat in view of Yankee Stadium and sold baseball, football, and basketball gear. Over time, they nursed that tiny enterprise into a big store with all the things you might need for ice camping in Alaska or kayaking down the wild Zambezi. It was Dad's policy to have fun every day with customers and to treat his staff—for better or worse—like family.

Dad reveled in success and in all things baseball. He organized a softball league in the neighborhood, starting with our home-store team. He got everyone into the act, young and old, skilled or spazzed. We called ourselves the Duelin' Durbins, and the fans waved cardboard swords wrapped in tinfoil to encourage us. I still keep a cardboard sword under my bed for emergencies.

Dad enjoyed telling about the Duelin' Durbins for the thousandth time over dinner, and Patrick earned much-needed points with him by showing interest. Time passed pleasantly until dessert, when Mom changed the subject. She reached over my father's jasmine ice cream to place a concerned hand over mine. Her voice was just loud enough for everyone to hear.

"Liza, darling, tell us. How are you doing?"

"Fine, Mom, just fine."

"No, really, how are you doing with *him*?"

I knew what she meant, but I looked right at Patrick and said we were doing great.

"No, not him," she said. "The other one. Is he still here?" Mom whispered this part, presumably so Franz wouldn't hear.

I was on the verge of a brilliant answer, but Cassie jumped in.

"*Franz*, sis, she means Franz Schubert, for God's sake. And he better still be here, because no one's coming to Carnegie Hall to hear you, that's for sure."

"That's not fair." Barry, my erstwhile boyfriend and current brother-in-law, leapt to my defense. "People believe they're coming to see Liza, so they are. Not everyone could do what she's doing. Let's give her credit."

Patrick looked like a cartoon character just after the anvil falls on its head. He tried to squeak out a question, but the Durbins were off and running.

"Oh, c'mon, Barry, what does she have to do?" Cassie said. "Just pray that Franz doesn't make a premature departure, is all."

"You think that's all there is to it?" Even as I spoke, I realized my strategic error of engaging in the fray.

"Liza, have you thought about that?" Barry looked worried. "What if he leaves? What then?"

"What the hell are you all talking about?" Patrick finally got his words in edgewise. "Are you all insane?"

"Yes, Patrick," I said, pulling on his arm to leave. "They are insane. How nice of you to notice. 'Night, everyone, gotta go, see you soon."

Patrick was stammering as I yanked him from his chair and pushed him like a battering ram through the restaurant. We reached the exit and realized that Fred was on our heels. He had urged me many times to tell Patrick about Franz. He alone understood Patrick's state of ignorance and justifiable shock.

"I know this is a bad time," he said, "but your sister had something special planned for after dinner. I wanted to tell you about it yesterday, Liza, that's why I called. We don't all have to go together, I guess, but I think you two should go by Times Square on your way home."

Patrick and I stared poison at him.

"I say this for your own good," Fred said. "Go by Times Square tonight, so you'll be prepared when your phone starts ringing."

We ran the whole way to Times Square.

You guessed it. Big as a house, lit like a horror movie, there I was, the star of my own billboard. It was Cassie's *New York Times* ad on sci-fi hormones—a giant me in the blue slut dress draped over the piano. Nouvelle classique.

I sank to my knees and hid my face in my hands. Franz spun around like an angry bee. I tried hard to shut everything out, to become one with the grime and dead chewing gum on the street. Patrick pulled me to my feet and packed me into the first available cab. He got in the seat beside me, I curled up in his lap, and he rocked me in silence all the way to Brooklyn.

***

Kann das sein? . . . Can this be? This absurd image is not about music. Why am I tied to this silly creature? We are trapped together, without explanation or even clues about our future. And how do they make a picture so large?

Patrick was waiting with fresh coffee when I woke up the next morning. I said I had an appointment, and he said he'd tie me to a chair if I tried to leave without an explanation. Time for full disclosure.

This was not my first time telling the tale of Franz and me. It was becoming my special story, like the favorite yarns people cultivate over years, ready to produce at a moment's notice. This would be my defining tale. When I was telling it to Patrick, the words flowed through a practiced groove. Patrick showed amazement, disbelief, delight, and worry in all the right places. My life felt like someone else's work of fiction.

Patrick barely said a word. His eyes asked the questions.

"Patrick, you heard me play," I said. "Did you really think I could pick up that talent while you were gone for a few months?"

"That's not any harder to believe than this story," he said.

I couldn't disagree. Mainly, though, Patrick wanted to know why I hadn't told him sooner.

"You were in Italy when it started," I said. "What would you have said if I called you from New York to say that Franz Schubert had invaded my soul? Literally invaded my soul?"

"But I've been home for weeks, Liza. When *were* you planning to tell me?"

"I thought about it every day. I didn't want to keep a secret, but I couldn't bear telling you."

"You told everyone else. Why keep it from me?"

"So you wouldn't look at me that way, like I'm some sort of alien. So you wouldn't change how you feel about me, like everyone else has. You saw my family last night—nothing's normal anymore. You were the one who just loved *me*. You could think I was just this great musician instead of some freak to fuss over."

"So we're never alone, are we? We've never been alone since I got back?"

"He sort of sleeps sometimes but he's always here." I still couldn't explain this well. "I'm pretty sure he didn't choose to be stuck in me, either. None of us has a choice here."

"Neither of you, you mean."

"Right. Neither of us has a choice. You do, of course." My throat tightened as the tears burst free. "Can you stand this, Patrick? Can you believe what's happened? I can't, I still can't believe it. It's made a mess of my old life, my *real* life. My new life scares me to death, and you're thinking I'm some freak from Pluto, and I don't blame you."

I was fighting off sobs and tremors. Somewhere inside, Franz Schubert was moved and tried to comfort me. Whether he felt distress or compassion I can't say, but he consoled me with sweet music. I settled down enough to continue talking.

"Nobody else has experienced this, as far as I know, so how can I go around talking about it? Eventually I'm going to have to tell the world. I can't pretend it's me playing forever. Schubert deserves the credit, anyway. So I feel crazy. Who wouldn't? I try every day to keep things under control, act like a sane person. I'm doing pretty well, really. You should've seen me a couple of months ago. You wouldn't believe the progress. But I don't know if things will ever go back to normal. And I don't know what happens with us, Patrick. Do you?"

"I don't know what to think, Liza. This thing that's happened to you obviously makes no sense, but I guess it explains your behavior. I just don't know what we do next. How do we think logically in a situation that makes no sense?"

Patrick rubbed his temples, struggling to stay calm when he had every right to go nuts. I sensed his fuse burning along a danger line of unfolding thoughts.

"This is the reason you couldn't say yes to Milan, isn't it?" Patrick's self-interest surfaced in his tart tone. "I thought you were hesitating about me, but it was about him. He's part of every decision and every moment between us. Isn't that right?"

I reminded him I had no choice in it.

Patrick stood up straight and froze in thought. "Shit, that guy's been in bed with us, Liza. Doesn't that strike you as kinky? I had a right to know. You should have told me about this, don't you think, Liza? Does he zone out when we're in bed, or close his eyes, or get off on it, or what?"

The truth is, I could feel the times when Franz was awake and enjoying the moment with us. Yes, it was kinky and I wish he'd stay away, but that was not an option. Hell, Franz watched me change my Tampax, bore witness to every belch, felt me go weak at the sight of Chase Barnes—I had no secrets from him. And, strangely enough, he still stuck by me.

"Don't worry, Patrick. I think he just tunes out our sex life. It's not what he's here for."

Patrick doubted this ridiculous lie, which really bugged me.

"Maybe he's a homophobe," I suggested.

"Maybe he's gay," Patrick countered.

Could be. Or maybe he got off on me in the mirror. Maybe this was the stuff of fantasy for most men—penetrating a woman's body in full, experiencing her pleasure, sampling things from the other way around. But it was definitely not the right time to pursue these thoughts with Patrick. He was having a hard enough time believing what he'd heard so far.

We talked about what it all might mean, and how it would affect us. Patrick knew I needed his support, but the situation was complex and he needed to adjust. We were deep in discussion, making a little progress, when the apartment buzzer called to us. My father's voice was on the other end.

"Paging Liza the Genius," he said. "Train leaving for Durbin's Sporting Goods, all aboard."

Patrick groaned, but I suspect he was as relieved as I was to have a distraction. Apparently the family had already forgotten about our sudden, awful departure from the Asian restaurant the night before. Dad had promised a trip to the Bronx, and he wasn't going to let us down. Within minutes my small apartment was brimming with Durbins.

Cameron and Brittany exclaimed over my awesome Times Square billboard. Cassie shared in their exuberance, safe in the knowledge that I wouldn't disembowel her in front of the kids. Barry looked embarrassed. My parents asked why I was still in my bathrobe at half past eleven.

"Just throw on some clothes, quickly, or we'll be late," Mom said.

"Sure, *just throw on some clothes, Liza.*" Cassie ran our mother's words through the scorn mill. "*Mo-om,* have you seen this sister of mine? *Sacré bleu!* She has a public to think of. There are reporters out there, photographers, potential fans. She can't go out in just anything."

Cassie looked stunning, as usual. And perfectly appropriate, if you consider a sporting goods store in the Bronx to be the social equivalent of high tea at the Plaza. Her red curls were bunched high on her head and dropped down to perfectly frame her face. The black sundress floated like a breeze around her svelte self. Even her many-strapped espadrilles were cunningly designed to make her feet appear slightly less enormous. She looked upon me with pity.

"Well, I'll go throw something on," I said. "Back in a minute."

I ran from the living room and locked the bedroom door before Cassie could follow me. She banged and pleaded, demanded to help me. I searched my drawers for something special. I chose the egregious mustard-colored sweater that Fred gave me for Christmas. It was too heavy for the day but the look of horror on my sister's face was worth a bucket of sweat. She nearly heaved at the sight of me. Even my father looked alarmed and inquired about my health. Barry discreetly suggested that I let Cassie fool with my hair. Instead, I pulled it into a ponytail, creating the effect of an abandoned eagle's nest hanging from the back of my head.

I enjoyed my fashion mayhem until we reached the front stoop and a photographer pointed his oversized lens at me. I instinctively slapped my forearm over my face, like the handcuffed criminals on the evening news. Very classy. The dreaded Norma Stein of *The Brooklyn Buzz* was there, too, in search of the truth, no doubt.

Professional Publicist Cassie Whitman sank to the occasion and handed Norma a copy of my bio (which I was curious to see myself) and a glossy photo of me slung over a piano wearing the blue dress and my sister's better body. Cassie gave a freshly minted business card to Norma and the photographer and said she'd be glad to talk to them at another time. We had a pressing engagement at Durbin's Sporting Goods, you see.

We walked past this media throng, all two of them, with the harried air of superstars. Mustn't be late for our fans in the Bronx.

The Whitmans' shiny silver vehicle was just a few blocks away— a sporty, luxurious tank that could fend off invading troops from Canada but was a snug fit for our crew. We were squished in unpleasant ways until Patrick suggested we split up. My parents jumped at the offer to ride with us in Patrick's mother's Cadillac.

"Aunt Frieda's sorry she couldn't make it today," Mom said, leaning toward the front seat to be heard. "She's so proud of you. She played a little piano, too, in her day. Nothing like you, Liza, but Uncle Seymour thought she was good."

"Is Frieda your sister?" Patrick said.

Mom appreciated Patrick's interest in our family, despite his record as a lousy home-wrecker.

"No, Frieda was married to my brother, Seymour. I wish you'd met him."

Mom was eager to acquaint Patrick with the wonders of Uncle Seymour. Smart, dashing, generous to a fault. Seymour, of course, was the relative who mysteriously became the U.S. Navy's table-tennis champion. He was also an ace businessman and an amateur inventor on the side.

When Seymour met Frieda, he and my parents had just opened Durbin's Sporting Goods as partners. He stopped in a hardware store one day and noticed her working on the ledger books. He invited her to lunch on the spot. They were secretly engaged before dessert arrived.

They were married less than three years when we lost Uncle Seymour. It happened in the basement of Durbin's, where he spent long hours inventing clever appliances. Seymour perished in a rare electric-mop accident, the details of which are so ludicrous that the family was sworn never to repeat the story to strangers, lest some boob laugh out loud at the tragic, "nothing-funny-about-it" demise of Uncle Seymour. (Ask me about it later.)

"And you stayed close all these years, even though she's not family." Patrick obviously admired this.

"Well, she inherited half the business. Lucky for us, too. A real knack for money. Besides, we consider her family. I think Frieda's always been family," my mother said. "Part of our soul group, so to speak. Do you know about that, Patrick?"

He did. She was talking about the reincarnation theory in which we travel from life to life with the same circle of souls around us. We find each other in different bodies, roles, sexes, and relationships—sometimes siblings, sometimes parent and child, friends or lovers. We repeat this until we get things right.

Franz might have found me that way, I suppose. Maybe he missed his cue to get reborn and hunted around till he caught up with his group. If he'd been on time, I might've been a child prodigy. Or maybe his spirit jumped centuries to call in a favor I owed him. If you believe in the theory, that is.

"It may not be true," my mother said, "but why not? Half the world believes in reincarnation. Haven't you met people you're sure you knew before?"

I didn't know about Frieda in previous lives, but I couldn't imagine this one without her.

Frieda missed her chance to have children with Seymour, and no man measured up to him afterward. So we were her family and I was her favorite. She made me feel special by offering odd and glamorous advice that other adults never seemed to mention: *Liza, whatever you do, don't become a female wrestler.* And *Liza, always remember to misbehave quietly.* And *Liza, you have invisible talents that only you and I can see through our special glasses.* Then we'd put on our matching shades with rhinestone trim. Unique in all the world, she said.

Aunt Frieda also gave me my first piano lesson, as my mother told Patrick.

"Liza wasn't six yet," she said. "Frieda had so much patience with her."

The brand-new piano was delivered on a weekday, the best surprise ever. Aunt Frieda sat me on the bench and held her hands over mine as I stretched my fingers across the bright new keys. She gave me one lesson a week and listened to me practice, too. At some point, my parents promoted me to lessons with Clara Wolf, an official piano teacher.

"Your aunt was very hurt by that," my father said. "She thought we were insulting her."

"I'm sorry, Max, but Liza needed a *professional* teacher." From my mother's tone, I knew why Frieda felt hurt. "And just look how those lessons are paying off today."

I laughed so hard I got hiccups.

CHAPTER ELEVEN

NEW YORK POST
March 23

Yanks' New Babe a Classical Hit

Yankees owner Greg Stronghurst and '60s pitching legend Rich Weber were among the Yankees and other Bronx fans greeting Liza Durbin, a fresh face in classical music, as she returned yesterday to her old neighborhood for a visit and impromptu concert.

Durbin has become a familiar name lately because of her upcoming piano concert at Carnegie Hall, which has surprised the classical music world.

Until January, Durbin was a lawyer at Stricker, Stricker & Feinsod. She's lived in the metropolitan area except for four years at Cornell University as an English major. Colleagues and friends say she didn't show any particular musical talent until recently.

"It's a total shock," said Myles Broadbent, a lawyer who worked closely with Durbin. "She was a competent lawyer, then she started acting really weird—like wearing her slippers to work. Then she took a leave of absence and all this started. We're thrilled for her, of course."

Durbin often practices at her boyfriend's apartment in Brooklyn, where neighbors first took notice. The Yankees say they loved her first.

"I've known Liza since she was born," said Stronghurst. "She's an all-American Yankee babe. I knew she'd go far."

Stronghurst, Weber, first baseman Joey Starr and catcher Rob Rosenberg were part of the surprise waiting for the pianist when she arrived at Durbin's Sporting Goods, the landmark store built by her father Max Durbin.

～～

I shouldn't have worn the egregious sweater. Even in the black-and-white photo, I looked awful. At least the smile was real.

Cassie had pulled off a great surprise, rounding up loads of old friends in the Bronx. I'd practically grown up in the family store, and there were several generations of Durbin's finest on hand. Like Oscar Wallace (still handsome at eighty), who used to play Motown records and show me cool dance steps, and Mr. Liakos, who let me play with the cash register, and some old classmates of mine who actually took time off from work to see me. Not to mention all the Yankees who showed up to give my dad his props.

The store was decorated with banners and too many posters of me in the blue slut dress. Alfie Durbin, my big cousin whom I once had a crush on, won my heart all over again by borrowing a piano from the music store down the block. I played a short Schubert piece to appease Franz, then Cassie handed me the sheet music for "Take Me Out to the Ball Game" and we really wowed the crowd.

Everything was perfect except for the media. I could have lived without cameras and reporters recording my every blink.

Greta the Grinch didn't care for the media, either. She called early on Wednesday to demand that we meet at her Juilliard studio later that afternoon. Fine with me, but her attitude was decidedly ungracious. Maybe she didn't like my mystery sexpot image (maybe it wasn't my first choice, either), but it was getting results. People were getting to know me, and they would learn to take me seriously.

On the way to Juilliard, I fortified myself with self-confidence, ready for a serious talk with Greta. She can be scary, but I planned to reason with her. As I entered the building, though, I was unnerved by a familiar voice.

"*Bonjour,* Liza, *comment ça va?* Pretty good coverage from yesterday, *non?*" My idiot sister caught up with me at the elevator, grinning as if she had any right in the world to be at Juilliard.

"Cassie, what are you doing here?"

"Nice greeting, sis," she said. "I was summoned by her majesty."

Greta?

"And if you ask me, Liza, that woman could use some time in charm school."

Greta.

"We've both been called to the office," I said. "Did she say anything else to you?"

"Nope, just insisted I come. She must've seen the papers today. Think she saw the billboard?"

Cassie actually seemed excited at the prospect. I warned her not to expect gratitude from Greta. She seemed not to hear me.

"We have a little time, Liza. Show me around. This place is really something. You know, I think I saw Itzhak Perlman just before."

"Yeah, I see him all the time." So blasé. "Why don't we go get a cup of coffee?"

The first time I had lunch at Juilliard, I must have looked the way Cassie did. She barely gave her eyes a rest, scanning the room feverishly. The dancers were as lovely as ever, the actors as magnetic, and the collective energy caused a power surge in an otherwise ordinary room. But this time I was consumed by my own circumstances, while my sister devoured the scene.

I told Cassie how much fun it was to see our old friends in the Bronx, that I appreciated all the effort it took on her part. I hoped Greta could see the upside of our situation.

"Oh my God, that *is* Itzhak Perlman over there," Cassie said. "Can you introduce me?"

I didn't have to answer because something even tastier showed up at our table. Unfortunately, he was with his dancing toothpick.

"Liza, where've you been lately?" Chase said. He kissed me on the cheek, then looked at Cassie. "You two must be sisters, right?"

Cassie did not seem flattered. I introduced them, and Cassie extended a hand as if waiting for a kiss. Chase shook it.

"And this is Chase's friend, Kathy," I said.

"That's *Katje*," said the toothpick.

"So sorry, Katje, of course. Katje is a dancer, Cassie." As if there could be any doubt. "And Chase is a very successful composer. He writes—"

"You think I don't know that?" Cassie answered. "We saw you perform in London, Mr. Barnes. *Magnifique*. We have your CDs."

Chase and Katje joined our table and we were a merry crowd, chatting about London and how lovely and talented we all were.

Chase informed Cassie and me that she must see Katje dance. He also mentioned that a contemporary piece would make a dandy encore for me. I reminded my sister that we had to go meet Greta. Chase and Cassie made farewells like old best friends.

Greta Pretsky was waiting for us when we arrived at her studio. Just seeing Cassie and Greta in the same room was jarring.

My svelte sister towered over Greta. Cassie wore Versace with pearls. Greta sported a stiff white blouse with conservative brown skirt and vest, looking like a Girl Scout leader without the badges. You'd need a DNA test to prove these two were members of the same species.

I made the introductions as they glared at each other.

"Mrs. Whitman, why are you making a spectacle of your sister and Franz Schubert?"

Greta's charm did not win over my sister.

"Dr. Pretsky, I'm sure we all have the same goal in mind here. Why don't we all sit down and talk about this?" Greta didn't budge. "Look, you want people to hear Liza. So do we. You want people to respect the music. Nothing could be more important to us. We have different approaches. It just so happens that ours is the one that's selling tickets."

"You are making a mockery of everything I hold dear. It is disgusting and I will not have anything to do with it. I insist you stop these foolish pranks immediately."

"Excuse me?" Cassie still smiled, but not so nicely. "By what right would you be saying this? Do you have a contract with my sister that I don't know about?"

Contract? The fact that I was a lawyer and hadn't even thought about a contract was proof of how deeply out of whack my life was. I was so swept up in being en-geniused that it never even occurred to me to ask about money, rights, and obligations for Carnegie Hall or thereafter. Greta had taken over my career, and I let her. Cassie took over my image, and I let her. They didn't even pretend to include me in their conversation.

"I will cancel this concert if I have to." Greta's apple cheeks turned a deeper red as she made her stand. "Then where will your sister be?"

"Carnegie Hall, of course," Cassie said. "I can easily finance this without you, Dr. Pretsky. But that's not what either of us really wants, is it? You've been wonderful to Liza. You're the one who got her this far. It would be a great shame if you didn't stick with us to the end."

Greta looked outplayed and frustrated. She turned away from us.

"Look, we've got the public's attention," Cassie said. "We may even sell out next week. I'll try to keep things more dignified. Don't you want to be part of this?"

Still no answer, but pulling back slightly.

"My people are working on the contracts. This will work out well for you, Dr. Pretsky, I promise. It'll work out well for all of us. Did you know that Liza may be recording on Sony Classical? I've been talking with John D. Doyle about it."

Suddenly Greta the Greedy got interested. She wanted to know about the recording deal, future concerts, promotions, and every other gory detail.

Franz, in a state of confused anxiety, added to my distress by spinning like a dervish inside my brain. I was suddenly enraged. Neither Cassie nor Greta remembered I was in the room, so they were surprised when I produced a scream that frightened the furniture.

"Franz and I are leaving." I switched to a tone of quiet menace. "It would be so good of you two to let me know what you've planned for my life. In fact, better if you talk directly to 'my people.' I'll have him call you. His name is Myles Broadbent."

I walked out, smiling. The thought of Cassie and Greta having to spend any time with that vile weasel would compensate for any lack of experience on the weasel's part.

※

My stand for emancipation gave me a temporary buzz, but it wasn't a convincing victory. Greta knew vastly more about the music world than I did, and Cassie actually cared about publicity and made things happen. I'd be in a stagnant mess without them. But where was the line of responsibility for me? Even if I trusted them with my future, could I trust them with Franz's? I didn't have the knowledge or tools to protect his interests or my own.

Chase Barnes, a man who knew plenty, bumped into me, literally, as I was leaving the building, as if he'd been waiting there to do just that. Thoroughly pleased with our collision, he suggested we head for happy hour. It was half past five and we hurried to a local pub. The place was dark, smoky, and adorned with old photos of revered writers and musicians. Mere proximity to these images infected the patrons with an air of intellectual achievement.

We took a corner table, where a flickering candle fought to shine through its filthy glass globe. We ordered a bottle of merlot and mussels in wine sauce. I described the encounter in Greta's studio. Chase oozed sympathy. He knew what could happen once a talent was recognized.

Chase was not among the child prodigies who never learned about normal life. As a boy in Syracuse, he played excellent piano when he wasn't busy with football, basketball, and messing around with his friends. He went to the University of Buffalo, where he was one of many music majors. His talent revealed itself in his first composition class. The professor saw something special and took time to work with an eager freshman. Their conversations went well beyond the usual undergraduate discourse.

"Dr. Kauber never doubted me," Chase said. "He always talked to me as a colleague. Not that I always understood him—he was in another orbit—but I learned so much from him. And I played my own work pretty damn well.

"Kauber got me into the good competitions. Before I finished college, I had a reputation as a young musician to watch. When I got to graduate school, people already knew about me. Most of the grad students and even some professors were threatened by me. I had the hangers-on, too. Lots of helpful people ready to share the glory, in case things went well."

Chase never made music for the Top 40 charts. There were not zillions to be made off his career, but plenty of interested parties lined up to get a piece of his respectable pie. The rewards would be prestige, power, and pretty good money. And everyone wanted to control him.

The people he trusted let him down. Chase didn't understand the business side of music and chose advisers simply because he liked them. His friends, it turned out, weren't much more knowledgeable than he was. So he got an agent who arranged for performances and a recording contract. It was years before he realized how much he was paying for questionable help.

Chase was booked for far too many concerts. He traveled all the time, performing with orchestras in the States, Europe, Asia, and Australia. He lived in a state of exhaustion. He finally became so depleted that he had to cancel concerts, sometimes with same-day notice. It hurt his career. Overnight he went from being the darling of serious music to an unpredictable brat. He used this downtime to think things over.

Chase fired the agent and cut his ties with anyone looking to control him. He took his current position at Juilliard, got back to serious music, and was master of his life again. And it took only twenty years to achieve all this.

The twenty-year timeline scared me into a second bottle of wine. We switched to less terrifying topics. Chase laughed at my Yankees stories. He gave me a full account of dinner with Mick Jagger in Singapore. We ranged over movies, art, embarrassing moments, and suddenly it was eight o'clock. Something rumbled in my memory banks.

Wednesday, eight o'clock: Nonie's Grill with Ruthie, Peter, Dan, and Fred. Except eight o'clock was wrong. I should have been there at six-thirty.

"I gotta go," I blurted. "It's been great but I gotta go, Chase. Really gotta go."

"Well, that's a shame because I could think of nicer ways to end this evening."

Yeah, yeah, very charming, but I *really* had to run.

I sprinted out the door and searched for a taxi. Nonie's Grill was way down in Soho, no chance of getting there in less than twenty minutes. I considered a subway until a cab pulled up and emptied its passengers right in front of me. I grabbed it.

The driver looked familiar. An African-looking man with a distinctive accent. The ID displayed in the front window said his name was Moreno Abdi.

"You gave me a ride once before." He looked back to see if he recognized me. "You sang for me and I bought a CD."

"I sell two or three CDs a day. Ha, if I am lucky!" he said. "You are musician?"

"Yes. Now I am. You drove me to Juilliard and sang for me. It was wonderful."

"Dat's right, I remember. You are 'sort of musician.' " He chuckled warmly. "Now you are real musician? Good, good. We can sing."

"I don't sing."

"Good, good. You can listen."

He serenaded us all the way downtown. His voice emanated from another place, where people dance to a lion's heartbeat.

The effect was mesmerizing. I forgot the anguish of having stood up Ruthie, Peter, Dan, and Fred. I would have to explain, to make things right again with my friends. But Moreno's voice was a lovely diversion, and I let those worries float away in his vibrato. I hardly noticed when he stopped the car in front of Nonie's Grill.

"We're here, miss."

I sighed in response.

"You like my CD, miss?"

His CD lay on a shelf in my apartment. I'd been meaning to play it.

"Oh, yes. How much do I owe you?" I reached for my wallet, then stopped. "Hang on a second. Let me peek in here and see if I'm staying."

No sign of Fred, Ruthie, Peter, or Dan.

I asked Moreno to drive me home. He made it an exotic journey with songs that brought sunshine and zebras into the cab.

I climbed the stairs to my apartment, dreading the aftermath of my no-show at Nonie's. Nasty messages on my machine, or worse, no response at all. Wrong again.

"Hey, Liza, it's about time," said Ruthie. She was comfortably curled on the sofa next to Peter. Fred and Dan lounged at the dining room table, and Patrick filled the big easy chair.

"Liza, we hear you're a possessed genius and a total mess," Dan said. His long blond hair was disheveled, as usual. "Grab a glass and spill your guts."

Some bottles of wine and an unopened Guinness sat on the coffee table. I filled a glass with something red and sat down with my friends.

They had given up on me at Nonie's, but Fred claimed extenuating circumstances on my behalf. Undependable was normal for me lately, he told them, probably beyond my control. He gave them the barest-bones account of me and Franz. They wanted to see for themselves and decided to wait for me in my apartment, so Patrick hosted an instant party.

With ridiculous eagerness, I filled my friends in on the events leading to Carnegie Hall. They may have laughed off Fred's version of the story, but they took mine seriously. My credibility was unquestioned, after all, based on my previous lack of talent.

While they wanted every detail of my amazing life, I wanted to hear everything about them. Ruthie and Peter, married six years, were still mad for each other and thinking about kids, or possibly a St. Bernard. Dan was secretly in love with someone at his genetics lab, so we gave him bad advice on how to get her attention. Someone asked Fred how he liked having his own ad company. He showed enthusiasm until he remembered that he and I had a few conflicts in that area, so suddenly he became interested in Patrick's career plans. Patrick stumbled on his answers, too, and it seemed a good time to call it a night. Anyway, we were out of wine and munchies.

We said good-bye with tipsy hugs and vows of secrecy. Franz added his contentment to the good cheer. Patrick and I went to bed happy—he even forgot to ask where I'd been until almost nine o'clock.

Gottseidank . . . Thank you, God, that I was not a woman. To be so duped by broad shoulders!

The next morning Patrick relayed a day-old message from my sister. She said I absolutely must watch *Gordy & Jill Talk!* on Thursday. Don't miss it, should be great.

I was already battling a headache, which worsened at the thought of this insipid talk show. Gordy Flims was the ex–Jet quarterback and quipping partner of Jill Camacho, a former Miss District of Columbia and professional blab-o-matic. Their show was taped in Manhattan and inflicted on viewers from Richmond to Honolulu.

GORDY: So, my driver took me past Times Square yesterday, and I gotta tell you, Jill—you've heard about this classical pianist, Liza Dublin?

JILL: Durbin, Gordy, I believe the name is Durbin.

GORDY: Whatever. In the middle of Times Square there's this billboard, more like a bill*broad,* if you want the truth. *(Audience giggles.)* I mean, this babe means business, Jilly. I'd listen to her play "Chopsticks" as long as she looks like that. *(Audience laughter.)*

JILL: Gordy, behave yourself. Your wife is watching! And yes, I've seen the billboard and the ads, too. I should explain for our fans across the country that Liza Durbin debuts at Carnegie Hall next week. She's a pianist, supposedly. And, by the way, I understand this whole thing is causing quite a stir in the music world.

GORDY: Hey, some of those musty old musicians probably could use a good stir once in a while. *(Audience hilarity.)* You, sir, in the third row, you know just what I mean. *(Such mirth!)*

JILL: Seriously, Gord. There are people who think this young woman, this Liza Durbin, is making a mockery of serious musicianship, of all the hard work musicians put into their work. Miss Durbin has no background as a pianist and one day she shows up in sexy ads and a billboard in Times Square, for Pete's sake. I don't want to say anything—

GORDY: No, not *you*, Jilly, you never say *any*thing! *(Still more laughter.)*

JILL: Well, no, I wouldn't criticize her. I've never even met the girl. I'm just saying a lot of people are wondering where she came from and if just anyone can buy their way into Carnegie Hall these days. That's what people are saying, anyway.

GORDY: There wouldn't be any jealousy because no one's asked you to sing there, right, Jilly?

JILL: Well, I'm not saying I'd turn down the gig. *(Mugging at the audience for applause.)*

GORDY: I hear you, Jilly, but I have to say this. I'm more a jock than a music lover—I mean, I miss the Spice Girls, right? If this gal can get my attention, maybe she can get some other slobs like me to take a listen. I hear she's big on Schumann.

JILL: That's Schu-*bert,* Gordy, as in Franz Schu-*bert.* And, yes, people say she has a special thing for him. Her publicist says Miss Durbin feels a special connection with Schubert, like they're mystically connected somehow. Isn't that interesting? Maybe we'll ask her on the show so she can explain that.

GORDY: Super. And speaking of mystically connected, did you hear about those Siamese triplets born in Sardinia?

JILL: *Conjoined,* Gordy, we don't call them Siamese anymore. They're conjoined. Folks, what am I gonna do with him? He's a dinosaur! *(More unexplainable laughter.)*

I had aspirin for breakfast. Patrick commiserated in a resigned way. This ball was rolling, he said, and no one could stop it. When he left for work, I checked my letters and messages.

A stack of mail on the kitchen counter swelled daily to new heights. The usual bills were joined by congratulatory notes, meeting requests, invitations from long-lost friends.

One Pacific-scene postcard with a scribbled note caught my eye: *"Liza, I'm thrilled to hear of your success. There's something I'd like to talk with you about. Please call me at your earliest convenience. My heartiest congratulations."* It was signed Abe Sturtz, and he wrote his phone number extra-large. I searched my memory and placed him at Nordstrom, when Franz first appeared. I set his card aside, along with the many messages I seriously meant to get back to. Then I turned to my answering machine.

Patrick had muted the phone the night before—a daily necessity by that time—but the calls had been rolling in. Some reporters. Ruthie (*"I'd like to see you arm-wrestle that Jilly Camacho twit"*). Cassie, wanting a serious talk with me. Greta, too. My mother wanted tickets to the show whenever I appeared on *Gordy & Jill Talk!* (*"That Jilly is adorable!"*). And Chase called.

I listened twice, then erased his dinner invitation. Life was complicated enough without dinner dates or awkward messages on my machine. I was not playing hard to get, even though it always works. Besides, what would Franz think?

Franz, the all-knowing and ever-present. Nobody since my baby days had observed every moment of my life as he did. No adult *should* be under constant scrutiny. It was embarrassing, when I dared to think about it.

It's like listing the foods you eat on any day. Most of us think we eat well, and would be shocked if we wrote down every morsel we consumed. A couple of chocolate Kisses off someone's desk (six), a sensible portion of pasta (enough to run a marathon on), the good intentions toward veggies, the near-absence of water. Luckily, the average body is pretty forgiving, and such lists are understandably unpopular. I, however, had an internal list-keeper for every aspect of my life. No way to simply slide my bad decisions or petty concerns past Franz. Whether or not he was judging me, he saw it all. This awareness bugged me. It also inspired me to something better.

I declared the rest of the day a gift to Franz and me. No Cassie, no Greta, no billboards or other silliness. Franz gave me something loftier than talk shows and books for dummies, when I was smart enough to let him.

I pulled on my jeans, a light sweatshirt, and sneakers. It was a brilliant day and I headed toward the Brooklyn Promenade. I dug my Discman out of a drawer so I could listen to Moreno Abdi's African music. I also grabbed one that Danny loaned me. It was Keith Jarrett, *The Köln Concert*, and I'd been meaning to listen to it for weeks. I slipped that into the Discman, put on the headphones, and took off.

The Promenade in Brooklyn Heights runs along the East River. It attracts people like an old town square, with pedestrian walks, play areas, park benches, and classic views. Nearby and to the right, the Brooklyn Bridge soars over the water and disappears into the Manhattan skyline.

Listening to Keith Jarrett's solo piano, we heard beauty, imagination, and a sense of freedom that was new to Franz. I doubt Jarrett ever played his compositions the same way twice, yet each piece was expertly turned and spun into silk. Sometimes the pianist let loose whoops of joy in the middle of a passage.

Walking down the Promenade, we set everything to music. Unwitting strangers glided by in tempo and sparked harmonies. Ancient men bantered about prostates in bittersweet *adagio*. Nannies strolled *allegro* with bundled babies. Grandmothers waltzed arm in arm, planning museum excursions. Lady Liberty swayed to the beat.

Franz and I strolled the Promenade for a long, lovely while. The last CD we played was Moreno Abdi's. His music filled us with a joy that pooled into something orgasmic. I know this because a gentle, blue-haired lady tapped me on the shoulder to ask if I was all right. She'd found me collapsed on a bench, drenched in tears and laughing like a loon. She just wanted to make sure I could take care of myself. Best to stay alert even in our nice neighborhood, she said. Can't trust everyone, dear, maybe it's best to go home and rest.

I had a better idea for our next stop.

I found Danny Carson's address in the phone book. He lived in an old brownstone on Chestnut Street. An elegant, fiftyish blonde answered the door and I asked to see her son.

"Danny?" she said. "You want to see Danny? Are you a teacher?"

"No, I'm a friend. Liza Durbin." Apparently this woman did not watch *Gordy & Jill Talk!* or get her news from *The Brooklyn Buzz.* "I'm a pianist, maybe Danny's mentioned me?"

She appeared disinterested. On closer inspection, I suspected certain facial expressions were beyond her abilities, thanks to too much cosmetic surgery.

"I'll see if he's home," she said at last, leaving me on the front step as she checked inside.

She returned without Danny.

"Who did you say you are?"

"Liza Durbin."

"Oh, yes, you were on the news. I remember you. Why don't you come in and wait? Danny should be home from school soon. I think it lets out at three."

The spacious apartment appeared surgically clean. Hardwood floors glowed aggressively, softened only by the Oriental rugs. Expensive pillows were arranged on chic Italian furniture. The dominant colors were crystal and platinum.

My hostess more than matched her environment. She might have been ordered from a catalog. But while her looks were perfect, she was socially unsure. I finally had to ask her name.

"Ilsa Shales," she said, as I instigated a handshake. "Danny and I have different last names. He's from my first husband, a nice man." Her German accent added to her sophisticated air.

"Danny's a great kid," I said. Mothers usually soften when you compliment their kids. "And talented. He's been listening to me play piano and he's played for me a few times, too."

She moved her mouth in smile mode. Her eyes sat still.

"He's a good musician," I said, still trying. "I hear he also plays flute. I haven't heard him yet." I wished I could tell her how strongly Franz Schubert was drawn to her talented son, that he sensed something magnificent in Danny.

"He plays flute well. And you must hear him sing. He has an excellent voice teacher," Ilsa said. "You know, I played second flute in my high school orchestra. I could have been first, I really think so."

"So Danny gets his talent from you."

"Yes, you could say that. I don't believe his father was a musician of any kind. A nice man, though."

"So, what time does Danny usually come home?" I asked.

"Soon, I'm sure. Sometimes he goes places after school, though."

Her vagueness was unsettling. Ilsa Shales resembled a mother in the way topiary might remind you of an animal. I was about to give up when I heard the front door open. I prayed it was Danny.

"Hey Moms, I'm home."

"Hello, *Liebling*, please don't call me that," she answered, then whispered to me: "Sounds awful, don't you think?"

"Wow, Liza, what are you doing here?"

Danny stopped short at the sight of me having iced tea with Moms. Something did not compute.

"I came to return the CD you loaned me," I said, "and see if you have anything else for me."

"Oh, sure." He was relieved that my business was with him. "In my room. This way."

I got up and followed Danny. In a confused maternal effort, Ilsa Shales yelled to her son not to close his door.

Danny's room had all the regalia of teenage décor, but it was scrubby clean. Someone dusted his treasures, framed his posters, and tightened his bed like an army cot. The glass in his window was spotless, like no one had ever pressed a nose against it. I wondered if the housekeeper kept things that way, or if Danny had chosen this compulsion for himself.

His CDs were stacked in five-foot-tall towers. They were organized by style, with various subsections. I ran my finger along the titles, wondering which of the shiny discs held revelations.

"Was my mother nice to you?" Danny asked.

I'd forgotten her by then.

"She was fine," I said. "She gave me iced tea."

"Did she talk about me?"

What did Danny need, a yes or a no? "We didn't talk much, really. I wasn't here that long. She's glad you play flute. And she said your father was very nice. Where does he live?"

"He doesn't," Danny said. "He died in a car accident."

"I'm so sorry. How old were you?"

"Three. I hardly remember him. We still lived in Austria then. Mom says he was her nicest husband. She thinks she might still be married to him if he lived. She gets married all the time."

"All the time?"

"Paul is number four. He's better than three but I liked two best, Alan. He still keeps in touch." Danny took a breath, then brightened. "At least they're rich. The last two have been millionaires."

Before I could respond, he turned to the CDs and engrossed himself in finding the right ones. He pulled from the classics, jazz, Celtic, and reggae sections. He offered me something played on a toy piano. Franz was giddy, sensing that good things were coming. Danny glowed in his milieu.

"Danny, *mein Liebes,* have you performed for your friend?"

We hadn't noticed Ilsa Shales standing at the open door.

"He hasn't played his flute for you, has he?" She was asking me while looking at him. "Danny's really good, you see. Better than I was, I think. Danny, why don't you play something for your friend?"

"I don't feel like playing, Mom." Sullen again.

"You should hear him, really," she insisted.

"I really don't want to, Moms. I'm not that good, anyway."

"That's not true. He's really good, Miss Durbin." She looked at her son, not knowing the magic words to use. "Maybe next time."

Danny thought just then that it would be great to go to Fred's to play piano. I agreed. He threw the CDs in his backpack. I asked him to bring his flute and he said sure.

Ilsa Shales was right. The boy could play.

Danny's flute and Franz's keyboard were a delicious match. We played impromptu duets until dusk. Fred would be home soon, so we had to wrap things up. He packed his flute away and I noticed how his demeanor shrank in the silence. He filled the moment by singing.

He was good at piano and flute, but nothing compared to his voice.

I didn't know the song—something sad about someone gone. Danny stared out the window and sang it straight through. Maybe he forgot I was listening.

Franz wanted to speak but I couldn't translate. I wanted to tell Danny about Schubert, so I could pass along higher praise than mine. But I heard Fred at the door and got sensible.

"Danny, that was incredible. I love your voice," I said.

"Oh, right," he said. "Thanks. That was fun. Do it again?"

"Anytime."

"Dieser Junge ist begabt . . . This boy is special," my mother said. "Can't he be a musician?"

"Music is fine for Franz now," my father answered, "but we are not rich and he'll need a profession. Teaching is honorable. He'll be glad in the end."

"But Franz is special."

Thank God for friends and patrons who kept me in music. How many gifts die of neglect, buried in unmarked hearts?

A special boy has found us, Liza. Pay attention.

CHAPTER THIRTEEN

With a week to go before Carnegie Hall, Franz's *Fantasia* dreams were spliced with my nightmares of getting stuck in traffic and missing our debut. Even worse, I dreamed that Franz left me.

This was my greatest fear, and the one most likely to occur. I had no assurance that Franz would stick around for my next breath, let alone another week. He had no obligation or, as far as I knew, any loyalty to me. Fear of desertion nailed itself to my chest and panted in my ear.

Desertion is part of everyone's life. Just live long enough and someone you love will die, move away, or choose another lover. A man tells a woman he can't live without her. Parents say they can't go on after losing a child. Kids feel like killing themselves when Mom dies. All heartfelt hyperbole. They'd be lonelier and sadder, but they'd brush their teeth every morning, finish school, go back to work, and life would get hold of them again. They almost certainly would not die. But I might.

Franz was not just with me, he was *of* me. He permeated my mind and body, absorbed me on an atomic level. For all I knew, Franz was a metastatic invasion that could not be extracted without killing its host.

If I did survive Franz's departure, everything afterward would be diminished. Even my desertion issues would return to the mundane. I'd torture myself with unoriginal regrets—wondering what I'd done to drive him out, how I could have made him stay. Heartfelt hyperbole.

Bolts of anxiety attacked me through the night. I'd lie still with eyes wide, concentrating on gravity, refusing to fly out the window and dissolve in the atmosphere. A baseless fear? Laws of nature were undone in my world. My comfort was Patrick.

I'd breathe in rhythm with him as he slept next to me, hold on to his warm back like a buoy. His wrist pulsed with life's secret code, and I kissed the beating spot. Patrick gave me what I needed and he never knew it.

~~~

On a rainy Saturday morning, Patrick and I drove to Upper Danville in his mother's Cadillac. I fully intended to act normal. But while Patrick crabbed about the weather, Franz found a melody in it. I guess we got loud.

"What the hell is that?"

I asked Patrick what he meant.

"That noise you're making." He made a face like he smelled a fart. "Are you okay?"

How humiliating. He hadn't heard me sing before. Franz was pushing a melody through me and the results were dreadful.

"Sorry, Patrick. Franz was writing a song."

"Are you sure, babe? I thought you were barking at me."

No denying my voice sucked, but that might not be the only problem. Franz had been thinking lately about his *lieder*—those popular songs that sparked the group-sing Schubertiads. Passionate *lieder* lovers still listen to and perform these pieces. Voice majors in college and professional soloists favor *lieder* as showcases for their talents. The most famous example is *Ave Maria*. Too bad they didn't all sound that good.

Call me a philistine; typical *lieder* made my eyes cross.

In those early months of inhabitation, I had raided the Juilliard library and listened to most of Schubert's work. I was regularly charmed, excited, moved, awed. But when I heard *lieder*, it took an effort not to laugh.

The first song I listened to sounded like a parody of classical music—a glacially paced dirge set to a poem by Goethe. The singer bellowed in German, his voice so low no dog could hear him. The next song was so bleak I thought Franz might be the Leonard Cohen of his day. I tried another one, a lilting ditty, but it was sung by the same rumbling behemoth—I thought of a rhino trying to knit. The next few songs were just as ridiculous to my modern, unsophisticated ears.

I'd set aside the whole issue of *lieder* then, not wanting to hurt Franz's feelings. I intended to get back to them someday. My inner composer was pushing the point. I explained the situation to Patrick.

"Fine, but don't sing again without warning me," he said. "I nearly drove off the road."

"Patrick, there's something else." My heart was suddenly pounding. "Did I sing in German?"

"German? Not even close. It sounded more like goose honks."

"Thank God."

We spent Saturday and most of Sunday at my sister's. We had big, noisy meals with Carnegie Hall as the invisible and oversized centerpiece.

I took Cassie and Fred aside to make our peace concerning their tacky, behind-my-back publicity scheming. They were meeting with Greta Pretsky and Myles Broadbent on Monday. I declined to join them. I had spoken to my weasel counsel already and given him the name of an entertainment lawyer to consult with. Myles was to review everything with a Stricker or Fiensod and come up with a nice deal for everyone. He was sending copies of everything for my approval and we would choose an agent soon. I had no interest in making Cassie, Fred, or Greta suffer financially just because they had embarrassed me in public or tried to run my life. Meeting Myles Broadbent was punishment enough to make me happy.

On Sunday morning, Cassie had a nice brunch planned. Just a little something for the family and a hundred best friends. I was the star attraction, natch, and everyone wanted to chat with me.

The room swarmed with upper-crusty types. They looked unnaturally swell for a Sunday morning—not an unshaved face or novelty T-shirt in the room. John D. Doyle, of Sony Classical fame, was among the crowd. Our first meeting was a pip.

I had escaped to the breakfast room. Franz was working on a melody in our head and needed a little quiet.

"Your sister's a persuasive woman; she about threatened my life if I didn't come today to meet you." A compact, fit-looking man in his sixties walked across the room and extended his hand to me. "John D. Doyle. Glad to see you're always practicing."

I followed his gaze to my fingers, which were busily planting a tune on the tabletop.

"Just working on some *lieder*," I said. "Nice to meet you, Mr. Doyle."

"Please, call me John D. I've listened to the tape Cassie sent me. You're quite something. And, of course, I know you're with Greta Pretsky." His bald head shone brightly and a neat white beard warmed his face. "So, which song are you working on?"

"Nothing you've heard, I'm sure."

"Actually, I know *lieder* quite well," he said. "I sang at Yale. 'Course, that was many years ago."

"Really. You must have a wonderful voice."

"So which *lied* were you thinking of?"

"Um, well, it was one of the Goethes," I said shakily.

"My old specialty!" John D. must have been a riot at frat parties. "Wait, don't tell me, let me guess."

John D. sucked in half the air in the room, then unleashed a few bars of song. He resonated like a barrel of dirty oil, thick and lumpy. But he delivered the passage with zeal.

"That was amazing," I said when he finished. "That's just the one I was thinking about. How did you know?"

He grinned conspiratorially at me. "*Lieder* lovers have a special bond, don't we?"

John D. led us to the Steinway and the brunch guests gathered around to hear us. John D. would sing a few bars of favorite music and we'd jump in and play with him. His voice warmed up decently and sounded really fine at times. I can't say the crowd sang along, but they got a kick out of the illustrious John D.'s performance. They cheered for both of us. We made music until our fans grew restless and headed for their limos.

Cassie considered the brunch a huge success. She was thoroughly impressed that I got John D. to sing with me. I explained it was his idea, which thrilled her even more. Making John D. Doyle happy was the perfect career strategy. I didn't bother to tell her I did it for Franz, or that I genuinely liked John D.

It occurred to me then that *lieder* might not be inherently bad. Some of them seemed dated and off-putting, but John D. sang some beauties, too. And making music with friends is a good thing.

I wondered if I could intentionally influence Franz's music. Obviously, I wasn't a creative source, but I was already introducing him to different music. Maybe I could encourage him to write new *lieder*, rethink the old form, incorporate a broader world of sensibilities. Anyway, he couldn't stop me from trying.

The brunch crowd was gone by two o'clock, just in time for the rest of us to catch a basketball game on TV. We gathered to enjoy the game together, sort of.

Cassie and Fred sat huddled on a couch in what was becoming their usual pose, speaking in whispers and scribbling notes. Mom and Aunt Frieda talked nonstop. Only my father and Patrick watched every play, occasionally shouting comments. Barry, the good son-in-law, stuck around mainly for the banter.

Cameron and Brittany lasted several minutes before getting bored. I suggested they help me bake cookies that we could sell for huge profits during time-outs. We retreated to the kitchen to whip up the only recipe I knew by heart.

The kids took turns measuring, mixing, and fighting over who would crack the eggs. They had washed their hands first, but their baking efforts included a hideous number of uncovered coughs and invasive contact with noses and hair. We'd have to boil those cookies to make them safe. I finally sent the little germs to their playroom to make cookies-for-sale signs. The cookies went into the oven, and the kitchen was transformed by the scents of melting chocolate, honey, and spices.

"Cloves are the secret. Always a pinch of cloves." I turned to find Barry behind me, quoting my secret for great chocolate chips.

"Good memory, Barry. It's been a long time since we baked cookies in college."

He sighed heavily and made a hug-me gesture. I obliged. He lingered a moment too long.

"What's up, Barry? Here to inspect my cookies?"

"No, Liza. I just thought, well, we never have any time alone anymore."

Because we're not supposed to, Barry, that's why.

"I haven't had a chance to say how proud I am of you. I know you downplay your role in this, Liza. I mean, Schubert's the guy, right? But this is a huge change for you. Your life is different in every way, and you're under a lot of pressure. I just want you to know I think you're doing great."

"Thanks, Barry."

I thought he'd leave then, but he sat at the kitchen table instead. More sighing.

"Cassie is like a different woman, you know," he said. "She's all energized over this. It's nice to see her excited about something that's not shopping."

"She's certainly done a lot on my behalf."

"You notice her and Fred?" The cookies were nearly done. Barry gestured me to come sit with him, please. "Suddenly those two have everything in common. Do you know how many times a day they talk on the phone? How often they meet?"

I didn't want to know.

"She's changed, too, Liza. It's like she's obsessed with making a name for herself. She's suddenly got to have her career back. It's not like she needs it, or like it's really meaningful work. And I'm sorry, Liza, but I don't think she's really doing it all for you. She just wants it. The kids and I are pretty much left out of it."

"We've all changed in the past few months, Barry. I'm shocked by how much."

"Yes, but some changes are for the better." A gaze and a sigh. "And others aren't."

The baking timer buzzed. Barry held me still with a hand on my shoulder.

"I have something for you." He handed me a small velvet box. "Nothing big, just something for luck."

In the box was a gold filigreed pendant shaped like a hand with the fingers pointing down and the thumb and pinkie curling up.

"Do you like it? It's the hand of Fatima, guaranteed to keep the evil spirits away." Barry flashed a grin I hadn't seen in years. "That's what the Gypsy woman said, anyway."

"You bought it from a Gypsy?"

"Well, nah, not really." He shrugged nicely. "But it sounded good, don't you think?"

Yes, for half a second this conversation sounded vaguely good. I remembered how it felt to love Barry without also hating him for marrying Cassie. He'd actually thought about me, bought me a gift, looked sincere. How tempting to slip back in time. So easy to shed years of resentment, but what would I do then? He'd still be my sister's husband and I needed to hate him a little.

"Aunt Liza! There's smoke! Where are the cookies?" Brittany came running back to the kitchen at her first whiff of burning cookies.

I tucked the pendant in the pocket of my blazer, smiled my thanks to Barry, and tended to a crisis I could believe in. We salvaged half the chocolate chips and sold them for twice the price.

Patrick was in a sunny mood as we drove home later in the rain. He said my family was growing on him. He liked their uninhibited commotion and affection. It was unlike his own family, which was small and definitely more proper. Plus, my father had stopped referring to Patrick as "that bum," even under his breath. He must've been hoping for an engagement soon.

"I talked with Barry for a while," Patrick said. "He's more interesting than I thought. I know your sister can be a pain, but she can be fun, too. Maybe we should all go out some night."

"Good idea." Dream on. "I'll set it up and let you know."

"By the way, your mother asked me about Milan."

I bet she did.

"I told her it's still up in the air," he said, "but you know it's coming right up, Liza."

Unfortunately, Patrick had been right when he once said that Franz affected everything between us. Before Franz, I held back in my relationship with Patrick. Afterward, I opened up to Patrick in new ways, partially thanks to Franz's overflow of passion. Then Patrick found out about Franz and a new gulf opened between us. Patrick was trying to adjust, though, and seemed more optimistic, at least for the moment. It made my overloaded heart hurt.

"I'm not pressuring you, babe," he said, "just reminding you that I don't have much time to decide in, okay? You're still thinking about it, right?"

"I think of nothing else, dear."

Schönheit lebt . . . Beauty lives, unstoppable in any age. I cannot be where I belong, but perhaps there is hope. I am not a stranger in this body when we have music.

CHAPTER FOURTEEN

THE NEW YORKER
March 28

THE TALK OF THE TOWN
Comment
You Can't Fight Carnegie Hall

Like good classical savants, New Yorkers are doing their bit to support the arts. They have questioned, debated about, and quite possibly become delusional on the topic of alleged Schubert-meister Liza Durbin. In a stunning hiatus of holy urban skepticism, they've looked upon her nubile image and questionable advertising and, lo, they found it good.

The impossibly late-blooming wunderkind will make her piano debut on Thursday night and the concert is sold out. You may ask how an unknown Brooklyn lawyer commands that kind of respect in a proudly wary city. I can only assume that the cachet of Carnegie Hall endures. Miss Durbin's talents will be unveiled in this most prestigious setting, under the sponsorship of the estimable Greta Pretsky, served up in a slinky dress; this combination of endorsements has proven irresistible to nearly three thousand ticket-holding music lovers already. The rest of us shall wait and see.

ᴧᴧᴧ

On Tuesday we picked out a piano.

I didn't know this was part of the process. Greta called that morning and instructed me to meet her at Steinway Hall on West Fifty-seventh Street. The sixteen-story building, home of the famous pianos, was built in the 1920s, beautifully suited to its purpose. The impressive façade is adorned with musical icons and tributes to classical composers. Distinctive embellishments and architectural elements are reminders that there's retail beyond the mall.

We were welcomed by a showroom greeter who ushered us to Steinway's "piano bank" in the basement, a well-known location to concert pianists. The goal was to select a concert grand for my debut. Franz lit up at the prospect, but I was stymied.

"There are so many," I said to Greta. "How's a person supposed to choose?"

"This is the way it is done, Liza. These are all marvelous instruments, of course. Pianists use these for concerts all the time. Franz must find the right one for him, yes? Then the Steinway people will deliver it to Carnegie Hall for the performance."

"Where do we start?"

"Try as many pianos as you like," she answered. "Franz will know."

Until then, Franz and I had played whatever pianos were available to us. He already understood that piano technology, design, and materials had changed dramatically since his lifetime. Given his chance, he wanted to try everything.

We went from one piano to the next, playing pieces of pieces, feeling the response of the keys and listening for differences. Franz could detect the subtlest variations in tone, brilliance, character. One piano seemed too dark, another required a lighter touch. Each had qualities that I wouldn't know how to describe.

The third one we tried was his favorite. He couldn't resist trying out others, but we always came back to this one. I remembered going to the park as a child and having a favorite swing. There were four swings in the set and I only wanted the second from the right. It suited me, I could go higher in it. Franz could go higher on this piano.

"Maybe we should try playing something together," I suggested to Greta. "Feel like the *Lebensstürme*?"

"We've practiced that many times, Liza. Perhaps the *Grande Sonata* instead."

Of course, the *Grande Sonata*. The duet/encore of Greta's dreams.

The music was wonderful and Greta played her part well. For a while, we each forgot to be stressed, nervous, stubborn. You could envision us as a happy team.

Then we finished and Greta's smiling apple cheeks collapsed into prunes again.

"It was good, yes? Makes an excellent encore," she said. "Only if you want, of course."

Of course, of course. No pressure, of course.

Wednesday morning choked me with panic. I woke up and immediately checked for Franz. Still there. Got the weather forecast—chance of rain Thursday, my hair might turn feral. Made a list of people to call, last-minute errands, things that could go horribly wrong. A long, long list. Finally noticed something missing—Patrick.

Patrick!

A note on the table:

Babe, don't panic—running errands. Back with bagels and coffee by ten. Love, P

Don't worry, you'll be great tomorrow. Try to relax.

I could barely breathe, let alone relax. I tried to draw on Franz as a source of wisdom and serenity. But he was in an agitated state, too, excited about our debut.

How could Carnegie Hall possibly be one day away? A person should have more time to prepare for such a thing. Twenty years of training, for instance, would help. This big event seemed thrilling in the abstract but nauseating in its imminence.

All week I'd been following Mikki's advice and visualizing the concert, tethering Franz to my future. I had no reason to think he would leave except that I had no reason to assume he'd stay. So I tried to stay positive in the face of terror. The effort was making me awfully cranky.

Patrick came home with bagels and fresh flowers for me. We had our breakfast, then he indulged me with a full-body massage. He kneaded my back and noticed I was a bit tight. Stiff as a board, is what he actually said, but he had to be exaggerating because I was immersed in positive thinking at the time.

"Does Franz know how lucky he was to find you?" Patrick said, stroking my cheek softly.

He was being incredibly tender and patient—and not in the obnoxious, know-it-all way. I saw him clearly for the first time in weeks. I focused on his face, my feelings, on us. Suddenly I felt a great wave of love. Here was a man with a body as well as a soul, who was with me as a matter of choice, not as a victim of fate. I pulled him into bed with me. Patrick had been somewhat reserved in bed ever since learning about Franz. This time, he wisely yielded and I made him a very happy man. We spent a good while in bed before Patrick noticed the time.

"Oh, jeez, I had no idea it was so late." He jumped up and grabbed his clothes. "I wanted to leave by noon."

"Where are you going?"

"I told you. I'm taking my mother's car back to her."

"You're going to Connecticut today?"

"Honey, I told you about this." Exasperation seeping through. "I'm going up today, take her out for her birthday, then we're driving in together tomorrow for the concert. Remember?"

"So you won't be here tonight?" *Don't panic.* "Did we talk about that, too?"

"Yes, as a matter of fact, we did," he said. "Liza, if this is a problem, I'll insist we drive back tonight. You said it was okay, but we can still change our plans."

I dimly remembered this talk about the car, a birthday, away overnight.

Too bad I didn't understand it would happen the night before Carnegie Hall. But everything was fine, really, so why would I fuss about a little thing like being left alone with my greatest fears the night before the scariest night of my life?

"Don't be silly," I said. "I'll be all right. Go."

"You're absolutely sure?"

Patrick looked nervous. You'd think he was walking in the jungle, afraid to step on the camouflaged elephant trap and get skewered on a spear. Was I that scary?

"Really, Patrick, it's perfectly fine." I thought I sounded serene and reasonable.

"Damn, Liza, if you're gonna be mad, tell me now." His steely voice had surfaced. "I don't want to go off thinking things are okay and come back to a big fight."

I assured him again that I was fine, admitted that I was on edge. He shook his head and started tossing his necessaries in an overnight bag. While he got ready to leave, I checked for phone messages.

We had switched to an unlisted number so the call count was down somewhat, but the anxiety factor remained high: Bonjour, *big sister.* C'est moi. *Have you changed your mind about interviews? Gordy and Jill want you on their show* . . . BEEP . . . *Darling, it's your mother. Hope you changed your mind and can come to dinner at Cassie's tonight.* (Not in a million years, thank you.) *We can't wait till tomorrow* . . . BEEP . . . *Patrick Florio, this is Susanne from Bon Voyage Travel. I've got those prices on flights to Milan* . . . BEEP . . .

I abandoned the messages for a relaxing assault on the breakfast dishes. No relief there.

"Patrick, can you come here a minute, please?"

"I gotta get going, babe. What's up?"

"What's this?" I dangled in front of his face the world's blackest, scummiest kitchen sponge.

Patrick regarded the sponge with obvious recognition. Embarrassment, too.

"Honey, you should probably rinse that out before you do the dishes," he said.

I made no move to rinse the abomination.

"Actually, I washed the car with it." He smiled weakly. "I guess you could throw it out."

I tried to be nice. This wasn't a bad omen, after all. It was just stupid— dare I say it?—*male* behavior. Nothing worth fussing about, on top of everything else going on.

"Yes, Patrick, I think I will throw out the sponge you used to wipe bird turds off your mother's car." He winced at my nice tone. "You know, that's a really good idea. When you think of it, this sponge probably shouldn't have gone back in the kitchen sink at all, huh? I mean, I think we can afford to break open a new sponge under the circumstances, don't you?"

"I'm sorry, Liza. Really, what can I say? It was stupid. Let's not fight before your concert, okay? It's kind of funny, really. You can call your friends and laugh about my guy behavior."

"Yes, I think I will, Patrick. And, by the way, you can call back your travel agent, Susanne." He double-winced. "*Going* somewhere?"

I don't know why I took such a bitchy tone. Of course he'd be checking out airfares to Milan by then. And a germ-infested, shit-ridden sponge in the sink was also not the end of the world.

I dredged up enough maturity to recognize my mood and let Patrick off the hook, sort of. We managed a semisweet good-bye.

Werde ich verblassen? . . . Will I fade away? I can't stay forever.

Maybe it will happen gradually, like the painted words on a sign, bleached by the sun until no trace remains. Or it could end quickly, in a great burst of energy. Then everything I am would break through this creature's husk to spray into the universe. Maybe pieces will land in other bodies in cherry-sized bits of song.

CHAPTER FIFTEEN

After Patrick left, I called Cassie back to decline dinner and absolutely refuse to appear on *Gordy & Jill Talk!* She was shocked by my lack of gratitude and good sense. All I had to do was drop by the studio for a cheery hello. What could be simpler? Believe it or not, I still said no.

The day was growing blustery. I pulled on a raincoat over jeans and a sweater, then headed to Fred's. He was just leaving when I got there. Things were different between Fred and me, mainly because things were different between Fred and Cassie. He had colluded with her, kept secrets from me, and I was afraid to know the details. But he was still my pal and I needed his love.

"Ready for your big day tomorrow?"

"Guess so."

"I'm sorry about, you know, things that have happened."

"Yeah, well, you let me keep a piano in your living room. That counts for a lot."

We fell into a comfortable hug, then Fred left with a wave.

Hoffman and Pardo were peering out from her apartment door. I said hello. They acted like my biggest fans, proud to know me from when I was a nobody. Cassie had sent me a handful of complimentary concert tickets. I'd given some to my writing students (I hadn't seen them in weeks!), but I still had four left. I offered Hoffman and Pardo a pair. They already had choice seats, but I gave them a pair anyway, to give to friends. Mrs. Pardo was going to call her daughter to see if she could come in from Baltimore for the concert. Maybe she could sit next to Fred.

My next stop was Danny's. He wasn't home but his mother was.

"Please tell Danny I'm sorry I missed him," I said. "I brought him tickets for my concert. I know he already has his, but I figured he could bring friends."

"He's already going with friends, I believe." Once again, Ilsa Shales looked awfully elegant for an afternoon at home.

"Of course. Well, I really wanted to thank him for being so helpful. He's been so nice, a real pleasure."

Ilsa studied me through ice-blue eyes. Her lipstick was perfect.

"Maybe you'd like two tickets?" I said. "For you and your husband, I mean. I need to give them away anyway. You're welcome to them."

Her first honest smile broke through, complete with dimples.

"Yes? That's very nice of you," she said. "Thank you so much."

She took the tickets and gazed at them with surprising joy. You'd have thought they were gold.

I caught the subway at Court Street. This trip felt nothing like my first jaunt uptown with Franz, when we walked across the Brooklyn Bridge and danced our way through Manhattan. The journey had become routine. Franz was no longer amazed by garish subway posters and dire smells. The only new thing was a nagging, can't-turn-back-now sense of dread. It followed me through the city, mocked my attempts at optimism, and enveloped me as I met Greta at her studio.

"You are late, Miss Durbin," Greta pointed out. "One hour late, yes? This is your habit, maybe, but not tomorrow. You understand?"

"I'll be there at six. I promise."

"No, you won't," she said, "but try."

Greta's nerves were showing, too. She insisted we go back to Carnegie Hall so she could give me, one last time, the Miss Manners version of concert protocol. Enter from here, walk this way, sit thus, play music, intermission, enter again, play more, bow gracefully, take an encore, go home.

Greta led me through it like a child, and I didn't object. I needed it badly. If only she would hold my hand as we walked across the stage. Empty seats gaped at us. Soon they would be filled with discerning music lovers paying big bucks to see the justifiably unknown Liza Durbin.

"Schubert will play for you," Greta said, noting my fear. "All you must do is behave well. You'll be fine, yes? Just comb your hair, remember your posture, and wear a decent dress, please."

"Don't worry, my sister's taken care of the dress."

I didn't say that to scare her, just to make myself laugh. Greta sneered.

"I plan to introduce you to the audience personally," she said. "A bit unusual, but necessary, I think. You don't mind?"

"No, I appreciate it. You'll know the right thing to say."

"Naturally."

Then Greta announced she had things to do in her studio and scurried toward an exit. I stayed behind, said I'd catch up with her later at Juilliard. She didn't seem to hear or care.

Most of the Carnegie Hall staff recognized me, either through personal introductions or news stories. They left me in peace as I circled the lobby, wandered through hallways, touched the walls, and climbed the stairs to explore the upper levels. I was searching for the building's soul.

Old signed photographs dotted the walls to show that Pablo Casals, George Gershwin, Prokofiev, and the Beatles never entirely left the building. As I passed these images, my brain volunteered snippets of their music. Franz begged for more. He tingled.

On the first tier, I found the Rose Museum with the door wide open. A heavyset black man in a sharp-looking suit was making notes on a yellow pad.

"Hello there, come on in." A deep voice, nurtured in the South. "Liza Durbin, right?"

"That's me," I said. "Nice museum."

"Glad to meet you, Liza. I'm Joseph Alexander." He had a full, warm handshake. A graying goatee outlined his smile and offset his glossy bald head. "You have good taste. The Rose is my baby. I'm curator here, see the stuff every day, and I still get a kick out of it. Check out these instruments. Benny Goodman's clarinet, Satchmo's horn, Toscanini's baton, a Stradivarius played by Paganini. Lots more, let me show you."

He walked me over to a glass case and pointed to his treasures. The room buzzed with the power of these mementos. My chest filled up with visiting spirits, leaving barely enough room for my breath.

"I suppose you'd want to see the Beethoven manuscripts," Joseph Alexander said.

"Beethoven? What do you have of Beethoven's?"

"A few pieces still on exhibit from a show we did last year. Original manuscripts, written by the man himself."

Joseph showed me to a case displaying several pages of music. No question of authenticity. Franz recognized the writing. He once received letters in that handwriting and deeply loved the man. Tears flowed, not for a dead genius but for lost friends.

For the first time, I understood Franz's extreme loneliness. My life and the people in it were not companions to Franz. Neither was I, really. We mostly communicated as necessary about music and logistics. He once had real friends who talked and joked and argued with him. They ate together and played music into the night. He was acquainted with the likes of Beethoven and Mendelssohn. I realized that the world I inhabited must seem stilted and depleted to him.

"Are you all right, Liza? Can I get you some water? Maybe you'd like to sit down."

I must have been a pathetic sight to Joseph Alexander, crying helplessly in his Rose Museum. I tried to pull myself together, without much success.

"Don't be embarrassed," Joseph said, handing me a monogrammed handkerchief. "I'm not a musician like you, but I am a music lover. Studied music myself but I didn't have the talent. It's not enough to love the music, is it? Gotta be blessed with the talent."

I nodded in understanding, having recently crossed that divide.

"Listen, I get emotional myself sometimes," he said. "I hear Marian Anderson's voice and that's it, I'm lost. Some other time, it's Dizzy Gillespie gets to me. Doesn't matter, when you love the music your soul is open to it. Wouldn't be fun if you couldn't feel it."

Was my soul door wide open when Franz first came to me? Maybe he had been floating in the ether, waiting for a receptive being to give him water and light to grow again. Maybe my core needed something to nourish.

"Yes, you have to be open to it," I agreed. "I think I've had enough fun here, though. I'm gonna do some more exploring, if that's okay."

"You do that." I started to leave when he called my name. "Just want you to know we're rooting for you tomorrow night. You knock 'em dead, all right?"

I walked downstairs to tour the orchestra level. Carnegie Hall had taken hold of me and Franz.

When you visit holy sites, whether it's in Jerusalem or Tibet, you can feel the energy of the millions of prayers that have settled in the stone. Music infused Carnegie Hall that way. Melody dripped from the curtains, the floors vibrated. Strands of song clung to the seats like stray hairs.

The main floor was deserted and I took a seat at third row, center. This was a chance to inhale Carnegie Hall air, to feel it race through my lungs and turn my blood a brighter red.

I threw my feet over the chair in front of me and leaned back to stargaze at the soaring ceiling. My eyes traveled across the upper tiers. Elegant boxes arced around the room, cradled in carved woodwork. The red carpet (what else?) and red velvet seats vibrated against the creamy tones and gold accents on wood and walls. Straight ahead, ornate columns and architectural flourishes framed the stage and wooden floor. Anyone on that stage would look glorious.

They knew how to build concert halls in the 1890s. New York has newer theaters that may be more comfortable or better equipped in some ways. Still, they aren't built today with the same loving, if impractical, grace. Our architects and technical wizards use effective, sometimes unaesthetic, tools for fuller acoustic effect. The Carnegie Hall builders had no techno-tricks to fall back on. They used lush, molded plaster, fine woods, and masterly construction. They created a structure that still feels alive after more than a century.

Of course, Carnegie Hall is more than building materials and design. It was the house of Mahler, Paderewski, Caruso, Isadora Duncan, Dvořák, Jascha Heifetz, Richard Strauss—and, soon enough, Franz Schubert. He was among peers here. His antenna sought them out, invited them in. We became aware of them, whispering among themselves and waltzing in the aisles. Wisps of music sighed in our ears. Visions rippled in the air, dissolving quicker than my eyes could focus.

An orchestra of vastly different sounds swelled together, rising from the stage and flooding the orchestra. The cacophony should have been awful; it was hypnotic. Floating chords and wild rhythms found one another, then moved on. Vivid colors melted into coral reefs, and living sounds swam through them.

More than ever before, Franz and I became *we*. We connected with otherworld spirits that would never have bothered with me on my own. Musicians, dancers, and singers drifted into our mind, summoning us to their dimension. Their voices were familiar to Franz, spoke a language he knew. They made him happy.

The usual barriers between body and mind dissolved of their own accord. Sound and sight splintered into uncountable facets, regrouping in fantastic manifestations. A thousand phantoms lifted us at their whim and tossed us around the room like a dry leaf on a windy day. From far above the balcony we inhaled symphonies. It was all quite marvelous until strange and terrifying words sprang from our mouth.

"Ich sehe. Ich höre!"

No!

"Ich bin lebendig."

No, Franz, no!

"Ich bin lebendig, ich bin lebendig!"

NO, NO, NO! STOP THIS, FRANZ, STOP IT!

Ich kann fliegen . . . I can fly. She doesn't realize it. The music makes it possible, and these friends. But I must not stay away long from her, my home, or I might get lost and vanish.

Wouldn't I?

CHAPTER SIXTEEN

A hand fell lightly on my right shoulder.

"*Sei ruhig,* Liza, *sei ruhig.* Calm down, you're all right."

It was Joseph Alexander, bending over me at third row, center, in Carnegie Hall. He patted my arm, spoke softly to me in German.

"I'm sorry, I don't understand."

"I'm afraid my German's pretty rusty," he said.

"I mean I don't understand German."

He looked surprised.

"Well, never mind." His voice was milk and honey. "I came to check on you 'cause you seemed a bit out of sorts. Guess you nodded off here. You were talking in your sleep."

I looked up and saw a small cluster of people onstage, all watching me with concern.

"Did I make a commotion?"

"No, no, not really," Joseph said. "A little. You know what it's like when you talk in your sleep."

Of course I do. When it's in English.

As I stood, I noticed my pant legs were wet and clinging to my inner thighs. A small puddle darkened the velvet seat, the scene of my appalling accident. If Joseph noticed, he didn't show it. I pulled on my raincoat and ran from the hall.

The street and the rain brought me back to me. Liquored up on adrenaline and fear, I chased Franz away with ferocious mental force. I walked with overboard physicality, exerting every muscle, pounding the concrete into submission.

I craved contact with real, flesh-style people. A bum spit on the street and I loved him. A businessman ran for a taxi and I wanted to kiss him. I bought an umbrella just to exchange money.

All I wanted in the world was normalcy. Ungifted, Franz-free normalcy. That, and a clean pair of pants. I stopped in Bergdorf Goodman, a wickedly priced, thoroughly normal store.

I stopped first in the ladies' room, where I all but showered in the sink. I talked to myself, visualized serenity, tried to scrub away the day.

In a plush designer department, I met and married a pair of purple leather pants in which I looked incredible. They cost half a month's rent, but they were size six and a perfect fit so I obviously had no choice. The matching jacket was wretched excess, but this was no time for good sense. Don't even ask about the red silk sweater.

I was wearing all my new gear when I presented my plastic for payment. The saleslady asked what I'd like done with my original clothes.

"Burn them," I said.

I felt stunning and dangerous when I reemerged on Fifth Avenue. Franz had infuriated me. Righteous anger brought me back to raging life. Franz was too much—too weak, too powerful, too much. He could destroy everything. The concert, our career, me.

He'd been overwhelmed by Carnegie Hall and its potent ghosts. Franz jumped to join them at the first opportunity, and nearly obliterated me in the process. This could not happen again, ever. I needed the kind of help that probably didn't exist. In any case, I wanted to vent about it.

I pulled out my cell phone and called Mikki for advice. No answer, left a message. I didn't want to call Patrick at his bitchy mother's house. Fred came to mind, but he didn't answer, either. I took my phone off mute mode in case someone called back, then I considered other options.

Cassie would be useless, and my parents would panic. That left only Greta. Not comforting exactly, but she did know about Franz from the start, and her steadiness would offset my emotional pitch. It was almost six and she was usually at Juilliard late. I caught a taxi and headed uptown.

Franz tried to surface a few times during the cab ride. I bullied him away. He may have been as confused as I was, or possibly frightened. Apologetic was a dim possibility. Or maybe he wanted desperately to go back and play with his dead friends some more. Fuck him.

It was raining heavily again when we got to Juilliard. I paid the cabbie and made a quick dash to the building, hoping to spare my new outfit. Just inside the entrance, I checked my reflection in a mirror. The purple leather had sprouted freckles and my hair looked like a bouquet of Slinkies. Naturally Chase Barnes was the first to notice me.

"Looks like someone could use a towel and hot coffee," he said. "Nasty out there."

"Yeah, it's pretty miserable. I need to see Greta, though."

"I'm pretty sure I saw her leave," he said. "Besides, haven't you seen enough of her lately? Have dinner with me instead."

"Sounds nice, but I think I'll check her studio, just to be sure. You understand."

"Sure. I'll come with you." Handsome, self-confident, *and* solid to the touch. Perfection. "If she's not there, you can pick the place for dinner. My treat, in celebration of your debut tomorrow. Unless you have other plans, of course."

Patrick (of the turdy sponge) was with his mother in Connecticut. The trek back to Brooklyn in the rain looked grim. I hungered for warm company and half hoped Greta would not be in her studio. I was wholly pleased when she wasn't.

"Where shall we go, m'dear?" Chase's eyes issued a lusty, full-contact invitation. "Restaurant or my place? I have a well-stocked pantry."

I wasn't *that* crazy. We started at a restaurant.

We walked three blocks to the Poca Cosa Cantina. I told Chase I wanted something spicy, the kind of food that makes your scalp sweat, something Franz was sure to hate. He told the waitress to bring on her hottest hot stuff.

The hip, gaudy restaurant was just what I needed. It was a noisy stew of loud colors, papier-mâché flowers (in Manhattan!), and raucous diners deep in the heart of Margaritaville. Strolling mariachis visited each table, singing in triple *forte* and playing odd-sized guitars. Out of respect for family heirlooms (I'm guessing), their instruments had apparently not been tuned since they were inherited. The result was enthusiastic, sometimes earsplitting chaos. The scene could be described as "anti-Schubert." Franz slinked into my right pinkie and left me alone with Chase.

Our young waitress, Tammy, brought us mega-margaritas and blue corn chips with salsa as starters. Chase tasted the salsa and immediately summoned her back.

"Tammy, I'm quite certain I specified hot." She shifted her stance, wary of Chase's genteel tone. He gestured at me and said, "The lady *must* have hot salsa. This is barely tepid."

She took back the salsa without a word.

"A toast," Chase said, raising his frosted glass to me. "To the start of something hot."

"Something hot," I mumbled back.

"What will you be wearing?"

His question surprised me. None of the men in my life had expressed interest in this detail. I should have realized that every part of a performance was important to Chase. I described my beautiful Armani.

"Sexy?"

"Tastefully alluring."

"Most women musicians look like frumps," he said. "Afraid they won't be taken seriously if they look too appealing. My opinion, anyway. I'd like to see you in something daring, Liza. People already expect it of you, so why—"

"I think you'll like this dress, Chase. Anyway, that's the least of my concerns."

"What on earth could you have to worry about? You're *it*, Liza, you're the real thing. You could wear pajamas tomorrow night and no one could deny you."

"I wish I felt that way, Chase. Things could go perfectly, but there's an outside chance that—"

Chase was distracted by a new batch of salsa, which he promptly tasted. Also not up to snuff. He called our waitress back again.

"Tammy, my dear, could you please send the maître d'?" Ever so polite. "I'd like to discuss the sad state of salsa with him."

Chase smiled warmly at me. "You were saying, Liza?"

"Nothing," I said. "I was saying nothing, really."

So Chase talked salsa with the maître d', who brought out some of the chef's private stock of melt-your-eyeballs brew. I grabbed the ice water after a single taste, and stuck to margaritas after that. Chase devoured every chip in the basket, along with the last drip of salsa. By the time our entrees showed up, a light sheen of perspiration coated his forehead and his cheeks flushed nicely.

Mikki returned my call just as the food and tequila took their calming hold on me. I told her I was fine, turned off my cell phone, and let the evening unfold.

"Where do you go after tomorrow, Liza?"

"Probably an insane asylum," I said. "But on the chance that all goes well and they don't put me away, I have no idea what I'll do."

"None?"

"No, of course, that's not exactly true," I said. "I'll probably be recording for Sony Classical, and people seem to think I'll get more concert dates."

"Well, people seem to be right about that, anyway. But what'll your career look like, Liza? What kind of music do you want to make? How will you make your mark?"

Chase posed the questions you'd ask of an intelligent, independent life form. These decisions were not mine to make, but Chase didn't know that. I took the luxury of pretending.

"I love the classics, of course. Schubert, obviously," I said. "But there's a lot of music I'm just beginning to learn about. Lots more that I'd like to learn about. Somehow it's all related. Opera, reggae, jazz—it's all related. I'd like to figure out how."

He watched closely as I spoke, encouraged me with his attention.

"I know everything comes out of somebody's soul." I felt emboldened. "The connecting thread may be organic, even spiritual. Doors are opening on all sides, and I have to be brave enough to go through them."

"Fascinating," Chase said.

I reveled in his praise of my musical insights.

"I've never met an accomplished musician with such simplistic thoughts," he continued. "It's astonishing that your skills so vastly surpass your musical depth."

"Yes, isn't it?" *Oh.* "But what about you, Chase? What have you got coming up?"

"Well, I've been writing for full orchestra again. I'm presenting new work this fall. Of course, there's my pet piece, which you already know."

"*Pantheon.* Right." He didn't ask his next question, so I answered it. "I've played the piece quite a few times. It gets more interesting each time."

He still didn't ask about the encore.

"Greta still wants me to play a duet with her for an encore."

"Well, that'd certainly be nice," Chase said sarcastically.

I quickly changed the subject to food. Shrimp enchiladas were exactly my speed.

The meal and drinks left me sated and silly. I'd already forgiven Chase's arrogance with the restaurant help. After all, this man had a lot *not* to be humble about. He was over-the-top attractive and told the kind of anecdotes that people get famous for telling. Time waltzed by unnoticed.

It was after nine when a concerned-looking young woman stopped at our table. Her black hair was pulled back in a ballet bun and her body was perilously slim.

"Chase, this is a surprise." The dancer glared at me as she said this. "Katje said you were playing bridge tonight."

"Obviously not, Aubrey." Chase's face tightened. "I wasn't aware that Katje discussed my schedule. How odd. Anyway, I'd like you to meet Liza Durbin."

Our hellos sailed past each other.

"This is Aubrey Schneidman, Liza. She's with the New York City Ballet. Katje Merrin's roommate. You remember Katje, don't you?"

"Of course, we've met several times." Who could forget the lovely toothpick so often at Chase's side? "I hear she's an extraordinary dancer."

"I'll tell her we met," Aubrey said. She gave Chase a punishing look and floated away.

He took my right hand and stroked my palm softly with his thumb, then kissed the spot.

"Katje's a sweet child with a vivid imagination," he said. "A little obsessive, it seems. Students often see faculty as glamorous. These things happen. Don't let it ruin our evening."

Chase was clearly lying, and not just to me. His thumb traced slow circles around my palm's soft, sensitive skin. Just enough pressure to tease without tickling—a favorite feeling that spread through my body. I felt myself slowly melting in sensual fever. Tammy arrived with dessert menus and Chase ordered something sinful in chocolate. We shared the rich, creamy concoction with the appreciative moans rarely heard outside of bed.

Then Chase asked me to go back to his place, to play music. I was finally that crazy.

CHAPTER SEVENTEEN

He lived on the fifth floor of the El Dorado building on Central Park West, in a classic apartment overlooking the reservoir. Every detail spoke of style, sophistication, and, let's be honest, money. To enjoy the spectacular view, a large telescope waited by the window. The leather furniture, silk rugs, and original artwork exuded dignity and taste. All in all, a fairly intimidating effect. The focal point of the living room was the Steinway grand, to which I ran for comfort.

"Wouldn't you like a glass of wine?" Chase asked.

He had already taken my jacket, shed his soggy raincoat, and regroomed himself. His hair was fluffed and he wore a fresh, dry T-shirt to great advantage. I was still dripping and frizzy-haired from the rain. In such situations, the best beauty treatment is to drink more wine.

"It's a nice night for a cabernet, I think," Chase said, "although I also have a bottle of Pouilly-Fuissé in the fridge. What's your preference?"

He could not have asked a deadlier question.

"Pouilly-Fuissé, please," I said. "My favorite."

Chase poured us each a glass. I had chosen the piano bench as the only sittable place in the living room, but Chase clearly did not like wine glasses near the instrument's glossy finish. He toured me around his apartment, finishing up at the window with the telescope.

"Well, you've got the million-dollar view, all right," I said.

"You do, too, tonight." He pulled me to his side, kissed the top of my head. "You're a remarkable woman, Liza. I want you to know you're doing just fine."

Doing fine? Was he grading me?

"This is where I hear my music, Liza." Chase looked out the window, over the traffic on Central Park West, and through the trees toward the lights of the East Side skyline. "It's different all the time, day and night, every season. I can silence the rest of the world up here. I just look outside and the music is waiting there."

"Yes, composing is a whole different experience in music, isn't it?"

"Yes, it's hard to explain to someone who plays but doesn't write. Have you composed at all?"

"Not really," I semi-lied. "I know the feeling, anyway."

As we stood by the window, I felt safe again. Not because of Chase, but because of his sturdy, bought-and-paid-for surroundings. Ethereal spirits would find nothing to cling to here. He had one of those giant TVs in his den, for God's sake.

Chase wrapped his arms around me from behind. He nibbled my ear and neck, softly licking the sweetest parts. Patrick leapt to mind. He had bugged me lately, yes, but so did a lot of things. How did that justify cheating? My one grand act of betrayal had been with Patrick, and I wanted to believe it was an exception to my faithful nature, triggered by great love. Besides, Patrick and I weren't doing so badly considering the charged circumstances. Chase Barnes was steamy fun but nothing serious. I pulled away and offered to play for him.

Inspired by our earlier Carnegie Hall encounter, Franz and I played Beethoven's *Moonlight Sonata,* a cliché perhaps, but irresistible. Chase observed me from the other side of the Steinway, tilting his head in appreciative surprise.

Moonlight Sonata begins with a heartbreaking *adagio* that made me ache for a lover I never met. Franz kissed each note he played, lingered where his memories lived.

This music had long ago built a home in Franz's heart. For the first time, his memories slid partially into my view. A glimpse of black hair, the tap of a dancing shoe on a wooden floor, a velvet coat with a deep red stain. The warmth of another body held close, praying that this one moment might never end.

In the last movement, Franz and I tore into the music until the whole piano glowed. We finished in sweaty collapse. Chase was moved to applaud.

"Thank God, Liza," he said. "I was beginning to think you were a one-man woman."

He caught me off guard with that.

"Yes, sure," I said. "What?"

"I thought Franz Schubert was your only love. I'm glad to hear you play something else."

"Thanks. I don't play enough Beethoven."

"Well, you're not as good at Beethoven, of course." *I'm not?* "Schubert is yours, obviously, and I'm sure you know that there are people who are better with Beethoven."

"I never thought about it."

"Not that many people play better than you, of course," Chase added, "but there are some. Natalie Frome, for instance. But, hey, Franz Schubert wasn't considered the greatest pianist of his day, either. He probably played his own work better than anyone, though."

His conjecture made me squirm. I wanted to defend our playing with pleas of Pouilly-Fuissé and margaritas. Instead, I offered to play Chase's *Pantheon.* He had no objection, even if others could perform it better.

Pantheon was not Schubert or Beethoven, but it was growing on me. The at-first discordant sounds coalesced gradually into an intricate structure. Great weights balanced on delicate melody. The composition changed currents while maintaining a mathematical purity. If you added its pluses and minuses, you'd arrive at a perfect balance. It wasn't without its hummable moments, either. A memorable segment emerged along the way, surfacing brilliantly in spots.

Pantheon takes thirty minutes to play, almost twice as long as the Beethoven. Halfway through it, Chase moved behind the piano bench and leaned against my swaying back. He slid his hands along my shoulders and music passed between us. He sang without words, vibrating with his score. Then his arms curled around my neck for greater contact as we traversed the keyboard together. I felt him hardening like a fist against my spine. The music intensified as we sped toward the finish in a sensual frenzy. I heard the zip of his fly and felt his weight against my back.

~~~

It was after two in the morning when I got back to Brooklyn in a state of emotional turmoil. I opened my apartment door, switched on the hall light, and heard a grunt come from the dark living room. Somebody turned on the lamp next to the end table. I froze, waiting for an attack. Nothing. I braved a closer look and found a sleep-tossed woman in a flannel nightgown sitting up in the folded-out sofa bed.

"And where *the hell* have you been?"

Through a blur of exhaustion and guilt, I recognized the furious face of Patrick's mother.

"Mrs. Florio, ha! This is a nice surprise. Ha! Well, I wasn't expecting to see you until tomorrow." Her spiky bed-head hair matched the expression on her face. "I hope Patrick's made you comfortable. He should have given you the bed. You shouldn't have to sleep on the sofa."

She glared silently like a pissed-off Sphinx.

"Well, I'll just say good night then, Mrs. Florio."

I attempted to walk toward the bedroom, a place I suddenly dreaded. Patrick emerged before I could enter. Oh, good, a family reunion.

"We've been worried, Liza. Where've you been?" Patrick's face signaled many emotions, none of them joy.

"I'm so sorry, Patrick. I thought you weren't coming home tonight."

"Right, and I assumed you were," he said. I noticed a bunch of budding yellow roses in a vase on the kitchen table. "I could tell you were upset about me leaving this morning—well, yesterday morning—so we came back early. Thought we'd all have dinner together."

"Well, I wish I'd known," I said.

"Liza, I started calling you on your cell phone around six, when I saw you weren't here. Actually, everyone was calling—your parents, Greta, Mikki. No one could reach you. You really need to call your folks back."

"Damn cell phone must be broken again."

"Oh, *puh-lease,* Liza, my son deserves a better answer than that." Mrs. Florio's unlovely voice dropped an octave: "Where the hell were you?"

"Mother, please," Patrick said.

"Let's talk in the bedroom," I said.

"You want me to come, too, Patrick?" Mrs. Florio stood up as she made the offer, fists curled at her chubby sides.

"No, Mother. That wouldn't be good."

"She shouldn't take advantage of you, that's all. I've always said—" We closed the door, forgoing the rest of Mrs. Florio's wisdom.

Our fight did not go well. He was right, and I was bad, and there wasn't much more to say. But we did.

"So, you like my new outfit?" I said.

"No." He puffed out his cheeks, blew frustration through puckered lips. "Where were you?"

"I had a long, scary day, Patrick. Traumatic, really." He wasn't buying it. I sat next to him on the bed and took his hands in mine. I told the truth.

"Something awful happened, sweetie. I had to meet Greta at Carnegie Hall. Then, I stayed after she left and—you won't believe this—Franz picked up on all these other dead spirits there, and they made contact. I could hear things and see things. Then I got swept up with them like something from a horror movie. Remember *The Haunting?*"

He gasped at the image.

"Liza, are you serious? Are you okay?"

"I'm fine now, but I was very shaken up, very. I shouted words in German, Patrick. In *German.*"

Just saying this out loud made me reel again.

"You should've called me. Why didn't you call? This could be serious, Liza. Maybe you shouldn't go back there. Maybe you should cancel tomorrow."

"No, Patrick, I can't do that. Besides, I think I'm okay. I know what to expect, so I can prepare mentally." Maybe. "I'm learning how strong my mind can be, that I can bully Franz away from me. I was extremely upset at first, but I'll be okay."

Patrick drew me into a cuddle and made brave talk about taking care of me. One nagging question was still out there, but sympathetic Patrick was hesitant to push me on it. Of course, he finally did.

"Where was I all night? Oh, Patrick, I was totally shaken after Carnegie Hall. I wasn't sure what to do. Bergdorf's is nearby, so I went there."

"You went *shopping*?"

"I needed to be somewhere familiar, not so spiritual. Then I went back up to Juilliard to see Greta. Then I met some friends who invited me out for a good-luck drink. You were gone, and I figured it would distract me from my craziness, so I went."

"Friends? You mean Greta?"

I shook my head, almost laughing at the thought.

"I didn't know you had other friends at Juilliard."

"Sure, well, you hang out in a place long enough and you meet people, right?"

Patrick wanted details.

"Oh, one of the composers, a dancer," I said. "There were some other people at the restaurant, too." I tried to be technically honest, and hoped that Patrick would want to believe.

"You had a little too much to drink, didn't you?" The answer was obvious and his tone was not nice. "This isn't the first time you've come home late. You missed Ruthie and Peter and the rest when you were out a couple of weeks ago."

No way was this going to improve, so I did something awful.

"Liza, honey, it's okay," Patrick drew me close as I began sobbing heavily. "I'm sorry. I didn't mean to make you cry."

"You can't imagine what it's been like, Patrick." Sniff, whimper, wail. "I've tried to tell you, but how could you know? How could *anyone* know? For the past three months, I've felt about to tip over. Any minute I could fall into this other person's existence and my own could be erased. Today I came so close to being sucked into another dimension. Please forgive me for acting crazy, Patrick. You have to forgive me."

The crying and the talk flowed freely. Patrick got me a box of tissues and occasionally kissed away a tear. My sadly manipulative act had turned into solemn honesty. I was truthful about everything except Chase Barnes. Not my proudest moment, but it was the best I could do at the time.

Finally, I threw my new clothes across the back of a chair and sank exhausted into bed. My head throbbed. My conscience ached. At some point I heard Patrick make a reassuring call to my parents. What had I done to deserve my blessings?

≡

Sie lebt auf diese Weise? . . . She lives like this? Her turmoil is appalling. Well, maybe I'm part of it. I once had my own reasons to laugh and worry and cry, all of them wonderful.

CHAPTER EIGHTEEN

Our big day started with the telephone rudely ringing on the night-stand. It was Cassie, which would be bad enough without the slight hang-over.

"*Bonjour, ma sœur,*" she trilled in my ear. "How's the genius superstar today?"

I moaned into the phone. My head felt like one big toothache.

"I was afraid of this." Cassie directed this comment away from the phone, probably toward my mother. "Listen, Liza, we're in the limo and we'll be at your place in half an hour. Mom and Dad are with me." Mom and Dad shouted greetings. "We'll have lunch, go over a few things, then we take you to Arla Shay's salon to work a miracle."

"What time is it?"

"Liza, you're not still in bed, are you?"

"Of course not." I pulled the covers over my head.

"Right, well, it's almost eleven. I *told* you I'd be there before noon. Were you planning to sleep through your concert tonight?"

"Not on purpose."

"Fine, be funny. Maybe you thought you'd do your own hair, too." In the background, Mom was talking nonstop to her. "Calm down, Ma, she's not cutting her own hair," Cassie said. "We'll be there soon, Liza. Wear something decent." Click.

I peeked out from under the blanket and daylight brutalized my eyes. Patrick came into the bedroom bearing a mug of coffee. He had obviously showered, dressed, and been waiting for me to wake up. The TV in the next room blared talk-show nonsense. Suddenly, I realized Patrick's mother was still in my living room. I dove under the covers again.

"Hey there, princess, time to wake up and snort the coffee," Patrick said, pulling the blanket off my face.

"I feel like a bad day in Hell."

"No surprise there," he said, "but this is not your day to languish in misery."

"Can I do that tomorrow?"

"Okay."

I guzzled caffeine, wrapped myself in a robe, and headed for the bathroom. Mrs. Florio barely looked up from the TV as I walked through the living room. With rare good grace, I was the first to say good morning. She pointed out that the morning was almost gone.

The hot shower had a slightly rejuvenating effect. I dressed in a dark blue cotton sweater and old pants that had grown big on me, then sat at the kitchen table waiting for my family. The yellow roses were fully opened and sweetly scented the room. I sighed at Patrick.

Cassie and my parents sensed the strain as soon as they arrived at my apartment. Patrick fidgeted and his mother seethed in my direction. Mom, my protector, bristled. She and Mrs. Florio locked eyes like rival cats on disputed turf.

"So nice to see you, Mrs. Florio," Mom said coolly. "I hope you'll be coming to our *après*-concert party tonight." *Parfait,* Mom was picking up Cassie's dopey French, too.

"We'll see" came the icy response.

A few more pleasantries passed before my father commented on the roses.

"Yes, Dad, gorgeous, aren't they?" I walked over to Patrick and hugged him around the waist.

"Don't thank me." He raised his hands in denial. "I can't take credit for those."

"I wish *someone* would take the credit," Mrs. Florio said. "Look at this card. Unsigned. '*I loved you before him.*' What kind of card is that, I'd like to know. Loved you before Patrick? What's that supposed to mean, Liza?"

Everyone but Mrs. Florio realized that "him" referred to Franz. Somebody loved me before Franz showed up. Cassie and my parents turned uncertain faces toward me, then looked at one another, then at their respective shoes. Patrick was unreadable.

"I have no idea who the flowers could be from, Mrs. Florio," I said. "Hey, it doesn't even say my name. Maybe it's a mistake."

A chorus of agreement from my family: *Sure, sure, that's it.*

"You could call the florist and find out," Mrs. Florio suggested.

"Forget it," Mom jumped in. "It was a *private* card for Liza in the first place. Anyway, there must be thousands of men out there who would send roses to our famous daughter. Right, Maxie?"

"Without a doubt, darling." My father was wearing a new black suit for my special day, the highest honor he could bestow. "Who could *not* love our Liza?"

Mrs. Florio, that's who. And possibly Mrs. Florio's little boy.

"Liza, why don't you get together whatever you need for tonight," my sister said. "We won't get back here before showtime."

Showtime. Cassie's casual reference to Carnegie Hall made my whole body go crumbly. Patrick grabbed my arm before I could sink to the floor. He escorted me to the bedroom.

I packed a small bag with things you take for an overnight stay in the hospital: fresh underwear, hairbrush, robe, a novel I'd been reading for months. I threw in some extras for later—jacket, shoes, jewelry—and soon I had actual luggage to haul around for my two-hour concert.

"You planning on moving into Carnegie Hall?" Patrick said. He'd observed my packing process in vague amusement, but he was also troubled. "You know, you don't have to do this."

"Pack?"

"Play," he said sharply. "You don't have to play tonight. As far as I'm concerned, you never have to go back to Carnegie Hall."

His face was resolute and marked with worry.

"I don't know what happened to you there yesterday," he said, "but why tempt the Fates? We've already seen one dead spirit commandeer your life. Who's to say that you can't be invaded again by other spirits? And that it couldn't be much worse than it is?"

This talk was too painful to hear. I tried unsuccessfully to blot it out. The combination of wine, Chase Barnes, and purple leather pants had made me cocky the night before, but my self-assurance vanished like starlight in the morning. I wasn't sure I could make it through a whole night among Franz's dead friends. On the other hand, I was so far down this path I wouldn't know the way home. Every scenario was scary, but turning back was not an option.

"Think good thoughts for me," I said.

"Always, babe."

Dad laughed at my luggage, while Cassie admired my restraint. We exchanged last-minute hugs with Patrick and his mother. She was still testy but wished me luck. I told Patrick he should come early and visit backstage before the performance. Anyway, I'd see him seated in the front row between my mother and his. He promised to wave and make funny faces. Then we set sail for Carnegie Hall.

After some discussion, we decided on lunch at the Stage Deli on Seventh Avenue. Cassie had wanted to drag us to yet another of her "absolute favorite" chichi bistros, but Dad spoke up for pastrami on rye. I added my vote for real food. The Stage is a place for carnivores and peasants like me.

The deli was packed, but the owner recognized me and found us a table within minutes. A taste of celebrity privilege. Our grizzled waiter bore a fresh mustard stain on his sleeve and an impatient twitch. The clank of dishes and silverware proclaimed this as a place for serious lunchers, not dawdlers. We all ordered the Stage's gargantuan sandwiches, except for Cassie, who never eats more than two peas at a sitting.

Throughout lunch, my parents rhapsodized over the food while Cassie fretted over last-minute minutiae. I barely noticed them. My corned beef on rye was too absorbing, succulent, thrilling in texture, taste, and all other aspects. When I wasn't terrified about Franz, his influence was magnificent. My simple sandwich had become ambrosia on stardust, a Gershwin tune with Picasso on the side.

"Liza, honey, does that man look familiar to you?" My father was pointing toward an elderly man wearing a tweed jacket and bow tie.

The man in tweed noticed us, too. He waved his fingertips at me.

"Liza, is that the man—?" Dad said.

He did look familiar. When the waiter cleared away our dishes, the man approached our table.

"I don't mean to disturb you, Miss Durbin. It's such a pleasure to see you again." *A-gayne,* he said. "You probably don't remember—"

"Yes, I do, actually," I said. "You're the man from Nordstrom's, aren't you?"

He nodded in courtly fashion. I introduced my family, though his name escaped me.

"It's Sturtz. Dr. Abraham Sturtz. I'm so pleased to meet all of you."

"What brings you to New York, Dr. Sturtz?" my father said.

"Can't you guess? I came to hear your daughter play." He turned his well-lined face toward me. "One can't play piano as you do and keep it a secret for long, can one? I bought my ticket as soon as I heard of your debut, my dear. I sent you a card. I hope you received it."

I had misplaced it, but I thanked him for sending it.

"Let me give you my card again," he said. "I don't mean to be pushy, but I'd love to talk with you about your experience. What a gift you've been given."

Dr. Sturtz bowed to each of us slightly, then returned to his table to finish his soup. The tweed jacket he wore was the one I had seen him in several months earlier, when all this started. Maybe he wore it in case we ran into each other, a marker to be remembered by. In any case, the power of my box-office draw was not in doubt.

We traversed the city in a white stretch limo chosen by Cassie to fit the day. In our lead-dog alpha car, we oozed entitlement. Cassie knew something about how to get noticed.

We pulled up at Shay Salon just after one o'clock. In the ultraposh waiting area, my father looked as comfortable as a U.S. Marine at a tea party. He checked his watch, promised to come back, and bolted for the exit. When he returned a few hours later, he was staggered by our transformations. Mom, Cassie, and I had been coiffed and buffed to a lovely glow. I got the shortest, best haircut of my life, plus a nice splash of red tint that brought me in line with the other Durbin women.

"Three gorgeous redheads, and they're all mine!" Dad said.

"Don't you *love* the red on Liza?" Cassie said. "My idea, of course. Lose a couple more pounds, Liza, and we could pass for sisters."

"It's not too red, is it?" I asked.

My mother and sister found the question too ridiculous to answer.

As we were leaving the salon, Arla Shay assured me that she and Gilda would meet us in plenty of time to do my makeup. They would come directly to my dressing room at Carnegie Hall.

An afternoon of pampering could not obliterate my terror. The out-loud mention of Carnegie Hall reminded me of the task ahead, and I fought the urge to cry.

It was close to six. Rain clouds crowded the sky. As we drove toward Carnegie Hall, my dread materialized as an extra creature in the car. It growled in my face and squeezed its tentacles around my torso. I sat in silent panic and watched the passing street numbers tick off my fate. Mom was talking to me. Dad, too. No discernible words, just talk. Fear paralyzed me, urged me to run. I might have, too, except for Franz.

Franz felt my fear, understood its source. He attempted to gentle my soul with his confidence. Nothing to be afraid of here. We will prevail. The concert will be brilliant. He would never leave me, his only living friend, to rejoin his dead ones. *Never.* Life was too spectacular to give up for a has-been past. Franz and I could only succeed together, so we would.

The limo stopped at the Carnegie Hall stage door and I stepped out, still not quite ready to communicate. My parents exchanged concerned looks. Cassie prodded me to say something, *anything*. It took all my energy to cross the sidewalk. A few plump raindrops fell on my nose and cheeks. My hair sensed a coming downpour and sent up antennae.

The backstage crew greeted me and we found Greta waiting for us. In the back of my mind was an expectation that my mother and Greta would exchange the sigh of long-lost friends. I was sure Mom had sent her to me in the first place. If they knew each other, though, they hid it well. Instead, Greta inquired about my health and readiness. She wore the same worried look as my parents. I hugged her for reassurance, which she did not enjoy. She led me onstage for a final reacquaintance with the concert grand I had chosen. She wisely insisted I warm up and get comfortable. The piano felt good, but being onstage brought back my dread. We returned to the dressing room, where my family waited.

"*Sacré bleu,* sis, you gonna walk around like the living dead all night?" My sensitive sister could see I was nervous. "Did you give them your list at the stage door?"

"List?"

"Your guest list, remember? Like I told you a million times?" Eye-rolling and a huffy sound. "So Arla and Gilda can get in. And so Barry and the kids can come back to see you. And Fred. Patrick, maybe? You said you'd make a list."

Cassie grabbed my purse to search it for the list in question. Amazingly, she found it.

"Fine. I'll just go deliver the list for you, Liza," she said. "How would that be? And you can sit here and stare at the walls with your mouth hanging open. Okay? Or, better yet, you can pull yourself together and act like this is the most important night of your life, which it is."

Cassie left with the list. My parents followed, probably to confer privately about my dumbstruck weirdness. I was alone in the Carnegie Hall dressing room ninety minutes before showtime.

The room was unexceptional, except for the many floral bouquets. I checked a couple of the cards to confirm they were for me. One was from Fred, another from Hoffman and Pardo.

There was something else about the room. In addition to the utilitarian mirrors, sink, chairs, and such, it had the ethereal imprint of history. I chose not to envision the performers who had dressed, primped, or warmed their vocal cords here. Sitting in front of the mirror, I swear I saw no remnants of blue eyes in heavy makeup, or damp blond hair in braids. No one made faces in the mirror, practicing expressions for dramatic effect. I absolutely did not see a young woman cry on her mother's shoulder—nor could I have said whether she cried before or after her performance.

I saw none of this because it was impossible. I closed my eyes to see none of it.

"There you are, Liza. How're you doing tonight?" I hadn't heard Mikki come into the room. She pulled up a chair beside me. Dressed in gray silk and pearls, she looked perfectly composed, as always. Following my gaze to the mirror, Mikki spoke to my reflection. "Your folks are a little concerned. Do you feel like talking?"

"It's been a rough couple of days, Mikki," I managed to say.

"Did you bring your SHOO blasters?"

They were in the luggage we'd hauled from Brooklyn that morning. I suddenly craved their comfort. I shoved a Girl Scout badge into my bra and spritzed myself with Shalimar.

I wanted to tell Mikki about the ghosts at Carnegie Hall the day before, and about Franz's reassurances. I would have told her about Chase and Patrick and his mother, too, but my parents walked in then with Cassie, Barry, and the kids. Instant commotion.

Brittany and Cameron jumped me like puppies. They asked questions about everything they saw and told me about their trip to the city. I found myself clutching them fiercely.

"Did you change your hair, Liza?" Barry asked.

"Only drastically," I said.

"Looks great." He gave me a proper brother-in-law hug and whispered in my ear: "Did you like the flowers?"

I looked around the room, hoping one of the arrangements was from Barry. My mind ricocheted to the yellow roses on my kitchen table at home.

Gilda arrived next with assorted powders and eyeliners. Brittany and Cameron couldn't sit still, so I gave them the job of reading the cards that came with the flower arrangements.

"Best of luck, Liza. Stricker, Stricker and Feinsod." Brittany struggled with the names on the card. "Who's that?"

"No one you'd want to know," I said. "Read me another."

"With the greatest admiration, Abraham Sturtz." Brittany pronounced it "Struts." "Who's he?"

"A man I met," I said. "A nice one, I think."

"Make her eyes look bigger," my sister said to Gilda. "Liza needs big eyes tonight."

I watched Gilda's progress in the mirror. It was like watching a Polaroid picture develop from its first washed-out image to its supercharged finale. To tell the truth, I looked like a painted toy. When I protested, Gilda patiently explained what it takes to glow from a distance. She promised that my everyday eyes were equipped to stun the balcony.

"This one says 'Chase Barnes' on it," Brittany said. She was holding a card plucked from a lavish arrangement. "That's my teacher's name, Mrs. Barnes. What kind of name is Chase?"

"A stupid name," I said. "Hey, has anyone seen Patrick yet?"

"Did I mention there might be some media at the party tonight?" Cassie said. "They're not officially invited, but they'll come if they want to. You're a celebrity tonight."

"Has anyone seen Patrick?"

And so it went.

CHAPTER NINETEEN

With a half hour to go, Cassie shooed all the nonvitals from the dressing room. Dad, Mikki, Barry, and the kids all went to claim their seats. Greta had already abandoned the dressing-room chaos. It was time to get dressed.

Cassie unzipped the Armani bag and pulled out my black velvet dress. Mom, Gilda, and Arla exclaimed over its beauty. I slipped into stockings and my new strapless bra, purchased to avoid strap slippage as I careened around the piano. To protect my hair, I stepped into the dress and let my mother zip it up. Then I presented myself to the full-length mirror.

A total dud.

The dress hung loosely from my frame like a sail waiting for wind. Everyone looked alarmed, except Cassie.

"Cassie, what have you done?" I screamed. "This isn't my dress, it's way too big!"

"Of course it is, Liza, I told you you should come try it on again."

True, but I hadn't felt like it. The last time I saw the dress was when we picked it out at the Armani store more than a month before. It fit perfectly and we just left it there for hemming. Cassie picked it up for me a week later.

"Cassie, do you swear this is the dress?"

"Oh, please. Of course it's your dress."

"I couldn't have lost that much weight. This looks ridiculous."

Serious fretting set in. Gilda suggested we stitch the shoulders to lift it a bit. Mom volunteered to make a quick alteration if we could find needle and thread—there had to be a sewing room for all the costumes. Only Cassie seemed unflustered. Smirking, in fact.

"Cassie, do you by chance have another plan?" I said.

"Now that you mention it, I was afraid of this happening." She reached into the Armani bag, where another garment lay in hiding. "Do you think I'd let you down, big sister? You've lost weight, so I brought a backup dress. Just in case."

I slammed my eyes shut, but not in time to miss a blur of blue satin emerging from the garment bag.

"This can't be happening," I moaned. "You can't make me wear that slutty dress tonight. I'll look like, like . . . a slut!"

"What's your alternative?"

"You're not unhappy about this, are you, Cassie?"

"This could be the best thing for you. You'll look great and the crowd'll love it," she said.

"If I look at the size tag, will I find that you switched dresses and got me a bigger one?"

"You think I would do that?"

It didn't matter either way. She had me.

The short blue dress floated around my body, settling in the curves and hinting at the rest. I'd gone from slightly lumpy to a streamline dream. Only my breasts were unfazed by weight loss. I looked spectacular.

My sister served up her loftiest praise: *"I hate you."*

The only problem seemed to be the regrettably low neckline, which was suspended by spaghetti straps that looked unlikely to survive the rigors of concert play. No one else mentioned this until Greta Pretsky returned to the dressing room.

"You can't be serious, Miss Durbin." Greta's mouth twitched. "Put on something decent."

"Sorry, Greta, my decent dress doesn't fit." I tried to sound disappointed. "I didn't realize how much weight I've lost. It's this dress or nothing."

Greta growled at my sister. "This is your doing, yes? It is what you wanted, this vulgar display." She pinched the thin blue silk between her tiny fingers. "This flimsy thing could fall off halfway through the concert. This is not a striptease!"

Cassie smiled sweetly. The blue dress of billboard fame and classical controversy was a publicist's dream.

"Look, we don't have a choice, do we?" I said. "Greta, I'm sorry, but I'm wearing this tonight." Her eyes bulged. "And, by the way, Greta, you look absolutely lovely."

She did, too, though she seemed surprised to hear it. Greta's hair was arranged in an elegant twist and she wore just-right makeup with almost-red lipstick. Her ankle-length dress was classic: long sleeves, black crepe with white cuffs and collar. No wonder I looked all wrong to her. We didn't appear to belong at the same party, let alone be about to play a duet onstage. Were tears gathering in her eyes?

"By the way, Liza, what's that necklace you're wearing?" Cassie said, inspecting the hand-of-Fatima pendant that Barry had given me for luck. "I picked up a bunch of these same necklaces in Chinatown last year, really cheap. We gave them to Barry's secretaries for Christmas."

"What a coincidence," I said.

Cassie disclosed that she'd brought me something that would look better with my dress. An extreme understatement. She handed me a sapphire-and-platinum necklace of her own, which I happily accepted.

"Your shoes don't match," Mom said to me. "Liza, you can't appear in black shoes with a blue dress."

My mother would rather eat dirt than wear shoes that didn't match her dress. Greta took a deep breath, afraid of drowning in our shallowness.

"You think I'd forget shoes?" my sister said, handing me a Manolo Blahnik box. Inside lay a devastating pair of blue satin heels with a clever spray of rhinestones.

"They're not yours, are they?" I asked.

"Don't worry, sis, they're your dainty little size," Cassie said. "I got them for you, just in case. You can thank me anytime."

They looked great on my feet and the high heels made my calves curve nicely. Perfect color, too. Cassie's not all bad.

"Don't complain to me if your feet hurt," said Greta childishly. "The house is starting to fill, Miss Durbin. Do you care to take a look?"

Oh, right. The audience, my debut, that's what we were here for. My mouth grew dry as I nodded weakly.

Peeking from stage left, the front row looked like home. Dad and Aunt Frieda were talking to the people behind him, no doubt bragging about me. Barry sat next to the kids, who were giggling with Fred on their other side. Mikki sat beside an older, bearded man—a date? Chase Barnes was on the right aisle beside the lovely toothpick, Katje. (How long ago did they buy their tickets together?) Ruthie, Peter, and Dan arrived as I watched, talking excitedly.

Dr. Abraham Sturtz sat a few rows back, not far from Joseph Alexander, the Rose Museum curator, who was reading the program. Danny and his friends were ushered to a row halfway back. I didn't see his mother and stepfather. Toward the back of the orchestra, I spotted the Duelin' Durbins from the old store in the Bronx.

I watched the scene develop. The hall was at first an unfinished puzzle. Gradually, the blank spaces were filled with color and animation. The growing crowd coalesced to become a living whole. Their clothes blended, their hair twined together, they breathed in unison.

Franz was looking for his friends, too. I felt him searching the corners, airshafts, columns. The spirits were still there, but not like the day before. They did not beckon him to play with them, but to play *for* them. They mingled with the audience, imbuing the lucky and unsuspecting crowd with their higher sensibilities.

Greta tugged me away with the news that we had ten minutes to go. I rushed back to the dressing room, where Mom, Cassie, Arla, and Gilda gave me a football-huddle hug for luck, then ran off to their seats. Greta was muttering her introduction speech to herself and walked out without a word to me. That left me and Franz on our own in the dressing room.

He and I had a little conversation. Nothing high-level, only two grateful souls bowing to each other. For better or worse, this would likely be the apex of my life. For Franz, it was an impossible comeback. I pulled a fresh blaster from my SHOO bag, a small framed picture of Cassie and me as children. Then I retrieved another memento, one that even Mikki didn't know about. It was a small plaster bust with the inscription *Franz Schubert, 19th Century Viennese composer,* probably awarded to a child for playing in a piano recital. I recently spotted it in an antique shop and knew that Franz needed it. A blaster of his own.

Someone knocked on the door: "Five minutes, Miss Durbin." I gulped a glass of water and made a quick bathroom stop. One last look in the mirror. The makeup was perfect, the hair defiantly lovely. Franz Schubert peered out of those eyes and into my reflection. What more could I ask for?

I waited near the curtain for my cue. Greta took the stage first to introduce me. She addressed the audience with enviable poise.

"Thank you, ladies and gentlemen, for joining us on this promise-filled evening." Her clear voice and Hansel-and-Gretel accent charmed the crowd. "I am Greta Pretsky and I welcome you to an evening like no other. I have been a concert pianist myself and have taught some of the world's finest pianists for many years.

"When I first met Liza Durbin, her talent was bold but unpolished. It took enormous effort, devotion, and resolve to take her from her starting point to this historic night. Naturally, there were frustrating times, when the effort seemed futile. But with determination, we kept going, until we reached the level you will witness tonight.

"I've trained Miss Durbin to play the music of Franz Schubert because her talents so clearly pointed that way. But you will hear that for yourselves. I thank each of you for having the faith in my judgment and the love of music that bring you here tonight. Liza Durbin may have been unknown to the music world a few months ago, but no one will forget her after tonight. Please welcome the finest student I have ever taught, Miss Liza Durbin."

The sound of applause merged with the roar of blood rushing through my veins. Somebody pushed me from behind, a gentle nudge that sent me into the bright circle of light in the great dark hall. I might have frozen in that spot if Franz hadn't pulled us both together.

I paused at the piano just long enough to look out at the audience. The applause had subsided. Across the dark audience, only two things stood out: Patrick's empty seat (next to his mother's empty seat) and a pair of lights like jack-o'-lantern eyes beaming from the balcony. Hard to say which bothered me more. Luckily, Franz took charge. He dispelled all thoughts but music and we sat at the piano bench.

The keyboard waited at attention. It begged for action, like a dog panting for its morning run. I rested my hands on the cool white keys. Franz snickered at my short red nails. Then we caught a wave of music and plunged in.

The Sonata No. 15 in D came first. It flowed smoothly through our body and onto the piano with warmth and technical bravura. For months, I'd worked to stay conscious, to retain a sense of self while playing. That didn't matter anymore. Franz's assurances filled my head: *Trust me, yield to me. We are safe.* So I yielded.

It was what I feared and wanted all along. Fully surrendering to Franz gave me a richer experience than I'd ever known. I was partner to a fantastic adventure, falling through space, riding a wave, sprouting wings. If I had hesitated at all, the momentum might have flagged. As it was, I heard every note but never felt the keyboard. With Franz in charge, we gave an astonishing performance.

The ending was met with the audience's unrestrained applause. They clapped and cheered and called my name. The spirit voices of Carnegie Hall whispered *yes.* In the midst of the clamor, I realized I was staring straight at the piano and needed to acknowledge the audience. I stood and turned for a brief bow and noticed my new blue heels were no longer on my feet, discarded at some point without my noticing. When I looked down in surprise, the audience responded with a wave of laughter.

Franz made a little room for me then, to wave at my parents and catch Greta's approving nod offstage. Chase Barnes made the showy gesture of standing but the crowd was not ready to follow quite yet. Katje pulled at his jacket to make him sit. Franz and I quickly returned to the bench and began the Sonata No. 19 in C Minor.

If anything, it was more beautiful. My surrender gave Franz unlimited freedom. His playing had changed in the past few months, perhaps influenced by hearing so much music that was new to him. In any case, he never played more magically. This might be, after all, his last chance. We didn't know if he'd be around for another concert—and Franz had already experienced the temporary nature of life. He held nothing in reserve, pushing himself through every risk.

The audience exploded at the end. This time I rose immediately for my bow, still barefoot and smiling. Franz did cartwheels in our heart.

Greta approached the piano while the ovation still echoed. She nodded to the audience, then slid beside me on the bench.

"Excellent, Miss Durbin," she said in my ear. "Now, on my count . . ."

We played the *Lebensstürme* with shine and synergy. Greta did extremely well, but was not at Franz's level. Hardly anybody could be. I knew he wasn't pleased to be sharing the bench with her on his big night. But Franz's annoyance aside, I must tell you that it sounded incredible.

The audience went wild for this union—Greta the Great meets the Unknown Pianist. Everyone felt like part of an event, witness to revelation. The ovation overwhelmed us. At the first opportunity, I sprinted offstage for the respite of intermission.

My dressing room was not an isle of tranquillity. Cassie and Arla were there to touch up my beauty. Family surrounded me with praise and advice. I asked for quiet, begged for privacy, was met with clamor:

C'est magnifique, *big sister. Arla, can you do something about her hair?*

Excellent, Miss Durbin, excellent. You must put on your shoes, yes? And we will tape those shoulder straps in place. Did you hear the applause for our duet?

Your mother and I are so proud, honey. You're doing just great.

Has anyone seen Patrick?

I sought refuge in the bathroom, lingering on the toilet seat in meditative pose. We were halfway through the concert, and Franz felt strong and I still existed. The frisky spirits of the day before respected their comrade and watched without touching.

Someone knocked on the bathroom door, checking that I was all right. I drew deep breaths. Not much left to the concert. Forty-five minutes, that's all. Forty-five minutes pass unnoticed all the time when you're watching TV or talking to a friend. I shut my eyes to envision the relief I'd feel forty-five minutes in my future. But what I saw was the space where Patrick should have been and a pair of jack-o'-lantern eyes watching from the balcony. I jumped up and went back into the dressing room, eager for the second half to start.

The audience cheered me just for returning to the stage. Franz responded emotionally. His tears streamed down my cheeks as I looked around to see where I'd left my shoes. One was under the bench, the other next to the pedals. I tried to slip them on inconspicuously, which the audience found amusing.

I gladly gave myself to Franz again. We played a rich and varied program—one piece to make them smile and another to make them cry. The ovation at the end was universal. People stood and yelled *"Brava!"* The Steinway screamed with joy. Near the back row, the Duelin' Durbins waved foil-covered cardboard swords above the heads of the standing crowd. We bowed to them all.

With the audience still on its feet, I left the stage for a minute. Then I returned for the encore.

Greta Pretsky beamed at me from stage right, one hand on the curtain, waiting to propel herself onstage for our *Grande Sonata* duet. She just needed my signal. In the front row, Chase Barnes swelled with confidence. He sent a good-luck thumbs-up, ready to hear his *Pantheon.* Their two faces implored me with expectations, not knowing that Franz and I had come to an agreement long ago.

Bild zweier kleiner Mädchen . . . A picture in a silver frame of two little girls. Laughing. One with bright red hair, the other with dark eyes and wild curls. This face is familiar—from home, from Vienna—often stopping outside my house to listen to music until rushed away by her mother or siblings.

"May I play, too, Herr Schubert?"

"Sorry, no."

But she is persistent.

Again: "May I play?"

"Maybe someday."

third movement

Ode to Kindred Spirits

CHAPTER ONE

THE NEW YORK TIMES
Friday, April 1

A Perplexing End to an Astonishing Evening
by Jonathan Porter-Cringe

Classical music aficionados can hardly recall a more thrilling or mystifying event than the much-ballyhooed debut of pianist Liza Durbin last night at Carnegie Hall. As expected, Ms. Durbin lived up to her billboard in overt sexuality, yet her musical gifts were supremely underestimated. Still, the surprise of her virtuosity was overshadowed by the shock of her encore.

Before the encore, Ms. Durbin delivered the all-Schubert evening with impressive emotional range and technical virtuosity. At one point, she shared the bench with the venerable Greta Pretsky for a powerfully rendered Lebensstürme. For her encore, however, Ms. Durbin played a mysterious composition called the Snow Sonata. When questioned afterward, she claimed that this, too, was the work of Franz Schubert. While the piece was indelibly Schubertesque, this critic has never heard the Snow Sonata. Ms. Durbin was unable to supply a catalog number and would only say that she had heard it before.

"Trust me, it's by Franz Schubert," said she. "I heard it once and never forgot it."

I'm not that trusting, Ms. Durbin.

I can find no mention of it in any reference source. This "new Schubert" can only be called magnificent, but corroboration is essential before accepting its authenticity. In the meantime, questions remain concerning its more likely origin and, more to the point, how any sophisticated musician could expect to dupe the public about a body of music that is so well documented.

Controversy aside, the evening itself was a musical miracle . . .

∿∿

Gordy & Jill Talk!
April 1

GORDY: So I stayed out late last night, Jilly. Couldn't miss the debut of Miss Liza Durbin, could I? And where were you, Jill?

JILL: Singing my kids to sleep, as usual. I may never sing at Carnegie Hall, but *some* people like my voice! *(Laughter, light applause.)* So, how was the lovely Miss Durbin, Gord?

GORDY: I'm no expert, Jilly, but I thought she was great. And I'm not the only one. That audience would still be cheering this morning if they didn't send everyone home. I tell you, that "nouvelle classique" is one tasty dish.

JILL: So tell us, Gordy, what was she wearing?

GORDY: You see that, folks? I try to give a serious music review and all she wants is to talk about the clothes! *(Beseeching expression.)* Well, I'll have you know I wasn't going to mention the sexy blue dress with the low front. Do I care if you could see down the neckline to her knees? *(Ho, ho, ho.)* Besides, that wasn't the sexiest part.

JILL: Don't tell me she took something off, Gordy!

GORDY: Good guess, Jilly. Seems little Miss Durbin can't keep her shoes on. Here she is, playing this big, important concert and she kicks her shoes off. Not once but twice!

JILL: Maybe she got tired of them. We've all done that. *(Turns to the audience for nods.)* And did I hear something about a strange encore? Like she made something up and called it Schumann?

GORDY: That's Schu-*bert,* Jilly, Schu-*bert.* And, yes, I guess there was some controversy about it. I wouldn't know, of course, but people say it was a fake Schubert. Sounded good to me, though, and I hate to accuse her.

JILL: Yeah, well, the Bee Gees sound good to you, Gord. And speaking of shoes, we have a well-known guest today who makes her own shoes out of rubber. You won't believe who it is *(big smile for the cameras),* and we'll tell you after this break.

∿∿

THE BROOKLYN BUZZ
Friday, April 1

Hitting the Heights with Norma Stein

Where were you when the lights went on? For weeks people have questioned whether Brooklyn Heights' own Liza Durbin was a serious pianist or not. Anyone who was at Carnegie Hall (and I *told* you to be there!) was duly enlightened.

Liza performed like a dream. I say if they taught her to do that in spy school in East Germany, then they should bring back the Cold War. I loved every minute of the concert, especially the Snow Sonata, which has always been my personal favorite.

∿∿

Hordes of people lay in wait at the stage-door exit after the concert. Their spontaneous cheer nearly toppled me. It knocked Greta off my left arm. (She had clamped herself onto me like an extra appendage, hissing in my ear, "What was that encore, Miss Durbin? What have you done? You've ruined everything, everything!")

The crowd was a mix of new fans and old friends. A mahogany face, last seen in a taxi. Danny and his friends vying for attention. Ruthie (surprisingly teary), Peter, Dan and his date. The Duelin' Durbins waving their weapons.

Chase Barnes glared from the sidelines with the dancing toothpick at his side. Fred rushed to hug me. People wanted autographs, a smile, a chance to touch my sleeve. The jack-o'-lantern eyes were there, too, set into the beefy face of a thickset man, possibly Hispanic, with a dark mustache streaked with white. To no one in particular, the man said, "Look at her eyes." People ignored his comment and, strangely, ignored his eyes. A well-dressed woman stepped in front of him. It was Mikki, smiling like a proud parent.

The limo pulled up and Cassie jumped out long enough to order me in. We were on our way to Castellano's. Still no sign of Patrick.

Between my parents and my big-mouth sister, the world knew about the party. The boisterous Bronx contingent, the sophisticated Juilliard types, a dozen teenagers, and assorted fans and media types all regarded one another as curiosities. They clumped themselves by species, the way monkeys and rhinos do on the African plain.

Norma Stein of *The Brooklyn Buzz* plowed her way toward me.

"Congratulations, Liza. Got a message for the folks back in Brooklyn?"

"I did it all for them."

"Seriously, Liza, can't I get some time alone with you?" Norma was short and stocky, with frizzy brown hair. Her long fuchsia fingernails dug into my arm, presumably as a friendly gesture. "Don't look so worried, I'm not out to hurt you. You kidding me, Liza? I feel like I discovered you. Besides, I know *bubkes* about music. All I want is a story about you."

"Sorry, Norma, spies never tell."

She smiled, undeterred.

"C'mon, Liza. No one believes you're a spy. No hard feelings, right?"

I gave her one of Cassie's cards just to make her go away.

Franz was nothing but euphoric with the evening. I felt him lapping up the adulation, enjoying the festivities from his unseen perch. This was his party, and I did my best to enjoy it for him.

We eavesdropped as my parents greeted each guest, demanding superlatives about the concert. Cassie introduced me to a dozen people I "absolutely had to meet." It seemed everyone there wanted a word with me. Except Chase Barnes, who wanted to have words.

Chase planted Katje at the bar and wormed his way to my side. He wore a look I didn't like, so I assumed an engrossed expression and directed it toward Ivan Stricker, who was telling me a boring story. This did not stop Chase.

"Thanks a lot, Liza." Chase stood inches from my face. His measured voice screamed with sarcasm. Stricker's eyebrows shot up.

"You're welcome, Chase. I'm glad you enjoyed the concert."

"I didn't say that."

"Chase, I want you to meet Ivan Stricker of Stricker, Stricker and Feinsod."

Stricker offered his hand, which Chase ignored.

"I thought we had a deal," Chase said.

"I never said anything was certain." I was still trying to sound pleasant. "Ivan, did you know that Chase Barnes is a famous composer?"

Stricker started to answer, but Chase was at full boil. "You owed me, Liza, you owed me that much."

"How do you figure?"

"I thought we had something special." Chase's voice did not convey the pain that you'd expect with personal anguish. "Do you know what you threw away, what I could have done for you?"

"I'll be just fine, Chase. Thanks for your concern." The embarrassed Ivan Stricker had slipped away, so I looked for another diversion to end my exchange with Chase. A white-haired man and a Chihuahua-like woman caught my eye.

"Well, look who's here!" I said. "Dr. Hoffman, Mrs. Pardo, I want you to meet Chase Barnes. Chase is a world-class composer."

"You were mesmerizing tonight, Liza. Absolutely mesmerizing." Dr. Hoffman turned to Chase. "And you, Mr. Barnes, as if you need introduction. Your *Composition in Stone*, a masterpiece, to be sure. Tell me about your inspiration."

Chase was torn between rage at me and his tickled vanity. I escaped on John D. Doyle's arm.

It was late in the night when the limo drove me back to Brooklyn Heights. The concert had been a huge success and people seemed to enjoy the party. Patrick had shown up for neither. While Franz was still elated, I was edging toward the other end of the emotional scale.

Bad enough that I treated Patrick badly, but did I mention Chase Barnes was the worst lover who ever lived?

No, really, *the* worst—if you could even think of him as a lover. At his apartment the night before, Chase had grown exponentially excited as I played his damn *Pantheon* on the Steinway. At first it was the rubbing and swaying against my back—admittedly erotic. Then he started grabbing my breasts in unpleasant ways. I said ouch but he was too fired up to hear. I told him to calm down but by then he was humping my back in dog-fashion. He was oblivious to me, even when I stopped playing and tried to stand up. He had each hand clamped painfully on a breast when he came in gushes all over the back of my new red sweater.

"What the *hell* was that?" I said.

"Don't worry, Liza, this is just the beginning."

"I don't think so, Chase. That was the end, believe me. The absolute end."

He tried to pull me back in his arms and persuade me to stay.

"Look, Chase, people get arrested on subways for doing that kind of thing," I said. "You can't just rub up against a person and grab at her and make a big mess. You acted like I wasn't even here."

"How can you say that, Liza? Can't you tell how I feel about you?"

"I'm pretty sure I do, yes, and I'm leaving."

"Stay."

"No."

"I'll see you tomorrow night. It'll be better next time, I promise."

He tried to kiss me. I pushed him away. Franz wanted to punch Chase but I was already out the door. That's when I ran home to safety and found Patrick and his mother instead.

A few hours after the concert, I climbed the stairs to my apartment, pray-ing I'd see a trace of light outlining my door, a sign that Patrick was wait-ing for me inside. But my apartment was dark and perfectly still. Switching on the light only made it darker. The corners grew unbearably black and the open bedroom door led to an abandoned universe. I felt Patrick's ab-sence the way I once felt his presence.

Lying facedown on the kitchen table, I noticed, was my new red sweater, the one I'd left hanging over a chair in the bedroom that morning. A blotchy stain stood out clearly on the back, slick and hazy against the textured fabric. The tangy bedroom scent was unmistakable. Patrick had left a note beside the sweater: *This thing needs cleaning.*

———

Niemals wunderbarer als an diesem Abend! . . . Never more glorious than tonight! She makes me better, though who would have believed it? We came together and became something new. I have everything I need now. If she only knew.

CHAPTER TWO

USA TODAY
Friday, April 8

Durbin's Surprise Ending—Schubert or Sham?
(with flattering photo, for a change)

The debut of pianist Liza Durbin at Carnegie Hall in New York on Thursday ended with a joke or a great new discovery, depending on your point of view. Her surprise encore of a "new piece" by Franz Schubert has launched the music world into heated public debate.

Musicologist Charles Morgan, Ph.D., of the Franklin School of Music in Manhattan, is a Schubert specialist who was skeptical at first. "I thought I knew the whole body of work," he said. "The Snow Sonata is new to me, but undoubtedly old."

Morgan bases this belief on a computer program he developed that reads the idiosyncrasies of composers.

"It's akin to handwriting analysis or fingerprinting," he said. "There are sequences or patterns that are distinctive to each musician, but they're so complicated that a computer analysis is the only way to be sure."

Nonsense, says respected Juilliard professor and composer Chase Barnes, Ph.D.

"If Miss Durbin says the Snow Sonata is by Schubert, it should be easy enough for her to prove," Barnes said. "She's a fair pianist and a good interpreter of Schubert but trotting out so-called new pieces is beyond the pale. Her ridiculous sexy image does not help her credibility, either."

People can make up their own minds about Durbin's authenticity when she begins her concert tour in May.

⌁

DATE: Friday, April 8
CLIENT: Liza Durbin

Patient is dealing better with Franz, but struggling with Patrick's sudden departure to Italy, lots of self-blame, uncontrollable crying. Also had a disturbing experience with a Juilliard composer, Chase Barnes. Relationship problems exaggerated by presence of Franz?—MK

NEXT APPOINTMENT: Friday, April 15

When I hired Myles Broadbent to be my legal weasel, I also acquired an agent. It's true I chose Myles mainly to annoy Cassie and Greta (knowing the big boys at Stricker, Stricker & Feinsod would watch out for me), but it happened that the young weasel had a cousin in the business. Despite my reluctance, I met Myles's cousin Jesse Edelstein and hired him on the spot.

Jesse was short, round, and balding before his time. He had a wife and identical preteen triplet girls at home. He chose to work very hard. His calm voice and soft body seemed safe compared to the many cutthroats who wanted a piece of my musical future. Also, Jesse had apprenticed with Lexter Sadler, who people say was the city's greatest music agent and who happened to be Jesse's mother's best friend's cousin.

Jesse kept out of my way until after Carnegie Hall. That was part of our agreement, based on my unreasonable demands. After my debut, Jesse planted himself on my front stoop, voice mail, and e-mail until I paid attention to him. He'd been working behind the scenes, lining up a summer concert schedule. Prestigious venues and music festivals in America and Europe.

On the other end of the dignity rainbow, my sister Cassie was again courting the folks at *Gordy & Jill Talk!* and setting me up for chat shows with late-night jokesters. Jesse and Cassie viewed each other as political rivals working on the same campaign. A week after my debut, we three met for lunch at an uptown restaurant.

"You think I treat her like a trained seal?" Cassie said. *"My own sister,* I would treat like a seal?"

"I think you need to consider her image." Jesse's tone was mild but unwavering. "If you sell her to the masses too soon, you lose her to the serious audience."

"Plenty of classical stars go mainstream."

"Yes, once they establish themselves. Liza has a ways to go yet." Still calm. Condescending? "Let's get the CD out, collect more reviews, build her performance credentials—then we can market her other assets."

"She's ready right now," Cassie said, probably afraid I'd gain back my lost weight. "People are dying to see her. She'll be old news in a month if we don't jump in while she's hot."

"She'll be a respected musician by winter, if we do this right," Jesse said. "Of course, there's this whole matter of the mystery sonata. Where'd that come from, anyway?"

I was tempted to tell Jesse about Franz, to avoid the lies that go with a big secret. For one thing, I was becoming aware of Franz's desire for recognition, which could be a problem. Besides, reasonable people would eventually require some explanation for my sudden explosion of talent. I might have said something, but Cassie jumped in with her point of view.

"It's the whole mystery thing that's our selling point," she said. "Liza is the genius from nowhere, a late-blooming wonder. She represents hope for millions of people who believe they've got great stuff inside them."

Jesse was not persuaded. He was looking instead for ways to pump up my résumé—my early training with Clara Wolf, an ongoing love of music temporarily sidetracked by other pursuits, the scrupulous tutelage of Greta Pretsky. Cassie thought we'd do better to call me a lucky duck and leave it at that. Jesse left us in the restaurant with a frustrated snort and the unpaid bill. Cassie and I stayed to discuss my spring schedule, which included recording studios, interviews, and way too many meetings.

~~~

After I proved myself in concert, people saw me differently. Old acquaintances sent little gifts, my snooty downstairs neighbors found reasons to chat, and Cassie's friends invited me to parties. I viewed it all with happy suspicion. Would these people rescind their kindnesses if I returned to the old me? Of course. Was it nice to be, even temporarily, admired by all? Franz seemed to like it, and I admit I found success pretty sweet. John D. Doyle was especially sweet.

He became a believer and pushed my first CD for immediate production. He showed up many days at the Sony studio in Manhattan just to check in on me. John D. never talked about my clothes, hair, or TV interviews (although he suggested I steer clear of investigative journalists and late-night quippers). He seemed enchanted by the music and endured many hours listening to me play the same piece again and again until we got the right take. I'm told this is not normal for a top Sony executive, but he had other matters on his mind.

"This first CD will be huge," John D. said, as we sipped coffee between takes. "It's all you, Liza. Comes straight from your heart."

"Thanks, John D."

He nodded slowly while searching in his coffee mug for his next words.

"I don't mean to push you, Liza, but I'm sure there'll be more CDs and I was wondering if you've thought more about *lieder*."

"Not really." Franz perked up at the mention of *lieder*. We hadn't had much time for it since the day at Cassie's when John D. sang and we played.

"You're thinking of singing again in public, John D.?" His eyes swung up to meet mine before he realized I was teasing. "Oh, right. Seriously, John D., do you want to sing professionally?"

"Certainly not, I'm not of that caliber, Liza. Not these days." His sharp blue eyes and trimmed white beard clashed with the aw-shucks tone. "Not good enough for the general public, at least. Maybe something private sometime. Did I tell you I have a voice teacher again? Anyway, we could think about *lieder* for one of your CDs. We have great singers to choose from. It doesn't have to be an all-*lieder* CD, of course. Maybe throw a couple in for variety."

"Great idea, John D. I'll definitely think about it."

Another awkward moment as John D. hunted for words.

"One more thing, Liza. Something serious. It's about the *Snow Sonata.*"

"I want it on this album."

"And I don't want us to look foolish."

"The *Snow Sonata* is by Schubert, and it's got to be on the CD."

John shifted in his chair, returned to studying his coffee mug. My happiness was important to him, most likely because of the *lieder.*

"I want to help you, Liza, but you have to give me something here," he said. "Some form of proof. Is there anything you can tell me?"

We were two weeks into recording this CD, and the *Snow Sonata* was tentatively scheduled for the following Monday. Franz wanted it to happen, and so did I.

"No problem, John D. I'll get you proof," I said.

∿∿∿

I was at home in Brooklyn thinking about the *Snow Sonata* dilemma when Patrick called. I would have called him first, but I didn't have his new number in Italy, and wasn't about to call Mrs. Florio to get it. He even changed his e-mail address. I'd been waiting for this moment, yet hearing his voice shocked my system. Franz went all fluttery.

"Patrick, oh God, Patrick, I'm so glad you called."

He asked me to mail his things to Milan.

"Okay, give me your address," I said, "but can't we talk?"

"How was your concert?"

As if he hadn't heard yet—the concert was three weeks ago.

"Good, Patrick, it was good. But I missed you there. Please let me explain—"

"No dead spirits attacked you?"

"No."

"All right, then. Write down this address, please."

He reeled out his new home in consonants, vowels, and numbers. It looked beautiful on paper but sounded cold in his voice.

"Listen, Patrick, I really want to apologize," I said. "And also let you know that things were not as bad as they looked."

Long-distance silence.

"I'm sorrier than you can believe. Things were bad enough, and life was pretty crazy, of course, but it was still not what you think."

"Did one of your spirits leave that nasty little deposit on your sweater?"

It was like talking to a stranger.

"I'm sorry about that, Patrick. Of course it wasn't a spirit. It wasn't anyone who matters."

"Bad answer, Liza."

I dug deep for another one.

"Look, we tried," Patrick said finally. "At least, I did. I think you did, too, for a while. But you really hurt me, Liza, when I was trying hard to keep things together. We were both dealing with lots of stuff, I know. But you're the one who cheated. I wish I could say it didn't matter but it does."

"I may be in Italy this summer," I said.

"Un-huh."

Un-huh. That's where we left things. The person I'd felt closest to had become a grunt. Strange how much I missed him.

When Patrick left for Italy the first time, I missed his company, the closeness, the sex. The second time he left, I missed him more. Worst of all, it was my stupid fault that he left, just when things might have been good.

But that doesn't explain how *much* I missed him this time. The grief and physical distress were, frankly, out of character for me. No person had ever affected me that way, not even Barry when he dumped me for my sister. I wouldn't have thought Patrick could rattle my soul this way. Then I realized that Franz made the difference.

Everything else in life felt richer since Franz arrived, so it made sense that my emotional ties—and my capacity for pain—would be deeper. Looking back, my connection with Patrick, despite all the distractions, became more intense when he first returned from Italy. Patrick had commented on it, too. Maybe that's why he tolerated Franz and all the craziness as long as he did.

I also realized that Franz missed Patrick. That was hard for me to ac-

knowledge at first. But Franz had only me and my world for companion-
ship. He liked Patrick. Maybe they would have been friends in another
life. Maybe lovers. I had no clue how sexuality fit into Franz's existence.
He was happy in bed with Patrick—but was that because he felt my pleasure or his own?

Of course, Franz didn't know about the way that Patrick and I got together, and I had no idea how he'd feel about affairs and broken marriages.
It was one of the secrets I could keep from him, which was a relief. I
wanted badly to see Patrick through Franz's eyes, uncluttered by stubborn
memories. His perspective could explain my pain.

That pain kept me awake most of the night. As the hours rolled by,
other concerns popped into view. Questions of a totally different nature
battled for attention. In a crucial moment between sleep and waking I figured out what to do about the *Snow Sonata*.

I awoke Saturday morning with loads of energy, a plan in hand. The Cal-
ligraphy Ink store on Clark Street had plenty of papers in all sizes, colors,
and textures. I bought an eighteen-inch ruler, three bottles of Higgins
black ink, brushes, and the kind of quill-style pens you dip in the ink—
the way Schubert once did.

Back in my kitchen, I spread the supplies on the kitchen table. I wrote
the words "Snow Sonata" on a yellow Post-it note and stuck it on the wall
in front of me. Then I put all my thought into the melody.

It was surprisingly easy to yield to Franz this time. He saturated my
mind. It felt good. His words floated in my head, mostly in German and
a few in English. I watched my hand as we watered down the ink and
brushed gray bars across the page, guided loosely by the ruler, preparing
the page for musical notation.

Music enveloped us. I couldn't distinguish between all the parts. Franz
could, though. He re-created the *Snow Sonata,* note for note, grabbing
bits of music from the air and drawing them on paper. He never corrected
himself.

When the last note was committed to paper, a thousand doves flew
from our chest. I felt sated, overjoyed, and ready to come back—to return
from "we" to "me." Franz wanted more. He dug his heels into my soul and

pushed on. Music splashed around the room, bouncing off the walls, creating wind.

No way to know how long this went on. One stack of pages filled up with new music, and another stack beckoned. Franz soared on, energized and ecstatic. Exhaustion crept into my bones, but he ignored it. The experience was too seductive. We could get lost in it. I suddenly realized that *I had to make it end.*

I sent my thoughts to Franz but he ignored them. I screamed in our head to drown out the music. No response. I tried to put down the pen. Franz's grip was stronger than mine. I had become the visitor in my body, peering through someone else's eyes. Trying to rise through the layers of Franz, I felt the weight of his soul. Fear filled my lungs and stole my breath. Franz showed no mercy.

"Please, Franz, let me out," I thought I said. But I was screaming in a dream.

Trust me, Liza, let this happen. His words were foreign but the meaning was clear: *I must do this. You must let me. Trust me.*

"Fuck 'trust me.' Let me out!"

I was drowning at my kitchen table. I clawed at my insides, struggling until a giant wave subdued me and darkness prevailed.

———

Ich verdiene es, hier zu sein . . . I deserve to be here.

She is my age, thirty-one. My final year. What did she achieve on her own? Whose end is near, whose beginning?

CHAPTER THREE

"Liza! Wake up, Liza! Can you hear me?"

Fred knelt beside me, yelling and shaking me. Strange that he would know me on sight. I was sure I'd been pressed into the mold of a nineteenth-century musician.

"Liza, can you get up?"

My body was curled like a sleeping cat in a corner on the floor. I wore the same T-shirt and pants I'd put on more than a day ago. They were obviously soiled. The shirt was ripped in spots, barely holding together at the neckline. There were scratch marks on my forearms. My fingernails fit in the grooves as I traced the lines. I tasted blood where I'd bitten my lip.

All I could manage to do was cry. It was full-out playground crying, with fell-off-the-swing-and-broke-an-arm sobs.

Fred dragged me to my feet and guided me into bed. He threw a blanket over me and kissed my forehead. I heard him make a call in the next room.

"Hi, Mikki? This is Fred Wilner. What? Oh, sorry. It's important."

A pause followed while presumably Mikki rubbed her eyes and pulled herself awake.

"I'm at Liza's. She's in bad shape." He lowered his voice so I heard just bits and pieces. *Dropped by with bagels . . . on the floor . . . yes, actual blood . . . needs you . . .* "Okay, so we'll see you at noon?" His voice returned to normal to make the good-byes. "Thanks, Mikki. Yes, I will. 'Bye."

Fred came back to check on me and looked relieved. He offered to draw me a bath, which sounded heavenly.

As my mind and body left the terror zone, I did a quick inner scan. No Franz. *Good,* I thought. *Maybe he's dead. Dead for real this time.*

"Feeling better?" Fred asked. He stroked my hand, then turned over my palm to look again at the marks on my forearm. "You frightened me, Liza. What's going on?"

"Franz took over," I said in a lumpy whisper. "Saturday morning we sat down to write out the *Snow Sonata.* He wouldn't let go after that. I tried to get back, but he wouldn't let me."

"Okay, you don't need to tell me everything. I can see it's upsetting you. Why don't you take your bath and we'll go see Mikki."

"Yes, okay," I said. "First the bath, okay?"

"Yes, first the bath."

I slid gingerly into the hot water. A memory of drowning nearly stopped me, but the water felt soothing. I searched again, more carefully, and found Franz nesting in my vertebrae, slumbering peacefully after his creative rampage. Let the beast sleep. Let him slip into a coma. Maybe I'd see a doctor and have him surgically removed.

I threw on the first clean clothes in sight, which sort of matched.

"I'm ready," I announced.

"Do you want to see this first?" Fred said.

I followed him to the living room, where handwritten music lay in stacks on the kitchen table, coffee table, couch, and floor. All the paper I'd bought the day before was covered in small black dots and lines. So were various envelopes, paper towels, and a photograph of Cameron. Each paper pile had a title at the top written in German. I only remembered the first one, "Die Schneesonate." The *Snow Sonata.*

The experience had been a debacle for me, a miracle by any other standard.

On Monday I met John D. Doyle at the studio and handed him proof of the *Snow Sonata*'s authenticity. He studied the papers through thick reading glasses. He was looking at a copy of a copy of a copy of Franz's handiwork. The quality was poor enough to bleach out most of the identifying marks in the parchment-like paper, yet the gray lines and his black musical notations were clear. It was not exactly like a modern manuscript, but familiar enough.

"Where did you get this?" John D. asked.

"The owner insists on anonymity."

He gave a small grumble as he inspected the German title and Franz Schubert's signature.

"I promise, any handwriting expert will recognize this as Schubert's," I said. "And the musicologists will tell you the same about the music."

John D. took off his glasses to study my face. He tilted his head and narrowed his eyes.

"Who are you, Liza Durbin? Where did this come from?"

"This manuscript wasn't easy to get, John D. Trust me, these are copies of the real thing. The originals are permanently unavailable." Shredded and burned by me. "Now can I record *Die Schneesonate*?"

He bounced on his toes and nodded happily. "Well, it's a start. I need to get these papers in the right hands. If even one expert buys it, we have a controversy at least, which is something more than we have now," he said.

"*Wunderbar.*"

Fred had accompanied me to the recording studio that day, where we finished the CD. Sony was working at warp speed to get it ready in time for my summer tour. Photos, liner notes, and other details were still in the works, but the important part was over for me.

It was early evening when Fred and I left for Sophie's, a quiet café where we could have "a good talk." The good talk, it turns out, included surprise dinner companions, Cassie and Mikki. They were worried about me.

"I don't think you should be alone," Cassie said. "Fred called and told me everything. He says you were a mess. Mikki thinks you might be losing it."

"Those weren't my exact words," Mikki said.

"Anyway, we think you ought to stay with one of us, for safety," Cassie said. "My house or Fred's, you choose."

"Don't you think you're all overreacting here?" I said.

I wished someone thought so. I wished *I* thought so.

Mikki spoke directly to me. "We understand your need for privacy and independence. The episode this weekend makes it clear that Franz wants independence, too, at least sometimes. He found a way to assert himself this time."

It's true that without Patrick in my home, Franz had more room to roam through my life at will. Add that to my list of regrets.

"I really should have seen this coming," Mikki said. "Franz has grown used to his surroundings, and he's experienced success in your concert. He can't get out of your body, Liza, but he wants some control in his life, such as it is. As long as you've got familiar faces around as lifelines, you have some protection. We can help pull you back to us, but being alone with Franz can be very dangerous."

"I told you that I gave in to him on purpose," I reasoned. "For that matter, I instigated it. I needed him to write music and that's what he did. Actually, he wrote a ton of it, so I don't think we'll have to do that again for a long time."

"What if Franz doesn't agree with you on that?" Fred said.

When Fred had found me on the floor the day before, I let him take me straight to Mikki. I later allowed Fred to sleep on my couch that night, apparently opening the floodgates for helpful loved ones to stand constant guard over me. I finally agreed to stay at Fred's temporarily.

The relief on their faces was nothing compared to the relief I was hiding.

Franz had not left me, but he was laying low. Fortified by protective attention from family and friends, I stayed in control while Franz went positively meek. No doubt he felt my anger toward him, not to mention my fear. Maybe he backed off to make amends. Or maybe he wore himself out with his music marathon.

Fred's apartment had an extra room that I took over as mine. It was almost fun playing house with Fred. I made waffles for breakfast, which he described as "buttered sawdust." He watched appalling TV shows, which I pretended not to enjoy. For the first few days, I barely acknowledged Franz, but then I realized he wasn't going away, so it was time to make peace and move on. I set aside a little time each day on the baby grand and gradually, carefully, let Franz show his face.

Cassie came one morning to dictate my life for the foreseeable future. Her elegant outfit seemed to mock Fred's apartment. I greeted her in faded gray sweatpants and an NYU sweatshirt plucked from Fred's unfolded-laundry pile. My hair was unspeakable. Cassie grimaced.

"Fred says you're doing fine," she said. "I hope that's true, because I met with your agent and we've got some dates lined up for you. Good ones, in just a few weeks. Will you be ready?"

"Don't worry, Cassie, under this unkempt façade is still your musical gold mine."

"Thank God," she said. "Now get out your calendar. If you have any last kinks to work out, do it quickly. We've got you at the War Memorial Opera House in San Francisco on May twenty-sixth. It's got prestige, a good location, but it's not like jumping right into the Kennedy Center. You're sure you can do it?"

I assured her I was.

"We also have tentative dates in L.A., Boston, D.C., Houston. Some of the best concert halls."

I went numb hearing this. Numb felt good.

"There are all the summer festivals, of course," Cassie said. "Wolf Trap, Tanglewood, a few others. They have them all over the country. How much are you up for?"

"I want to play a lot." Suddenly it seemed important to perform as much as possible. This was a game without a clock, likely to end in sudden death. "What about Europe?"

"Europe in the fall. Paris, Amsterdam, Milan." *Milan?* "And you'll want Vienna, of course."

Vienna. The word zoomed through my body. "I definitely have to go there."

"Well, the Schubert thing and all," Cassie said. "People will expect it."

"I expect it," I said. "So does Franz."

As Cassie described the next few months of my life, I felt my body los-

ing line and form. It was a lovely, amorphous feeling. I hated when Franz
took charge of me, but I was oddly happy to have my bossy sister make
plans for me this time. Happy not to be fretting over what on earth I
should do next with my life.

Cassie brought up the travel arrangements. Sony was putting up
money to promote my CD and we'd negotiated for me to travel with some
staff. Well, one staff.

"Fred and I will take turns with you on the road whenever we can."
Cassie spoke in reassuring tones to me, her mental-case sister. "But this
paid staff person could be more like your assistant, a gofer to get you to
the airport on time and help with other arrangements."

Cassie had spoken with my agent, Jesse, about this. He said solo pianists don't need much of an entourage because the logistics were pretty
straightforward. Still, it's nice to have someone to run errands and make
sure that things go smoothly. Jesse had a couple of people to recommend.

"I want Greta," I said, which surprised me. "At first, anyway. Not as
my gofer, of course. She knows the music world, so I'll need her. And I already know who I want as my assistant."

Franz filled my head with a powerful, irresistible image. It was the face
of an eager boy who loved music and needed friends.

Danny stopped by after school a few times a week. I was practicing long
hours every day, until my back hurt and my arms screamed for mercy.
Danny's visits brought fresh energy into our boot-camp practice schedule.
He was always ready to listen, play, sing, joke.

"Danny, what are you up to this summer?" I asked.

"My mom's taking off somewhere. She's sending me to the relatives in
Maine."

"Sounds nice."

"It sucks."

"Excellent," I said. "I have a better offer."

I explained about the gofer concept.

"So this person just travels with you and helps out with things?" he
said.

"Pretty much," I said. "It's a little more complicated in my case."

I was scared to tell Danny about Franz, but he needed to know the truth before he signed on for more. I hadn't told the inhabitation story to anyone since Patrick. I'd almost gotten used to it, and the few people I'd told about it had grown out of their shock by that time. The tale had always elicited disbelief, confusion, and general astonishment. Danny's response was distinctly his own.

"This is *totally* awesome, Liza!" He hadn't blinked in minutes, not wanting to miss a thing. "You gotta tell people about this. This is the coolest thing ever."

Maybe it was because he'd heard me play. Until this news, he assumed I was born with genius, but he was open to any possibility.

"I'm glad you're so excited," I said.

"Well, aren't you?"

"Sure, but this hasn't been exactly easy. My life has changed totally, and it's not all good."

But Danny was too jazzed to listen to me. (Why don't people enjoy my whining?) He was bouncing around the room, exulting. His enthusiasm spurred me on.

"Want to see something Franz wrote himself?" I offered.

"Oh, man, the *Snow Sonata*—that was you, of course! I gotta see it. Show me everything!"

There was a small stack of Franz's music on the piano, some pieces we'd been playing that day. Danny wanted to touch it all, absorb it through his skin.

"Schubert's handwriting! This is the real thing—I can't *believe* it!"

He spotted some *lieder* in the pile, written to poems by Schiller. Danny stopped, smiled.

"You play, I'll sing," he said.

"You know German?"

"My mother, *Ilsa,* remember her?" Danny underlined my forgetfulness. "She's only from Austria, is all. She never speaks English to me at home."

"Never?"

"She heard it was the way to make me bilingual. German at home, English everywhere else."

I picked a song and played the melody line for Danny. He read through the lyrics. After a while we put the pieces together. Danny sang beautifully

in strong, succulent German. With the last note, he whooped like he'd
scored three points at the buzzer. Franz forgot all about the rumbling bass
voice he'd once had in mind for that song.

Naturally, Danny couldn't wait to be my gofer. I explained how weird
things could get, that we'd have to share a suite so he could guard over me
in case Franz's spirit got feisty. Every worrisome detail struck Danny as
flat-out cool. He suggested I be the one to ask his mother if he could be
my summer gofer.

"She'll say yes to you," Danny said confidently. "She loves you since
you gave her tickets to your concert. Hey, maybe I'll give her tickets to
something."

<center>~~~</center>

Franz joined in the happiness of our day. In fact, he added his own touch
that night.

I had recently noticed a change in Franz's spectacular dreams. They
were losing their slippery, random quality. Dreams are supposed to be un-
grabbable, like trying to write on fur, but his were growing startlingly real.
I saw coherent scenes and stories, with beginning, middle, and end. In this
dream, I saw Franz's best friends:

*Franz lives in a large home that doubles as the school where his father teaches.
Franz has four siblings, though many others were lost in infancy. The Schuberts are a musical clan and the house whirs with gorgeous sounds.*

*(While dreaming, I know what Franz knows, including the who-and-how
details of his history. I understand what is said, too, not even noticing which
language is spoken.)*

*Franz is eight, and distant relatives have come to live with them. Cheerless
Aunt Mathilde, who has no husband (Franz does not know why), arrived
with her wonderful twins who were born the same day, same year, as Franz.
Dainty Marta has blond curls and an untamable laugh. Peter makes swell
jokes and allows his springy, coppery hair to run rampant.*

*Franz, Marta, and Peter are best friends. They are fiercely loyal and close,
as you're likely to see only among children and soldiers. In this dream, the family has gathered for an evening of music. Franz plays violin, and Marta and
Peter get into the act, too. She dances like a tipsy spider. He sings in a voice*

*that could melt glaciers, warm and sunny, with a hidden giggle (very much
like his hair). The three are loved by all.*

*After the musicale, the children eat sugared raspberry tortes. They make a
game of the jelly messes on their hands and faces. Just before bedtime, the best
friends hide under a staircase for their nightly secret meeting. They make a
vow that Franz and Marta will marry as soon as they're old enough. That way,
the three will be inseparable forever. They lick one another's cheeks to seal the
deal. Once you've done something that gross, there's no turning back.*

I was awakened by Franz laughing out loud.

CHAPTER FOUR

SAN FRANCISCO CHRONICLE
Friday, May 27

Hearing Schubert Anew
by Ross L. Fine

Just when I thought I knew Franz Schubert, along comes Liza Durbin. Playing with technical prowess and sensual lyricism, Durbin gave new life to a well-worn program last night. The predictably assembled works were enlivened by inventive interpretation and, of course, by the much-debated Snow Sonata—a work of power, texture and mystery.

LOS ANGELES TIMES
Saturday, June 4

Stunned, at Last, by Schubert
by Rebecca Klein

After 41 years of reviewing classical performances, I thought I was beyond being stunned. Least of all by Schubert, not my favorite composer. And certainly not by a nobody pianist in a sexy dress.

HOUSTON CHRONICLE
Wednesday, June 8

Who Is Liza Durbin and How Does She Do It?
by Andrea Bevier

With shocking ease, Liza Durbin has taken the classic Schubert repertoire into the stratosphere.

NEW YORK MAGAZINE
June 10

Who the Hell Is Liza Durbin?
by Chase Barnes, Ph.D.

It's hard to believe that reasonable people can embrace this obvious fraud.

~~~

When I was in second grade, my parents let me have a sleepover party with friends from school. We played games, ate ice cream, and drew pictures with my new color-marker set. After everyone left, my mother picked up a picture left behind by Alisa Hyatt, the class artist. It was a portrait of our teacher, Mrs. Josephson. My mother exclaimed over its loveliness and asked who drew it.

"I did!" I blurted.

I regretted my lie as soon as I heard it. Before I had a chance to take it back, Mom was running upstairs to show the picture to Aunt Frieda.

From that day, my mother attributed great artistic talent to me. She found something ingenious in all my mediocre pictures, until my guilt made me stop drawing. Mom had Alisa's picture framed and hung it in our living room. I never invited Alisa to our house again, afraid she would expose me. When Alisa moved away in the third grade, it felt like divine reprieve. I vowed never to lie like that again, but I never forgot how easily the lie had worked.

I didn't mean to break that vow by accepting Franz's credit, but that's how it was. Strange that the guilt I felt as an adult was no different from what I felt as a child. Maybe pure emotions don't mature, we just handle them differently. And because I hadn't initiated the lie myself, I managed to enjoy the attention a little more this time. There was actually quite a lot to enjoy, when I wasn't feeling guilty.

Danny missed the first few weeks of my concert tour because of school. Greta was with me, and either Fred or Cassie accompanied us until Danny met us in Chicago. By that time I was an old hand at concert life.

"God, Liza, you're a star!" Danny's enthusiasm lit up my twelfth-floor suite in the Chicago Hilton. "I saw you on *Gordy and Jill Talk!* You were a hoot."

"You watch Gordy and Jill?"

"Please, what do I look like?" he protested. "I only watched it to see you. Some friends came and we watched it together. You were awesome."

"You didn't tell your friends about Franz, right?"

"Hey, I'm no rat," he said. "Tell me about the tour so far."

I had arrived in San Francisco with nauseating jitters. Luckily, I was flanked by Cassie, Greta, and Franz Schubert. This time I was sure the concert would go well, but my life was another story. My familiar surroundings were far away, and Franz kept rapping at my mind's door with creative surges and dream-tales of childhood. I needed my cohorts to keep me in my own head.

The first couple of concerts were critical successes, but there were plenty of empty seats. Apparently it takes more than a Carnegie Hall triumph and a new CD to get people to classical piano concerts outside of New York. Cassie took action by arranging more dramatic promotions to precede us in each city. To Greta's horror, Cassie resurrected the "Durbin Does Schubert" ads. She kept the "nouvelle classique" line and added quotes:

Impressive emotional range, technical bravura!—Jonathan Porter-Cringe, *The New York Times*

Liza Durbin, a dazzling pianist!—Andrea Bevier, *Houston Chronicle*

Durbin kicks classical ass!—Gordy Flims, *Gordy & Jill Talk!*

Cassie also booked me on local radio and TV shows, and made plans to bring back the Times Square billboard for bigger cities. Greta met us in Milwaukee and went livid when she spotted an ad with me in the sexy blue dress in the paper's calendar section. She cooled down when she learned we nearly sold out that night. Business was picking up.

"It's scary to be the star," I told Danny. "There's only so much that advertising takes care of. After that, it all depends on me. I'm not that nervous about the music anymore. There are other things, though. Like finding a crowd of strangers waiting outside the theater to see me. Or going to a restaurant and people sending over flowers or champagne."

"Yeah, tough life," Danny said. "How does your pal Franz like it?"

"I'm sorry to say he enjoys it. I guess he likes the limelight after being away so long."

Franz seemed not to care about our mixed-up identities, but I did. Our fans didn't know they were in love with a sideshow freak. I was a living ventriloquist's dummy—and some really smart person might detect the truth at any time.

Then there was my paranoia. Who were all these fans? How could you tell the good guys from the twisted? And why did I see jack-o'-lantern eyes again in the audience in Milwaukee?

"C'mon, Liza, I *know* you have fun. Big star, lots of attention. You can admit it."

"It has its moments, Danny. Good and bad, it has its moments."

We were a fine team, Danny and I. He was a city kid, instantly at home in Chicago, Philadelphia, Buffalo, or Cleveland. We'd take a walk around each new town before I settled in for a couple of hours of practice. He liked my rehearsals better than the concerts because I played different pieces and he could yell out comments or applaud whenever he felt like it.

My concert repertoire was pretty set. The *Snow Sonata* was always the last piece, a natural finale. I alternated encores for variety. Greta came to some performances in June. We played our duet and audiences loved it.

But Franz was aching for new music. Luckily, Danny came with a good supply of CDs—he said it was his duty to educate Schubert. We listened to the likes of Louis Armstrong, Ravi Shankar, Tito Puente, and Emmylou Harris. Franz listened to everything with intensity. He particu-

larly loved tango music, and we indulged in truly awful dancing. Sometimes Danny sang along in his excellent voice.

Franz became increasingly experimental during our practices. He
wanted to elaborate on the music he composed on that notorious night in
Brooklyn. I yielded—but only so far—and gave him the freedom he
needed. Danny was always nearby. He loved Franz's new pieces. They had
a different sound, classically rooted with a contemporary tint.

"What was that last one?" Danny asked, after hearing Franz's newest
favorite. "Something new?"

"Yep. You like it?"

"Totally. Much better than that one yesterday." He sang a reminder.
"Much better."

He was right. Franz had hit a distinctive stride in this composition,
adding sharp steps to his choreography.

"Why don't you play that in concert?" Danny asked.

"I'd love to, Danny, but unfortunately it's in the same boat as the *Snow
Sonata*. People are just accepting that piece. I can't just spring another unknown Schubert on them."

"Sure you can. You're a star. People respect you. Major music critics,
academic types, almost everyone. Hey, you've got Franz Schubert behind
you. Why not play what you want?"

His enthusiasm yanked a laugh from me. We'd been taking everything
so seriously. The music world took me ultra-seriously. They accepted me
as consistent and professional, even if I was a mystery. My reputation was
riding a smooth crest. This was all to the good, but somewhat limiting.
Also, Franz figured out what we were talking about and warmed to
Danny's suggestion.

On the other hand, John D., Greta, and a few others might have a
communal heart attack if I sprung another surprise like the *Snow Sonata*.
Besides, I didn't have a name for the new one yet.

Toward the end of June, I was adjusting better to the fan reaction and loss
of privacy. We did several performances a week, which meant a hectic
travel schedule. I would not have insisted on deluxe hotels and limos, but
I didn't protest when Cassie did.

The concert routine felt familiar by that time: backstage smells, squeaky wooden floors, testing the piano for tune, fussing with hair and makeup, and last-minute to-dos over sound, promos, or panty-hose. Danny helped with countless tasks. He was impressively organized and a good companion for late-night pizza.

I felt more and more comfortable performing. Franz took over to play but did not completely bury me. I asserted myself in small ways. For one thing, I broke with classical tradition by requesting a mike onstage so I could talk to the audience. Usually it was just a welcome and a few words about the music. Sometimes I told an amusing story about my day in the audience's fair city. They loved it. A few reviewers mentioned it (". . . refreshing when a classical artist shows the confidence to be human onstage . . ."). I heard that the famous pianist Natalie Frome, who was losing some fans to me, tried it herself afterward. My audiences kept growing.

The jack-o'-lantern eyes still got to me. They showed up again in Omaha. Outside the theater, I saw the security guard escorting away an unruly, bright-eyed fan who demanded to see me. When it happened again in Sacramento, I turned to my gofer for help.

"So, Danny, what's up with Miss Bright Eyes in the fourth row?" This was during an intermission. A long-haired woman with the jack-o'-lantern eyes was close enough so Danny couldn't possibly have missed her from his backstage view.

"Bright eyes?"

"You know, Danny, the light-up eyes I told you about. That stupid novelty thing—I can't believe you haven't noticed them."

"Liza, I don't know what you mean. Who were you looking at?"

"Fourth row, left side. You can't miss her. Long, straight hair and super-bright eyes. Like a jack-o'-lantern. Must be some kind of glasses or contact lenses."

Danny squinted into the audience.

"Anyway, they're distracting. Maybe you could ask her to remove them for the second half." Danny looked at a loss. "Well, try anyway, okay? Hurry."

She was still in the audience, bright-eyed and annoying, in the second act. Danny said he couldn't find her. Franz had noticed her, too, though.

· · ·

Later that night Franz gave me something I wanted all my life.

In this dream, he is singing. I feel my throat vibrate. His voice is far too lovely to be mine, but he is sharing it with me.

Franz is singing with the choir at Liechtental Church, in the town where he lives, just outside Vienna. This is a normal Sunday, though the music sounds extraordinary to me. Voices swell and mingle with immeasurable grace.

Marta sits in a pew near the front. When her mother looks away, she makes silly faces at Peter. He is also a chorister, and sings better than Franz. Peter never sees his twin sister's funny faces because he dares not look away from the choirmaster. You wouldn't, either—he is sternness itself. Besides, Peter has a solo this morning, and he's too nervous to think of anything else.

After the service, there is a big meal at the Schuberts'. The adults make a fuss over Franz and Peter. Marta spills something on the tablecloth, to be sure she is noticed. Everyone will perform in one way or another that evening.

These people don't know that I can see them, that Franz has invited me into this scene. A dream, a vision, a visit . . . I can't tell. But it feels like a gift from Franz, my only chance to sing with beauty and feel the joy of very young genius.

We woke from this dream still drenched in the spirit of daring and cama-raderie. A few hours later we flew to San Diego to play at Copley Symphony Hall. The audience included my family, friends, and other enthusiastic fans. They were ready to love whatever I played. Franz and I both felt it. That's why the encore felt right.

"Thank you so much," I said to the appreciative crowd after the *Snow Sonata* finale. "How would you folks feel about hearing something new?" *(Cheers.)* "Not really new, of course, but I know you haven't heard it. It's *Das Nachtsonate*—the *Night Sonata*—by Franz Schubert. It was written late in his career and it's never been performed in public before."

A charge ran through the audience as they realized what was about to happen. The *Snow Sonata* had been a glorious find—the first audience felt special and told all their friends about being there. This crowd was about to welcome the newest undiscovered Schubert. They would worry about authenticity later. For the next eighteen minutes, they would be the only earthlings with the privilege of hearing it. A few enthusiasts offered *bravas* even before the first note. Some college kids (obvious music nerds) made howler-monkey noises. I signaled everyone to sit down, then put a finger to my lips to shush them.

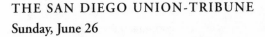

CHAPTER FIVE

THE SAN DIEGO UNION-TRIBUNE
Sunday, June 26

Durbin Reveals Another "Unknown Schubert"

Concertgoers who heard Liza Durbin last night at Copley Symphony Hall witnessed a fine performance with another of the pianist's surprise endings. The recently discovered pianist capped off her program with another "previously unknown" piece by Franz Schubert, the Night Sonata.

Durbin is known for her mastery of Schubert's repertoire and for introducing the composer's Snow Sonata, another newly uncovered piece, at Carnegie Hall in March. Last night's performance was an equally stunning surprise.

THE SEATTLE TIMES
Wednesday, June 29

Liza Durbin—The Reviewer's Dilemma
by Stephen Chasson

. . . Yet aside from the aforementioned accolades for technique and expression, I must address the issue on everyone's mind: Schubert's Italian Impromptu. This is the third "new Schubert" performed by Durbin in concert. The first, the Snow Sonata, is believed authentic by reasonable scholars who have studied the music and seen copies of original manuscripts (whose owners demand anonymity). The Night Sonata, the second new piece, just premiered last week and has yet to be studied. Last night's Italian Impromptu is a reviewer's dilemma—a classical piece, of controversial origins, that no one's heard before.

I can't replay this complex piece well enough in my mind to analyze the music and performance with the scrutiny it deserves. However, Schubert was my specialty in my own short, forgettable performing career, so I draw from an intimate feeling for the composer. If this is an elaborate hoax we may all feel foolish in the end; on the other hand, great music is great music and my job is to give you my impressions.

Picture an orange, the color and texture familiar in every way. Then peel away the rind. The fruit is succulent and glistening, networked with fuzzy white veins, everything as expected. It tastes like an orange, too—but there are hints of salsa, curry, whiskey and spice. The flavor is intoxicating. At the point of satiation, the rind somehow rewraps around the orange and seals itself seamlessly once again. The fruit inside was richer and stranger than any orange ever tasted, but it remains unmistakably an orange.

The Italian Impromptu is unmistakably Schubert.

∿

"*Three* more unknowns? You played *three* more unknowns while I was gone?"

"Hi, John D.," I said. "How was your trip?"

John D. had just finished a ten-day raft trip on the Colorado with his grandson. They emerged at the south rim of the Grand Canyon and within fifteen minutes overheard two Australian tourists talking about the American pianist who keeps coming up with "new Schuberts." John D. phoned immediately. His voice was strained with the effort not to scream at me.

"I'm glad you called, John D. It's been incredible." Sometimes you have to ignore a person's bad temper. "You wouldn't believe the response. We're sold out here in Minneapolis, and we're practically sold out for the next month."

"You didn't think to pass this by anyone first?" John D. said. "Three new Schuberts and you don't even warn me? Don't I deserve that much?"

"What'd you want me to do, send a carrier pigeon to Utah?"

"The Grand Canyon's in Arizona, Liza. And you could've waited."

"The moment was right, John D., really, just what we needed. People are scooping up tickets, hoping they'll be at a concert when I play something new. They wear these pins that say, 'What's new, Liza?' Cassie thinks I'm a marketing wizard. Fred and Jake built a killer website and fans are chatting about me day and night."

"Who's Jake?"

"Fred's graphic artist. I'm sure I told you."

"Why would you tell *me* anything? Liza, has any of this been authenticated? The music, I mean." His voice transitioned from anger to worry. "Where did you get this music? Is this the same source, because I'd really like to know who—"

"Of course, the same source," I said. "It's all the same source, isn't it? Franz Schubert."

By way of anonymous donors, he reminded me.

"You're gonna love this stuff, trust me."

"I don't doubt that, Liza. But you've got to be honest with me about your sources. I don't want to look like a fool."

"You'll look like a genius."

His breathing slowed and his voice approached normal again.

"Did I mention that those Australians got tickets to see you next month?" he said.

"You see? Not so bad."

"Well, not yet," he said, pausing before his next question. "Any chance there's some *lieder* among these undiscovered treasures?"

I didn't mean to embarrass John D. or anyone else. My dilemma was how to carry on with our nicely packaged show while letting Franz move forward. Surely he was not here for my glorification. Taking chances on his behalf felt like a responsibility I couldn't ignore. It caused both great excitement and escalated pressure.

Luckily, we had ten days back in New York, with a concert scheduled on Long Island and another in New Jersey. I could set aside time to transcribe and photocopy the new Schuberts for authentication.

I stopped in at my apartment, which still felt strange. I'd never cozied into the place again after my terrible night with Franz. I checked on the usual maintenance and upkeep duties. Two weeks into my tour I'd stopped calling home for messages, and I keep my cell number top secret, so the answering machine was overloaded. Old friends, Chase Barnes twice (*creep*), Ruthie three times, Patrick never. *(I sent him two postcards. What more could I do?)* I packed a few things and we left.

I stayed at Fred's apartment, both for the company and the piano. Hoffman and Pardo dropped by to snoop, I phoned a few friends, and I learned more about Franz every day. He showed me glimpses of his life story, and he seemed more interested in my life as well. I often worried that my behavior must seem wrongheaded or absurd to him. He proved I was right about that.

Franz called Patrick in Italy.

I found this out when I woke at a dark, unnamed hour to find the phone in my hand and Patrick's voice in my ear.

"*Pronto! Pronto?* Anyone there?"

Patrick's voice swept through me like a warm island breeze.

"It's me, Patrick."

"Liza? How are you?"

"We really need to talk, Patrick. Please, *please,* don't hang up. Let me explain this time."

"It was Chase Barnes, wasn't it?"

Patrick's unexpected statement made me sit up in bed.

"Not exactly," I said. "Sort of, but not the way you think. How do you know, anyway?"

"He's the blowhard from Juilliard who writes such nasty things about you. Childish, stupid crap, very personal. I figure you dumped him."

"You're nearly right. I ended it before we ever got started, though. The night before Carnegie Hall, when I was mad at you and he was this great, successful musician who wanted to help me."

Patrick grunted. He sounded more jaded than hurt after all this time.

"Chase was using me, Patrick. He knew I was hot—musically, I mean—even though he didn't know about Franz. He wanted me to debut a piece he wrote but I didn't do it. I played the *Snow Sonata* instead."

"Why were you even flirting with this guy? We were together then." Patrick spoke with the neutrality of an inquiring journalist.

"I was crazy and frightened. He knew everything about music. I was dumb as a rock." Then another drop of truth sought daylight. "And when you came back to me from Italy, Patrick, how dumb had you been without me around for all those months?"

Patrick exhaled loudly.

"Not that dumb, really. I always meant to come back to you. There was one minor flirtation—"

"With a contessa?"

"A waitress. An aspiring opera singer, actually. It also ended before it began."

"Before it began, Patrick?"

"All right," he said, "almost as soon as it began. A little while later. Not more than a month."

"One month?"

"Well, October to December, maybe. Totally casual and meaningless."

Other people's honesty can be so annoying, except when it relieves you of your own guilt.

"So we're even?" I asked.

Even, yes, but not the same. We both knew it.

We had fulfilled our own prophesies: Cheaters cheat. A crusty layer of mistrust had kept us less than committed, and obviously open to temptations that neither of us really wanted. But here we were again, attempting to chip away at that crust with taps of honesty. We agreed to keep in touch until September, when I'd be in Milan. Then we'd see.

I did not tell Patrick that Franz was the one who called him. He could reasonably say that Franz had crossed a serious line, despite any good intentions. I might have said that Franz's meddling was excusable this one time. After all, everyone felt good about the result, even hopeful. At least this time Franz was helpful instead of trying to take over my life for himself.

In my optimistic and grateful mood, I wanted to be nice to Franz in return. We all deserved some normal, healthy fun. It was the Fourth of July, so I grabbed Fred and we went out to enjoy the day.

It was summer at its steamiest. I put on a light denim skirt with a sleeveless top. Then I shoveled my hair into an extra-large baseball cap and wore big dark glasses to avoid recognition. Fred and I could have gotten a good view of the fireworks from Brooklyn Heights, but we went into the city for a day of free concerts and outdoor festivities.

Manhattan had, as usual, gone overboard to prove that New York was the center of the Fourth of July universe. Historic sailing ships had arrived from around the world to parade through the harbor in tribute to the city's greatness. A knockout fireworks display—with the Statue of Liberty at the center—would depict the history of the United States, set to the music of great American rock stars.

Franz was dizzied by the sounds and smells, the texture and heat of so many people. He prickled at the nonchalant intimacy of random crowd contact—the brush of my arm against a stranger's sweaty back, the odor of someone's breath.

And there was the street scene. Performance stages were set up along the route from Greenwich Village to the river. Street musicians lit up the corners. Franz wanted to see everything, but that would have overwhelmed him. We concentrated instead on a few standouts—the guitarist who looked like an accountant but played like B.B. King, a college girl singing Puccini, four black kids crooning nearly perfect doo-wop.

By late afternoon, it looked like everyone in the city had migrated to lower Manhattan to get a look at the tall ships. As we neared the water, the crowd became so dense that independent movement was out of the question. The heat and humidity melted us into a vast bionic blob inching south. I removed my Yankees cap and fanned myself with the brim. Franz was hyperventilating and produced frightening sounds.

"Don't sing, Liza," Fred said. "You'll just make matters worse."

"It's not me, Freddie. Franz is on the verge of a panic attack and I don't know what to do."

"You look overheated," he said. "Maybe you and Franz are both overheated. Everyone feels crappy in this heat."

Fred gave me his water bottle, and I poured the contents down my back. We were carried by the crowd another ten yards.

"Liza, I feel fresh air!" Fred's neck was stretched high and he was sniffing loudly. Salt air. "Try to veer right," he said. "And don't sing anymore. People are looking."

Fifteen minutes later, the source of the fresh air was less than a block away. The crowd had bumped up against a chain-link fence enclosing prime waterfront property. The sandy lot was bare, probably cleared for new construction. A stretch of what might have been beach beckoned from the other side of the fence, perfect for a holiday party. But the PRIVATE PROPERTY sign and, more important, the four cops standing nearby encouraged the crowd to keep searching for a better view.

We must have been there at the right time, though. The cops were surely as miserable as the rest of the hot, frustrated crowd. They took a long look at the empty lot, in which there was not a single thing to destroy or deface. They conferred briefly and gave unverifiable nods. A minute later, the cops looked away as the first person scrambled up the fence and jumped over into fresh air and a priceless view. Soon five or six people at a time were crawling up and jumping over. Most New Yorkers have jumped fences in childhood. This seven-foot fence looked like fun to me.

The grip of a shoe toe in chain-link was a familiar childhood feeling. I pulled myself up and stopped at the top to show Franz the view. We sang with joy (seagulls sound better). Then I pulled one leg after the other and jumped over.

The world went black.

The hem of my skirt was caught on the top of the fence, and my upper body was wrapped like a mummy in denim. My legs flailed around searching for ground. Finally, I felt Fred reach up and rip my hem, dropping me in a pile on the sand. I pushed my skirt back in place and the first thing I saw was a Japanese tourist aiming a camera in my face. His T-shirt read: *DURBIN DOES SCHUBERT, Copley Symphony Hall, San Diego.*

Was für ein Tag! . . . What a day! When have I laughed so much?

CHAPTER SIX

NEW YORK POST
Tuesday, July 5

Moon over Manhattan
(photo of Liza Durbin—hanging by hem from chain-link fence,
upper torso covered by skirt, bottom half in bikini underwear)

Liza Durbin went over the top for the Fourth of July, showing her patriotic spirit by mooning lower Manhattan. Japanese tourist Akira Koziki, who snapped this photo, says Liza walked away unhurt but was cursing a blue streak—in German.

Jay Leno, The Tonight Show

You heard about the latest from our favorite classical piano babe? Liza Durbin was photographed at New York's fireworks celebration, hanging by her skirt from a fence, with her dress pulled up over her head. Gave us a great view of her nonmusical talent. Liza's publicist says it was a silly accident that could happen to anyone. Liza is planning to accidentally perform topless in a karaoke bar in Queens Saturday night.

∧∧∧

John D. Doyle called, concerned about my July Fourth mishap.

"What the hell is wrong with you, Liza? This is not the way to build credibility."

"Don't worry, John D., I wasn't badly hurt. Just my pride, mostly."

"Liza, you *have* seen the papers, haven't you?" John D. can be so earnest.

"Yes, we were just talking about it."

Danny was huddled in my kitchen with Fred, who was filling him in on every awful detail. Fred was worried about my reputation and my state of mind, yet he somehow summoned the courage to laugh like a hyena. Danny, too.

"I'm glad someone finds this funny." John D. had good hearing, even over the phone. "Liza, I fight this battle all the time. Musicians and marketing people who consider any publicity to be good."

"Don't worry. I already talked with Cassie about this." Who took it a lot better than John D., I might add. "She sent a press release and explained it was just an accident, that it could happen to anyone."

John D. let that slide.

"Liza, someone has to stand up for quality and standards, and that happens to be me. If you're a laughingstock, that makes it harder for people to believe in your new Schuberts. It makes it harder for me to believe. You need to authenticate them immediately."

"I'll have them in a few days," I said. "By the way, John D., just so you know, there might be some actual tape of my tush on the evening news."

He expletived me, harshly.

John D. was right, of course. The new music needed to be authenticated quickly. Some of it was already on paper, produced on the night that Franz took over. Newer pieces were not yet transcribed. Based on our history, the writing process itself scared me.

I asked Fred for help. I told him that Franz needed some time "out" for writing. There was about a day's worth of work to do, and all I needed was for Fred to stay with me. He could pull me back if things went too far. If he had to, he could plain scare the shit out of Franz.

I arranged my most powerful SHOO blasters around the piano. Family photos, an old crocheted pillow, Girl Scout badge, Shalimar, stinky sneakers, and a bag of M&M's (in case I got hungry).

Fred was anxious about his role as protector. Nobody had actually seen me in this totally submerged state before. Even I hadn't been able to see myself that way. Having an observer was a jarring necessity.

"Should I videotape you?" Fred asked, as we drank coffee in his living room.

"Tape me writing music? Freddie, are you kidding? Haven't I been taped enough for one week?"

"Liza, I'm serious. This could be important." He looked over my shoulder and out the window. "I've been thinking that what's happened to you, that it might be a miracle."

He ran a shaky hand through his dark curls.

"Hasn't that occurred to you, Liza, really? I mean, how else can you explain it?"

Somehow I preferred to think of Franz as supernatural, not directly related to God or religion. Spirits and poltergeists are simply from some other realm, if they even exist. In a supernatural realm, regular people like me might be worth tormenting. But what interest would God—*the* God—have in me? God had long ago shown partiality toward Schubert, but how did my name pop up?

"I know it's hard for you to even consider this possibility. Maybe we'll never know. I do know you're okay, though, Liza," he said gently. "I'm sure of that. I'm sure this is a good thing."

A good thing. That should be my mantra, I thought. A constant reminder that I'm not inhabited by Lizzie Borden or Richard Nixon. *This is a good thing.*

As for the videotape, the idea made me nervous.

"What would we do with a videotape, Fred? I'm not ready to tell the world about Franz and I certainly don't want a tape floating around."

"Well, I'm not going to show it to anyone, that's for sure." He seemed offended that I even mentioned it. "Look, we can lock it up safely—you keep the key. But it might be something you want for later. Scientists or theologians or musicians might want to study it. Who knows? A hundred years from now your great-great-grandchildren might want to see your miracle on tape. Besides, you might want to take a look at the tape yourself."

A scary thought. For all I knew, composing "under the influence" might involve drooling, nude dancing, and other visions not meant for human eyes—that's how little I remembered of the last time it happened. In the end, it was my vanity pitted against Fred's once-in-forever chance to catch a miracle on tape. He promised to take me for ice cream afterward, and I said yes.

It was less grueling this time—partly because of the time limit. We started at nine and Fred's job was to retrieve me at six, no matter what. Before we began, I threatened Franz with angry mental images. He winked at me. During the day, Fred broke through to my submerged state with an occasional pat on the shoulder or a handful of M&M's.

Afterward, I looked at the tape, just to get the general idea. I was startled by the elation I saw. Clearly, the torture of our previous writing adventure was not part of the composing process but was caused by my battle to end it. As I watched the tape, I was jealous of my own ecstasy. When had I felt that blissful on my own? Had I ever seen *any* adult that happy? Some vestigial impulse made me want to remove that smile, *his smile,* from my face and look the way I looked in other pictures— reasonably happy, reasonably content, a reasonable portrait of me. But I was also mesmerized.

What I saw was Franz's emotions on my face. This was a level of intimacy that shouldn't be possible. It contradicted everything we learn, often painfully, about relationships—that we are each alone in the end, and that no one can ever see with another person's eyes or heart. But I did.

Until then, I had assumed that Franz was a compassionate observer in my life, but maybe the transference went both ways. Franz's dreams could have been his way of drawing us even closer. They were seductive and addictive, an intimate exchange that erased a natural taboo. Franz's storytelling transferred feelings directly to me as well as knowledge. Though an inner voice warned me to protect my independence, I was entranced again that night by another vision from Franz's sleepy, time-free world:

"Mother wanted me to be a musician. Doesn't that mean something, Father?"

"I know what your mother wanted, Franz. I know what you want. But you can't expect to feed a family on music."

Exquisite sorrow in his father's voice, but Franz hears only "No."

"Salieri says I should continue."

"Of course he does, Franz. He believes you're taught by God Almighty. But Antonio Salieri will not pay your bills. We must be practical. You will train as a teacher, then you can always have a job in my school or in another."

This is not even the worst news of Franz's week. In his pocket he carries a terrible letter from Marta. After living with the Schuberts for nearly five years, Marta and Peter moved to another town when their mother married a widower with seven children. After that, Franz and the twins sent heartfelt letters to one another.

At thirteen, Franz became a student at the prestigious Stadtkonvict, where he studied music and made new friends, but he never forgot who his truly best friends were. He held their vow as sacred.

Franz reads Marta's letter one more time, on the off chance that the words have changed. But no, Peter has still eloped with a girl from a hated family. Seventeen and married. Marta asks if she and Franz should now marry, but Franz no longer wants the deal. It was all three or nothing to him. Marta will be glad about this, I think, but Franz will feel imprisoned by teacher's training without the sunshine of their secret betrothal.

His sorrow fills our bed.

~~~

We delivered our photocopied proofs of the new Schuberts to John D. at Sony Classical, who received them with great relief. They had the same look and feel as the previously accepted evidence, and we all felt confident that they could pass the same tests. John D. swore I would give him a coronary yet. He promised to be at my concert Saturday night on Long Island.

Sony marketing wasted no time distributing news releases and excerpts of the latest Schubert manuscripts. I was all over the newspapers and daily news shows. Even people who didn't like classical music talked about the newfound work. After all, if this old music could be discovered, why not Atlantis or the Lost Ark? People everywhere excavated their attics and cellars to find remnants of genius—preferably the kind that sells for a fortune at auction. Talk-show hosts theorized with guests about the anonymous source of the manuscript—a long-lost Schubert heir? A billionaire recluse who re-created nineteenth-century Vienna in her Hollywood home?

The excitement over the new manuscripts made most people forget that I had displayed my butt to all of Manhattan just a few days before. I remained controversial, but with greater dignity.

The concert on Long Island that Saturday was standing-room-only. My parents flew in with Aunt Frieda. Cassie and her gang were there, along with Greta, Fred, and Danny. There were Duelin' Durbins, John D. Doyle, and many others from my recent past. Only Mikki was missing. This seemed odd, since I'd sent her tickets in advance and left a message saying I hoped she could be there.

Naturally, the crowd was dying for something new. I tortured them with traditional repertoire, teased them about what I might do next.

"How many of you came to hear the classics tonight?"

Enthusiastic applause.

"And how many of you came hoping to hear something new?"

Bigger applause.

"And, honest, you can tell me—who came here hoping to see my underwear?"

The biggest applause of all. By the time I introduced Schubert's *Lost River Sonata,* the audience lost control. Their wild response was unbecoming to such a refined group, and I told them so. As I finally left the stage, some people threw flowers in appreciation. Some people threw underwear onstage, too. They appeared to be clean, so all I could do was laugh.

The reviews the next day were over the top. Several of us were staying at Cassie's, which was not far from the concert hall, and everyone was in high spirits for her dinner party Sunday evening. A good time to relax, catch up, and congratulate one another.

"Your hair looks like tumbleweed," Cassie announced. She didn't like the way I'd swept my hair up and away from my face. "Maybe we should shave it off and make you wear wigs."

I suggested we cut off her toes so she'd have normal-sized feet.

"Could you girls talk nicely to each other on this special occasion?" Mom's chastising tone hadn't changed in decades.

We were gathered for pre-dinner schmoozing in what Cassie called her *apéritif* room. Everyone but the kids had a wineglass or cocktail in hand. Brittany and Cameron were spitting cranberry juice at each other. John D. arrived with roses.

"Normally I would have sent these," he said, "but you must be receiving flowers every day. I wanted to give these to you personally."

John D. kissed my cheek, the old charmer. I went squishy inside (or maybe Franz did).

"John D., have you met my assistant, Danny Carson?" Danny was walking by in search of munchies. He stopped to shake hands.

"Pleasure to meet you, Danny. Must be exciting to be on the road with Liza."

"Best summer gig in the world," he said.

"Liza, I'm happy to see *lieder* with this latest batch of Schubert," John D. said. "Can't wait to hear it."

"Hey, I know the *lieder*," Danny piped in. "Liza and I do *lieder* together."

"Really, Danny? Are you a singer?" John D. wore the frown of a betrayed lover.

"Liza and I just goof around with it."

"Tell me, Liza, how good is this young man?" John D. said. "Shall we have a listen?"

John D. saw himself as my *lieder* guy, so he wanted to hate Danny.

"Danny has a wonderful voice. Nothing like yours, of course." He was relieved by that. He morphed into a puppy waiting for a treat. "Maybe I'll play later and you can sing, John D."

He wagged an invisible tail. As we sat down for dinner, John D. offered a toast.

"As some of you know, I lost my wife, Florence, several years ago," he said. "I thought about retiring after that, but what would I do then? I've been in this industry so long, it was mostly business to me, just something to do every day."

He turned his eyes on me.

"Then this one, with the wild hair and sexy dresses, shows up. No résumé, no training, a totally inexplicable gift. Even with all that talent, I didn't guess we'd get this far, this fast. I'll be honest, I've been pretty shocked by some of the antics we've all witnessed. And that thing with the underwear, well . . ." John D. gave a good-natured grimace. "But people seem to like Liza even more for it. In fact, everything seems to be more than we hoped for with Liza. And on top of everything, we've got *lieder* on the way, for which I am truly grateful. So, here's to you, Liza Durbin. Thank you for surprising me again."

After dessert we gathered around the Steinway. I played "Heart & Soul" with Cameron, *Für Elise* with Brittany. Then Danny, John D., and I made beautiful *lieder* together, late into the night.

I went to sleep on a cushion of love and optimism.

〰

VIDEOTAPE? . . . I didn't know, are . . . UNFORGIVABLE . . . Where did . . . Why can't she . . . but Liza . . . Who's responsible . . . What kind of video . . . ? . . . OUTRAGEOUS . . .

Raised voices crashed through my sleep the next morning. Cassie, Fred, John D., and possibly others were arguing in the kitchen. I grabbed a robe and ran toward the storm.

"*There* you are, Liza," John D. thundered. "What the hell do you know about a videotape? Another one of your little surprises?"

My head spun to Fred.

"Fred, you *promised*."

"Liza, you think that I . . . ? You actually believe I'd do that?"

"What's all this about, John D.?"

He slapped a newspaper on the breakfast table. We all circled around to read the morning news.

CHAPTER SEVEN

THE TOWN CRIER—AMERICA'S LOCAL NEWSPAPER
July 11

Music Phenom Channeled by Dead Composer
"Franz Schubert Is Living in My Body!" Cries Liza Durbin

For months, The Town Crier has brought you stories about Liza Durbin, the music sensation who seemingly came out of nowhere. Where was this piano wizard keeping herself all these years? And how does she come up with all these "brand-new pieces" by the late Franz Schubert?

This mystery, which stumped the classical music experts, is finally explained by channeler Patty Flanders in an exclusive Town Crier interview. On March 11, Liza Durbin, along with psychologist Mikki Kloster, went to Flanders's retreat in Clupperville, New Jersey, for a clandestine meeting. All was revealed at their fateful meeting.

"Nobody even heard of Liza Durbin back then," Flanders says. "You

can imagine my surprise when I heard she was channeled by Franz Schubert! I was thrilled for her and assumed she would be, too."

But four months passed and Flanders didn't hear another word from
Liza Durbin. What's more, Durbin became famous and never mentioned
the channeling to anyone.

"She had a duty to disclose the source of her gift," Flanders says.
"Luckily, I videotape all my encounters for scientific purposes. Liza's
exact words were, 'Franz Schubert is living in my body.' I have that in her
own writing and she said it on tape, too."

A Secret Too Long

Flanders can't explain why Liza Durbin withheld the truth so long. She
says she brought her story to The Town Crier because Schubert deserves
better.

"People like Liza and myself are merely the recipients of our entities'
gifts," Flanders says. "I'm going public about Liza because it's wrong for
anyone to take credit for their entity's power. Liza should be proud to tell
the truth, not steal the glory for herself."

Flanders says she's been channeled for the last eight years by Zazer, a
2,000-year-old entity who, in the form of a miniature dachshund, be-
friended a famous Bible figure. She's written several books on channeling
and is considered an expert in the field. The MegaNetwork's Entertaining
News Tonight has bought the rights to the videotape for an undisclosed
sum. (Durbin, who is a lawyer herself, signed a full release the day of the
taping.) You can see the tape for yourself on EN Tonight tomorrow, but you
read it here first in The Town Crier!

~~~

Like millions of people, John D. had heard the story on the news that
morning. He ran out and bought *The Town Crier* to torture himself—and
me—with the full pictorial spread. In one picture I was talking with Patty
Flanders and wearing a twisted expression that had to be a reaction to the
puppy-shit stench. In another shot, Mikki and I were being chased by
miniature dachshunds, which was pretty hilarious—but John D. didn't
see it that way. And he wasn't the only one taking it badly.

Greta learned about the tape and hopped a train, then a taxi, to

Cassie's. She showed up in a tizzy not long after John D. My parents and Aunt Frieda added to the chaos. There were lots of strong feelings (like Franz screaming in my ear), but none greater than John D.'s fury.

"You *admit* this, Liza? You're telling me you *did* this insane thing?"

"I did, John D., but I have a good reason."

"And what the hell could that possibly be?"

"It happens to be true." Confession felt liberating and, as usual, terrifying. "Not that I'm channeled, of course. But something happened to me, John D. It happened over Christmas. Franz Schubert really did land in my body, and he's been here ever since."

Of all the people in the room, only John D. had never heard the truth. Despite his appalled reaction, the truth felt right. After all, wasn't this always the plan? Start a career, build a reputation, and, when the time is right, tell everyone about Franz. I hadn't picked the time— maybe I had let the right time pass—and the choice was taken out of my hands.

"What are you saying, Liza?" John D. said. "People will think you're insane. *I* think you're insane."

"Some people will think that, I'm sure. But will anyone think the music is bad?" I said. "Shouldn't we all put our heads together and come up with a plan?"

"We'll need a news conference." Cassie was already in PR mode. "A chance to show that you're sane and coherent, before they air the *Entertaining News* segment. Then we'll take you out of the public eye for a few days, watch the reaction, and figure out our strategy."

"Excuse me, Cassie." John D.'s cold tone sliced through her calculations. "You're talking like this little crisis might just disappear. This is not about underwear or pulling new Schuberts out of the air." Then, turning to me: "Do you actually think I'd risk Sony Classical's reputation on you?"

This was my first glimpse of John D. Doyle at full power.

"I'm sorry you feel this way, really," I said. "I can't change what's true, and I don't know how to prove it to you."

Nor could I deny John D.'s perfectly normal response. It's one thing to be accepted by family and close friends who know me and my history, but what could I expect from others? If this were happening to somebody else, I would be making jokes myself.

"Liza, I'm sure there are people at Sony who'll think this is just fine, as long as it boosts your CD sales. I'm not one of them." Then he relented, but just a hair. "Liza, everything was going so right. If I'd known you were in trouble, that you were so—"

John D. left his thought unfinished, though any number of unpleasant words would have worked. Greta placed herself beside John D., close enough to join hands, if they wanted.

"I have a concert Thursday night," I said. "Should I cancel?"

Lots of headshaking and murmuring. Except for Mom: "Cancel, what, are you nuts? You'll be bigger than ever."

Mother knew best.

The news was too much for some people—their minds couldn't operate in such a strange gear. But millions of people loved it.

Cassie called a news conference immediately. She got me on TV before *EN Tonight* could show the tape that made me look insane. Calmly, coherently, I told my story. I answered questions with complete honesty: No, I wouldn't call it channeling. Inhabitation is what we'd been calling it, though I couldn't explain the difference. Yes, Franz was with me all the time, but he didn't speak through my voice—only through music. No, I didn't know how it happened. Did I know Chase Barnes and other music scholars were calling me a fraud? Of course. I expected that to happen. People were free to draw their own conclusions.

What most people drew was hope.

They took heart knowing that a nobody like me could acquire a guy like Schubert. They loved the concept of waking up different, better than before, with no effort whatsoever. Maybe it could happen to them. Anyway, they could have fun watching me. And who knows—maybe I'd have a meltdown in public or Schubert might jump out of my body and parade around onstage like the living dead. That would be cool, too.

They lined up to see me in concert after that. I got fan mail and weird mail and e-mails from Tibet. Little girls formed fan clubs. Some misguided women even tried to copy my hair.

Reporters had an easy story, always an update to close the show with. Someone located my old piano teacher, Clara Wolf, retired and living in

Jericho, Long Island. It was a hoot to see her on TV after twenty years. She'd grown shorter and grayer but her voice was the same.

"Of course I remember Liza Durbin. A lovely child." She smiled briefly, presumably at me. "She played nicely. But gifted? Only her mother said that."

"So you believe the Schubert story?" asked the perky reporter, smirking at the camera.

"Trust me, dear," Clara Wolf said, "if you'd ever heard Liza play, you'd believe it, too."

The public quickly became fascinated with all things Durbin. Cassie called me one morning to tell me to turn on the TV. There were our parents on *Gordy & Jill Talk!*, spouting about my glories.

"Our Liza was always special," my father said. "But becoming inhabited by Franz Schubert, well, that changed everything."

"Well, it's not like Schubert does it all," Mom added. "Where would he be without Liza?"

"Mrs. Durbin, are you saying that your daughter is the talented one in this partnership?" Jill's voice was sugared irony.

"What I'm saying, Jilly, is that there's a reason Schubert picked Liza." Gordy and Jill nodded encouragement. "There are billions of people in the world. Why her? Think about it."

"Well, we want to thank the Durbins for this fascinating discussion," Gordy said. "Stay with us, folks, because after this break we're going to interview a woman who set up a website from hell. That's *the* hell, ladies and gentlemen. No joke. I gotta see this one, and so do you."

<div align="center">~~~</div>

In this dream, Franz is at Marta's country house, which overlooks a perfectly round lake. He's been working on a symphony there. Old friends have gathered for the weekend. A Schubertiad is planned for the evening, with music by Franz and others. It's springtime at its best, the first day when warm definitively defeats cold. The party has just moved into Marta's well-appointed parlor for cognac and late-afternoon snacks.

Franz is delighted to be among good friends. Anselm Hüttenbrenner is telling a bawdy story to Marta's husband. Franz von Schober shows a water-

*color he made that morning. Johann Vogl, the opera singer, warms up his
voice.*

*A door opens and everyone's attention pivots toward Marta's little girl,
Brita, as she runs into the room ostentatiously crying. She was petting a neighbor's horse and it sneezed on her head. In any historical period, it would be hard
to keep a straight face in the presence of that much horse snot. Brita is distressed
by the hilarity that her misery causes. She runs to her mother for comfort.*

*Franz is the first to stop laughing. He's studying Brita's profile. Who does she
look like?*

*He never sees Brita without remembering a day in this same country house,
not long before Marta's marriage. Her fiancé was a solid sort, she said, who
never laughed at her jokes. He was considered a good match, though.*

*"I will always remember you and me," she said that day, "and Peter, of
course. Our funny game, the secret engagement."*

*Franz remembers how Marta couldn't smile at the memory. Her eyes glis-
tened evenly, without tears. She calmly reached for his hand.*

"Marta, we mustn't."

"Why not? It ends today, either way."

*She fell on Franz with the clumsy hunger of a novice. He thinks he said no,
but maybe he imagined that. He might have imagined the whole thing, except
that every time he sees Brita, he recalls Marta's breath against his neck. And he
studies the little girl's profile.*

*Brita continues crying over the horse incident. Franz Schober and Johann offer
to slay the villainous steed who offended their princess. They leave just long
enough for another swig of cognac, then return with good news.*

*"Dear Brita, the horse has apologized most deeply," Schober reports. "He is
mortified by his bad conduct and pledges to honor you from this day forward.
What shall we do?"*

*Princess Brita is inclined toward mercy, and the horse lives on. Everybody
is happy. Nobody suspects how Franz suffers.*

*Surely the aches and weariness will go away, he thinks. I'm only twenty-six,
strong and healthy. This will pass and I will be fine.*

*When Brita asks Uncle Franz to carry her upstairs, he wonders if he has the
strength. (You can, I whisper. You have years to go, you can do this.) He carries Brita to her frilly bedroom and rests awhile there, admiring her profile.*

Welch merkwürdiges Spiel dies ist! . . . What a strange game this is! She dreams of my life now. My memories become hers, she sees through my eyes. We might slide past each other on our journeys one night and never find our ways back.

Such an unholy thought, I am ashamed to pray for it.

Once I became aware of Franz's pain, it permeated my thoughts, even as real life got easier in many ways. The world knew about Franz, so we could play whatever he wanted in concert. We had no more lies to keep track of, and enjoyed the freedom. I just couldn't forget his pain.

With full understanding of its futility, I started exercising on Franz's behalf. Compulsively perhaps. When I wasn't playing piano, I ran or did push-ups. Making us stronger, *running and push-ups*. Doing *something*.

Fred noticed the change, and so did Danny. Cassie asked if I was doing something different, and complimented my arms. Interesting that they re-marked on these outward changes without noting the deeper one, the one that haunted me.

With all the attention Franz and I got, not a single person—no friend or relation—remarked on the gradual fading away of the original Liza. My first life, the one I'd created with my own experiences, tastes, and neu-roses, slipped quietly into retreat. Franz was the benevolent body snatcher, and I was the lucky donor.

As our popularity grew, I looked for ways to be a real participant, to justify my existence in our pairing. I needed to add something distinctive, to provide something of greater value than a warm body for Franz's use. I worked at polishing our performances, making my presentation more interesting, at making us proud. Franz and I became a better team, more willing to help each other, to learn and to take chances.

At a late-July concert at Tanglewood in Massachusetts, Franz felt compelled to give the receptive audience a surprise encore of *lieder*. Without hesitation, I called Danny onstage. He was not exactly dressed for the occasion, but completely ready to sing. We took the chance.

His was not the voice people expected with this music, but Danny won them over. He had confidence, training, and, of course, he'd been singing with Franz for months.

The piece we performed was a new one, composed by Franz to suit Danny's young voice. The crowd responded with Super Bowl cheering. The most traditional music lovers probably weren't in the crowd that night, but our expanded, open-minded audience was wild for updated *lieder*.

Danny instantly made the evening news. He was another nontraditional twist in our saga. Plus, he was the kind of good-looking, appealing kid that magazines and TV love to shine lights on. He sang at all the remaining concerts that summer and the media featured him as a new teen heartthrob.

Celebrity took Danny completely by surprise, and he thought it was a total kick. Franz beamed like a proud parent. Later, Danny would likely find that fame had its price. I had already learned to hate its intrusive aspects. I warned Danny that the aggressive behavior of fans and tabloids could be downright spooky. He simply reminded me that there are worse things than being adored and sought after, and he was right.

Late in the summer I had a two-week break and decided to spend it at home in Brooklyn, alone in my apartment again. I read books, listened to music, watched old movies, ran a lot, and did many push-ups *(one for me, one for Franz, another for me, another for Franz . . .)*. The solitude also gave me plenty of chances to visit Franz in dreams.

Franz was in the hospital a few times in his last years of life. I couldn't claim that my exercise mania helped him, but I refused to assume it did not. He needed something from me.

Franz feels a little better today, strong enough to stroll through Vienna on a sunny day. He regrets that he never married. It's hard to be sick alone, but it's too late to choose a mate.

He had dabbled in love a few times, but not with his full heart. Franz cared briefly for a beauty named Thérèse, but she married someone else. There were others, too, whom he'd rather not think about. None of them equaled the love he expected to share with Marta and Peter. A juvenile expectation, yes, but juvenile expectations are famously resilient.

As Franz walks through the park in Vienna, he spots someone he thinks he recognizes, at least from behind. The man wears a light coat, and his hat rests on a mass of bushy red hair. His stride and the slope of his shoulders are distinctive, familiar, even after all these years. Even though people assume he is dead.

He must have been killed when he ran away to elope. How else could he fail to contact his family, especially his twin? Peter and his bride ran off, naïve and defenseless, to an unknown and therefore dangerous place where—Marta felt sure—Peter must have died. But at this moment, Franz is not so sure.

The man is less than thirty yards from Franz, walking away from him at a brisk pace. Franz last saw Peter at age seventeen, more than a dozen years ago, so it's hard to be certain. This may be Franz's only chance to know. He starts to run toward the man. Pain shoots up his weakened legs, each breath is a knife wound. Still, he tries to reach the man.

"Peter! Peter, is that you?"

The man keeps walking. He doesn't hear Franz weakly calling after him.

"Peter, please turn around."

The man stops to check his watch but does not turn around. He walks on.

"Is it you? Is that you, Danny?" I woke up sweating and shaky.

"Yes, Liza, it's me." Danny was crouching next to me, where I'd fallen asleep on the couch. He had a hand on my shoulder, either to wake me or to calm me. "It's me. Who were you expecting?"

"Was I expecting you?"

"You asked me to stop by, remember? It's almost five. We were gonna go running together before dinner. I think you were having another bad dream."

Right, another dream. Danny stood there in standard running gear. Not dreamlike or mysterious. Just a solid, amazing teenage boy who had found me, as usual, exactly when I needed him.

"Danny, why do you think you and I are here together?"

"Huh?"

I swung my feet around and sat up on the couch to face him. He was understandably confused.

"I mean, you're not very close with your mother, are you? And you have friends your own age, but you still hang out with me. Why?"

Danny shifted on his feet uncomfortably. "Are you mad about something?"

"No, not at all," I said. "You haven't done anything wrong."

"Fine then. Let's forget the run, though. Franz driving you nuts again? Hey, let's order a pizza."

I looked into Danny's direct blue eyes and gave up on the conversation. He was my loyal pal, cohort in music, and all-round protector. He didn't question any of it. Why should I?

We watched a classic movie with our pizza (Franz had developed a thing for Myrna Loy). I was determined not to think about Franz's life, and to enjoy my real life instead. I got a reminder of real life when the phone rang halfway through Myrna's romantic scene with William Powell. The call was one I had been expecting and dreading, a luncheon invitation from a flesh-and-blood nightmare.

~~~

I arrived early for lunch the next day at Mrs. Z's Café on Lexington Avenue. It was chic and dimly lit, popular with celebrities. This would be my first meeting with Mikki Kloster since she conspired with Patty Flanders to sell me to the tabloids.

Mikki was running late, which gave me time to marinate in my anger toward her. As soon as I saw the *Town Crier* article all those weeks earlier, I knew that Mikki and Patty Flanders had cashed in on me. I called Mikki and raged at her for being a traitorous, manipulative monster who was too cowardly to come to my Long Island concert (even though I sent her tickets!) because she would have had to face me the next morning when *The Town Crier* came out—when Mikki's demon nature would be revealed to everyone, including the sainted genius Franz Schubert. Or something like that. You can imagine how mad I was.

I was enjoying my simmer when Mikki plunked herself in the chair across from me. Cheerful and chipper, she was.

"Sorry I'm late, Liza. Are you okay? You look stressed."

Mikki had tinted her salt-and-pepper hair with a bit of cinnamon. She looked trimmer, too.

"We have some things to talk about," I said.

"Don't we, though?" Mikki sparkled at me. She wore smart reading glasses that matched her new hair. Her necklace was a rich concoction of silver and jade. "So much has happened, Liza. And I'm sure you'll agree it's only getting better."

"*Better,* Mikki? That's an interesting way to look at it."

She rested her menu and looked at me, hands on her thighs, elbows crooked out like wings.

"Are you still mad at me, Liza?" Her famously soothing voice had a bit of tease in it. "C'mon, are you actually saying things aren't better than before?"

I got busy shredding a dinner roll and not looking at Mikki.

"You were a mess of self-doubt and fears when you came to me. You were living with this huge secret, a monumental lie. Keeping Franz a secret was an unbearable burden for you, Liza. You always meant to go public, but you never got around to it."

"So you went ahead and did it for me."

My poor dinner roll was disintegrating badly.

"I didn't do it, Liza. Patty Flanders did, and she believed it was the right thing to do."

"You planned it all with her."

"Who says so? Not me and not Patty."

"I'm not some idiot reporter, Mikki. I *know* you told her to tape me."

"Patty tapes lots of people. You signed the release, after all, and you *are* a lawyer. Channelers aren't bound to confidentiality like doctors or attorneys. Anyway, it's worked out well for everyone. The world loves Franz Schubert again, and you're a star. It's time to be happy, Liza."

"I'm not unhappy with everything," I said. "Mostly it's *you,* Mikki."

Mikki was wearing more makeup than usual. Also, her manicure was perfect.

"I see you're ready for your book tour, aren't you, Mikki?"

"Damn! I wanted to surprise you. Who told you?"

I explained that her publicist had called asking me for kind words to use on the book cover. Mikki reached into her large purse and pulled out a slim, hardcover copy of *Inhabitism—Attract the Spirit That's Right for You!* She pushed it across the table to me with absurd pride.

"An early copy for you. Don't worry, you're never mentioned by name," Mikki purred. "Professional ethics and all. It's just anonymous case studies and advice."

"Case studies, Mikki? Plural? I *am* your case study. I'm pretty sure people will figure that out."

"How can you say you're my only case?" A cagey smile, tilt of the head. "You can't know that."

My dead dinner roll was mashed back into a doughy lump, so I started shredding it again.

"You're a phony, Mikki. A deceitful, self-serving phony."

"Whoa, Liza. Before you call anyone else a phony, I'd ask you to look at your own behavior. How long were you willing to pass yourself off as something you weren't? You might still be acting like you were the musical genius if someone hadn't forced your hand."

"The difference is, I wasn't betraying anyone."

"No? What about Schubert?" she said. "What about the truth?"

I threw a handful of dinner roll crumbs in her face. She made a show of wiping her face.

"That was childish, Liza. I'm concerned about your hostility."

"Mikki, just tell me one thing. Why did you do it? Why did you use me this way?"

She folded her hands primly on the table, but her foot thumped rhythmically on the floor.

"I helped you, Liza, and you can't deny that. It's what I'm supposed to do. Being a therapist is draining. Exhausting, really. And the rewards aren't all that great, monetarily, I mean."

She sat back and struck a new pose to indicate we were moving to a new conversation.

"Did I tell you I'm giving up my practice? I've been needing a change. I'll be promoting my book, of course, and I've got a contract to start my next one. I'm looking into many opportunities."

"Mikki, how much money did you get for your book, the one everyone will guess is about me?"

Contentment graced her face.

"Let's order, shall we?" she said. "My treat."

———

Ich habe diese Frau nie gemocht . . . I never liked that woman. She is cold and has that irritating voice.

Mikki was not altogether wrong in suggesting I was a fraud, and my life may indeed have been better in some ways, but not because of her treachery. For unknown reasons, I had received stupendous gifts in the form of music, genius, and people like Danny and John D. The price for all this, of course, had been high. You'd think that after my "fraud" was exposed, the debt might be forgiven, but the hidden costs were mounting.

My excursions into Franz's world were getting trickier. I felt drawn to them, but wary of their power. What would happen to a person whose dreams grew stronger than life? Had it happened to Franz—is that how he found me? I wanted to sleep, to check in on Franz often. But I needed to stay in my own life, where *real* events were occurring and I was part of things.

I intended not to tell anybody about this. Someone might give me good advice that I wouldn't like to hear. Patrick was the one who finally drew out my secret.

We were talking once a week or so, thanks to Franz's first bold phone call. Patrick and I would see each other again soon in Milan, and we were building toward that. One night Patrick said I sounded tense and distracted. He was right, so I took a chance.

"I'm worried about Franz," I said. "He's sick."

"Sick, like he's leaving you?" Patrick did not sound sad about this.

"Not now. Then."

I tried to explain, but it was probably a mistake to refer to these episodes as dreams. Patrick, like most people, had had dreams of his own that felt intensely real. Naturally, he was skeptical about mine.

I played with this thought, wondering how I could prove what was happening. Could I grab a book or a candlestick and wake up with a memento in hand? Franz was able to move my body, so I could try it in reverse. On the other hand, it might be more proof than I could bear. While there was a sliver of uncertainty, I could ignore the warning lights along this road.

"Liza, haven't you learned yet how dangerous Franz can be?" Patrick said. "You've got to get out of that apartment and live in this century. How much are you supposed to give up for this guy?"

"Cassie wants me at her house for a few days. I don't want to go."

"Go."

"She wants me to meet with my agent and stuff. It sounds horrible."

"GO!"

I rented a red Mustang convertible, which was great fun, although my hair was reduced to postwar rubble before we reached the expressway. Danny came with me, at Cassie's request. He had become an integral part of our marketable package.

On the winding driveway to Cassie's home, the trees on either side were in their assigned places, arching their branches into a perfect canopy. But while Cassie's house was its usual immaculate self on the outside, something was different inside. Her pristine domain had sprung to life with the soft commotion of people at work.

I said hi to Fred, who was there with his graphic artist, Jake, a twenty-something charmer of near-sumo-wrestler build. They had made themselves cozy at the dining-room table, with laptops, photographs, and colorful papers in loose piles. Brittany and Cameron quickly pulled me away to their playroom, where they were assembling the latest of many official Liza Durbin scrapbooks—this one with Danny on the cover. I excused myself to find a cold drink and found the fridge covered with me-related newspaper clippings held in place with cheap refrigerator magnets. *(Magnets on Cassie's zillion-dollar fridge?)* A grease board with scribbled notes sat on an easel between two sofas in the living room. *(Grease boards in Cassie's living room?)* My agent, Jesse Edelstein, was talking on the phone in another room.

Somebody had hung a Yankee cap on the Remington.

"Cassie, what's going on?" I pulled her aside for privacy. "I hardly recognize the place."

She had to think about what I meant. From the other room, I heard Jesse hang up the phone and talk to someone whose voice I didn't recognize.

"We're working, that's all," she said. "You never believed I could pull this off, did you? Well, you're a huge celebrity now, and getting bigger. I can't wait to fill you in on all the ideas and endorsements and licensing possibilities. You won't believe it."

She was right about that. I'd been wrapped up in music and Franz for months. This behind-the-scenes procession had been barreling along without me.

"This seems a bit much, Cass. And why is everyone here, in the middle of your house? Don't they have offices of their own somewhere?"

"Sure, but we all need to meet together sometimes. For some reason people like to come here." *Could it be the pool, the grounds, the cook, the maid?* "I don't mind having them here. There's so much work to do, and we have fun together, like a team. I think I might give away the Navajo loom and make a real office out of that room."

I marveled at all the changes. This sloppy, convivial energy was exactly what had been missing from my sister's showcase home.

"Is Barry around?" I ventured.

"Overworking at the office, as usual. Should be home for dinner," she said. "Let's get Danny. We can all meet in the living room and see where things stand."

We arranged ourselves in a semicircle facing the grease board. Jesse introduced Danny and me to his assistant, Frenchie. She was a late-twenties, ripe-banana blonde, as taut-looking as Jesse was soft. Her lightly accented voice had the deep chafe of a devoted smoker.

"I'm not sure where Myles is," Cassie said, "but let's start. He's pretty much up to speed anyway."

"Myles *Broadbent?*" I said. "The weasel is coming here, too?"

"Actually, I'm already here," Myles said, walking into the room. "I was just in the bathroom. Good to see you, Liza."

"Right, Myles, a pleasure," I said. "Sorry about that."

"It's okay, you were a weasel, too."

Jesse rose to point at the grease board and stun us with flip charts. Merchandising rights, recording contracts, movie-of-the-week scripts, incorporation, logo, promotions, and too much more. Fred and Jake showed us spiffy Web designs and artwork for other promotions.

"Why didn't I know you were working on all this, Cassie?" I asked.

"I tried to tell you. You're never interested. Besides, we've got experts for this."

Jesse was an experienced agent, and initially he had wanted a dignified classical image for me. Apparently he was flexible, though, and saw my broader potential. Myles Broadbent had been working closely with entertainment lawyers on my behalf, and saw this as his burgeoning specialty. Cassie, Fred, and Jake were taking care of image and publicity. I had people to call other people's people.

"Everyone wants your story, Liza," Cassie assured me.

I'd heard enough. I asked to see any strategies they had in writing. I already knew I didn't want to read such things, but it seemed like the responsible request to make. Their long-term plans included Danny, which was good. Counting on Franz for anything in the future was iffy at best. Had these rational people forgotten the surreal nature of my situation?

I excused myself and left Danny in their expert hands. They were plotting his future and I wished them luck.

Not everyone stayed for dinner, thank goodness. It was just Cassie and the kids, Danny, Fred, and me. Everyone had the good sense to steer clear of work talk. I felt Franz relax along with the rest of us—he was really pretty social. Barry came home as we finished dessert.

"*Bonsoir, chéri,* about time you got home. It's after eight." Cassie did not get up to kiss her husband. "How many late meetings can a person have in a week?"

Barry tried to look patient but he looked pissed.

"I told you this morning that I had to go to Philly for the day."

His voice was tight but he smiled gamely. Cameron and Brittany supplied his welcome hugs.

"You're not working tomorrow, right?" Cassie said. "Saturday. You said you'd be home."

"I may have to make some calls from here, but I promise I won't go anywhere."

With that, Barry earned his honey-I'm-home kiss from Cassie. I got the next hug.

"It's great to see you, Liza. It's been way too long."

As everyone else left the dinner table, Barry pulled up a chair and sat beside me. In a low voice, he said, "How come you don't wear the hand of Fatima necklace I gave you? I thought you'd wear it at Carnegie Hall."

You mean that piece of crap you also gave to your secretaries for Christmas, you cheapskate?

"Wow, Barry, I'm surprised you even remember that detail."

"Of course, I remember everything," he said. "I was hoping we'd have a chance to talk while you're here."

"Sure, we'll talk," I said. "Why wouldn't we talk?"

He gazed at me strangely, so I got up from the table and offered Cameron a piano lesson.

Franz didn't bother me with dreams that night. Maybe I was too preoccupied with my own thoughts. I didn't even go running in the morning (though I did twice as many push-ups, just because). I attempted to concentrate on my own life, which was quite enough.

The new ritual at Cassie's was to start the day by checking the morning papers, online news services, and TV shows for mention of me or Franz or Danny. They kept track of everything.

I had not seen most of it. The news was filled with bizarre tidbits:

- Neurotic parents around the world were scooping up Mikki Kloster's idiot book to learn "how to attract the right inhabitee" for their extraordinary children. Mikki was often referred to as "therapist to the stars—living and dead."

- Professor Ludwig Manheim of Frankfurt, Germany, announced that he'd been my "secret piano teacher" in the Bronx for years, and the whole Schubert thing was a hoax. He showed an old photo of himself with a young girl at the piano. She looked just like me, except for the silky blond hair, blue eyes, and different face.

- Church groups in Arkansas fought fiercely about me. One side thought I was the incarnation of holiness. Another wanted me burned at the stake as a you-know-what.

- Herbert J. Schubert of Milwaukee claimed to be the unacknowledged descendant of Franz and wanted a percentage of the action.

- Musicologists analyzed my work—most were impressed. Chase Barnes led a tiny crusade against me and my "misguided minions."

- Mothers Against Something-or-Other wanted to know more about me and the teenage boy.

- MTV veejay Andrea Sweet: *Calling Jimi, Janis, Kurt, Tupac! You out there, dudes? Invade me!*

New Orleans sweltered toward the end of August. Giant magnolia leaves dripped sweat and everyone's clothing turned two shades darker. My hair soared to new depths. Danny panted in muggy despair, and Franz took a long, long siesta. Only John D. Doyle seemed untouched by the heat.

Danny and I were in New Orleans on the last leg of the summer tour. John D. just happened to be in town, too, and I was glad for the chance to spend time together.

The mercantile majority at Sony Classical was thrilled with my CD sales, but John D. was still having a hard time with my image. I felt like I had disappointed him more than once, and wanted to show him that I was serious, too. As it turned out, John D. wasn't all that stodgy himself.

"Don't you love this city?" He was on his second bowl of jambalaya at the Royal Café. "Liza, you're not drinking your mint julep."

"Mint juleps sound better than they taste, especially with dinner. I'm switching to wine."

"Waiter, bring the young lady a Hurricane, please." John D. grinned at me. "You'll probably hate that, too, but you must try the local treats."

"I'll try a Hurricane," Danny volunteered.

John D. snorted at him, but good-naturedly. He was in the finest of moods, reporting on the music he'd heard around town and who was playing at what clubs. Everything about John D. seemed transformed here, like he'd stepped through the looking glass. He was wearing actual blue jeans and a garish Hawaiian shirt. Danny finally asked John D. what the hell had come over him.

It was New Orleans. John D. said he first visited in his junior year at Harvard. His roommate grew up in the Garden District and flew home for every holiday because he missed the music, the food, and his eccentric Southern family. He talked it up so much that John D. (of the *Newport* Doyles) finally traveled south of the Mason-Dixon line to see what all the fuss was about. He never got over it.

John D. heard masters of jazz, blues, and zydeco, magicians who made the moon glow brighter. He prowled the bars with his buddy, sucked the brains out of crawfish, threw up on a cop's shoes, and saw naked breasts on Bourbon Street balconies. Over the years, John D. returned to New Orleans many times for Jazz Fest, Mardi Gras, wild parties in the bayou, and for no reason at all.

"So why do you spend all your time with classical music?" Danny asked. "Why not produce the stuff you love?"

"I love classical music," John D. said. "I studied music, you know. I wanted to be a musicologist, but my family expected me to join the business world. Family obligations were everything then. And I didn't give up music. Classical was right for me, and it turned out to be right for me in business." A sly smile turned his face young again. "This music, this life in New Orleans, it's a private joy. I'd hate to think of it as business."

"I like its effect on you," I said.

He and Danny had sung together at rehearsal earlier. John D. sounded great, and I told him so.

"Our voices aren't bad together," John D. agreed, "and I like the new *lieder.*"

"Yeah, Franz and I worked some things out together," Danny said.

John D. shuddered slightly, as always, at the mention of Franz. He still found it hard to accept him as a presence at our table. "Yes, Danny, I assumed that the English translation came from you. I think it was the 'Oh, baby' part that clued me in."

"Liza said it was stupid," Danny said.

"I think we'll dispense with the 'Oh, baby' in any actual recordings, okay?"

We finished our meal with bread pudding in whiskey sauce, then set off into the night. Danny was dying to see Bourbon Street (*naked breasts on the balconies!*) so we cruised the blocks, bathed in the music streaming from doorways. Life-force rhythm shimmied through the gumbo of tourists, cigarette smoke, booze, and happy sweat. Franz swelled inside me, absorbing every sensation.

Everything that was touched by music—the gorgeous and the grotesque—was drawn into the grander experience. I looked at Danny and John D. with pity. They were thrilled to hear and see it—but their senses were limited, as mine had been before Franz. I pitied the mere mortals.

Danny's one complaint was that he couldn't go in the bars. He wanted to get close enough to the music to blow a good eardrum or two. John D. had the solution.

"Let's go bowling," he said.

Danny was appalled. "Have you gone, like, totally senile?"

John D. did not care for the characterization. "Believe me, kid, you won't be disappointed."

The Mid-City Lanes Rock 'n' Bowl is a New Orleans classic, and it's just what it sounds like. Bring the family for a wholesome night of bowling as you stuff your face with barbecue, then dance until your feet burn up. The sounds of pins falling and kids shouting went well with the music. The Cajun fiddle and bouncing rhythm crept into the central nervous system of the crowd. A thousand people tapped one toe. Old ladies danced with young boys, men in love glowed like moonbeams, and one bald tycoon in faded jeans twirled me until I fell down laughing.

The Midnight Crawlers played until eleven, then Maggie Sunshine and Her Bayou Bo Bos took the stage. The sound shifted from zydeco to blues, and someone played guitar like God's favorite demon. The crowd drifted toward the stage for a closer look. The band included three men of unkempt persuasion and a scrawny young woman on a cherry-red electric guitar.

She had jack-o'-lantern eyes.

This was no novelty gag. Franz was on high alert, sniffing something familiar. Part of me wanted to run but we couldn't resist her. When the set ended, I followed the band to a rear door. I was vaguely aware of Danny and John D. right behind me.

Maggie Sunshine was the first to leave the main room through the rear door. I grabbed the last band member as he was about to walk out.

"I need to talk to Maggie Sunshine, please. Can I come back there for a few minutes?"

The bearded man sized me up by sticking his nose in my face, then directing his head up and down several times. His body seemed constructed of coiled wire. He wore black jeans and a plaid shirt with pearly buttons. His breath smelled swampy.

"Well, will you look at this? I know you—you're the gal from TV," he said.

"Please, I just want to talk with Maggie."

"Ha! Nobody ever wanted to talk to Maggie before!" The man drew back his mouth in what I assumed was a smile. His teeth sprouted in random directions. "All that's changed. She got talent and gonna be a star. We're going to the top."

"*We?* Are you related?"

"She's my niece. I'm Paulie Sunshine. She's been livin' with me since her mother passed," he said. "She ain't too friendly these days, but I'll go fetch her for you."

Danny and John D. asked me what exactly I was doing. As if I knew.

Paulie came back a minute later with Maggie. She was a stick figure in a shiny silver blouse and tight velvet pants. Paulie had to drag her to us. She stared at her own boots.

"Okay, Maggie, you say hello to Miss Liza Durbin. She's like you, girl. Suddenly got took over by something," Paulie said. "Say hello, Maggie, and be nice."

Maggie finally looked at me. Her face dissolved in fear.

"Sweet Jesus!" Maggie pointed at me, stepping back in fear. "What is she, Uncle Paulie? Those eyes! *She got voodoo eyes, Uncle Paulie!*"

"What you talkin' about, Maggie?" he said. "She got no such thing."

"You just look, Uncle Paulie! That witch got the Devil in her eyes!"

"Wait, you can't be serious," I said. "You're saying *I* have a light in my eyes? What about *your* eyes, Maggie? You're the one with light in your eyes!"

She froze at my words. We both felt the blow of unwanted truth.

"You're wrong, lady." Maggie could barely whisper. "Ain't nothing wrong with me."

She turned to run, but I grabbed her by the shoulders. I stared into Maggie's eyes and she looked back into mine. Hers were hypnotic up close, so bright it should have been painful. Instead, I was pulled into their center, where a white flame swirled through an abstract dance. We were connected by an energy that only we could see.

Maggie broke contact first, ripping her eyes away like a Band-Aid off a wound. Franz felt sucker-punched by the brief encounter and almost relieved by Maggie's rejection of us.

"There's somethin' wrong with you, lady, that's for sure," she said, "but I don't got whatever you got, so leave me alone. *Please,* just leave me alone."

"Maggie, don't be crazy," Paulie said. "This is Liza Durbin from TV. She's possessed, like you."

"I ain't possessed, Uncle Paulie! I got a gift, a God-given gift. She's a monster!"

Maggie struggled to leave and Paulie tried to control her. Finally, she bit him hard on the cheek and made her escape. Franz was wobbling badly. We trembled in unison.

I apologized to Paulie. Clearly, I'd chosen a bad time.

"Don't worry 'bout me," he said, wiping Maggie's saliva from his face. "She bit my dog last year—got all oozy but he lived. Maggie's just stubborn as a stump. Two months ago, that girl didn't know a guitar from a toothbrush. Wakes up one morning, picks up my guitar, and holy shit! She's so crazy she thinks that's how it works for everyone."

I confirmed that a thing like this could make anyone feel crazy.

"I tell her I heard all about this on the news, how you got rich this same way. 'This here's our gold mine,' I tell her. She says, 'Well, *I'm* the gold mine, not some spook.' Hell, I know what happened to Maggie ain't normal."

"No, it's not." I was regaining composure since Maggie had left the room. "It's hard to accept and much more complicated than you think. It's not all about money. I'd really like to talk to her."

"Humph . . . I don't see you turning down money, Missy," he said. "For your information, we're talking to a record producer next week. We've always been poor and ugly, Lord knows, but at least we don't gotta stay poor."

I asked Paulie to at least give me Maggie's phone number.

"You can have it, but seems to me like she don't wanna talk to you. Can't force the girl."

I gave him my number, too, saying she could call me anytime.

Danny and John D. had witnessed my scene with Maggie Sunshine in helpless silence. They treated me gently as we headed back toward our hotel. Sitting in the taxi, they asked repeatedly how I was. Danny had an inkling about what had happened.

"I guess the jack-o'-lantern eyes are for real," he said. "Only not everyone can see them."

"I guess you can't even see your own," I said, "if you happen to have them."

"Will someone please tell me what I'm missing here?" John D. said.

Danny told John D. about the jack-o'-lantern eyes I'd seen on the road. I also told them about a bright-eyed man waiting outside Carnegie Hall after my debut. He had said, "Look at her eyes," but no one listened. So it shouldn't have been a total surprise to me, but I was about as eager to have these eyes as Maggie was.

This was the first indicator that I was not unique, but it wasn't a rewarding meeting. Franz was more agitated than happy about finding this fellow spirit. Whatever he saw in Maggie Sunshine's eyes was not an old friend.

Danny and John D. stayed with me for a while in my hotel room to make sure I was all right. At one point, we piled into the bathroom to study my eyes in the mirror. We checked them from every angle. Danny shined a penlight into them. Standard-issue peepers.

John D. wrote a list of everything we knew, which wasn't much. He did not believe it was coincidence that both Maggie and I made music. He suggested creativity as the link.

"Maybe they're oversized, creative spirits," I said, "what we think of as genius. Spirits too big for one body or one lifetime."

"But people would recognize them eventually," Danny said, "like Schubert."

"Not necessarily," I said. "I bet we don't know most geniuses by name. Probably a tiny fraction, when you think of it."

"But they stand out, don't they? That's the point—they're special," Danny said.

Maybe in their own surroundings, I agreed, but that could be very limited. Think of a woman painter in the Middle Ages, or a poet slave in Egypt, or an elephant driver in rural India who thinks in logarithms— anyone, anytime, might be the living definition of genius, but how many people would know it? Not to mention the potential geniuses who died as babies or were forced into the family fish business. The greatest singer in the world today might live in a remote Amazon village. The opportunity for fame almost certainly has nothing to do with possessing genius.

"I could believe that Maggie Sunshine has genius in her," John D. said thoughtfully. "She's an unlikely carrier, but she's got a spark."

"Yeah, but that girl's totally crazy," Danny said. "She can't handle it."

Danny obviously assumed I could handle it better, but circumstances mattered there, too. It's doubtful that Maggie Sunshine had a therapist to call on when things got rough, and her uncle Paulie lacked empathy and a lot of other good qualities. I hoped that Maggie had more of a support system somewhere. I'd be in endless trouble without mine.

When John D. and Danny finally left my room, I went straight to bed, as if sleep were possible. Maggie and other unknown people ran drag races in my head, shining their brights in my face. I'd already seen eyes like mine more than once, so I had to assume there were others. I wanted to feel an innate connection with them, but it wasn't there with Maggie. Either she and I were too different or our spirits were at odds. Certainly Franz was in a dark mood.

I wondered if spiritual inhabitation was a recent phenomenon or traceable through history. I pictured traveling souls descending on people in every era. How many of them wound up in asylums or sleeping in subways, arguing loudly with nobody? It might work out smoothly if it happened to someone in infancy, when the mind and body are wide open, and there could be absorption with no resistance. Maybe that explains Mozart's childhood compositions, or why Yehudi Menuhin played violin with a life's worth of passion when he was only a little boy. Some of the world's acknowledged "geniuses" might have had blinding-bright eyes all their lives, but no one saw.

I wanted very much to talk with Maggie Sunshine, to compare notes and assemble our bits of knowledge. I called her first thing next morning and several times that day. I went back to the Rock 'n' Bowl and left tickets for her and Uncle Paulie for my concert that night. She never responded. We left the next day for Austin.

John D. came through with heightened loyalty and empathy for me after the Maggie Sunshine incident. He believed in Franz and was energized by the musical possibilities. He even came to Austin with us, where Danny debuted one new song and a brazen John D. joined him in another. *Oh, baby, oh, baby.* On our last night, we went to a rowdy club and listened to Charlie Drew's Frayed Knot play classic Western songs. Franz was entranced and Danny threatened to write lyrics for the world's first cowboy *lieder.*

We all flew back to New York together, and John D. began aging again somewhere over Virginia. He must have realized it because he did something spontaneous, a last-moment gesture to his wild side.

"What would you think of a label of your own, Liza? Well, not really your own, but a subsidiary of Sony Classical." He gulped the cheap airline wine like he was chugging beer. "Not just for you, but you'd be the first. We'll record serious, innovative, outrageous artists like you. I can do that, Liza, and I think we'd all be happier. How about we call it Sony Classical Vision?"

"I like it, John D." We clinked plastic cups of airline wine and drank to Vision.

Wie enttäuschend . . . How disappointing, to discover another one such as I and find the meeting disagreeable.

That poor girl is visited by a buffoon. Talented, to be sure, but eternally dreadful. She is weak and will go mad with him.

Now I know there are others, at least. They can't all be buffoons.

CHAPTER ELEVEN

Gordy & Jill Talk!
Friday, August 26

GORDY: Well, you heard about her here first, folks, didn't you?

JILL: You're talking about Liza Durbin, Gord?

GORDY: Of course. The whole world is talking about Liza Durbin these days, and I was the first to tell you about her.

JILL: Not that you're bragging, right? *(Subdued chuckles in the audience.)*

GORDY: Me? Never. Well, listen, a lot's happened to the lovely Miss Durbin since then. Everyone knows that she claims to be inhabited by the spirit of Franz Schubert. This whole "inhabitation" thing has become a big deal around the country, and we've got a lady with us today who can explain it all to us.

JILL: That's right, Gordy. She's the world-famous therapist and bestselling author of *Inhabitism—Attract the Spirit That's Right for You!* Please welcome Dr. Mikki Kloster! *(Mikki takes a seat between Gordy and Jill.)*

MIKKI: Thank you so much for having me.

GORDY: Okay, Mikki, just between you and me, you *are* Liza Durbin's therapist, right?

MIKKI: Let me say first that Liza Durbin and I know each other. Professional ethics keep me from discussing my clients by name. But Miss Durbin is obviously the kind of case I specialize in.

GORDY: Well, I guess so. Of course, there is that videotape of you and Liza at the channeler's house, but we won't go there, right?

(A silent, unrockable nonsmile from Mikki.)

GORDY: Can't blame me for trying! Well, what we do know is that you've studied this phenomenon more than anyone.

JILL: I've read your book cover-to-cover, Mikki, and I'm simply fascinated.

MIKKI: Thank you, Jill, that's what I'm really here to talk about. Anyone can learn something from the case studies in my book. I've already heard from people across the country who think they've attracted a spirit for themselves or their children.

JILL: Wow. I'm hoping to attract a spirit that'll teach my nine-year-old to make her bed.

GORDY: Seriously, Mikki, tell our audience about one of your cases.

JILL: Oh, Mikki, I love the one about the little girl who hardly spoke until she was three, then opens her mouth one day and sings an aria from *Carmen*.

(Jill explodes into an operatic sound bite, to the audience's delight.)

MIKKI: Yes, that little girl was a favorite of mine, too. She's so young that her parents still protect her identity. I also had a recent letter from a woman in the Midwest whose twelve-year-old son built a working car. Can you imagine? They read my chapter called "Focused Meditative Magnetism" and followed the suggestions. It has all the instructions for connecting with a potential inhabitant—I call them "available spirits"—and finding the one that resonates to the child's creative energy. Does that make sense?

JILL: Oh, absolutely. But why is it so important to select the spirit and not leave it to chance? Is it true that wild things happen with the wrong spirits?

MIKKI: Well, I hate to call them the "wrong" spirits, but you do want something compatible. For instance, an ancient spirit's behavior might not always be acceptable by modern standards. I know of a man inhabited by a Minoan fisherman who insisted on vaulting over the horns of charging bulls as part of a ritual dance. There were unfortunate consequences.

GORDY: Ouch! Well, you know, Mikki, we're going to talk with someone who
claims to be inhabited herself, right after this commercial break. Folks,
you won't want to miss this because it marks the return of one of our most
beloved stars.

(*After the break, a Toto dog wearing a checkered dress and ruby slippers yelps
to "Somewhere over the Rainbow."*)

◊◊◊

As soon as we got back to New York, John D. made arrangements to
record our new CD. We were also leaving for Europe in a month, so I was
quickly submerged in rehearsals and preparations. With everything I
needed to do—practice, running and push-ups, more practice, running,
push-ups—I again left the business particulars in Cassie's hands. Greta,
who had distanced herself from me because of my public image, rejoined
the fold, purely for the sake of music.

I resumed my habit of playing at Fred's whenever possible. My first day
back, Mrs. Pardo spotted me coming down the street and met me on the
front stoop. After her obligatory fawning (I was *her* discovery, after all),
she told me that Fred wasn't there and she hadn't seen much of him recently. He was apparently spending a lot of time working with Cassie in
Upper Danville. Mrs. Pardo mentioned once or thrice that her daughter
would be visiting soon. She hoped Fred and Lovely Daughter could spend
some time together. Wouldn't that be nice?

Ever so nice, I agreed. I double-bolted Fred's door behind me, only
opening it for Danny at lunchtime. He bore sandwiches and good news.

Danny had worked it out so he could live in Vienna during fall semester, staying with his grandmother and going to school. He would join us
for concerts whenever he could.

We celebrated Danny's announcement with ice cream and raucous
music. Franz was still floating on the sounds we'd heard in New Orleans
and Austin. He added new spices as we banged around the keyboard.
Danny took a turn at the piano and sang brash, audacious tunes. When
we left Fred's apartment, Mrs. Pardo happened to be at the mailbox in the
hall (where I suspect she'd been getting her mail for hours). She smiled
weakly and looked worried about our competence. Apparently the commotion we'd made was not fit for the unimaginative or the tasteful.

In the weeks before Europe, Franz and I were getting along pretty nicely. We were both heavily focused on our recording, and we knew enough to appreciate these days of high creativity and relative peace.

Danny recorded some awfully good *lieder* with us, including new songs by Schubert, one of them with lyrics by Danny Carson: *"I got hot love ready for making, and a heart that's ripe for breakin', Pretty mama, won't you teach me to regret you."* You'd think Franz would recoil at this tripe, but it must be hard to recognize corn in a language you're just learning. Besides, Franz was loving country tunes since we heard Charlie Drew in Austin. He even found a way to make the piano "twang." (Don't worry, John D. sanely cut the whole thing from the CD.)

John D. Doyle was also at most recording sessions. Because he let Danny sing new *lieder,* we asked John D. to sing a traditional song himself. He had resurrected his voice to a more than pleasant level through many hours of training with the famous vocal coach Pamela Alvera. She was at the recording studio, too, guiding him through the process, tending to every nuance.

In the evenings, we went in search of more music. Salsa clubs in Harlem, uptown cabarets, jazz in the Village, and *Porgy and Bess* at Lincoln Center. Franz never ran low on interest or energy. He educated my spirit, opened my heart—and he continued to draw me into his life.

Lying in bed, Franz is thinking about the F Minor Fantasie, something he'd like to dedicate to a friend. He hears the tune and sees the written music at the same time, the way other people picture written words in their heads. It looks and sounds beautiful in his mind.

He wants to play the new piece on the piano, to fully enjoy it, and perhaps tinker a bit. But this is a bad day. Franz is weak and queasy, lacks the will even to stand up.

This about kills me, watching Franz's enormous spirit brought down by a feeble body and one insolent microbe. He is almost thirty, a little younger than I am. I'm so strong, far stronger than a city girl needs to be. I could give him half my strength and we'd both be fine. I would do that, gladly.

"Get out of bed, Franz! Now, just try!" My throat hurts from screaming

through time. I will his limbs to move. "Please, Franz, pull back the covers and
walk to the piano!"

And, I swear to God, he does it.

~~~

Cassie called to summon me for Labor Day festivities at her house. I was
protective of my solitude at that time, but she persisted.

"Sorry, Liza, you can't get out of this one. Family and all that. Besides,
there are plans to discuss, decisions to make before you leave for Europe.
Some nice new possibilities you should—"

"Okay, I get it, Cassie. Will this be torture?"

"Nope. We have a surprise for you."

"Mom and Dad?"

"You dragged it out of me."

"Aunt Frieda, too?"

"She can be the surprise."

I arrived at Cassie's in a limo, a luxury I was growing way too fond of. A
cluster of relatives met me at Cassie's front door with the usual Durbin
hoopla. When we stepped inside, I felt again the buzz of people at work in
my sister's home. I still wasn't used to that.

Jesse Edelstein, Frenchie, and Fred were huddled around a table, waiting to show me mock-ups for T-shirts, Web pages, programs, and other
paraphernalia. They were arranging media coverage in each city on my fall
tour. Frenchie had experience in this and would come along as my assistant. Also, being Dutch, she spoke enough languages to be comfortable
anywhere in Europe.

I told everyone that Danny was coming to Europe, which warmed
their marketing hearts. I also told them that Greta Pretsky had agreed
(after making me beg) to accompany me for the first few weeks. Nobody's
heart seemed warmed, but I would be happy to have her musical support.

We hammered away at the logistics. We didn't stop long enough to eat
or to notice it was getting dark outside. When Barry came home after
nine, we were nearing the bottom of our discussion list. He was either
tired from his day or tired of seeing Fred, Jesse, and Frenchie planted in his
dining room.

"Hi, Barry," Cassie said, glancing at her watch. "Guess we lost track of time."

"What else is new?" Barry said. "Don't worry about it, Cassie, I had a pretty long day myself."

He dispensed one hello wave for everyone, then headed for the kitchen, loosening his tie on the way. Jesse and Frenchie got busy pulling their papers together. Apparently this was not the first indication that their marathon meetings got on Barry's nerves. They left within minutes. Fred was staying for the weekend for a little bit of work and for the pleasure of the Durbin company. When Cassie left the room, I asked Fred about the tension in the house.

"Your brother-in-law's a little tightly wound, that's all," he said. "Nothing to worry about."

Fred was not convincing, but I wanted to believe him.

Trying to fall asleep that night, thoughts of merchandising and schedules and Barry rattled noisily around in my head. My mind battled to stay awake, just to torture me. Finally, I got out of bed and did push-ups until exhaustion got me. Couldn't hurt, right?

When I crawled back in bed, Franz took me in his care. He soothed me with his song about a round lake near the mountains, and took me there in our dreams.

———

Sie versucht, freundlich zu sein . . . She tries to be kind. I can see what I've done to her life, and still she tries to be kind. She must know she can't help me. What a fine, stubborn thing she is.

I woke early and stepped outside to inhale the end of summer. An erratic wind ruffled the air, not quite allowing the day to settle. Birds squawked from tree to tree, tart and discordant.

My mother was on the great lawn, finishing her sun salutations. She seemed immune to the blustery day. Franz was transfixed by the grace of the yoga and her bloom of red hair in the hazy light. I told her how beautiful she looked.

"I didn't start till I was over forty, you know." Yes, I knew. "I guess late-blooming runs in the family. Much later for me than you, of course."

Mom started her fabric-art career in her fifties, so I had to agree.

"I didn't have to bloom so late," she said. "I put everything aside for you kids and for the store and all. I'm not laying guilt on anyone, but that's why I've always encouraged your talents, Liza. I know I sound overboard sometimes, but I never wanted you or your sister to wait."

"Why are you bringing this up now, Mom?"

"Why did you say I look beautiful?"

We did a sun salutation together, then Mom went inside to shower. She left me wondering whether I ever would have bloomed without Franz. I found it hard to imagine the last few months or next fifty years without him.

If Franz hadn't diverted me from my path, I might have gone back to writing, eventually. Maybe even attempted a novel. But, barring marriage to a really rich guy, it wouldn't have happened for a very long time. I'd grown so practical that by age thirty-one, I thought a dull job at a law firm was almost fine. Franz ended my waiting.

We spent most of the day working on a new sonata, one of my favorites to date. The edginess in the air gusted around the keyboard, infusing the melody with skittish tension. Franz and I were playing in shared joy. I didn't need another person in my world just then, but I got one.

"God, Liza, you look as great as you sound."

Barry tried a little too hard to be hearty. He lacked his usual summer bronze, and light lines across his forehead were planting permanent roots.

"I hear you've been working like crazy," I said. "Had any time for tennis this summer?"

He searched my eyes, as if looking for an ally. He wanted sympathy. Everyone around him, he said, was involved in my big bright light, while he labored every day at a boring bank. I didn't point out that most people would be thrilled to have his gigantic income and palatial home in return for a few hours at a bank. But I'd never seen Barry in a mope, and his genuine sadness doused my sarcasm.

"I always found you special," he said, "way before any of this happened. You were *always* special, Liza."

Barry's chest bellowed deeply. Sweat brightened the baby wrinkles in his brow.

"Do you ever think that we made a mistake, Liza?"

We? We made a mistake, you cheating, heartbreaking, dump-me-and-marry-my-sister prick?

"What mistake? What on earth are you talking about, Barry?"

He grabbed my arms and leaned toward me, resting his head against my hair.

"She doesn't need me anymore, Liza. Maybe she never needed me, really. Maybe she liked my money, my name."

I tried to pull back, a little.

"Don't be an ass, Barry," I said. "Cassie loves you."

"She's happier than she's been in years, and it has nothing to do with me. She's happy with Fred and the rest of them. I'm the background scenery."

"Cassie's just found a purpose," I said. "She's growing. I think that's good."

He was nuzzling my neck. I really did protest this time, but not that strongly.

"You and I were totally connected once. You were for *me*, Liza," he said, "just me. And that's the way I felt about you, too. Wherever we were, even if there were thousands of other people in the place, you and I were the ones *together*."

"Barry, that was a long, long time ago. Cassie's just going through—"

I couldn't finish because I found his lips covering mine. This time I really did try to push him off. After a moment of nostalgia.

His taste, his touch, the full lower lip, were too familiar not to ring bells. The first time we kissed had been a surprise, too.

We were freshmen at Cornell, first semester. We met because we both had leftover high-school steadies at Syracuse University. I found Barry's name on the ride board for students looking to share weekend transportation. We went to Syracuse in his MG Midget three times in the fall.

On the drives to Syracuse we talked school, books, movies, and everything else. The return drives were always about my boyfriend or his girlfriend. Hard to say who was the bigger pill. Barry's girlfriend was an earnest left-wing world-changer who considered it a triumph to have a corruptible boyfriend from a rich family. My guy, Stan, was a football star in my high school graduating class. We'd known each other since kindergarten and he managed to ignore me until senior year. He discovered my inner charms right after my breasts popped out in their C-cup grandeur.

Stan was well on his way to a starting position on the Syracuse football team. The cheerleaders, who had C-cups of their own, made quite a public fuss over him. Someone had made a private fuss over him, too, which I realized when I found lacy underwear in his dresser drawer.

As it turned out, Barry and I broke up with our steadies on the same weekend at Syracuse. On the drive back, it felt good to talk with someone who understood (and was really cute himself). It felt even better when he dropped me off outside my dorm and kissed me so sweetly that it made me cry. His taste and feel eventually became as familiar as my own, although I had set aside that memory until this surprise kiss in Cassie's living room a thousand years later.

"Liza, what the hell are you doing with my husband!"

My sister's voice hit like a meteor landing between Barry and me. We jumped apart. Cassie glared through steaming eyes. Fred stood beside her, speechless. Barry found his voice first.

"You're asking what *we're* doing? You ignore me for months and carry on with this, this *person* in my own house!" Barry gestured rudely toward Fred. "And you're asking what we're doing!"

Cassie's face went from a surprised oval to squashed repulsion.

"Is *that* what you think?" she said. "Fred and me? You think *that*? Are you crazy?"

Fred shrank three sizes.

"You think I would throw away you and my family and our life?" Fred shriveled further, to a wisp. "Barry, I just have something new in my life, something I'm excited about." Cassie's voice got snagged on a tear. "I keep hoping you'll . . . I mean, you're all I ever—"

Barry's sudden relief erased years from his face. I heard a light thud as he dumped me once again for my sister.

"Oh, baby, do you mean it?" Barry said as he walked straight toward Cassie. "I couldn't stand the thought of you and that guy. You know nothing's going on with me and Liza. You *do* know that, don't you?"

"Well, I didn't think you'd fall for her crap." Cassie turned toward me coldly. "Liza, could you please *not* be so pathetic?"

Fred and I watched in silence as Barry and Cassie went up the grand staircase to discuss their feelings in private.

Even after they left the room, their shadows remained stubbornly stretched across the floor. Fred and I wanted to disappear, so we ran to his car and drove away. We stopped in a restaurant where we could sit at the bar and recount our humiliation. Fred felt it necessary to assure me that nothing in fact *had* happened.

"Not a thing, I swear," he said. "But she's lying if she says she was never tempted. I was maybe waiting for a sign, I admit that much, but she always pulled back in the end."

I believed him. Not because Fred was unsmitten with Cassie, but because of my sister's agenda. Of course she liked Fred. Why not? She relished his attentiveness—especially considering he had once found her ridiculous. But a flirtation was just for fun, certainly nothing for Cassie to risk home, family, and fortune over.

Fred and I labored over whether we could just go back to Brooklyn. We decided we'd look even more pitiful if we ran away. We would have to face Cassie and Barry again sometime. We fortified this mature point of view with a decent wine and went back to the House of Embarrassment.

Cassie deserved an apology. I found her in one of the many unexplained rooms in her house.

"Cassie, I'm so sorry for what you saw," I said. "You have to believe me, it was nothing."

"Of course I believe you, Liza." Dismissive ennui. "Do you think I'd worry about a little kiss? *Sacré bleu!* A stupid little kiss between Barry and *you?*"

The "you" stung.

"Well, I'd understand if you were worried, Cassie."

"You mean because of your history as a cheat and a home-wrecker?"

"No, I mean because Barry and I have a history. He's been feeling neglected by you lately. Is it impossible to imagine he'd be drawn to me?"

She looked to the ceiling for guidance, then bestowed a pitying look on me.

"Liza, I know I did a bad thing to you once, 'stealing your boyfriend.' " She etched quotation marks in the air. "At least, you've always thought I was the bad one, isn't that right?"

"We don't need to talk about that."

"No, let's talk about it, Liza. It's about time we did. You've always thought that Barry belonged with you."

Well, maybe a tiny bit.

"Wrong, Liza. You wouldn't have lasted a year with his family and their million-dollar traditions."

That "old family" bullshit had indeed gotten on my nerves when we were together. Barry always seemed vaguely amused by the uprooted Durbin family tree, which could not be traced back past 1900 or so. On the other hand, he'd probably claim that the cave paintings at Lascaux were signed by Barry the First.

"You think I don't know the things you say about all this pretension?" Cassie said. "What you say about the damn Remington?" She *knew*? "You would have sold the Remington at a garage sale years ago. Did you know that Barry is the one who insists that it be front and center? He shows the damn thing to everyone who comes in the house."

"Barry does that?"

"Not in words, of course. His native language is WASP. He just makes sure that everyone who visits walks by the Remington at some point. If the guest is discerning enough to ask about it, Barry bores them with the details. 'A gift from Senator LaSalle to my great-grandfather Barton Ward Whitman III, who passed it to my grandfather,' and so forth. Get it?"

Yes, I finally got it.

"I know Barry's been fantasizing about the past." The slightest concern crossed Cassie's lovely face. "About you and him and all that nonsense. He's mad because he's not the center of my universe all the time. He'll get over it. And he'd never leave me for you, Liza. *Never.* So let's just end this visit to Fantasyland, okay?"

No amount of protest could persuade Cassie that I had no designs—fantasy or otherwise—on her husband. Her lack of concern about me as a threat was an infuriating relief. I couldn't say she was wrong. Cassie and Barry were a match made in escrow, joined for life in merging interests.

I hid comfortably under the covers that night. Franz treated me to an entertaining dream in which he concealed himself under a lover's bed while someone's oblivious spouse snored between the sheets just above him. He must have known I was embarrassed by the whole Barry incident and graciously showed me his own reckless side. Stupid is eternal.

I would have been happy hiding in bed the whole day, but Fred came knocking on my door. He couldn't stay in his room all day, he said, but he didn't want to face Cassie or Barry alone, either. Fred and I braved the kitchen together in search of caffeine. We both dreaded the awkwardness of meeting a Whitman.

Cassie was already at the kitchen table, sipping her coffee. Luckily, she forgot to feel awkward. She was her sisterly self the moment she saw us.

"God, Liza, your hair is a fire hazard." Cassie looked haphazardly stunning with her red mane loosely gathered in a black velvet ribbon. "Get it cut before it explodes."

"Thanks," I said, "and may I say your feet look large today."

She gifted Fred with a cordial *"Bonjour."*

"Listen, Liza, we have to plan some power shopping," Cassie said. "You need a new concert wardrobe for Europe. You'll take the famous blue dress, of course, but you need warm stuff for the fall. Let's go this week so we leave time for alterations."

In Cassie's shallow, self-centered way, she showed no after-grudge from the day before. Shallowness may be underrated, after all.

Barry did not feel so good about it. When he apologized to me later, I said it was no big deal.

"But I sort of hurt you again."

"Not at all, Barry."

I was honestly delighted by how much it didn't hurt. That sort of hurt him, I think.

"Besides, Cassie's not mad at me," I said, "and I'm not mad at her anymore, so that's good."

"Great. Peace between sisters."

"Don't get too excited. She has a million ways to annoy me. You're just not one of them."

"No, of course not. Liza, I'm sorry I was such a jerk."

"Barry, we're fine. This is the way it's supposed to be. You might want to make nice with Fred, though, before permanent weirdness sets in."

Barry and Fred did chat briefly. I watched from across the living room later as they shook hands in manly resolution. They didn't exchange sharp words, and they considerately avoided each other all weekend. I wouldn't be surprised, though, if they sprayed their chosen corners like tomcats, but politely.

The rest of the family never knew about our melodrama. My parents and Aunt Frieda were excitedly plotting their own fall trip to Europe. They planned to catch my concerts in several cities and see every monument ever built. Aunt Frieda also heard they sold shoes there.

Brittany and Cameron made the most of the warm, bright days. We splashed in the pool and ran around barefoot. Brittany invited me to be in their Labor Day Spectacular, an original show starring Brittany on the piano and Cameron standing on his head (*ten minutes without stopping!*). Brittany asked if I would play a duet with her.

"Well, not really *you*, Aunt Liza," Brittany said. "You know."

"Franz? You want to play with Franz?"

"Should I ask him myself?"

"You don't need to talk him directly." Too strange a concept. "I'll pull strings for you, Brit."

"But does he know me?" Brittany craned her neck, trying to see inside me. "Does he know I'm here? Can I speak to him?"

"He hears you. Why don't you play something for him?"

We went inside and Brittany played *Für Elise*, the same piece she'd played months before. The first time Franz heard her play it, he was horrified. This time he listened like a proud uncle.

A few days before leaving for Europe, I received a late-night phone call. She probably didn't think of the time difference before calling.

"How do you stand it?" This was instead of hello. "I got what you got, Miss Durbin, I know it for sure. I think it's killing me."

"Maggie, thank God it's you. I've left so many messages. I was hoping you'd call."

I was not hoping she'd sound so frightened.

"He's in my head all the time," she said. "I can't do a thing but what he's lookin' at me and laughing. Gotta be the Devil himself in me."

"It's not the Devil, and nobody's laughing at you, Maggie. If you're inhabited, you're very important to that spirit. You're still Maggie Sunshine. Nothing changes that."

"I want this to end." The saddest voice you can imagine. "I pray and pray, but it just don't end. Uncle Paulie, he says I gotta go onstage. He tells people I got the spirit of Jimi Hendrix. Heck, I know it ain't him. Don't sound a thing like him. But Uncle Paulie says Jimi Hendrix is the famous one to have. Miss Durbin? Liza? Please, do you know why the Lord has cursed us?"

I told her that it took a while for me to work things out with Franz, and that she could do the same thing. I felt sure it wasn't God's curse.

Maggie just cried softly, not bothering with words.

"Can you come to New York?" I asked. "I'll send you a ticket. We can spend time together, help each other."

She mumbled something that sounded like an excuse. I offered to fly to New Orleans to see her, but she didn't respond. I heard a click, then a dial tone.

Maggie didn't return my calls after that.

fourth movement

Finale

Why did I think it would be nice to fly to Milan with Greta Pretsky? She spoke only to the flight attendant *("Miss, please make that child stop crying, yes?")* until we were somewhere over Greenland. Then she asked me to move my elbow.

I could have sat with Danny, who was a row behind us, exclaiming to a Midwestern couple about the outrageous beaches they *gotta* see in Spain. But I was honestly hoping to make amends with Greta.

In Greta's eyes, Franz was my only validation, the sole reason she would sit in the same jumbo jet as me. On her lap lay a folded newspaper. She did not remove it during lunch, dinner, or the movie. When she tried to sleep, she lay the paper on top of the American Airlines blanket. A silent reminder of my gross inadequacy as host of the great Franz Schubert.

THE TOWN CRIER—AMERICA'S LOCAL NEWSPAPER
September 7

When Schubert Met Hendrix—Liza Finds a Protégée

A phenom in New Orleans is doing for guitar what Liza Durbin does for classical piano. Twenty-year-old Maggie Sunshine can be heard at local clubs most nights with her band, the Bayou Bo Bos. This stupendous guitarist couldn't play at all before her "inhabitation" three months ago, when she first discovered her gift. Then, in August, she met Liza Durbin and her career took off. Maggie's uncle and agent, Paul B. Sunshine, gave The Town Crier the exclusive, inside story.

"Maggie had no talent at all, then she wakes up one morning and starts playing like the dickens," Sunshine said. "I realized it had to be the spirit of Jimi Hendrix. I already heard about Liza Durbin and figured it was the same thing."

Sunshine, who read about Liza right here in The Town Crier, was wise enough to arrange a meeting between his talented niece and Liza Durbin when the Schubert diva herself was in New Orleans. He says they've stayed in contact ever since.

"Maggie idolizes Liza Durbin. She's like her hero," Sunshine said. "They have so much in common. I'd like to see them play together someday."

A spokesperson for Durbin says the pianist is thrilled at this prospect, and will look into it after her European tour. By then, Maggie Sunshine will have released her first album, according to her uncle, who is negotiating the contract with an unnamed recording company. Meanwhile, take heart: If there's a classic/rock heaven, we'll all hear one hell of a band.

Keep checking The Town Crier for updates on Maggie, Liza and any other ghosts we meet on the comeback trail.

～～～

Greta actually tried to back out of her promise to come to Europe with me when she read this article. I swore it was nonsense, that I knew nothing about it. She made me vow to behave decently, attract no improper headlines, or embarrass myself in any way while in Europe. I promised not to be me whatsoever. She had the puniest faith left in me, but she was still loyal to Franz. So I had Greta's sour, so-much-better-than-thou company for the next few weeks with me in Europe. Oh boy.

Frenchie had flown to Italy before us and was waiting at Malpensa Airport with a limo, driver, and refreshments in the car. Her hair had gone plum-colored and her tight body was wrapped in Euro-looking scarves and rings. She tried to light a Gauloise in the car but was loudly vetoed by all. As we drove toward the city, she went over our schedule for the week. A few days to readjust to the time and settle in (at my insistence), then some interviews, photos, a concert, and off to the next city. She rattled off the details as we watched the scenery.

I had only passed through Milan before on vacation, not choosing to linger. As we entered the city, I remembered why: Milan lacks charm.

Milan has energy, rhythm, culture, history, smarts, art, and money. What it lacks is charm. The most style-centric city in Europe has defaced its own loveliness with every thoughtless modern affliction. Inside the famous shops, the fine merchandise serves as counterpoint to the surrounding insults. Hideous modern buildings hide the city's beauty like barnacles.

Since Milan had never moved me before, my sobs as we drove through the streets could only be attributed to Franz. Frenchie seemed startled by my behavior, but Greta and Danny were used to it by then.

This was Franz's homecoming, sort of. He knew Europe by feel and breath. He'd been in Milan at least once before. As we drove toward the Hotel Rossini on via Scarpetti, bits of scenery nipped at his senses. The glimpse of a building with an unchanged façade transported us to sometime else, to a busy street at dusk . . . Horse-drawn carriages and pedestrians in winter clothes. A sniffling child tugging at his mother's skirt. A tall man and a plump woman in evening clothes arguing in whispers as they hurry along. Church bells, stray cats, cooking smells, a gargoyle carver singing opera as he works . . . All of this was happening within and beside the whining motor scooters, honking drivers, Cineplex movie signs, and political posters for the Italian government-of-the-week.

Franz was tilting badly. Excited and appalled by his reentry to Europe, he lost all bearings. I grabbed Danny's hand so hard he yowled.

"I think Liza needs to lie down," Danny said, trying to rescue his wounded paw from my grip. Did I see a trace of blood? "Are we almost at the hotel, *signore?*"

The driver stopped just then in front of the Hotel Rossini. A bellman swept our luggage away as Frenchie paid the driver and Danny pulled me from the car. I was not what you'd call compliant. Danny later told me I scratched his cheek, but he didn't have any clear marks to prove it.

The hotel centered on a classic grand lobby, immaculately maintained in hundred-year-old splendor. Behind the scenes (and in the bathrooms, where it counts) lay all the modern luxuries, but it had an old-world look by American standards. By Franz's standards—early-nineteenth-century Austria—this was a futuristic Europe, but still his Europe. The weight of his memories made my knees droop, so Danny and Frenchie each grabbed an elbow and led me to the elevator. I don't remember entering my hotel room or falling into bed, but the dream I had has stayed with me.

Franz has moved into the home of Franz von Schober, who recently married the round, freckle-faced Justine. Another close friend, Johann Vogl, has also married, and the old crowd doesn't hang out the way it once did. On this wintry afternoon, though, the Schobers have invited friends to celebrate Franz's thirtieth birthday. Vogl is there, and so is Justine's gregarious brother. Marta has just arrived, too, with her husband and children.

Justine has cooked her lamb-and-dumpling specialty for lunch. It's disgusting. Even so, it surpasses her usual cooking, so she gets compliments. Before she can inflict a dessert on her guests, Vogl offers a song. Franz is delighted to accompany him on the piano. At age sixty or so, Vogl's operatic voice is imperfect but nicely mellowed. It resonates like good port.

Next to perform is Marta's daughter, Brita (she of the sneezing horse incident). She's probably nine or ten, and tries to look serious in her flouncy dress and hair ribbons. She has decided to sing Für Brita, *which Franz wrote just for her. Brita is nearly tone-deaf and yells out every note. The adults brace themselves as they sense a high note coming . . . ouch. The applause is meant to acknowledge but not encourage the child. Surely she has other talents.*

Vogl volunteers another song, one he sang years ago when he, Franz, and Schober vacationed in Italy—back in their invincible years. During that trip,

Schober introduced himself to the Italians as an Austrian count, which he was not, and set his sights on meeting contessas.

The search for contessas ended one evening with an overweight, half-drunk Italian policeman chasing them through the city streets. By the time the policeman caught up to Vogl, Franz, and Schober, nobody had the energy for an arrest. Instead, they all piled into a trattoria, where they drank grappa and swapped songs. Vogl sang one of his favorites.

Franz wants to play this song again with Vogl, but suddenly he feels so tired. He almost declines, is ready to excuse himself.

You should do this, Franz, I say. You'll live almost two more years, no matter what you do tonight. These friends make you happy. Play for them.

The phone's sharp ring tore me out of the past and woke me up in Milan. Danny rolled off the couch (where he'd stood guard over me, apparently) and grabbed the phone. Mutter, mutter, click.

"Get dressed, Liza," he said. "Company's on the way up."

"Frenchie?"

"Better than that." He pulled an NYU sweatshirt over his head, finger-combed his hair, then slipped away to change from pj bottoms to jeans. "Patrick's here."

"Patrick?" I clenched the blanket around my chin. "Patrick's here already? He's not supposed to come until dinner."

"That was last night, Liza. You slept all day yesterday. We couldn't bulldoze you awake, so Patrick said he'd come back this morning. I stayed nearby because you were so out of it. So, what is it, jet lag or a bad case of Franz?"

I ignored his question as Patrick's knock on the door propelled me out of bed. In one motion, I pulled the sheets around me and lunged toward the bathroom. I morning-croaked *"Buon giorno"* to Patrick and slammed the door behind me. Not the touching reunion scene I had hoped for. Jet-lagged and disoriented are not words normally associated with good looks. I looked in the mirror to assess the situation.

My hair was engaged in a great battle. I'd slept on my side, so half my hair was massed around the right ear, waiting to spring on the undisciplined troops leaping from the left. Dark bags hung under my eyes—

partly exhaustion, partly the remnants of yesterday's makeup. Also, a slightly fetid odor followed me from the bed to the bathroom to the sink. All in all, a regular goddess.

Danny rapped softly and asked if I was okay. I said I was fine, yelled more greetings through the door to Patrick, promised to be out soon.

A hot shower knocked off the top layers of grit and weariness. Skin creams and makeup helped. I pulled my hair into a ponytail—it resembled wet kindling, but at least it smelled good.

Unfortunately, I hadn't brought any real clothing into the bathroom. My nightshirt and sheet were not an option, but a terry-cloth robe with the Hotel Rossini insignia hung from a hook on the wall. Good enough.

Patrick and Danny were in easy conversation when I finally emerged. They stopped talking abruptly when they saw me, adding to my discomfort. Danny recovered quickly.

"Well, hey, I think I'm gonna go find some food downstairs," he said. "See you guys later."

"Danny, really, you don't need to run," I said.

"No, you and Patrick have a lot to catch up on. I'll go have a look around the city." He waved as he rushed out.

After a moment's hesitation, Patrick stood up and gave me a long, swaying hug, which made me soft and weepy. We ordered room service and sat together at the small round table beside the window. With our top-floor view, we could see the spires of Milan's great cathedral. Franz knew it by sight and could barely look away from it.

"You look wonderful," Patrick said.

"Liar. I'll accept the compliment."

Neither of us knew yet where our bodies and boundaries belonged. We had agreed to take things slowly, so we were off to the right start.

"How's it going with Franz? We were worried about you last night. Do you remember I was here?"

"Sure, of course I do." He didn't believe me. "It's been a rough landing for Franz, coming back to Europe and all."

Rough for me, too. A thought had occurred to me during recent, intensely real dream encounters—the possibility of getting stuck, maybe trading spiritual places with Franz. An outrageous notion, of course, but the whole situation was outrageous. Besides, even this fear did not keep me from wanting more. If I'm honest, the danger may have been the slightest bit exciting. I didn't dare be that honest out loud.

The weather went strange as Patrick took me on a walking tour of Milan. He wanted to show me what he'd found to love in the city, the nooks and buttresses that made his architect's heart sing.

We roamed the streets through an indecisive precipitation. That whole day it never rained quite hard enough to wash the buildings properly. Grime slid down the façades like tear-smudged mascara. You might have found it gloomy, but not Patrick.

Patrick provided the sunshine. He guided me to obscure beauty and reveled in the aroma of wet leaves. In the corners of a small dark church, he illuminated the space with aesthetic passion. We marveled over the Caravaggios and Tintorettos in the Pinacoteca di Brera, and touched rain-dripped statues in the parks. Patrick liked this gray day. With no sun to bleach the colors out, everything looked richer. The wetness added depth and character to flat buildings, he said.

Wherever we went, I held tight to some part of Patrick's tall, hard frame. Part of it was affection, and a lot of it was fear. He was a physical anchor to keep me grounded while Franz bounced off the rooftops and lunged through strange doorways.

The five-star cathedral, *Il Duomo,* was one of Patrick's obvious destinations that day. Just the thought made Franz hyperventilate. I kept putting it off, though I knew we'd go eventually. I insisted we stop for a late lunch in the Galleria Vittorio Emmanuele II, the glass-domed mall of shops and cafés built into a thoroughfare of historic buildings and frescoes. It sits across from the cathedral, and Franz could sense its closeness. His excitement took over.

"Liza, how about a glass of wine to calm down?" Patrick said. "You seem kind of jumpy."

"I'm okay. Really, I'm fine."

"By jumpy, Liza, I mean that you're actually jumping around."

I sat back and clutched the bottom of my chair.

"A glass of Chianti would be nice," I said. "I'm a little nervous. It's the cathedral, I think. Franz is all worked up."

We lingered over our meal, watching the well-dressed Italians click by in smart shoes. This was not a warm, ebullient Roman piazza but a cool, style-as-business scene. Franz saw many familiar-looking faces passing by, thanks to the resiliency of this good-looking Italian gene pool. The noise and pace and feel of the city were radically changed since his last visit, which was, literally, ages ago. Franz had been with me too long to be stunned by twenty-first-century life but he still felt the sting of loss, the distance between this time and his own. He wore me down with impatience and we finally went to visit *Il Duomo*.

〰

In 1386, one Italian said to another, "Let's start it here."

The other said, "A little to the right, I think."

"Okay," said the first.

He put shovel to ground and began building a cathedral in Milan. More than four hundred years later, when Franz Schubert was a teenager, work crews were still fussing with the finishing touches. Every sculptor in northern Italy and countless artists and artisans made their contributions along the way. It grew into the largest cathedral in Italy and one of the most spectacular in Europe.

Walking out of the mercantile world of Galleria Vittorio Emmanuele II, we were faced with this mountain of Gothic achievement, weighted in triangular might and adorned with a bristle of spiky pinnacles. On either side of its pointed center, still higher spires appeared ready for liftoff, aiming straight toward heaven. Franz swooned at the sight.

"Liza, I can take you back to the hotel." Patrick threw a strong arm around me. "We can save this for another day."

"No, let's go in," I said, but in German.

We walked slowly but my heart raced ahead of us. Things could easily get out of control. My fear was that we'd enter the cathedral and Franz would totally lose it. Instead he was found.

The immense cathedral has its own atmosphere inside. The feeble forces of weather, politics, fashion, and glitz all wither on contact. Franz knew where he wanted to go and respectfully bypassed beckoning saints and altars. He chose a pew with a perfect view of a stained-glass Crucifixion scene. It was huge yet weightless, staying aloft on color and light. Franz closed our eyes to experience it.

Ave Maria . . .

Ave Maria, the melody streamed through us in a pure and seamless voice. Not male or female, young or old, just perfect. An organ played in elegant simplicity. Twice I pried an eye open to find the source of the music. The stained-glass window stared back silently. No one else in the cathedral seemed to notice it. Nor did they hear Franz Schubert's impassioned prayer, delivered in perfect, voiceless clarity:

Heavenly Father, I thank you for so many blessings, for giving me this second chance, though I did not deserve or ask for it.

Please, Dear God, release me.

Give me strength, Almighty Father. I ask only for help to finish my work so my soul may return where it belongs, and this lonely madness can end. I pray this of you, Almighty God.

Ave Maria.

"Hüttenbrenner." I pronounced the name with extra care, though our overseas connection was fine. "That's H-Ü-T-T-E-N-B-R-E-N-N-E-R, two dots over the *u*. Did you get it?"

"H-Ü-T-T-E-N-B-R-E-N-N-E-R, dots over *u*, got it," Cassie said. "Now, what do I do with it?"

"There's a chance we can find the rest of Franz's 'Unfinished Symphony.' He may have left it with these friends in Vienna, brothers actually, Anselm and Josef Hüttenbrenner. There've always been rumors that Franz finished the symphony and left the manuscript with one of them. Some people think it got mislaid in his house. It was never found, but it could still exist."

"Franz told you that?"

"No, but I read about it." This was weak-sounding, even to me. "Most people think it's nonsense, but I don't know where else to start. Even Greta says it's worth a try. We need to help Franz find it."

"Why doesn't he just rewrite it himself? That should be easy for him."

"I don't know why he doesn't do it. I've tried to suggest that myself. I just know he has to finish something, and I'm pretty sure this is it."

No need to discuss my recent revelation at *Il Duomo* with my spiritually reluctant sister. She promised to make this happen, and I believed her.

Before we hung up, Cassie passed along news about Maggie Sunshine. She'd gotten in trouble with the police. Drug possession and firing a gun at a concert.

"At a *concert,* for God's sake," Cassie said. "Her hillbilly uncle's been on the news saying the spirit made her do it. He swears she never did drugs until she got inhabited. Says she never had a drink, either. Religious or something. They look like quite a pair on the news. I guess her spirit wasn't too picky."

I gave Maggie's phone number to Cassie. I told her to offer Maggie help with money, a lawyer, or whatever she needed. Cassie groaned, but I knew she would do that, too.

As it turned out, Maggie Sunshine wouldn't accept our calls or help. People were laughing at Maggie in public ways, and my heart broke for her. She was on drugs, and her uncle Paulie blamed it on Jimi Hendrix. Ridiculous on the face of it, but it made me wonder how much an inhabiting spirit could change the basic nature of a person—and whether a person was stained forever, for better or worse, by a visiting spirit, even if that spirit eventually left.

If I looked objectively at myself (as if that could happen), I might admit to being ever-so-slightly affected by Franz, in a zillion ways. Was he changing my nature permanently? Franz was still with me, but I never assumed that he would stay, and I didn't know who I would be afterward. Maggie Sunshine acquired a drug habit. I didn't want everything that Franz had.

~~~

La Scala, the world-famous opera house, proudly wears its age. No revamped, ultra-styled furnishings or juxtaposed architecture. In this concert hall, music is its rich, original self. The sophisticated Milan audience was dressed for the place and occasion, not gussied up like Americans but tastefully matching the ambience.

The full house included my parents and Aunt Frieda, who had arrived that morning. A few rows behind them, Patrick had finally come to hear me in concert.

Franz breathed in the atmosphere and grew serene. When the house-lights dimmed, I walked onstage. The floor made no sound underfoot, and something smelled of orange blossoms. The piano glowed like a harvest moon.

I yielded to Franz as I had before in many other performances. As at Carnegie Hall, the spirits of great musicians inhabited the woodwork of La Scala. I was used to their presence by then, had expected to see these old friends there. They brightened the place with a tangible light. It became so glaring I wondered how the audience could bear it with open eyes.

We started with the *Snow Sonata,* followed by classic pieces, then another new one. A musical breeze floated through the hall, caressing every listener. Playing never came more naturally. There seemed no separation between hands and keyboard—the piano might have been playing us.

Danny joined us for a conservative, classic *lied* before encoring with something new. His natural gifts and glowing youth charmed the audience. The reception was *stupendo.*

We had a family celebration afterward at a local restaurant. Greta was invited but declined to come. She was not highly social to begin with and had grown positively allergic to Aunt Frieda.

"Darling, this was your best night yet," Dad said. "I've never heard you better."

"It's true, Liza," Patrick said. "You were brilliant. You *are* brilliant. I can't believe what I've been missing."

Since finding each other again in Milan, Patrick and I had danced around our relationship. Occasionally, one of us advanced or retreated in the romance arena, but we were out of phase and insecure. Our evening at La Scala was like prom night, though—all dressed up with magic to spare. Maybe we'd been building for a special occasion. Under the dinner table, Patrick's fingers crawling up my thigh hinted that he was willing to take a risk.

We all walked back together to the Hotel Rossini after dinner. Only Patrick lived elsewhere. In a sweet show of parental protectiveness, my father insisted on seeing me to my room himself. After all, it was late and Patrick didn't need to escort me, right?

Patrick responded to my father's dismissal like a good prom boy. Deprived, but respectful of family honor. Everyone said good night, then I went to my room and counted the minutes until Patrick phoned me. Eighteen, exactly. Enough time to send my folks to bed and make a place in mine for Patrick. 'Bout time, too.

The next morning, I woke with Patrick beside me and a fresh dream of Franz still clear in my head. Somewhere, sometime, Franz was growing steadily weaker. While Patrick snored peacefully, I crept out of bed. I washed up, stretched my limbs, then got down on the floor.

"One for me, one for Franz, one for me, one for Franz . . ."

Out of habit, I counted out loud to keep track. I kept my voice down so I wouldn't wake Patrick. Maybe he was about to wake up anyway.

"Liza? What are you doing?" Patrick squinted warily at me.

"Push-ups. Just a few push-ups."

I jumped up quickly to dispel the image in Patrick's head. Too late. He was sitting up in bed, staring at my biceps, which bulged with the evidence of obsessive push-ups.

"What have you been doing, babe? What does Franz have to do with this?"

Patrick acted as if I'd done something awful. I told him that Franz was getting sicker, that I wanted to be strong for him. That brought Patrick fully awake.

"Are you listening to yourself, Liza? Franz is *dead,* totally dead. He's been dead a long time, and nothing you do will change that. Please, tell me you understand that."

"I'm not deluding myself, Patrick. I don't do this to make Franz feel better. It makes me feel better to do something, okay? Isn't that enough?"

Patrick sank back against the headboard, shaking his head slowly.

"Liza, I know you can't stop dreaming, but promise me you'll stay away from push-ups and trying to help Franz," he said. "As much as you can, anyway. And promise you'll have someone with you all the time. Who's going with you to Geneva?"

"I'll have plenty of people around," I said. "I always take a suite, and someone sleeps nearby."

He promised to meet me in different cities when he could. I crawled back into bed and slid my body over Patrick's. His concern touched me, though he couldn't really understand. We made love to chase away the spooks, to capture each other's spirits, to thrill our bodies with forgetfulness. Franz did not look away.

Danny went back to Vienna, and we took the train to Geneva. I shared a compartment with my parents, Aunt Frieda, and Greta. We left Patrick behind, but his taste and feel came along for the ride.

Chugging out of gritty Milan (*Patrick's tongue tracing a line down my back*), past industrial debris (*stubbled cheek tickling my neck, warmth spreading from my center*), soft rain streaking across the windows (*hair brushing against belly, tongue seeking secrets*), the Alps bursting through the scenery, transforming the horizon (*arched back, spontaneous, unstoppable*), mountains surround us, luring us higher, no escape (*bodies entwined, enjoined, frenzied, spent*) . . . ah, what a ride.

I tried to read, tried to nap, but the Alps were too magnificent to ignore. Franz might have enjoyed the view, too, but he compulsively looked eastward. We could have turned the train around and Franz would be home in Vienna in hours. He felt the proximity, would have run there barefoot. I placated him with promises that soon we would finish. He sneered at me and made unhappy music in my head.

In the next weeks, we prevailed in Paris, Nice, Brussels, Amsterdam, and other choice spots. Frenchie oversaw the logistics of our tour with tart efficiency. Every morning she checked on my needs and handed me a detailed schedule. She got us everywhere on time, dealt with the locals, and was first to check out the concert halls. Her professional demeanor ended promptly at the finish of our workday, when she became a rabid party girl, exploring the men and other danger zones of Europe. She often came back to the hotel when the rest of us were waking. Her smile was on crooked and she smelled of cigarettes. Between work and play she somehow found time to change her hair color frequently. But she never missed our morning check-in and always got the job done. My attempts to bond with her went nowhere.

"So how'd you get the name 'Frenchie'?" I asked once while we waited for a train.

"I speak French," she said.

"But you speak lots of languages, and you're Dutch. Why 'Frenchie'?"

She shrugged and began the search for her next cigarette.

So much for bonding. Greta was a bosom buddy by comparison. When Greta went home two weeks into our tour, I was surprisingly sorry to see her go. I went to the airport to see her off. Greta told me I was doing well, mighty praise from my teacher. I told her how important she was to me, that she helped me in ways that no one else could. Then I gave her a book of poetry by Goethe as a thank-you gift. She told me she already had the book at home, but she took it with her to read on the plane. I bet she was happy.

My parents and Aunt Frieda rented a car and took a leisurely tour of Europe, meeting us in the cities they wanted to visit. Danny flew in for the weekend concerts and his hip, heartthrobby image appeared on TV and in the papers. Despite my assurances to Patrick that I'd never be alone, it was sometimes just me and Franz at night. I tried not to obsess over Franz's health, but that wasn't easy. Fortunately, Franz was doing fine in our life together, safely on this side of the time line. Things went surprisingly smoothly until Cassie called.

"Fred found the house in Vienna. He thinks it's bullshit, though," she said.

"Well, he's wrong," I said. "I'm sure Hüttenbrenner had something. The manuscript exists."

"Fred traced the ownership of the most likely Hüttenbrenner home. You know, there were quite a few Hüttenbrenners around," she said. "Anyway, this house is over two hundred years old, but somehow only four other families have owned it. Can you believe the way people hang on to things in Europe?"

I urged her to get to the point.

"The current owner is Frau Gerta Schmidt. I don't like her."

"You don't like her? How do you know her?"

"We talked. She wants money to let you in the house," Cassie said. "Lots of money, whether you find anything or not."

I told Cassie to pay.

"She's obnoxious and greedy. I don't like her attitude. Neither does Fred."

"Give her whatever she wants, *anything* she wants," I said. "We have to do this."

Was soll dieser Umweg? . . . What is this detour? Wondrous in ways, but it's time to go home. Liza, it's time to go home! *Liza, are you listening?*

Patrick met me in Lisbon when I had a break at the end of September. We took a few days to ride up the coast and back. It was nice to be away from performing and Frenchie, but sightseeing was hard for me (*when soon we would finish*) and simple conversation could be a challenge (*when Franz was getting sicker*). We stayed one night in the dreamy Hotel Palacio de Setais in the hill town of Sintra. You couldn't find a more romantic setting. Too bad Franz couldn't stop composing.

"Liza, I think they wanted to use that tablecloth again," Patrick said.

I looked down to see a tangle of musical doodles on the restaurant's white linens. The ink matched the pen that had somehow found its way to my hand.

"Sorry, Patrick. Franz can't stop composing lately." I covered the scribbles with my napkin and made a note to tip heavily. "It's about Vienna, about finishing the symphony. He's dying to be there. He's in a writing frenzy. The whole thing makes me nervous."

"Do you think he'll leave you there? Maybe you'll find the manuscript and he'll finally be able to go back to wherever he came from."

I'd thought about this many times. I was scared of Franz staying and scared of him leaving.

"Liza, if you're not sure, let's take a vote." Patrick raised a hand as if swearing in court. "I vote he leaves forever."

I reminded Patrick that I might be the unremarkable me again without Franz. We'd all grown used to more than that.

"Not me, babe," he said. "I say, 'So long, Franz, it's been weird to know you.'" He put down his forkful of pasta and leaned so close I could feel his breath. "You're all I want, Liza."

Patrick was the first person to say that unequivocally. He loved the music, but he still liked me better. How'd I get so lucky?

"By the way, did you hear about Alison?"

"Your Alison?" Patrick and I hardly ever discussed ex-spouses.

"Not mine anymore, but yeah. She's pregnant."

"Wow. Married?"

"Don't know. I heard it through the Manischewitz vine, so it's a little vague."

I'd just recently learned that Jeff, my onetime husband, had married again. I didn't want to picture my ex with his next, but I was glad to know that both Jeff and Alison had been wounded but not broken by Patrick and me. They'd moved on quite nicely, in fact. It felt odd to be discussing their faraway lives over dinner in a Portuguese castle. Patrick and I knew it was significant news, though we didn't dwell on the topic.

I fell asleep warm and secure that night, with Patrick at my side.

I woke the next morning in Franz's bed. I spent most of the day there.

Franz awakens when Justine von Schober enters his room to check on him. She sees his eyes flutter and spreads the curtains to let in the morning. It's autumn. Everything about it, the colors, the smells, infinitely autumn.

"No breakfast for me, Justine," he says. "Just coffee, please."

"I've made a treat for you," she says brightly. "Apple dumplings. You must have a little."

A polite protest. Justine is good-hearted, but her treats could sicken a rat.

Franz doesn't like to ask for help, so Justine offers a hand without waiting.

She props him up against the pillows, then slices and serves his food without a word.

"We've had a message from Marta," she says. "You'll have company today."

Franz smiles. Always a smile for Marta. Too bad the husband is so ordinary. She could have done better.

Marta arrives in late morning. Franz is disappointed because she has not brought little Brita. Marta normally brings Brita because she makes Franz happy.

"I have news about Peter," Marta says.

News about a dead man?

"Our cousin Rudolf went to Trieste on his wedding trip. He saw Peter singing in a theater there. He uses another name, but it's Peter."

"He spoke to him?"

"Only briefly. Rudolf was on his honeymoon, after all, and Peter is the family scandal."

Franz demands every detail. He finds out that Peter has lived in Italy all these years. People pay well to hear him sing. He never did marry the girl he ran off with.

"Didn't marry? Then why did he stay away?"

"Running away was the idea, I suppose," Marta explains. "He and the girl wanted to run away, they never really wanted each other."

Franz can't imagine why Peter would want to run away at all.

"I think it was my fault, Franz." Marta looks at her chubby hands, squeezed into a ball on her knees. "We argued before he left."

A blush spreads across Marta's soft cheeks and soon covers her body. Her blond curls go pinkish.

"I never wanted to say, Franz, but now, well . . ." Marta fights the truth to the end. "We argued about you. I don't suppose it matters anymore, but that's what happened."

Franz is shocked by this. What had he done that caused Peter to leave?

"You know how it was then," Marta says. "We both loved you, we loved each other, and you loved us. A child's game at first, but it was real, too. Three is wrong, Franz. Three is impossible, isn't it?"

"I have found that two is too difficult for me, Marta."

"Can you forgive me, Franz? How much have we hurt you?"

"I'm not hurt, Marta." And, after years of hurt, Franz can say this honestly.

"Things have turned out well for us, haven't they? You have a good husband and your children. It's my bad luck to be so ill, but my life has been blessed."

"What you must have thought of Peter! And of me."

"I'm glad you told me," Franz says. "It seems that there was too much love, not a lack of it. This is better."

As Marta leaves, Franz makes the farewell special. He vows to always love her, and he will.

Franz stays in bed after that, coming to terms with what he's heard. He stares out the window, where clouds are ganging up for a storm. Flocks of birds speed by on serious migratory business. They will soon be in Italy for the winter, where Peter will serenade them for free.

Predictably, Franz translates Marta's revelations into music. He hums a tune, not bitter but blue. I've heard the melody before: Franz will transcribe it almost two hundred years later at my kitchen table. But he aches to play it now. He doesn't have the strength to leave his bed. I concentrate on his hands, willing them to move toward his lap. In the manner of music students forever, he plays piano on the imaginary keyboard that I lay before him.

I think I was singing along in my dreams—perhaps in German—when Patrick shook me awake. A ruddy-faced man stood beside him, bent over me with a stethoscope and a concerned look.

"Liza, thank God! We thought you were in a coma."

Patrick pulled me to him for the hug of a lifetime. He'll never know how grateful I was that he tugged me back into time. I didn't know enough to be afraid while I was gone.

"I would like, please, to take you to hospital in Lisbon," the doctor said. "Is best to be safe."

"Thank you anyway, doctor. I'm fine."

He frowned as he checked my pulse and shined light in my eyes. Patrick argued for me to go to the hospital and get a barrage of medical tests (which would certainly not detect Franz). Patrick said I slept like the dead until noon, then refused to wake up when he yelled and poked at me. The doctor was a last resort, and he was also worried when he couldn't rouse me. The fact that I woke up in perfect health should have pleased everyone, but I understood their concern. Still, I flatly refused hospitals and tests, and sent the doctor away.

"Now what, Liza?" Patrick said. "Now what do we do?"

"Nothing, really. I'm fine."

"You can't be alone, Liza. I'll stay a few more days, until Danny's back at least."

"I'm happy to have you here, Patrick, but there's nothing to be afraid of anymore," I said. "I don't think this will happen again. Everything Franz needs is here. That's what I think, what I believe, so don't worry."

Right. Not a worry in the world.

Patrick stayed four more days, and even he admitted I seemed less shaky. Franz had found a sort of peace in his conversation with Marta. He was glad to know, at last, that Marta and Peter had been as confused as he once was. Peter's escape was not a rejection, and it spared all of them from who-knows-what. With years behind them and weeks to live, Franz loved and felt loved by them again.

Franz's dreams became fewer and sparser after that, and too sad to retell. I accepted that I could not help him through his ex-life except in minor ways. A whispered wish or extra push-up—small gifts, to be sure. In this life, though, I was Franz's vessel for something urgent. *Finishing.* As we resumed touring, it permeated every day and action.

Danny met me and Frenchie in Madrid, where we performed to a delirious crowd. As the audience yelled for more, Franz's thoughts were on finishing. On the train to Seville, Danny chattered while Franz fell into the train's rhythm and filled our head with finishing. It's three o'clock, *and soon we will finish.* It's cold in the train, *and soon we will finish.* The food is stale, *and soon we will finish.* A late evening at a flamenco club grabbed Franz's attention, but not fully. Beyond the raw music and heart-stealing dancers, I clearly heard *and soon we will finish.*

The final weeks of the tour whipped by quickly. After two sold-out concerts in Edinburgh, we finally flew to Vienna. My parents and Aunt Frieda were on the same plane, which bounced dramatically through hundreds of miles of filthy weather. Because of our own agitation, Franz and I were oblivious to the abundant bumps and dips until we heard other passengers' shrieks. The ever-cool Frenchie pulled out a cigarette and rolled it lovingly between her hands, unlit, to ease her distress. People prayed loudly in a patchwork of languages. The nervous-Nellie pilot announced that we must stay buckled in our seats, and issued earnest assurances that nothing was wrong. What a weenie. Even Franz, still a nineteenth-century guy at heart, knew that a few potholes in the sky meant nothing compared to the task at hand. No way could a simple force of nature interfere with our plans to reach Vienna and *finish*.

———

Daheim sein . . . Home . . . I can't recall the moment I left, nor anything else until I opened my eyes and saw bright red fingernails playing my music on a strange piano.

She has become my home, too. A person can have many houses, but two homes? My heart is torn, and my mind is of no use in this. At least we will be there soon and I can finish my task.

My symphony will be whole again—right and left hand interlaced, his and her halves locked in union. I can wait just a little bit, though. I must see the city and eat schnitzel. I am ravenous for Vienna.

Don't ask me to describe seeing Vienna through Franz's eyes. I never felt that version of joy before or since, so I don't know the words for it. Same for the anguish, the gratitude of homecoming, the solitude, and an overwhelming hunger for something unnameable.

Through blurry sheets of rain the city itself was, of course, instantly recognizable. Vienna voraciously clings to its historic looks. The love of antiquity may lie in the population's reluctance to embrace big chunks of the last hundred years. Vienna's glory lay long before the days of Hitler, war, fascism, and other miseries. The recent past could not compare with the times of Schubert, Beethoven, Liszt, Strauss, Mozart, and the rest.

During the limo ride from airport to hotel, my parents and Aunt Frieda lavished Cassie with the details of their European adventure—the fabulous paella that made Dad sick, the shocking public toilet in a Belgian park, Liza's devoted fans, and the Frenchman who fell hard for Frieda. Cassie tried to interrupt the travelogue to discuss business with me, but I waved away her attempts. Talking would have distracted from the view.

Vienna's Baroque and Gothic architecture is made of whipped cream and garnished in gold. With their showy swirls and dress-up demeanor, the buildings could be ladies at a ball. The whole city has a toe stepped forward, ready to waltz.

Franz cheered the sound of Austrians speaking his language. He read every street sign, greeted each landmark with an applauding heartbeat.

We passed the Musikverein, the nineteenth-century building where we would perform the next night. I plucked one of the tourist brochures sprouting from the limo's side pockets. It said that the immense Musik-verein, with its Greek Renaissance façade, wasn't completed until 1870, well after Franz's death. Many of the all-time greats had played there. I should have put the brochure away then and there, but instead I leafed through it a page too far.

"This is much too strange."

My intensity got everyone's attention.

"This Stadtpark, the city park, we just passed—it's filled with statues of great musicians," I said. "There's a whole cemetery dedicated to com-posers."

Dad caught the significance. He guessed that Franz was there.

"Oh, yes," I said. "Statue in the park and a place in the cemetery. He's right next to Beethoven. Pretty strange, huh?"

"How's Franz doing?" Dad asked.

"I can't be sure. It seems he's fainted, and I can't stop shaking." I handed Dad the open brochure. "We saw this picture of his statue, of him and his friends, all in their graves, and he kind of vacated my premises. Isn't it true you can't see yourself dead in dreams?"

"Freud said that," Mom said.

"God, poor Franz," I said. "Do you think he saw his own grave and went insane?"

"Only if *we're* the characters in *his* dream," Dad reasoned. "I say we're all real. Anyway, everything's different with Franz. Do you think he can handle being here?"

I honestly didn't know, which made Cassie nervous. She was thinking about the concert.

"Don't worry. I'd know it if he were gone for good." *Wouldn't I?* "He's not always up and awake, anyway. When he first came, he slept half the time. This is just overwhelming for him all at once, don't you think?"

Unanimous *uh-huh*s.

"Liza, is there any chance that this is exactly what Schubert wanted all along?" my father suggested. "That you brought him home, and now he doesn't need you anymore?"

Maybe we were close to our goal but, no, the game wasn't over. I assumed Franz would be back any minute. I couldn't guess how long he'd stay.

The Hotel Imperial is a huge, ornate pastry. The exterior is held up by more columns than there are pigeons to poop on them. Inside and out, no elaborateness of design is too much for this converted Württemberg Palace, whose first resident was Emperor Franz Joseph I. The hotel staff acted as if we guests were a bunch of emperors ourselves. In my opulent suite, I removed my wet clothes, stood in a hot shower, and searched for Franz. He seemed to be stirring. I wrapped myself in the courtesy Hotel Imperial bathrobe (where was my courtesy Hotel Imperial tiara?) and studied the city from my window, trying to envision what Franz once saw there.

There was a knock at the door and, happily, it was Patrick. He dropped his travel bags on the floor and whistled at the grandness of the suite. We barely had time for hugs when Cassie showed up for a business update. We arranged ourselves at an antique table under a crystal chandelier that complemented the brocade wall coverings and carved moldings on the cloud-painted ceiling. Just like home.

Cassie spread important-looking papers across the elegant table. "CD sales are strong," she told me, "and we're finalizing your spring tour. That'll bump sales even higher."

Another tour was too much to think of at the moment. I wanted to know about taking Franz to the Hüttenbrenner home, where we could finish. Cassie said it was all arranged for Sunday. Fred would be arriving soon with the details. I almost protested the two-day wait, but I understood.

Vienna had been purposely scheduled as our last stop in Europe. No one was willing to say so, but we all knew it might be Franz's last stop anywhere. For the same unspoken reason, we had to go to the Hüttenbrenner home *after* our concert. I was okay with that. We had reached Vienna, so we would definitively finish.

Fred called from the lobby while we were still meeting. Long flight, but he'd come right up to see us.

He brought a date.

My sister stared at Fred's companion as if she were a poodle on its hind legs. In fact, she sort of resembled a Chihuahua, with bright blue pop-out eyes. There was something familiar about her.

"Fred, I had no idea you were bringing someone." I extended a hand to his friend. "I don't think we've met."

"Actually, we have." She set her dimpled chin in a self-possessed position. "I'm Leslie Pardo. My mother lives upstairs from Fred. We met once last year."

She looped a hand comfortably through Fred's arm. Her lopsided smile was endearing.

"Of course. Leslie, have you met my sister, Cassie?"

They exchanged nods. Cassie had not uttered a sound. She was gaping loudly, though.

"How did you two get together?" I ventured.

Fred and Leslie traded off telling the story of how they met when she was in Brooklyn Heights visiting her mother. They really did hit it off from the start. Her mother had been hinting for them to get together ever since. When Fred returned home from Upper Danville (after the confrontation with Barry and Cassie, when Cassie pretty much called him an inconsequential nobody), Leslie was in town for a visit. They stayed in contact after that. Leslie made a point to visit more often. Mission accomplished, Mrs. Pardo.

Leslie was honestly cute, bug eyes and all. A sprinkle of freckles across her nose was all that stood between her and a flawless complexion. And everything about her was petite—Fred's compact body would easily wrap around hers. She really was damn cute and likable. Franz thought so, too.

We all went to dinner that night at Zu Den Drei Hacken, an old Vienna restaurant. So old, in fact, that Franz himself picked it. The hotel concierge was directing us to his personal favorite when "Zu Den Drei Hacken" jumped from my mouth. My inner composer woke suddenly, craving greasy foods and beer.

Danny met us at the restaurant and brought his grandmother, whose matched pearls were as perfect as her posture. Her regal bearing triggered a vestigial curtsy reflex in me.

The festive feel of the dinner was perfect for the end of my parents' and Aunt Frieda's trip. We talked about great cities, the foul weather, Danny's school, and the dearth of crime in Vienna—everything but our impending drama at Hüttenbrenner's.

Leslie charmed everyone, almost. I nearly felt sorry for Cassie, who tried desperately to outdazzle her. Her eyes flitted between Fred and Patrick to see which man was more vulnerable to a knockout redhead with limitless finances. She discovered the existence of Cassie-proof men. Leslie commanded more attention with her sly accounts of life as an ER nurse. Patrick and Fred weren't even aware enough to enjoy Cassie's anguish, so I had to do it for all of us.

After dinner I asked Patrick to stroll around the city with me. The rain had lapsed into a halfhearted sprinkle, and we could catch a cab if it got worse.

I thought Franz might lead us straight to the Hüttenbrenner house, but he didn't. Instead, we wandered the town, from memory to memory. Patrick indulged our meandering. He looked where we pointed, sniffed when we sniffed.

Franz was prepared to see the changes in Vienna, but he chose not to. His view slid past the new and saw the old things he preferred to see. A door to a butcher shop he knew well. The window of a friend's house, bright with a stranger's light. A tailor shop, where the owner made his brown suit a tad too small. Cracks and cobbles of familiar design.

In a city of monumental buildings, Franz made time for only one grand structure, St. Stephen's Cathedral. It was built in the twelfth century in Romanesque style in the time of Ottokar II of Bohemia. Centuries later it was reconstructed in Gothic detail. Baroque embellishments and art treasures were added later. For nine hundred years, truly devout or overly rich people have sought their way into Heaven by depositing prayers and fortunes in this church. You'd call the style gaudy if you saw it in your neighbor's house. Franz found it splendid. We spent a good part of the evening there. Patrick was content to study the architecture. Franz felt inspired. He prayed with an open heart: *Thank you, God, please let me finish.*

I was more nervous about my Vienna concert than I had been about any in a long while. According to the news, the locals were not unanimous in their support of me. Franz was their special guy. If I was the real thing, they couldn't love me more, but if I was a phony, watch out. I felt like a child trying to please an ultra-strict parent.

Every detail of this concert seemed crucial, my hair included.

"I'm having it cut short," I said.

"You can't do that," Cassie stated.

"It never stops raining here. My hair is twice its normal size. I have to cut it."

We were already at the beauty salon and our patient stylist stood at chairside, waiting for instructions. Cassie wouldn't budge.

"Odious as it is, you're famous for your hair, Liza," she said. "You can't cut it."

"Really? Hair is what I'm famous for? I thought it was the music."

"Stop being juvenile." Cassie folded her arms resolutely. "No cut, no way."

My mother jumped in on Cassie's side. I pleaded for reason.

Our stylist settled the matter with a compromise. In nicely accented English, she recommended a hair ornament. She'd pull my hair back in a halo-sized band so we could maintain control but keep the length. We picked a gold band with elegant leaf-and-pearl embellishments. It gave a tasteful tiara effect—perfect for courtly Vienna.

The performance was sold out, but we arrived to find a small group of people marching outside the theater with homemade signs. A couple of words were similar to English: "*blasphemy*" and "*imposter*," though they could mean something totally different in German. Danny was with us, but he declined to translate.

This concert hall felt different from the others. The crowd exuded a spotty leeriness at first, as they decided whether to applaud or scold. Franz found it disconcerting, since he was especially eager to please this audience. Danny was a huge help. On most of our tour, I missed bantering with English-speaking audiences. Danny jumped in as *der Banterer.* When he came onstage for the *lieder,* the crowd responded immediately. They had heard about him and knew he lived in their city. He talked to the audience just a little, and whatever he said was good enough to warm the room several degrees. By intermission, I felt almost safe.

Unfortunately, I made a mirror check during the short break. As I suspected, the nonstop rain had transformed my hair to a bundle of mohair yarn. Encircling it was my hair ornament, which looked less like a tiara and more like the Crown of Thorns. This did not build my confidence.

So Franz and I both felt a little off that night, not to mention keyed up about our mission to Hüttenbrenner's the next day. That explained a few mistakes during the performance. Nothing most people would notice, but exactly what nasty music critics live for. And wouldn't you guess there were a couple in the audience, most notably—you won't believe this— Chase Barnes. My rejected lover and crusading debunker was on special assignment for a cable TV show. Not long after our performance, we caught Chase's review on the all-news channel in our hotel suite.

Special Report to **Entertaining News Tonight,** *October 22*

Good evening, this is Chase Barnes in Vienna, where, depending on your opinion, I just attended a concert by pianist Liza Durbin or the comeback of Franz Schubert.

If you've kept your wits about you through the hoopla of the past year, you should not be surprised to hear that Miss Durbin, who claims to be possessed by Schubert, embarrassed herself and a susceptible Viennese audience tonight. It was an evening marked by blatant mistakes and a perverse version of *lieder*—a traditional German song style—delivered by Danny Carson, Miss Durbin's ever-present wunderkind. She did little to convince discerning people that she is the living embodiment of Schubert. It would be easier to believe she carried the spirit of Liberace.

Still, people love to be fooled. This little fantasy appealed to the sappy audience, which cheered her efforts. They all but threw kisses at young Mr. Carson as well, for presenting what he called "collaborative *lieder*" in his pleasant but unripe voice.

As a side note, the potentially attractive pianist wore the most vulgar sort of tiara—a crass parody of Austrian monarchy, perhaps? I'd say a parody of music was more on the mark. Take this excerpt from the opening piece, the much-talked-about *Snow Sonata* . . . *(Tape rolls, highlighting the single mistake in the first half. Instant replays ensue.)*

~~~

Most of the reviews were not like that. The few missed notes were generally forgiven, and the concert was well received by critics, particularly by the ones who were not personally spurned by me. They mostly reviewed the concert on its merits and sidestepped the Franz controversy.

Cassie gave us the full report the following morning. She was laying out the plans for our trip to Hüttenbrenner's. I should have been riveted by these details, but I was still recovering from a strange night's sleep. Following our concert, I had taken a terrible chance and made one last effort to find the ailing Franz in my dreams.

Lying in bed, I silently called his name and searched for a shred of his prior existence. I caught a glimpse of his room, a snatch of music, sunbeams bouncing off a pitcher. I saw nothing of Franz, but I thought I heard something—a distant, frightened voice, in what could only be a prayer. I could make out the tone, if not the words. It was similar, no doubt, to prayers offered by dying people throughout time. A lifetime expressed in a few fading heartbeats.

"*Franz, I will finish for you,*" I said. "*You will not end here. There's much more, I promise you.*"

Maybe Franz thought he heard something, too. Maybe my promise wedged itself in his spirit, triggering our merger in the far future, when the time was right. That's my theory, anyway, which is as good as any.

I knew I'd never visit Franz that way again. I withdrew, feeling lucky to return to my own life, whole and for good. Despite all reason and historical fact, I added my own prayerful appeal on Franz's behalf, requesting a change of heavenly plans, just this once. It didn't work, of course. When I woke up, Franz had still died in 1828. He knew I tried, though, which had to count for something.

"They'll meet us there at three, and we'll go into the house together," Cassie was saying. She was pointing at something on a piece of paper. "Liza, are you listening?"

Cassie had arranged for media coverage, but I forgot until that moment. We had discussed it in advance and she convinced me it was necessary. This event would happen only once, and it called for documentation. With rare sensitivity, Cassie had opted to keep the party small.

"Just a *New York Times* reporter, someone from CNN, and that guy you like from NPR," she said. "They won't interfere or bug you with questions until it's over."

That's when the reality of the moment gripped us. This was what we had been aiming for, charging toward, but the journey itself would be hard to give up. Does the hiker sprint the last mile or drag his feet a bit to admire a tree that he'll never see again? I felt the slightest hesitation in Franz as doubt and conviction and great possibilities all roared through us at once. No matter, though, it was time to go.

Franz could barely contain himself as we started out. If I checked a mirror, I might see him leaking out of my eyes and ears. There were other people in the limo with us, but who? All our senses were lasered into one task, nothing to spare on nonessentials.

The twenty-minute ride dragged in Franz time. When we stopped at a red light, I had to fight him to stay in the car and not carry on by foot. There was great relief when we reached Hüttenbrenner's street.

Frau Gerta Schmidt stood waiting at the door, the proud treasure-keeper. The media people were already there with her. She welcomed us in memorized English and gestured toward the threshold. A smell of roasted meat came wafting from inside. I heard myself stifle a whimper.

Earnest faces were urging me into the house. Cassie, my parents, Patrick, Aunt Frieda, Fred, Danny, the news strangers. They appeared to be concerned, their lips were moving and their faces darkened with concern. I couldn't distinguish among the people or their words. That's when we snapped.

"*No, no!* This is *wrong!*" I yelled. "This is *definitely* wrong!"

For the second time in my life, I fainted.

I didn't like my second faint any better than my first. I woke up surrounded by worried looks. Patrick cradled my head and I mumbled that I was okay. The newspeople scribbled and muttered. Cassie exhorted me to get up and come in the house, for God's sake.

Franz would not budge. He knew for certain this was wrong. He clued me in during the faint.

"You don't understand," I said. "This is the wrong place."

Blinks of sudden comprehension.

"Get me a map," I demanded. "I need a map."

The limo driver quickly fetched one from his glove box. I looked at the detailed map and found the spot right away. Ostwiese was a tiny dot on the map, southwest of Vienna, a village that ringed a perfectly round lake. A wonderful calm overtook us. I apologized for upsetting everyone. We piled in our vehicles and took off again.

The town lay less than thirty miles away, in view of the Alps. As we drove though the pale autumn day, Franz drew me a picture of how this countryside once looked, with trees stretched high on a summer afternoon. I grabbed the first hand I could find, maybe Patrick's, maybe Danny's.

"Will you know the house when you see it?" Cassie asked.

We had spotted the village in a valley just a few hills away. "I'll know it."

"Remember, Liza, they don't know we're coming," she said gently. "We don't even know if the house is still there. You might be disappointed."

"We'll find it. If no one's home, we'll break in," I said.

The houses circling the lake looked ancient. Any one of them could have been there for centuries. I asked the driver to slowly circle the water until I said to stop.

Moments later . . . *"STOP!"*

It sat about thirty yards back from the lake, just as we pictured it. A two-story stone building, larger than remembered, with a great lawn leading to a strip of beach. A sign outside read GASTHAUS MÜLLER.

I jumped from the car before it completely stopped. My entourage followed closely. A young blond boy answered the front door with his little sister hiding behind him. He studied me for a moment before his face brightened with recognition.

"Sind Sie Liza Durbin?" He yelled over his shoulder, *"Mutter, Papa! Es ist Liza Durbin!"*

The parents ran to the door. They looked more awed than surprised.

"Good evening, Miss Durbin," the man said. "I'm so glad you've come."

How far back can you remember? Do you recall standing in your crib or being carried on your father's shoulders? My early days run like an out-of-order slideshow. One image dissolves into another without reason, overlapping and bleeding into one another. They are random moments, stuck in my brain before I had a filing system for time and relationships.

That's how it felt to arrive at Gasthaus Müller. Distorted, familiar, soft around the edges. Crossing the threshold, *I* was left behind and Franz and I entered the house as *we*. Our thoughts, memories, feelings, all twined in absolute harmony.

Zu klein, viel zu klein. Too small. The rooms seemed too small, and new ones stretched beyond the original space, some with odd modern touches. A television flickered and blared nearby—*schrecklich!*—we walked across the living room and shut it off. We planted ourself in the room's center and banished the cameras and company from our mind.

Wo sind meine Freunde, meine Lieben? The familiar voice of a welcoming spirit, asking where we'd been so long.

The large stone fireplace still roared with its original purpose and the unchanging smell. *Holz, Rauch, Glück* . . . The happiness of wood burning. A large bay window peered over the lake, where it had witnessed every bird and leaf that flew by for more than two centuries. The pictures on the walls were new, except for a small framed etching that was once quite a bargain in a dingy shop in Salzburg. *Zwanzig Schilling* and not a penny more.

People were talking nonstop to us, those in the room and others unseen. *Willkommen, lieber Freund. Zu lang warst du weg,* dear friend, gone so long. Questions, greetings, Brita's woeful singing. The murmur blended into an amorphous call for human contact, which we ignored.

We toured the main living room with our eyes until we found the path. A cherrywood staircase banister, partially obscured by an archway. *Dort* . . . there . . . *Das ist der Weg.* We went upstairs.

Bitte Gott, lass es mich finden. Please, God, let me find it.

Despite the sturdy banister, we navigated the stairs by tracing the wall with our right hand. Something powerful lived within that stone. At the top of the stairs we turned right without pause, walked into the little girl's frilly room, and turned on the light.

This wasn't originally a child's room. In the days of weekend Schubertiads, it was a guest room. Our room . . . *Unser Zimmer.* Stepping into it was like switching on an old-fashioned radio and spinning the tuner dial back and forth. Snatches of trill and thump, *Musik,* warbling voices, piano riffs, Marta's laugh, a baby crying. Beer, a wretched stomach flu, candlelight. A night of card playing, a swim in the icy lake, *ein Mann und eine Frau*—a couple fighting, crying. A hiding place . . . *Ein geheimer Platz.*

A large wooden wardrobe covered most of one wall. Of course it would still be there—it was built for the room and was far too bulky to justify ever moving it again. The top two thirds consisted of a double-door closet filled, no doubt, with linens and blankets and a hanging rack for little-girl clothes. Under the closet section were three exterior drawers with newish brass knobs. At the bottom of the wardrobe was a foot-high decorative panel with carved scrollwork that matched a carved angel on the panel that graced the top. They weren't just decorative.

Engel der Gnade . . . Angel of Mercy.

We reached high and pushed a small lever behind the angel's outstretched wing. The bottom panel popped open. *Aha!*

Legal papers, love letters, bits of jewelry, and intimate mementos lay in their secret bed, just as remembered. We brushed our fingers along them only in passing as we reached for a leather tube containing a rolled packet of deeply yellowed papers.

Gottseidank . . . Thank you, God.

With shaky hands, we pulled the ancient music out of its nest. The tied cord that had faithfully held it scrolled fell open with a sigh. The rolled pages uncurled of their own accord. The smoke-dry paper pulled itself together, regained its brightness, and felt fresh again in our hands.

The hand-drawn musical notes refused to sit still on the pages. They cavorted freely, pounding out the rhythm, sailing through the melody, *schöne Vögel,* colliding and chorus-lining. We watched their antics from beginning to end . . . *Ende.*

To this day, people debate what they saw that night. Whose hands flattened the tightly rolled sheets? Did the decrepit paper turn whiter or did the camera lie? And surely it was Liza Durbin's trembling hands that made the notes appear to dance across the pages. They never even mention the moment the cameras didn't catch—when the young-again papers gathered themselves into wings and fluttered, not much, but enough. We dropped the pages on the floor before they could fly away. Cassie took possession then of the manuscript, dry and yellowed, incorrigibly curled and fragile again.

Franz and I didn't need it anymore.
Gottseidank.

Solch ein Empfang . . . Such a homecoming for me, for her. Beautiful still, but no longer perfect. I would make changes now. First, the wallpaper. Other things, too.

CHAPTER SEVEN

Sunday Edition, National Public Radio
October 23

TOM WISEMAN: Mr. Müller, help me, if you will, by explaining in your own way what happened today.

MR. MÜLLER: It's as you have said. Liza Durbin came to our house, unexpected. She appeared, I think, to be in some sort of trance. She walked through our home and found music hidden in an old furniture.

TOM WISEMAN: Had you met Miss Durbin before? You obviously recognized her.

MR. MÜLLER: No, no. We went to her concert, the whole family. That's all.

TOM WISEMAN: You know, Mr. Müller, that your house wasn't the first stop on Miss Durbin's search. We followed a dramatic sequence of events. Forgive me, but skeptics may yet ask if this was all staged in advance.

MR. MÜLLER: Certainly not.

TOM WISEMAN: Yet you didn't seem completely surprised to find Liza Durbin at your door.

MR. MÜLLER: We have always heard rumors that Franz Schubert stayed here and wrote music here. When I heard Miss Durbin play, I thought, yes, she might be connected to him. She would know this place, of course, but really it was still a surprise to me.

TOM WISEMAN: Mr. Müller, do you believe now that Liza Durbin is inhabited by Franz Schubert?

MR. MÜLLER: The house felt entirely different when she was here. You felt it, no? How could we not believe?

Gordy & Jill Talk!
October 24

GORDY: So, did you catch our gal Liza on CNN?

JILL: Or read about her in the paper or hear it on the radio, you mean? We've all heard about Liza Durbin by now.

GORDY: And do you believe the whole thing was for real?

JILL: Absolutely, don't you? *(Tentative applause.)* How could Liza Durbin be that good an actress? She about fell apart halfway through. I was afraid for the poor thing.

GORDY: But, Jilly, didn't you think it was a bit *too* perfect? Like maybe someone planned it?

JILL: I refuse to be as cynical as you. I believe in miracles and this feels like one to me. How about it, folks? *(Bigger applause.)*

GORDY: Well, according to the *USA Today* polls, most Americans agree with you, Jilly. They think it's the real thing. And I like Liza Durbin very much, so I hope it's true.

JILL: Will you be at her New Year's Eve concert to hear the "Finished Symphony," Gord?

GORDY: You bet, if the network can get me in. That'll be the hot ticket of the season. And speaking of gals with spirit, wait'll you meet our next guest.

JILL: You must mean the UCLA cheerleader Corky Spright, who wrote her memoirs about her years with the squad.

GORDY: A fascinating book, Jilly.

JILL: That means he read the captions with the steamy photos, folks. *(Snort, laugh, wink.)*

NEW YORK POST
December 21

Symphony Found—Liza Lost?

It's been two months since Liza Durbin's dramatic recovery of Franz Schubert's manuscript of the Unfinished Symphony, and she's dropped completely out of the public eye ever since. Durbin had been a highly visible figure since last spring.

Durbin's sister and publicist, Cassie Whitman, canceled all public appearances and declined interviews leading up to the unveiling of the Finished Symphony at Lincoln Center on New Year's Eve. The sold-out event will be broadcast worldwide. Durbin's unpredictable behavior and sudden withdrawal from the public arena have raised questions about her health and state of mind.

"Liza will definitely be here on New Year's," Whitman said. "So will Franz. People will hear something that's completely new but already a classic."

But experts worry that finding the lost symphony pages may have been an overpowering emotional experience for Durbin. On her nationally syndicated talk show, inhabitism expert Mikki Kloster says it's also possible that Franz fulfilled his purpose and departed. She says this may explain Durbin's disappearance.

It's good to have friends who are rich. John D.'s personal fortune was in the Stagger Zone. As a child, he and his extended family summered with the Doyle matriarch at her Rhode Island estate. John D. was lord of the manor these days, and told me "no one ever winters there." (People of his social set use the seasons as verbs.) Therefore, he explained, the old place was empty and at my disposal. That meant thirty or forty rooms, tennis courts, and—just what I needed—a ballroom.

The ballroom was the exact right size for sixty-four musicians and me.

John D. contacted stellar and trustworthy Sony artists for me, and Greta lined up some people she admired. I called a few I'd met along the way, and Danny returned in early December from his semester in Vienna. Soon we had the makings of an orchestra in a secluded estate. Frenchie stuck around to manage the details, freeing the artists to make music without distractions. Reports say she distracted them in other ways after hours.

This was nirvana for Franz—a Schubertiad that lasted more than a month. He even returned to his old, gloriously creative dreams. No more visits to another time, always looking straight ahead. Franz was a wide-open source and a receptor for musical revelation.

The wide artistic differences among the musicians caused a few initial problems. Because I'd never performed with more than one other person, I was amazed at the passion of their arguments. After all, these were professionals who were used to playing with other musicians. But trying to move so many creative minds in one direction was like teaching synchronized swimming to cats. Maybe it was because of the circumstances—collaborating with Schubert and all—and everyone's eagerness to add something personal. More than one musician stomped off in the first two weeks, vowing never to come back. But "never" is a relative term that usually lasted a sulky hour or so.

The group needed to find its vision, so we could all see the one star in a billion that we were shooting for. It was hard to achieve with our stacks of music, my limited vocabulary, and Franz's occasional German outbursts. Greta came to my rescue more than once, translating our intentions into directions that the group could follow. It all came together when we started asking questions—not about what the musicians *were* doing but about what they *could* do. Things started sizzling. We listened and absorbed and knitted our souls together—at some point, each person crossed from *I* to *we,* at least for a little while.

⌁

Lincoln Center felt like the right place to debut Schubert's "Finished Symphony." It's where Greta and I teamed up, for one thing. It also had prestige and a modern image that fit the occasion.

The evening before the concert, I stayed at my apartment in Brooklyn Heights. I hadn't spent much time there in the past months. Patrick was flying in from Milan in the morning, and I didn't want anyone else's company that night.

Alone in my home, memories swarmed around me. Everywhere I looked were clues about my almost-deserted life. I visualized my little railway apartment taped off like a crime scene: white-chalk outlines of me at the kitchen table, Patrick in my bed, Franz writing music, Greta at my door, me calling Mikki in a panic, Fred trying to save my life, me going insane as Franz sank into my soul. I also saw images of me dressing for work, chatting on the phone with Ruthie, and of Patrick and me before he left for Italy—last year, when we were young. These last images were so deep in the memory pool that I couldn't stay with them for long without coming up for air.

New Year's would be a landmark night. Franz would finish his work, yet I knew I couldn't return to mine. Whatever happened, we'd be forever bonded. A great sentimental wave pushed me down on the bed as I felt Franz get emotional, too. A year of intimacy had passed between us, but how and why we were brought together remained a mystery.

I lay back in bed, stunned at realizing how much I loved Franz. My transformed life was juicier and more exquisite because of him. I crossed my arms around my chest to hug him. I stroked my sides and breasts and legs to caress him. My mind went to steamy, hungry, adoring places, and my body sang out in love *lieder*. Time lost its coordinates. The laws of nature were redefined and greatly improved.

A strange thing happened just hours before the concert.

The day was a rush of phone calls, media nonsense, hair care, and last-minute details. My parents had asked me to meet them and Aunt Frieda for lunch at the Stage Deli. With all the public commotion, this would likely be our only chance for a private New Year's moment. I was meeting with Greta in her studio at Juilliard when I noticed it was after twelve forty-five, so I invited her to join us.

My family displayed the impressive Durbin appetite while Greta munched on a salad twice her size. She was friendlier than usual, though she avoided Aunt Frieda, of course. Her face warmed when my father asked how she thought the concert would go.

"It will be a great accomplishment, of this I am sure. Your daughter has worked very hard for Schubert's sake," she said. "They did well to find each other, yes."

"Do you think that's how it happened, Dr. Pretsky? That our daughter and Franz were looking for each other?"

"In a way, Mr. Durbin," she said. "I think perhaps that's how it might happen, yes?" Then she shrugged and returned to her salad. "Opposite poles that need each other, perhaps. But what do I know of this? It's only a feeling. You must have your own guesses."

We downed our sodas and suddenly it was after two, time to rush to my hair appointment. It was a crisp, dry day, the weather least likely to craze my hair. Still, attention must be paid. We left the table as a group, with me in the lead. In my state of hurry and distraction, I nearly knocked over a man who was walking into the restaurant as we were leaving. He was an attractive elderly man with a tweed overcoat and white hair.

"My goodness, Miss Durbin," he said. "How nice to run into you again."

"*A-gayne*" was how he said it. Of course, the man from Nordstrom, my first real fan. What was his name again?

"*Abe Sturtz!*"

Two voices cried his name in unison—Greta Pretsky and Aunt Frieda, a shocked and shocking duet.

A momentary silence followed, then Greta wheeled on Aunt Frieda and uttered, "Slut."

Aunt Frieda retaliated, "Bitch."

Dr. Abe Sturtz, refined to the core, interrupted with a "*Tut-tut*" and expressed his delight at seeing them both.

"Mom, I want *every detail*," I said to my mother. "I'm late for my hair appointment. I have to go but I want every detail. Remember, Mom, every word. It's important."

Dr. Sturtz chuckled at my reaction. "Miss Durbin, please, take my card again. Do call this time, won't you?"

Lincoln Center buzzed that night. If no one moved or made a sound, there still would have been an audible beat emanating from the people waiting to be astonished.

In the last minutes before the concert, I chased everyone out of the dressing room. Me and Franz alone again.

We watched each other in the mirror, studying our single reflection. The hair was good for a change. Definitely good. And the dress was great—the blue slut model, unworn for months and resurrected for this occasion. When the knock came on the door and it was time to go on-stage, I looked deep in the mirror, waved at the face in there, and left the room.

———

Wenn ich sie liebe heisst das ich liebe auch mich? . . . Is loving her the same as loving me? Surely this is a sin of pride as well as lust. To be so complete— at once to surrender and conquer, to enter and envelop!

I fear I am eternally damned, for I certainly won't repent. In that case, one more time, please, before we sleep.

CHAPTER EIGHT

THE NEW YORK TIMES
January 1

The Night the Music Changed
by Jonathan Porter-Cringe

If you are one of the two or three people on Earth who slept through the Renaissance last night, let me tell you about the world today. The New Year begins with a sound born in an 18th-century soul, emerging through a 21st-century heart and mind. While the core of Franz Schubert's Unfinished Symphony remained intact, its completed expression via Liza Durbin and company was altered in unexpected and undeniably smashing form.

The Finished Symphony was delivered by 64 consummate musicians. They were not a traditional orchestra but a composition of their own. Yes, there were strings, horns, woodwinds and two pianos. Also a few surprises, like Wynton Marsalis on trumpet, Don Byron on clarinet, Anoushka Shankar on sitar, a baritone from Kenya named Moreno Abdi, cellist Yo-Yo Ma, James Galway on flute, Maggie Sunshine on guitar and Bobby McFerrin conducting. The engaging Danny Carson added to the mix. In fact, the only obvious missing player was Liza Durbin herself. She was onstage as a semi-conductor of sorts, but never sat at a piano. The benches were reserved for the highly talented and recently neglected pianist Natalie Frome, for Durbin's mentor Greta Pretsky and for another, most surprising guest star. Chase Barnes—the publicly sworn Durbin-hater—played a passage of startling originality, referred to as Pantheon in the program notes.

The seemingly mismatched mélange of players had every reason to be terrible. They could have fought their differences and clashed in every measure. Instead, something wound them together as they carried the familiar Unfinished Symphony theme into another realm. Each musician had glowing moments. Latin sounds melded into Celtic history that swayed to a Balinese beat. If the real Franz Schubert choreographed this incarnation of his masterpiece, I reel at his generosity and vision.

The original movements of his symphony, while instantly recognizable, have been translated into contemporary terms. The additions to the work, referred to as the Twin Movements, rivaled their predecessors in . . .

USA TODAY—EUROPEAN EDITION
Friday, January 20

The Greatest Comeback Ever—Schubert Rocks On

Almost a month after the premiere of the Finished Symphony, a thing called "Schu music" has planted itself in every part of the world. Musicians young and old, fans of every stripe, are playing with the synthesis of styles and instruments that stunned them at Liza Durbin's New Year's Eve concert.

The concert recording is hugely popular. Musicologists debate its content and form. Wherever you go, people talk about what they heard. Musicians are retuning their ears to absorb and play it.

"I can't believe my mother and I are listening to the same music," said 17-year-old Larry Cantor, a junior at Clarke High School in Westbury, New

York. "I play in the hottest band on Long Island and I'm suddenly listening to Mozart with Mom. Strange times."

Larry's mother, Erica Cantor, was not always a fan of the music played by Fly Zone, her son's band.

"A month ago I could barely stand to listen. Last night he played his guitar—something he wrote himself—and it brought tears to my eyes."

This kind of intergenerational, cross-cultural musical exchange has become a phenomenon around the country.

But while the clamor for Schu music is high, people may have to use their own creative resources if they want to hear more. Depending on what you believe, the Finished Symphony was created either by Liza Durbin or, through her, by Franz Schubert. They've both dropped out of sight since then. There are no plans for a spring tour or other recordings at this time.

Yet Schu music thrives.

"We definitely won't let it die," said Larry Cantor. "My band has gone totally Schu, and a lot of others are, too."

When asked what made Schu music special to him, Larry took a minute to think about it. "I never heard anything like it before," he said. "It was like seeing new colors."

⌁⌁⌁

What did people expect to hear? I guess they thought we'd play the notes we found on those missing pages at the Müllers' home. I probably thought so, too. When Franz held the music in his hands again, he still liked some parts quite well. We had simply found the manuscript too late. A year in my life had radically changed his perception.

Genius carries over time. Franz was a musical sponge in his century and remained one in ours. Everything he heard expanded his arsenal, ignited his creativity.

After the New Year's concert, I gave copies of all the manuscripts we'd written during the past year to Greta Pretsky and to my sister. Greta would do something noble with them and Cassie could make them famous. It was important that they got a good home because they were the last that Franz would ever write.

He left even before the concert ended. In the ecstasy of a perfect phrase, Franz Schubert's spirit lifted lightly from my body and floated away. No pain or struggle, just the rightness of the moment, the lightness of a kiss.

I'd felt this coming for weeks. We'd said our version of farewell many times, just in case. When it finally happened, I was prepared.

I had asked Natalie Frome to play piano instead of me. Hell, she had actual talent of her own. Greta also played a part, one that was completely unlike her usual repertoire. It was a jazzy, unruly section that drove her crazy at first. But when she put it together with the orchestra and heard the iridescence, she made the music her own. She improvised, flourished and pumped the piece to a higher level. I'd never seen her giggle before.

Chase Barnes was Franz's idea, too. Not because he liked Chase—the man was an undisputed asshole—but a minor theme from Chase Barnes's *Pantheon* had been running through our head for months. Something in it perfectly complemented the "Finished Symphony," maybe even was crucial to it. When I called Chase to invite him to join us in Rhode Island with some of the world's best musicians, he played hard to get for nearly a heartbeat. Then he was good enough to forgive me for being "a sad, semitalented fraud with offensive, possibly psychopathic, delusions" (*Time* magazine, June 25). Only Franz could have made me call him, but not a thing in the world could make me like him again. His music, though, really was something.

The most reluctant musician was Maggie Sunshine. I had to go to New Orleans to persuade her. She was not performing regularly because of "personal problems," but I tracked her down through someone at the Rock 'n' Bowl. She was ashamed to tell me that her spirit had left her. I knew it anyway because the light had left her eyes. Oddly, she could still see my light—a residual ability left by her visitor. She told me that she could still play some, too. She underestimated herself by miles. Whoever had inhabited Maggie left her with a gift. Not the same as the original, but something of her own, something we needed for our symphony. When she finally came to understand this, Maggie flowered. You wouldn't recognize her today.

· · ·

Nobody seemed to notice when Franz took his leave with ten minutes to go in the symphony. The concert finished in expert hands and a world-wide audience cheered. Only one person met me backstage to acknowledge my loss. I live with him today on a small island in Washington's Puget Sound. The natural beauty here inspires me, and the abysmal weather keeps me indoors, working on this book.

When Greta was fresh out of the conservatory, she had begun a career as a concert pianist in Europe and the States. Her lovely face with the round apple cheeks appeared in photographs announcing her recitals. Young Abraham Sturtz saw her play and thought she looked approachable. He told her he'd recently discovered that he had a talent for piano, though he couldn't explain where it came from. The two of them eventually guessed that he'd been found by the wandering spirit of Robert Schumann. The prospect terrified them. They kept it a secret rather than risk public humiliation or worse. Abe's behavior was sometimes overtly weird then, though I don't know if he ever went to work in his bedroom slippers.

Greta and Abe saw his inhabitation as a cursed blessing. They anguished over how to nurture and present his talent. After a while, they shared the stage for extremely well-received performances of classical work, particularly that of Robert Schumann. Things went well until Abe got distracted.

Apparently Aunt Frieda was quite a distraction in her young and single days. Being an at-home pianist herself, she often attended recitals. She sat in the front row one night when the adorable Greta Pretsky performed with the still-more-adorable Abraham Sturtz. The next day, Frieda and Abe happened to meet in the store where she worked. That's all it took.

To hear Greta tell it, Aunt Frieda was a wild floozy who didn't take Abe's work seriously. He swears he never stopped playing music while they were together. Maybe Greta's perspective was bent by her broken heart.

Frieda and Abe were on the verge of engagement when Greta Pretsky foolishly announced her love for him. Abe was genuinely distraught. The women in his life went to war, including a hideous argument in public. Within a week, Abe left New York without a good-bye. The next time he spoke to Greta was forty years later, soon after he heard me play piano in women's shoes at Nordstrom. He called to say that it had happened to someone else—that he saw the light in my eyes, the light he'd seen in only two other people, a light he realized he once had. That's how Greta found me. She never divulged this history to me because it was part of her private and most painful past—and because she didn't know the ending herself.

Greta liked to blame Frieda for Abe leaving town. The truth is, Abe left them because Schumann left him. He felt devastated and unworthy, so he retreated.

Abe eventually got a doctorate in music in San Francisco. Schumann had left traces of genius behind, enough to help him understand music on another plane. I also feel stained by my inhabitant. Abe understood and reached out to me.

So that's how I wound up living on this island, in the home of Abraham Sturtz. He offered this as my retreat, a place to record my thoughts and recover from my gift. Since I'm almost done, the alternatives are waving around in my face like willow branches on a breezy day. I like my options.

Franz rearranged my soul and supercharged my mind. I don't have his genius anymore, but I have more of me to work with. Music will always be with me, and I intend to study it in a serious way. But writing seems right for now. More than right, actually, it's my passion. I even connected with a local high school and helped it establish a Young Writers Program.

Mom and Dad come often to visit me and Abe and Aunt Frieda on the island. Did I mention that true love never dies? Abe and Frieda are absurdly happy together. He seems years younger and she looks less like a schnauzer every day.

And Patrick. He's almost finished with his stint in Italy. He and I plan to regroup then and see where we stand. We might stand pretty well, since we've shed our useless issues and traded guilt for trust. I certainly pull from a deeper well. The passionate highs I experienced with Franz have mellowed into an honest engagement in life—with *staccato*s and *legato*s and all the emotions in between.

I'm not done yet with my journey with Schubert. He gave me something I needed and I think I did the same for him. His spirit was unfinished and needed a place to lodge. He found a tiny crack in my soul, where perhaps I had a slow leak. He slipped in and filled me up.

I don't know what I'll do next, but I'll do it better and more fully—and I promise to finish.

———

Woher kam es? . . . Where did it come from, and where did it go? I expected nothing and got everything. How'd I get so lucky?

ACKNOWLEDGMENTS

A heart full of thanks to my husband, Steve Sadler, who acted like it was perfectly normal for me to write a novel, and who read each page— hot off the printer—late into many nights. And to my parents, Ed and Sylvia Marson, for exuberant and unlimited belief in me. And Deborah Hoffman, my Evil Twin, and a splendid writer, for saying, "just keep writing till it's finished."

I fell in with a good crowd by way of this book. My agent, Richard Pine, easily lives up to his reputation as "best in the business." He's a great reader, professional guide, and, lucky for me, has abundant patience. Big thanks, too, to Lori Andiman and the entire staff at Arthur Pine Associates.

And at Random House: I can't imagine there's a better editor than Jonathan Karp, who gently and clearly guided me toward a much better book. He has the gift of patience, too, for which I'm grateful. Thank you also to Gina Centrello, Vincent La Scala, Casey Hampton, Jonathan Jao, Kate Blum, Sherry Huber, and so many others who are part of the effort.

Special appreciation to Howie Sanders, Lorenzo di Bonaventura, Mark Rosenthal, and Larry Konner, who see the big picture.

Thank you, Paul Cremo and Sony Classicals for sharing the music.

And to my earliest readers, cheerleaders, and indispensables: David Marson, perceptive reader and fabulous nephew; Joe Marson, swell musician and fabulous nephew; and Linda Edeiken, who has always been there; Ruth, my sister of choice, and all the amazing Safirsteins at Schubert East; Bennye Sadler, great champion of books and authors; Carol, Sedge, and Lela Schneidman, a family of wonders; Daniel Guss, for his meticulous and fascinating comments; Burgess and Barbara Needle; Katalina McGlone; Brenda Gadd; Lana Holstein; Ann Pardo; Jan and Dan McIntire; Alyssa Cohen and Scott Friedmann; Susan Doyle; Ashley and Wilson Whitaker; Bernie Marson; Carole Hyatt; Robert Israel; Peter Ott; Karin Malzan; Anne Parker; Cousin Johnny Rosenberg; Dan Baker; Susan Hall and Bob Scholz; Teri Bingham; Julie Kembel; Rose Brandt; Anna and Dean Schoff; Chief Inspector Clouseau; and to Gargoyle Carvers everywhere.

Finally, there's my unfinished, ever-growing love for Franz Schubert. Genius is all around us. Listen.

Bonnie Marson is an artist who has worked in many media—painting, drawing, photography, ceramics, and mosaics. She has sold her work in galleries and to collectors around the country. Film rights to *Sleeping with Schubert,* her first novel, have been acquired by Paramount Pictures. The author lives in Tucson, Arizona, with her husband, Stephen Sadler. She can be reached via her website: www.bonniemarson.com.

ABOUT THE TYPE

This book was set in Garamond, a typeface designed by the French printer Jean Jannon. It is styled after Garamond's original models. The face is dignified, and is light but without fragile lines. The italic is modeled after a font of Granjon, which was probably cut in the middle of the sixteenth century.

Southern Lehigh Public Library
3200 Preston Lane
P. O. Box 279
Center Valley, PA   18034